Midnight Rose

DANI HART

Midnight Rose

Dedication

I want to dedicate this book to everyone out there who has ever been afraid to follow their hearts and chase their dreams. The only one who can make you feel like a failure is you.

Other Books By
DANI HART

The Midnight Trilogy

Midnight Rose

Midnight Winters

Midnight Hunter

The Arie Chronicles

Reality

Dreams

Contemporary

A Firefighter's Flame

Forgotten Treasures

1

THE EARLY MORNING SUN warmed my pale cheeks as I stood in front of my open window. Summer break was officially ending, and I longed to soak in the last few days of freedom. Pounding footsteps drew my attention to the driveway where my best friend, Kendra, was jogging up, huffing and puffing dramatically. By the time she reached the house, I was in absolute hysterics.

"How…can…you…laugh at me…in this…state?" She stopped just below my window. Her hands were gripping tightly around her bony hips, and her head hung between her knees as she tried to catch her breath.

Still smiling wildly at her expense, I pulled my long hair up into a knot, catching every chestnut strand, and wrapped a hairband tightly around it. "Come on, Kendra.

You're building character."

"Abby, I barely know how to put one foot in front of the other quick enough to make actual strides, let alone build character."

Stress creased her forehead as her lungs expanded and contracted quickly. "I think…I'm having a heart attack," she choked on her words. "One more month, Abby. One more month."

Kendra had failed her driver's test three times, so her mom made her wait six months until she could take it again. *To build character.*

"What are you waiting for? Me to let down my hair? Come in," I teased.

True friends were hard to come by in high school. The slightest things made you an outsider, but nothing would ever come between our friendship. She moved here just in time to save me from drowning in a thick sea of depression. We were one in the same in so many ways. We were seventeen, neither of us had ever been on a date, and we spent most of our time watching old movies. I had become accustomed to being alone before I met Kendra. I even liked it, but it was nice having someone again.

My dad traveled quite a bit for business, and my mom kept herself busy with her knitting club. I didn't know something like a knitting club even existed, but it did, and my mom filled my closet with a plethora of proof, not that any made it out of the house.

"I'm still perfecting my technique, sweetie," my mom

would say each time she presented me with one of her latest creations. She raised my uncool meter by many degrees, not that it was low by any means.

I joined Kendra at the bottom of the stairs, grabbing my messenger bag and slinging it over my neck. "I take it you aren't going to miss walking to the bridge?"

Wide eyes met mine. "You're kidding, right? I still think it's weird your parents won't let you drive."

Interlocking my arm in hers, I pulled her out the front door. "I have a closet full of knitted sweaters with one arm noticeably larger than the other. Weird is my life."

As we started our ten-block walk to the Cedar Street Bridge Marketplace, I relished in the last month of earth-producing warmth in my little town of Sandpoint, Idaho. The population boasted less than 8,000 people. Small was an understatement. For example, Spokane, which was the closest major city to us by seventy miles, housed over 200,000 people.

I grew up here, so all I knew was small-town living where everyone kept tabs on everything, and you couldn't look at a boy without it spreading through the whole student body within minutes. Learning the art of silence at a young age saved me from a lot of humiliation at the end of eighth grade when my world crumbled like a stale cookie. I became distant from my childhood friends, trying to hide the emotional devastation that hung around me like a dark cloud. Those friends quickly turned on me, taking personal offense when I chose a complete stranger over them. Kendra had moved to town near the end of summer before ninth grade, and we had stuck together ever since. She was the only one who cared enough to not ask questions and to just be there for me. The rest of my so-called friends were too wrapped up in boys, fashion, and who the next top model would be. Kendra was an enigma—the mysterious and beautiful new girl—and could have been friends with anybody, but she chose me. And I chose her.

"What are you thinking about?" Little Miss Enigma inquired after we logged a few blocks on our trip.

I gave her a grateful side hug. "What a great friend you are."

"You got that right! I wouldn't walk to town for just anyone."

Her long white hair was flatiron straight, contrasting her bright blue eyes, and blending with her rosy cheeks and soft pink lips. She was naturally beautiful, not needing a speck of makeup. I, on the other hand, was completely ordinary, and I could probably benefit from a little blush and lipstick to offset the fair skin I had inherited from my mother.

"Your parents seriously have to get over this no-driving-until-you're-eighteen thing," Kendra whined.

I didn't tell her driving wasn't high on my priority list, but it was easier to blame it on my parents. Divulging my inexplicable fear would dig up my past, and I just wasn't ready to talk about the worst day of my life. Besides, everything was within walking distance in Sandpoint, and

I loved the fresh air. I planned on prolonging the inevitable as long as I could stretch it.

"Can we at least stop at the shoe boutique? I want a killer pair of heels for the first day of school."

The excitement rose in her voice while my stomach flipped with nausea. The start of junior year was only a few days away. This was the year when all the important dances took place: junior prom, winter formal, spring fling, and then as if those weren't enough, they threw in a Sadie Hawkins dance the first month of school. A dreadful sigh left my lungs.

"Oh, come on, Abby. You have no idea how pretty you are. Any guy would give their pitching arm to take you to a dance if you'd give them the chance."

Kendra had me laughing uncontrollably, to which my clumsy self ended up tripping over my own two feet, causing a domino effect of disaster. I landed hard on my knees, and my messenger bag twisted over my face.

"Oh...my...word!" Kendra exclaimed loudly.

Something in Kendra's tone and the exaggerated spaces between words tipped me off that she wasn't talking about my less than graceful plummet to the ground.

"Who...are...they?" Kendra's voice drifted softly to my ears.

I pushed the messenger bag away from my eyes, but complete removal called for more effort since the strap buckle was tangled in my hair. I followed her line of sight to the red light where a flashy, slate gray Mercedes convertible idled. I had missed whatever view Kendra was drooling over, getting rearview only now, but I was able to definitively discern there were two boys and a girl, because the convertible top was down. The girl's hair was golden, held securely in a ponytail, the driver's hair as dark as lava rock, and the boy who rode in the back had auburn hair. They seemed oddly familiar, and my stomach swirled with unease.

"I don't recognize the car. Can you help me get my hair out of this thing?" I begged my stupefied, unmoving friend. "Earth to Kendra!" I shouted.

It only took a second for the world to slow down as the boy in the back seat turned to us, alerted by my obnoxious demand for help. The boy with auburn hair met my eyes, trapping me in a flood of memories—laughing, crying, screaming. A lump formed in my throat, and all the moisture in my mouth dissipated along with the air in my lungs. The light turned green, and the convertible roared to life, taking away two years of progress.

Breathing had now completely failed me.

"Abby?" A faint plea penetrated the pounding in my ears. "Abby, breathe."

But I couldn't. I didn't want to. My face melted into the warm concrete, Wes' face being the last image burning in my retinas before I blacked out.

"ABBY, ARE YOU ALL RIGHT?"

My eyes blinked open and were met with blue-eyed worry. Kendra's long lashes pulsed rapidly as she shook me gently in her lap. I was mortified to see Mrs. Baker and her daughter Natalie hovering worriedly above us.

"I called 911," Mrs. Baker said quickly.

I groaned in response to my complete mortification and, of course, Miss Popular would be here to witness it.

"I think she's okay." Kendra's knowing wide eyes fixed on mine.

"Wow, what happened, Abby?" Natalie feigned concern.

I sat up slowly, my head spinning slightly. "It must be the heat," I lied.

"Oh. It doesn't seem that hot to me. Are you hot, Mom?" Natalie turned to her mom.

"No, honey, but Abby has always been a bit fragile. Stay put, sweetie. Let the paramedics take a look at you."

I glowered at the mother-daughter duo. Kendra blocked the view before they noticed.

"This is ridiculous. I'm fine," I protested, crossing my arms over my chest. The sirens filled the midafternoon air, getting closer by the second.

I hid my face in my hands. This would be all over school on Monday and what if Wes was there, too? Two years without a word and he just drives back into my life. I could already feel him inching back into what was left of my heart.

After the paramedics released me, Natalie made a hundred phone calls to let everyone know I was okay.

"How else would they know? You're welcome." Natalie flashed her beauty pageant smile and sauntered away with her mom, disappearing into a dress shop on the corner of First Avenue, leaving Kendra and me alone once again. We were only a block away from Cedar Street Bridge Marketplace.

"What the hell happened?" Kendra's voice was still unsteady as she interlocked her arm in mine.

"I can walk without your help, Ken," I assured her.

"Maybe, but I'm not letting you get away until you tell me why you just passed out." Her eyebrow raised in curiosity.

My shoulders dropped, not wanting to start a conversation that would take longer than the walk we had left. "Can you just let it go for now?" I asked softly.

She squeezed my arm. "Of course," she accepted sympathetically.

"I don't feel like shopping anymore. Would you mind if I had my mom pick me up?" We stood at the corner of the best shopping our town had to offer. It wasn't much, but it was better than nothing. Spokane was a huge trek, and without a car, impossible.

"I'll come with you," she offered.

"No, really. It's okay. I'd like to be alone anyway." My chest filled with the familiar ache of the past.

"Uh, okay. If you're sure."

"I am." I couldn't bear to break down in front of her again. She had seen enough unanswered tears from me over the years, and my mom was already on her way because, thankfully, Mrs. Baker had thought to call her and tell her what happened. *Thankfully.*

My mom and I drove in silence. We didn't have a lot in common these days. She liked to knit and talk about tulips and begonias while I enjoyed reading, watching the classics, writing, and most of all, silence.

"Are you sure you're okay, honey? Mrs. Baker had me very worried, telling me the paramedics came and all."

She reached out to comfort me, placing her hand over mine hesitantly. It had been a long time since we showed much physical affection toward each other, but she was a good mom and always had the best intentions for me, no matter how misguided at times.

"Mrs. Baker is a drama queen. I felt a little dizzy, so I lay down on the sidewalk. That was it." My answer seemed to have satisfied her, because she didn't pry further. My concentration was solely on keeping my heartache from pushing tears down my cheeks. Then the questions would never end.

My mom left the engine idling in the driveway. "I'm going to go to the store and get some things to make us dinner. If you're feeling okay, that is?"

I opened the door, already stepping out. "Mom, I'm fine. I promise. Dinner sounds great." I forced a smile for her benefit. She only cooked when she was stressed.

"I'll be back in no time."

I shut the door and waved with a plastered smile until

she was out of sight. That was when I noticed the sun wasn't quite as warm as it was before. Dark clouds had rolled in, foreshadowing the cooler weather on its way. A breeze whistled through the trees, shaking dead leaves to the piles already forming below. Fall was upon us, its beauty undeniable, but the feeling that overwhelmed me, idling at that red light, stole a piece of that serenity.

Goose bumps sprawled across my skin like a band of scurrying spiders. Nothing good could come from the Hunters returning. Trouble followed them, tragedy left in their wake, and I was at the top of the victim list.

I slowly stalked up the stairs to my bedroom. It not only overlooked the driveway, but also the perimeter of thick forest that encircled our property. Our house was nestled up on a steep hill at the end of a small neighborhood at the edge of town. I loved the seclusion.

My footsteps felt heavy, carrying the weight of so many tears shed over the auburn-haired boy. I kicked off my shoes and replaced my jeans for my favorite pair of sweats. Frozen in the middle of my room, time stood still. I had imagined this day so many times, in so many ways, but it had faded as days turned into months and then into years. I had finally stopped hoping for his return, but he was always in my thoughts, burning hell into every sleepless night. He had enchanted me all those years ago and haunted me for the years after.

Dizziness swirled around me again, so I sought stability on my window bench and let the cool breeze coat my skin.

The clouds were getting darker and more threatening by the minute, and the wind was strong enough to pick up the top layer of leaves and spin them like a tornado, much like the feelings weighing down my chest.

I had so many questions for Wes. Ones that I had etched into my journal day after day after day, but I wasn't sure I'd be brave enough to ask him even one. Where had he been for the past two years? Why did he leave me, bloody and broken? And the least likely to be asked, did he ever really care about me?

First love was a hard habit to kick. It was an addiction like any other. An obsession that plagued a mind endlessly. Only worse because, once it was stolen, it was gone, taking with it all signs of rationality. And I was hopelessly in love with Wes. He had consumed my thoughts with his endearing smile. There was a time when I had even thought that he felt the same for me, but then he disappeared, leaving my heart overflowing with doubt and an emptiness I swore would never fill again. It was laughable to ever imagine Wes with someone like me. The Hunters were perfect—beautiful, wealthy, and rarely entertained company.   They were considered to be out of everyone's league in Sandpoint, and many questioned why they chose to settle here, so no one was surprised when they left.

It was silly to think I would be special when I had nothing to offer, but my heart had succumbed to Wes, and I had taken a chance, only to be gutted and left for dead because that was what it felt like. *Death*. My confidence sank below sea level, and my insecurities layered thicker than the snow on our local mountains. How was I going to face him when my heart already hurt from the mere thought of being in the same town as him?

My back found comfort against the wall, my eyelids closed, feeling heavy from the mentally exhausting day, and I tried hard to remember why I hated him so much so I could be strong on Monday. *So I could be strong today.* So many memories I had fought hard to stash away filled my weakening mind.

"This is it, you know?" iridescent eyes whispered.

My heart fluttered as I closed my eyes and sucked in a quiet breath, grasping my hands tightly together to mask the trembling. Wes' lips grazed mine, stopping the world around me. Then screams yanked me from my fantasy, and those iridescent eyes were gone.

I jolted from the window seat, my fingers digging into my chest as my frightened heart pounded fiercely in retaliation. A flock of squawking birds outside pulled me back to the safety of my room, reminding me it was just another nightmare. They flew wildly as they took flight, beautiful with fully extended wings and snow-white feathers. One of the feathers was lost, and I followed it as it drifted slowly to the ground, swirling in circles with the breeze, landing on what was left of the disturbed pile of leaves. As I lifted my chin, a pair of eyes stared back at me. My muscles tensed and a scream stuck in my throat, and before it could escape, the eyes were gone. I searched the forest manically, but it was empty. Nothing moved, not even the air, and the silence was palpable. *It was just a wolf,* I tried to convince myself. We had a lot in the area, but I had never seen one so close to the house.

My mom pulled into the driveway, so whatever was in the woods was surely scared off, leaving me wondering what I really saw.

2

I WAS BACK AT MY WINDOW the next morning, my sleepless nights having returned with Wes, along with a darkness that I feared would take me down for good this time. The anticipation for school tomorrow was debilitating. The last time Wes and I saw each other was intense. Too intense. *Earth-shattering intense.* Did he blame me for what happened? It was a horrible accident. Even now, pain radiated throughout my body like a radioactive time bomb as my muscle memory relived the injury. I hurt everywhere.

"Knock, knock."

Incapable of moving my head in Kendra's direction, I fixated on the raindrops that pounded my window fiercely. It was ominous outside, foreshadowing my impending doom tomorrow.

"Your mom called me to stage an intervention." She crawled onto my bed.

"An intervention is normally attended by more than one person." I smiled weakly.

"Your lack of social competence changed the rules," she responded smartly.

"Ouch. Nice intervention."

"I'm sorry. I didn't mean it like that. Besides, I have the same social ineptness." She sat back on the bed.

"By choice," I reminded her. "All the girls want to be you, and all the boys want to be *with* you. I'm just your wing girl." I kept my voice absent of any petulance. In all honesty, I didn't envy Kendra. I saw how uncomfortable the attention made her. I was convinced she became my friend so she could hide behind me—her invisible cloak.

She sighed. "I'm not joining your pity party. I'm here to get your butt out of bed."

"What if I don't want to?" I challenged her. "Besides, I am out of bed. See?" I waved to the window seat I was perched on. However, the bed did sound much better right now, so I crawled under the blanket. "Now I'm in bed."

"Fine. Then I'm going to get under the covers with you and breathe loudly in your ear until I drive you absolutely insane."

Keeping her promise when I didn't move, she climbed beneath my sheets, throwing her arm around me, positioning her mouth as close to my ear as possible, and breathed in and out deeply. Her breath tickled, eliciting a laugh rather than the annoyance she was hoping for.

"Even your breath is perfect. Is that mint?" I finally sat up, surrendering to her serious lack of intervention skills.

"Yes." Her smile was bigger-than-life.

"Yes, you're perfect, or yes, it's mint?"

"Both." She winked.

Amused disbelief forced a smile. Throwing my blankets off, I shuffled back to the window seat. The chill from the storm outside penetrated the glass.

"Is that the same shirt you wore shopping?" she asked, disgusted.

Sheepishly, I turned to her and showed her my best innocent smile.

"Gross. Shower. Now." Kendra pointed her finger to the bathroom.

"Seriously?" I raised one of my eyebrows in defiance.

"Yes! Go, or I'm telling everyone you fainted because of a boy." Her arms crossed tightly over her chest and her lips pressed in a promise.

My heart stopped at the mention of *him*.

"You're turning white." Her eyes widened in recognition. "That's why you fainted?" She threw her hand over her mouth. "Are you going to faint again?"

With rushing speed, Kendra ran to my side. If I hadn't been sitting, I probably would have fallen to the floor.

"I…I think a shower's a good idea." My voice cracked. I stumbled off the window seat and made my way to the bathroom and locked myself inside.

Memories of the eighth grade, when my world first came crashing down, rushed me. A young heart shattered to pieces and confidence stripped. I knew what was coming. It was familiar and painful, and its wrath would be quick and merciless.

An anxiety attack.

I quickly turned the shower on, before the sadness consumed me, and curled into a fetal position on the shower floor, hot water dissolving my tears while my chest heaved wildly, the breaths hard to catch in between. Horror at what tomorrow would bring filled my head with gut-wrenching clarity. I would be invisible to him, proving an ordinary girl could never be good enough for someone so extraordinary. It was something I had always feared. My feelings would remain unrequited.

Kendra stayed with me, reminding me when it was time to eat, something I had barely done all weekend. She even sat in absolute silence with me as we watched the growing storm outside. The storm I would face tomorrow would be worse. Maybe Mrs. Know-It-All was right. Maybe I *was* fragile.

DOOMSDAY MORNING HAD arrived too quickly, my routine being my only saving grace, eating my usual cereal while my mom hummed over a cup of coffee. She was knitting, but also watching me carefully. Her eyes followed me everywhere around the kitchen.

"I was worried I would have to drag you to school," she spoke carefully.

"I'm not in kindergarten." A surprisingly unpleasant tone inflicted my words. The hurt registered on her face immediately, flushing my cheeks with regret. "I'm sorry. I'm just a little on edge."

"Do you want to talk about it?"

I knew what she was thinking. That I was sinking again. I wondered the same thing, but wasn't I stronger now? Hadn't I grown in two years? My dark days had nearly broken our family last time. My parents were so worried about me and couldn't agree on how to proceed, creating a tumultuous atmosphere around the house. My dad had finally accepted work out of the country to escape it, leaving my mom to try to drag the broken pieces of me back together. Now I felt worse for snapping at her. I took a bite of cereal, apologizing silently.

"Do you want me to drive you to school today?"

"Kendra's probably already waiting for me." I caught her disappointment. "Thank you, though." I stood up and put my bowl into the sink, having only taken one bite, still absent of an appetite, and headed out the door with my book bag.

Kendra and I started walking to school sophomore year, saving us from unnecessary embarrassment. Neither one of us wanted to show up with our parents. It would prompt all the questions about why I didn't drive yet, and while

Kendra had a valid reason, I didn't. At least not any I was willing to share. I could lie and say I didn't have my license yet, but then there would be more questions. *Why not? Did you fail the test?* Awkward conversations from nosy peers. No thanks. So instead, we would walk through the parking lot as if we had driven.

I met Kendra at the bottom of my driveway. We were off to start our junior year at Sandpoint High where our class was only 159 students strong. One hundred sixty now that Wes was back. The senior class growing by two, courtesy of the Hunter twins.

"Do you like?" My naturally beautiful friend waved her hands across her new outfit from our failed shopping trip. Well, *my* failed shopping trip. She did quite well from what I could see.

"It looks great on you. Orange is definitely your color, and the dress hugs your best features," I said as cheerfully as possible to show my support.

I, on the other hand, wore a plain black V-neck and jeans. I was never much of a fashionista, and luckily, it didn't bother my friend. My goals today were simple—go unnoticed and don't faint.

Kendra had an uncharacteristic bounce in her step today. Her excitement would have been infectious had dread not been increasing with each stride that brought me closer to the longest seven hours of my life.

"This is our year, Abby. I can feel it."

She interlocked her confidence with my apprehension,

dragging us more quickly to the first day of my glum future, predictability falling to the wayside. Every car that passed by had my heart palpitating, only brave enough to peek up to see its taillights. My stomach was painfully tight, and my nerves riled up as I looked for the steely gray convertible that had turned my perfectly predictable world upside down.

We made it to the parking lot in record time, and I searched nervously for *his* car, sucking in a deep breath of relief when it was absent. My muscles finally relaxed a bit. Maybe today wouldn't be so bad after all.

My self-assurance lasted all of three minutes from the time my foot hit the parking lot pavement to the moment it entered the halls of my own claustrophobic nightmare filled with a herd of students. It was impossible to move without grazing a shoulder or stepping on a heel. The eyes of my peers followed me in the hallway, my invisibility temporarily broken because of my fainting episode. I tucked my head down to my red Chucks and shuffled quickly to my locker.

"I guess Natalie's tall tale wasn't overshadowed by some other magnificent event."

I peered up to catch Kendra glaring at the onlookers and catching a whisper close by.

"Do you think she knows?" The squirrely girl with accusatory eyes stared straight at me, her words mocking me.

The hall doors suddenly slammed open, and the fear

on the top of my list manifested. Eyes were no longer fixed upon me. They were on the trio that drifted gracefully into the front office. *The Hunter siblings.* My stomach churned, and I felt like I was going to be sick.

A copious amount of apologetic eyes met mine. Except for a group of condescending ones that I was ashamed were associated with my former best friends. They stood in a tight circle smirking at my misfortune.

My breakdown when the Hunters left town was no secret and neither were my feelings for Wes. *Obsession.* I wanted to scream at all of them to leave me alone, but I slammed my locker closed instead and walked quickly to the girls' bathroom, careful not to breathe, fearing that would cause an uproar of chatter to break through the rare silence that plagued a high school hall. I hid in a stall, sitting on the seat and lifting my knees to my chest, waiting for the bell to ring and the halls to clear. I pulled on the laces of my shoes, bringing me back to that horrible day when everything changed. I was so caught up in my head, I didn't realize I was crying until the drops stained my favorite pair of shoes a darker shade of red.

"Abby, what's going on?" Concern echoed off the bathroom walls.

"Nothing. I'm fine." I wiped under my eyes.

"The whispered gossip in the hallway would beg to differ."

Kendra's cute little pink flats peeked under the stall.

Luckily, the bell rang, saving me from any confessions for a little while longer.

"I don't want to be late," she pleaded as one of her pink flats tapped anxiously.

"Just go, please. I'll be okay. I just need a minute." I steadied my voice as best as I could.

Without another word, her flats disappeared and the door shut. Confident I was alone, I peeked out the bathroom door to an empty hallway. I sped to my first class, the white soles of my shoes squeaking across the smooth linoleum. When several pairs of footsteps chorused with mine, I broke into a slow jog, not daring a glance over my shoulder. I slipped into creative writing just in time to avoid potential disaster in the hallway. Not that it couldn't have been anyone other than Wes, but I wasn't ready to take that chance. *Not yet.* When I turned from the door, the class went silent. The first day of school and I had become the center of attention.

"Miss Rose?"

At Mr. Dixon's confused stare, I realized I hadn't moved. I scanned the room and found an empty seat next to a girl named Sandy. She was Switzerland in the land of Sandpoint High. She kept to herself and never engaged in gossip. She was safe.

Creative writing was my favorite subject, but my thoughts wandered elsewhere as I tapped my pencil nervously on the desk.

"Abby, do you mind?" Sandy was glaring at my pencil.

"Sorry." I bit my lip and put down the pencil, the nervous energy traveling to my foot.

Annoyance stared at me out of the corner of Sandy's eye.

"Sorry," I mumbled again. Keeping my body still for forty-eight minutes was torturous, and I hadn't even written my name on my paper when Mr. Dixon came around collecting our assignments. He stopped at my table and stared at my blank paper.

"You can finish it after school," he said as he continued walking around the classroom. Shrugging pathetically, I gathered my things when the bell rang. One class down and I had already managed to earn detention. I didn't even know what the assignment was, so I glanced at the board as I walked by.

What are you most looking forward to this year?

It took every last ounce of strength in me to focus on the rest of my classes before lunch. I wasn't in the market for racking up detentions my first week. The whispers around me continued, and I prayed something catastrophic would happen to someone else to take the attention off of me.

"Hey, how did the morning go?" Kendra's larger-than-life smile met me at my locker.

She was a walking bubble of positivity. It was no wonder why she was able to pull me out of that deep hole I dove into years ago. I handed her my detention slip.

"Already? That's gotta be a record." She handed it back to me.

"Not a record I wanted," I grumbled.

As hard as I tried to keep my head to the floor as we walked to the cafeteria, the urge to see if *he* was around tempted me enough to peer up every so often. I stood behind Kendra at the salad bar, not picking up anything.

"You have to eat something, Abby. You're practically skin and bones."

"Thanks, Mom, but I prefer to keep the contents of my stomach securely in place." However, I did grab an orange. I didn't want to risk a fainting episode in front of the whole student body.

We found an empty table tucked in the corner of the lunchroom where I preferred sitting when the weather was bad. It had started raining again.

"It's really coming down." Kendra took a bite of her salad.

"Yeah, and I forgot my jacket at home." I peeled the skin off my orange absentmindedly, cringing every time someone walked into the cafeteria.

"At some point, you're going to have to tell me what's up with you and the new kids." Kendra waved her fork in my direction, spinach and tomato threatening to fly off with each syllable.

"I will. And they aren't new." She looked at me curiously, but kept quiet.

I resigned to the fact that keeping this from her was not only wrong, but doing me a disservice. I could use someone to confide in, and I had never spoken about what happened.

I never thought I would need to.

The Hunters didn't grace us with their presence at lunch, which made my nerves frantic. At least if I had tabs on where he was I could go out of my way to avoid him, but I had the nagging feeling that he was doing just that. Avoiding me. The thought stung in places that had been dead for so long. He was reviving a part of me I didn't want to resurrect.

By the end of the day, I hadn't run into the enchanting trio, and the stares subsided as word got around that Natalie and Donny had broken up. It was the event I hoped for. I checked into Mr. Dixon's class after school and concentrated hard on what to write. I began by writing my name and the title of the assignment.

Abigail Rose
Period 1
8/15

What are you most looking forward to this year?

Surviving.

I didn't know what else to write, so I handed Mr. Dixon an unfinished assignment and walked out into the rain. The parking lot became deserted in those thirty long minutes. I told Kendra not to wait for me, so I was on my own.

Stepping out into the rain from the protection of the

overhang, I crossed my arms for warmth and ran across the parking lot, miraculously managing not to slip and fall in the process. I slowed my pace slightly when I reached the sidewalk. Running or not, it was inevitable that I was going to be drenched, and I really didn't want to scrape my knees up any further. They were still pretty bruised from the other day.

My socks were already wet from the puddles I hadn't been lucky enough to miss in my sprint. The slick sidewalk glowed brightly as headlights drifted up slowly behind me, standing the hairs up on the back of my neck. My mind was chanting *please don't be him, please don't be him,* but my heart was screaming *please be him, please be him.* I let out a deep breath when a blue truck passed me, one part of me relieved, the other part disappointed. I was less than pleased when it sprayed me with water that had collected at the curb.

"Jerk," I huffed.

The chill set into my bones as I trudged on slowly. Finally lifting my eyes from the ground, I saw it. The gray convertible parked along the residential street across from the school. My breath hitched, and my heart froze. I wrapped my arms tighter around my body as tremors rolled through me. Not from the cold, but from the mere presence of him. I hated him and tears immediately trailed down my cheeks mixing with the rain. I wanted to storm over to his flashy car, yank open his door, and scream at him for all the pain he made me endure for the past two years.

I had one foot to the street, ready to make good on the

promise, when the door opened and Wes slid out. We were more than a street width a part, but I could still feel his eyes burning into my soul. Neither one of us moved, the rain pounding us harder. My heart was racing painfully.

What was he waiting for?

As we stood there, unmoving, flashes of our past kept me company in the quiet. My heart laughed, but also cried. My hate roared fiercely while my love burned brightly. I was conflicted, and the only thing I was sure of right now was that he did this to me and that I would never forgive him. I should have just walked away, leaving him to ponder my silence, but I couldn't.

"I hate you, Wes Hunter," I choked back my tears as I yelled across the street, my words muffled with the storm. "I hate you for abandoning me, and I hate you for coming back." He didn't move. I shook my head in disgust and continued home, weaving around puddles and overflowing gutters through the old neighborhood where I lived, which consisted mainly of senior citizens. When Kendra moved next door, I was more than pleased to not be the only teenager in a half-mile radius anymore.

The first moment shared between Wes and me in two years was horrific and it was digging a deep hole in the pit of my stomach. I didn't know what to make of it. It was strange and uncharacteristic of him, but maybe the Wes that had run away wasn't the same Wes that had returned. No matter which Wes stood on the street silently breaking my heart, I was angry just the same. Fuming now, I ran up the driveway, narrowly missing my mom's car as she backed out.

She rolled down the window. "Honey, I was getting worried. I was just going to look for you."

"Sorry. I had to stay after to finish a paper. I'm fine." I ran into the house, stripped out of my soaked clothes, and hopped into the shower.

I had barely survived my first day of junior year.

3

THE REST OF THE WEEK WAS uneventful, if you didn't count Kendra asking Donny to the Sadie Hawkins dance, becoming Natalie's newest target of hatred while simultaneously putting Kendra back on every guy's radar. Donny accepted, of course, dispersing the line of guys at our lunch table.

"Hey, so I heard those kids are being homeschooled. They were just here on the first day to meet with the counselor."

Kendra studied my reaction that I tried so hard to keep steady. To be honest, I wasn't sure how I felt about the news. I was relieved I wouldn't have to see them at every corner, but I was also disappointed because I wouldn't see *him* at every corner.

"Ready to spill yet?" Patience waned.

THE WEATHER HAD LET up, so Kendra and I were back to our traditional walk home from school. We made it to Friday, and I promised her a sleepover full of wild tales and unrequited love. She laughed at my attempt to make light of an obviously difficult predicament for me.

My dad finally returned home from out of the country, so he and my mom went out for the evening. Nervous about confessing my deepest and darkest secrets to my best friend, I set up our usual spot on the couch with a blanket, sodas, too much candy, and popcorn. She wouldn't be here for another thirty minutes, and I had run out of things to keep me busy, having already folded my laundry and cleaned the kitchen. I really wanted to tell Kendra the whole truth, but I didn't know how. Not to mention how terrified I was that reliving all of that would force me back into a place I didn't want to be. She still wouldn't be here for another twenty-nine minutes, and the anxious energy made me pace erratically.

A light tap on the front door brought a huge sigh of relief.

Before I had completely opened the door, I was already greeting her. "Kendra, I'm so glad you came early—" And then my heart jumped out of my throat and took a nosedive at Wes' feet. Wide-eyed and stunned, I was paralyzed, half in the present and half two years in the past.

"Hey." Wes smiled coyly.

His eyes were still the unique iridescent I remembered, changing colors slightly depending on the angle and light, and still mesmerizing even after all this time. He watched me carefully, standing poised and confident, the light catching every breathtaking feature his face had to offer. I hated him for being so…so…him. Once the initial shock of him standing in front of me passed, I slammed the door in his face, only his shoe caught it.

"I can see you're mad." He pushed the door open slowly, being careful against the weight I still had on it.

"And I can see you're still observant," I snapped, trying to kick his foot out of the way, only bruising my socked toes in the process. I threw my hands up in defeat. "Fine." I took a few steps back, letting trouble walk back into my life.

When he stepped inside, I took in his mature look. He was no longer the skinny boy I had been so infatuated with. He was a young man. Taller and had gained muscle mass. If it weren't for his eyes, I should hardly recognize him on the street. But I had, even from the convertible at the red light. I had, because my body would never forget how I felt whenever he was around. It was as if my insides were drawn to him out of necessity. Much like they screamed now, my body heating up and my hands shaking.

"You've changed," he said, a seducing smile tugging at his mouth.

"Funny how two years can do that to a person." I

shoved my hands into my sweats pockets to hide the effect he was having on me. Sweats. No, no, no. First the drowned cat look, and now a depressed teenager look. Not how I envisioned looking when I saw him. And to further my humiliation, my hair was in a messy knot on top of my head. *This is fantastic*, I thought sarcastically.

"Yes, well, you look great."

His compliment was quickly followed by his fingers reaching for my face, something he had done so many times in the past that it almost didn't faze me. A part of me longed to feel his touch again, the comfort it brought, but the smarter part slapped it away.

"What are you doing here, Wes?" I snapped as I fluidly pulled down my hair, combing it out with my fingers, feeling extremely self-conscious.

"I wanted to see you." His reply was so ordinary, as if nothing had transpired between us.

"I meant, what are you doing back in Sandpoint?"

"I wanted to see you." His answer unchanging, but softer this time as if it pained him just as much to have been separated all this time.

His present hold on me was stronger than I thought possible. My willpower was weakening and begging for me to let go of the past and forgive him, but I couldn't. How could I? I wasn't some stupid teenage girl anymore, and he was responsible for that. He gave me my first good dose of the consequences associated with letting someone get too close. I trusted my heart to him, and it was one of my biggest regrets.

"I think you should go. My friend will be here any minute." My tone deceived my words as I looked away to hide the inner turmoil of finally having him here in front of me again, close enough to touch.

"Is that what you really want?" His head turned just a bit, exposing vulnerability within his eyes.

My fortress against his enchantment was falling quickly. "Yes," I said with resigned indifference as I bit my bottom lip.

"It's probably best." He turned to leave, but then spun back around gracefully. "Abby…"

I held my breath for some big revelation that would answer the millions of questions swimming wildly in my head.

"You can't tell anyone about that night. You know that, don't you?"

A lump formed in my throat, and my heart stopped beating. Tears immediately welled in my eyes. The last shred of hope I had that maybe he did miss me disappeared. I wanted to believe he was here to apologize, but all he wanted was to make sure I had kept our secret.

"You haven't told anyone, have you?" He carefully treaded the waves of my emotions.

I shook my head, my hands forming fists in my pockets, digging my nails into my palms to hold back the pain he was inflicting with every second that passed.

"Thank you," he whispered just before gliding out of my house and closing the door securely.

I crumbled to the floor, losing sight of my sanity. I was losing the will to live again, but I was stronger. *I am stronger.* I had to find a way to be okay. I couldn't fall again because I knew I wouldn't have the strength to come back a second time. I loved Wes with every beat of my heart, but it was time to let go and move on. It was time to love myself more.

I called Kendra, canceling on my loyal friend, needing time alone to process why in the world Wes needed me to keep that night a secret. I wasn't even sure what I remembered. What was real and what was caused by my concussion. But Wes knew, and he didn't want anyone else to know.

My memory from that night was hazy at best, but I tried to go through the minutes leading up to the crash again. Maybe this time I would remember something else. I was driving without a license, and I wrapped Ben Hunter's car around a tree. There was a lot of blood and screams from me. But what I remembered most were those eyes— iridescent swirling with black—glowing hungrily at me. Wes' eyes. Then I blacked out and woke up in the hospital and the Hunters were long gone. Those eyes haunted my dreams almost every night, not knowing if they were real. There was so much menace behind the beauty. Dark and dangerous, thirsting for something.

It was exhausting reliving that night. I had crawled upstairs and snuggled up to my window staring at the storm still brewing. My lids were heavy, so I relented and fell asleep, thinking about those eyes.

"Abby."

A whisper slithered through the darkness. I became keenly aware of three things. First, I was asleep. Second, I wasn't alone. And third, I might die.

My feet fumbled with sheer terror as I ran into nothingness, falling to the ground, dried leaves manifesting under the grip of my fingernails. Popping my head up, a thick forest of trees appeared around me, and the sound of lapping water reached me from afar.

"Abby."

Fear surged through me, filling me with adrenaline to run toward the water. Somehow I felt I would be safe there. Safe from whatever was chasing me—hunting me.

Jumping over fallen trees struck down by lightning and cutting my bare feet on sharp rocks and scattered twigs, I ran as fast as my heart was racing. I pushed my burning muscles to the max. I wouldn't go down without a fight.

The rippling of gentle waves amplified as I neared water, seeing the light of the moon just ahead, my predator not far behind. Thrashing through the last of the trees, I fell down a tall ditch bank, rolling hard over storm debris and cutting my cheek, my arms, and every exposed part of my body. It felt like I was falling down Alice's endless rabbit hole, possibly falling to my death, but then my palms sank into dry sand. I recognized this beach. It was Sandpoint City Beach. I hadn't been here since—

"Aaaaabbbbbbbyyyyy."

The hunger was more pronounced as my name stretched along a timeless moment.

Scrambling to my feet, I headed to the water, glancing back several times to see how far away my predator was. The water would save me. I was sure of it. My instincts screamed for it. Finally, the icy water covered my feet and then my knees until I was treading in the black lake. The surface glistened like ice crystals, my reflection revealing a gash on my forehead.

I spun around, breathing hard as my arms tried effortlessly to keep my head above water. I scanned the beach and stopped dead on a pair of eyes glowing at the top of the cliff, fixated on me. I couldn't look away, and in those few seconds I saw my hunter, but I also saw my savior.

Covered in sweat, I rolled off the window bench, landing hard on the carpet and panting frantically. It was still dark outside and rain tapped vigorously on the window.

Resigning to sleepless defeat and shaking off the nightmare, I crawled back onto the window seat and stared out into the blackness, the familiar dull ache pounding relentlessly in my chest as I watched lightning bolt after lightning bolt strike in the forest beyond. My thoughts quickly traveled back to Wes. The nightmares had dissipated over the months after he left, but had started up again with a vengeance now that he was back.

I had worked so hard for an ordinary high school experience. To blend in and get by without complications, avoiding boys and ignoring gossip. Until recently, I had been delightfully successful. But now, how was I going to live in a town where a piece of my heart walked around, overlooking me at every turn?

The tears fell slowly. Once again, I was living in a world where Wes was a boy that I was unforgivably in love with. I rested my head against the cold glass and let the sounds of the storm roaring outside lull me back to sleep.

"Abby?"

My dad shook me awake.

"Did you sleep like this?"

I looked around, confused. "I guess so." Sleep still hanging on.

"Is everything okay?"

He rarely showed much emotion, so his concern was refreshing. The last time was when he found me in the hospital—bloody, bruised, and disoriented.

"I just had a nightmare. I'm fine." I shrugged it off for his sake.

"It's Saturday. Do you have any plans?" This was his attempt at small talk.

It only took me a split second to run through my schedule for the day. Sleep, eat, sleep, eat, and sleep again.

"No, not really," I said, figuring that was a better response. I rubbed at a painful kink in my neck.

He shifted uncomfortably. "Maybe we could grab lunch or go to the movies or something. Like old times."

When I didn't immediately respond, he continued.

"I mean, I know you're a teenager and all, and hanging out with your old man isn't the coolest thing to do."

"No, Dad, sure. Like old times." I forced a smile. The last thing I wanted to do today was leave the house, but maybe that was exactly what I needed to keep my mind off other things. "I just need to shower."

"Okay then. Great." He backed out of the room and closed the door.

I stayed at the window for a little longer, watching the weight of the rain bend the smaller branches on the trees. The leaves were glossy from the rain, highlighting the turning of the leaves from green to hues of orange, red, and yellow. Fall always reminded me of Wes.

"Are you excited for ninth grade? Only one more year and we'll officially be in high school." Wes turned to me.

We were lying under the cover of a large tree, some of its leaves yellow and others pink.

"I'm not sure how it's any different. It's not like a separate school or anything. We've been going there since seventh grade."

"I guess you're right." His eyes squinted, and the enchanting smile that melted my heart every time we were together rose.

I looked away shyly, trying to hide the blush heating my cheeks. "What kind of tree is this again?"

He shifted slightly, his shoulder accidentally brushing mine, the thrill catching my breath. I closed my eyes, trying to get a grip on the overwhelming sensation consuming me as tingles dispersed across my skin.

His eyes studied the tree above. "Katsura." A small chuckle escaped him.

"Right. You've told me that before. Katsura." I repeated the name several times, finding an escape from the heaviness constricting my lungs. It was getting harder to be around him like this, only being friends. I wanted more, but Natalie's words rang in my ears like a song on repeat.

"He's not into you, Abby. If he were, he would have kissed you by now. You've been hanging out since you were kids. Besides, look at him. He's gorgeous."

Her words bit at my confidence. She accused me of being obsessed. She even called me a stalker once, but she was my best friend and I trusted her opinion. Maybe I was crazy thinking that somebody so extraordinary could like somebody so ordinary.

"Abby?"

Wes' voice entrapped me. He rolled onto his side, facing me.

"Yeah?" My insides screamed. Maybe Natalie was wrong after all. The tingles on my skin rushed to my stomach, spinning around erratically.

He reached his hand over, moving toward my face slowly, his body moving with it, our lips so close I could smell the spice of the tree left on his skin when he climbed up to shake more leaves off. His breath was warm on my cheek, and his iridescent eyes burned right through me. His lips curled slightly upward, sucking me into a hypnotic state. I closed my eyes, bracing for what was to come next, but instead of his lips on mine, I felt a tugging on my hair. I opened my eyes quickly as he brushed through my long strands strewn about the leaves.

"There was a bug in your hair," he whispered close to my ear.

"Oh…yeah…thanks." The disappointment burned, and I sat up, mortified. How could I be so stupid? Natalie was right. Look at him. It was hard to even believe someone could be so perfect.

"What's wrong?" Wes sat up, too.

"I just remembered my dad is coming home today. I have to go." I jumped up, slipping my brand new red Chucks on quickly.

Wes stood up gracefully, pulling up the blanket and folding it neatly. He handed it to me, his hand touching mine, sending my body ablaze with adoration.

"Abby, can I take you somewhere tonight? There's something I want to talk to you about."

How could I deny those smoldering eyes?

"Sure. I'll meet you at the end of the driveway after my parents go to sleep."

"I'll be waiting." His voice carried a bit of desperation with it.

"Tonight then." I tucked my head sheepishly and ran to my house.

I thought that night was going to be the best night of my life, full of wishes come true and promised love. I couldn't have been more wrong. The memory of that day was still painfully vivid.

I searched the forest for those eyes. The ones I thought I saw the other day. The ones from my nightmare. I needed to convince myself the nightmare wasn't real. That it *was* just a dream.

"Abby." My dad knocked. "Almost ready? I thought we could catch the two o'clock showing."

I slid off the window seat. "Yeah, Dad. Almost." I turned one last time to the window, getting an eerie feeling that I was being watched, but the downpour made it impossible to see anything. I grabbed my robe hanging over my desk chair and headed slowly to the bathroom, still looking over my shoulder cautiously.

4

AFTER THE MOVIE, MY DAD TOOK me to our favorite place to eat, Sandpoint Bistro, where they had the best stone-baked pizzas. We used to come here every Saturday night with my mom, but then the accident happened.

"I miss this," my dad said as he took a large bite of barbecue chicken pizza.

I looked at him in disgust. "Seriously, Dad, how can you eat that?"

"What?" His puzzled look was followed by a mischievous grin because we'd had this conversation at least a dozen times.

"Barbecue sauce does not belong on pizza. It belongs on a barbecue. That's why it's called barbecue sauce." I took a bite of my completely normal and plain cheese pizza with *pizza* sauce.

"Well, then somebody forgot to tell the owner." He winked.

"Tell me what, James?" Mr. Hunter stood tall next to our table.

I nearly choked on my pizza as I looked up at yet another reminder of the past.

"William, when did you get back?" My dad wiped his hands on a napkin and stood to shake Mr. Hunter's hand, also known as Wes' dad.

It was dumb to feel somewhat shocked by his presence since he owned the bistro, but I wasn't ready to see the Hunters back to business as usual like their absence went unnoticed. Wes looked a lot like his dad. Maybe he looked like his mom, too, but I would never know because she died when Wes was born. I had never even seen a picture of her, as if the memory of her was erased.

"I got your application, Abigail." Mr. Hunter offered a positive smile.

I squirmed in my seat. I hadn't told my parents that I was looking for a job, and in light of recent events, I had completely forgotten. Plus, had I known the Hunters were running the business again, I would have avoided applying at the bistro like the plague.

"Oh, Abby, you didn't tell me you were looking for a job. You know if you need money you can just ask." My dad's jaw clenched.

My parents wanted me to focus on school and not worry about money, but I didn't think he'd have such a revulsion to me working. His glare was making me uneasy.

"You've been gone," I said uncomfortably.

Mr. Hunter broke the tension. "Well, I think it's a great idea. Work builds character."

There was that adult phrase again. *Builds character.* I smiled apprehensively, avoiding eye contact with my dad.

Mr. Hunter continued, "Why don't you come in Monday after school for an interview?" He looked at my dad and then back to me.

"Sure. Monday," I confirmed and took a large gulp of soda, fearing any more words would cause this situation to erupt.

"It was good catching up, James." Mr. Hunter went for a handshake, my dad hesitating for just a second before he reciprocated this time. "Welcome back, William," he finally replied politely and sat back down.

My pizza became the most fascinating thing in the universe as I tried to avoid the glare that was surely burning a hole in my forehead.

"Something you want to tell me?" my dad said as he laid his arms on the table.

"Dad, look, I know you and Mom said you would pay for everything that I needed, but I really want to save up my own money." I searched his eyes to see if anything I was saying was softening the hard edge in the creases of his forehead.

"Okay, then tell me what you're saving for." He sat up even straighter, business-like.

"Well...umm." I was starting to hyperventilate. I knew how this was going to go. The same way it always did. "A car." I closed my eyes quickly and scrunched down in my seat. Surprisingly, my dad kept quiet, which was a vast improvement to the fight that exploded the last time I brought it up.

"Okay." He smiled slightly.

"Okay?" Had I just heard that right? I peeked one eye open cautiously, searching his eyes for some sort of reverse psychology.

"You're seventeen now, so maybe it is time for you to start driving."

I released the deepest breath of my life. I hadn't even planned this conversation, and it went way better than the ones I had rehearsed for days. I sat up straight and more confident.

"On one condition." He lifted his finger.

My shoulders tensed. There it was. I knew it was too easy.

"I get to teach you. No one else. And especially not that Wes kid." He took a bite of his barbecue pizza.

Not that Wes kid. He was the reason I hadn't wanted to drive. The reason my parents never wanted me to drive again. My first time driving had been a monumental disaster that almost resulted in my death and had Wes fleeing. That was probably why he hesitated shaking Mr. Hunter's hand. My dad never told me how that conversation went after the accident. I can't imagine it went well.

As we walked to the car after dinner, a prickly sensation traveled down my spine. I glanced back at the restaurant and locked eyes with Wes who was leaning on the wall of the building, watching me. The intensity of his stare was as if he was trying to communicate something, but what was a complete mystery to me. I was never good at reading Wes, which was why when he left I was completely blindsided. I walked slowly, trying to savor his presence, my mind not fully convinced this was all real. Wes was back, but he was no longer *my* Wes.

He held his gaze on me as my dad backed out of the parking space, my heart barely beating. I peered over my shoulder as we pulled out of the lot, and sure enough, Wes was still watching me, and at the same time, ripping out my soul piece by piece.

When we got home, I had an unwelcomed guest. Natalie was waiting in my living room.

"Abigail," she squealed as she jumped up from the couch, hugging me.

"Natalie, it's been too long," my dad acknowledged her warmly.

I glared in his direction. *Traitor*.

"It really has been." She smiled widely.

"Well, I'll leave you two to chat." He disappeared into the kitchen where I heard him greet my mom.

I turned back to Natalie, grumbling to myself. "What are you doing here?" I was biting back what I really wanted to say.

"I thought I would just come by and see how you're doing."

The shrill in her voice was already getting on my nerves. Of course, she would come over and rub it in my face that Wes was back.

"I'm fine." Not hiding the bitterness.

"I was just so worried after you fainted." Her eyes widened with feigned concern.

"That was over a week ago." She bounced around as if it was completely normal for her to be here talking to me.

He's too good for you.

She walked around the room touching everything. Why was she here? Natalie Baker always had a reason, and it was usually because she wanted something.

"So, I know I don't have to ask your permission or anything, but I wanted to be a good friend."

A good friend? Who was she kidding?

"Wes is back in town, which you already know, and I just wanted to make sure you guys weren't a thing. I mean, you were pretty obsessed with him before he left." She flipped her hair over her shoulder, letting her sentence hang without closure.

If blood could boil, mine would be bubbling over. "Yes,

I know he's back. No, you don't need my permission."
Permission for what?

"Anyway, if you aren't going out or anything..." she
continued again, leaving the sentence unfinished.

It irritated me back when we were friends just as much
as it did now. It was like she was showing her control of the
conversation by leaving me hanging to wonder what she
was going to say next, but really it was because she was
too dumb to formulate full sentences. That was my guess
anyway. "Are we done here?"

Natalie put her hand on her chest, feigning shock. "Well,
excuse me. You don't have to be so rude." With her head up
high, Natalie made her way to the door, throwing it open.
"It was nice chatting, Abigail," she mocked my dad's words.

I slammed the door as she sauntered out, exaggerating
the sway in her hips. Anger was fuming out of my ears, but
visualizing Wes and Natalie together made me nauseous.
And here I thought I couldn't hate her any more than I
already did. Every muscle in my body was clenched tightly.
My nails were puncturing through the skin of my palms.

The doorbell rang, and I had just enough time to gain
the courage to punch Natalie in the face. I threw it open and
was poised to let loose when Kendra's face met mine. She
covered herself protectively.

"What the—Abby, what are you doing?" She waved her
hands in front defensively.

"Kendra! I'm so sorry. I thought you were Natalie."

"So that *was* her." Disgust filled her baby blues.

"Unfortunately. She wanted to tell me she was asking out Wes. Like I care." I scoffed as bravely as I could muster.

Kendra squinted. "Hmmm. Okay, so what *is* the deal with you and Mr. Perfect?"

She slid by me and made herself comfortable on the couch. This conversation was inevitable, and it had finally caught up with me.

"Let's go to my room."

"Ooooh, it's one of *those* conversations." She jumped up gleefully.

"It doesn't have an HEA, so settle down." I led Little Miss Overexcited up the stairs.

"HEA?" she inquired.

"Seriously? Happily Ever After." How could she not know that?

"Oh," she said thoughtfully, followed by a less enthusiastic, "oh," when realization hit her.

I listened for my parents to make sure they were still downstairs and then closed my door softly and headed immediately over to my window seat. Kendra sat on the bed across from me, watching. *Waiting.*

"Wes and I were close." A blush overtook me as I admitted it aloud for the first time.

"Define *close*." Her head tilted toward me curiously.

"Not like that. We never even kissed." Disappointment hovered over my words. "We were just really good friends." There was silence as we both digested the information.

"But you wanted to kiss him," she stated.

Shamefully looking out the window, I whispered, "Yes."
Kendra joined me on the window seat.

"Abby, there's nothing to be ashamed of. We're teenagers. We were built to be boy crazy. So you liked a guy who happened to be a friend, and happened to be drop-dead gorgeous. I bet every girl was crazy about him. *Is* crazy about him."

"Not helping." I was on the precipice of a breakdown, and I didn't want to be. I just wanted… I don't know what I wanted. Or maybe I did, and that was what scared me.

"You love him." Kendra's eyes searched carefully for the answer.

She didn't say *loved*, as in past tense. She said *love*, as in right now.

"Yeah." Simple. I was in love with Wes Hunter whether he loved me back or not.

Being the great friend she was, Kendra let it go. We sat and watched the winds whip around the defenseless trees, breaking off branches and stripping them of leaves. Storms were both magnificent and terrifying to watch, unpredictable and unforgiving. It seemed like the storms would never end.

After Kendra left, I kept replaying Wes' visit, analyzing every word he said and how he said it.

I wanted to see you.

He said it twice, unflinching and confident. He wasn't the same Wes who had left me. He had somehow changed. Matured. But there was something else. The way he looked at me. I couldn't put my finger on it, but it almost felt like desperation. When he was standing in my living room, something so surreal that I had imagined for years, I knew I felt the same way. I was a fraction of myself without him, hollowed and broken. His mixed signals were maddening. If he missed me, why was he avoiding me? Was he embarrassed of me? My ordinary couldn't stand up to his extraordinary? Were we doomed from the start? Our friendship was so unlikely, yet we were drawn to each other from day one. The day he came to town felt like the first day of the rest of my life.

I kicked my feet out as hard as I could, wanting to fly high with the birds, loving the wind in my hair.

Back and forth, sand then sky, giggling as my legs took me higher.

The clanking of chain on chain pulled me from my imaginary flight, and looking over at Wes Hunter, who had come out of nowhere and was pumping his legs, trying effortlessly to catch up with me, a small smile crossed his mouth. Without a word, we swung side by side, the energy increasing between us as our feet touched the sky.

Back and forth, sand then sky, no longer alone.

Then the bell rang, alerting us to the world that expected our return. Feet to sand, we slowed down in sync, hanging onto the gentle rocking as our eyes met and unspoken words crossed from him to me and me to him. The strangeness of his eyes sucked me in, and only when the bell rang again did they release their hold on me. He slid off his swing gracefully and held out his hand. I took it obediently, beguiled by this beautiful boy who stood in front of me, who chose to join me in the sky rather than with the boys in the yard. Goose bumps traveled up my arm as his fingers interlaced with mine, leading me back to reality.

SUNDAY MORNING BREAKFAST with both of my parents was a rare event, but nice. I exchanged cereal for my dad's famous pancakes. It was his life's purpose to try to replicate the perfect restaurant pancake buttered with crispy edges. My mom and I teased him incessantly about it.

He placed two pancakes onto my plate.

"I still can't figure out how they cook it so evenly. Maybe it's those industrial griddles." His brows furrowed as he tried to uncover the big pancake secret.

My mom and I shared a laugh. "Dad, they're great."

"Oh, James, really. You have been to restaurants all over the world. It's hard to compare pancakes from France, to Greece, to here. You've obsessed over this for years," my mom teased.

"Lucinda, I am a chef at heart, and I swear on my grave that I will get them perfect." The frustration from his face faded. "Okay, maybe not my grave." He cracked a smile. "This is nice. We should do it more often." He shared a knowing look with Mom.

"It is," my mom agreed.

"So, Dad, when do you leave again?"

My dad was never around for very long. He was a highly sought-after software engineer, so companies flew him all over the world to work with him. I always assumed if it was computer related it could be done from home, but apparently not. He made good money, but I could tell it wasn't about the money for him. He loved to travel, and when he went to new places, he would always bring me home something. Well, he used to, anyway. It dwindled as I reached puberty. I kind of missed it now.

My dad sat down with a pile of pancakes on his plate.

"Dad!" We all stared at the Eiffel Tower of pancakes and laughed.

"What? I'm hungry," he teased defensively.

I took another bite, waiting for him to answer my question.

"Your mom and I have been talking…"

Oh no. Nothing good ever came out of a conversation starting with *your mom and I have been talking*.

"Okay," I dragged out slowly, putting my fork down, losing my appetite.

My parents exchanged looks again.

"I'm not going to travel as much. I'm only going to accept local jobs and work from home as much as I can."

To say I was shocked would be grossly understated. Ever since I could remember, he'd been gone more than he'd been home.

"That's great, Dad, but why?"

The timing seemed odd, what with the Hunters back in town. I knew how he felt about Wes, and he didn't seem to buddy up to Mr. Hunter last night.

"I'm getting too old to travel, and I feel like I've missed so much of you growing up. You'll be eighteen next year, and I want to spend as much time with you as possible before something swoops you off your feet."

Or some*one*.

"Dad, you're only thirty-seven." I laughed.

My mom had me when she was eighteen and my father twenty. They were very young and still got rude comments about it.

"Have you applied to any colleges yet?" he inquired.

"Colleges? No, not yet. It's too early." I pushed my plate away, no longer hungry. He was phishing, but what bothered me most was not knowing why. He couldn't be that concerned about Wes, could he? Or was he really just feeling nostalgic? My foot fidget started as seconds suddenly felt like minutes.

"Maybe we can start driving tomorrow after school," he suggested.

His voice was more of a challenge than a suggestion. He knew I had the job interview.

"I have that interview at the bistro tomorrow, remember?" I dug my hands in my lap and chewed on the inside of my lip, waiting for an argument.

"That's right. I forgot." He dug into his pancakes.

"Your father told me the Hunters were back. Have you seen Wes?"

My mom always liked Wes, but she never mentioned him again after the accident. I think them leaving was a relief on everyone, except me.

"No, I haven't," I lied, not divulging that he stood in our living room only two days ago. They seemed satisfied with my answer and left me alone the rest of breakfast. The second my dad stood up, I jumped out of my seat, put my plate into the dishwasher, and raced out of the kitchen.

5

"HOW WAS THE DANCE?" I asked Kendra who bounced beside me on our way to school.

The storms were taking a break, and the temperature was forecasted to reach mid-seventies. I could use some sunshine and less sloshing in my shoes.

"Honestly? Kind of lame, and Donny was a complete dud. Natalie can have him back. I'm pretty sure I'm within the thirty-day return policy." She laughed.

"I'm sure he's already groveling at her feet."

"Speaking of feet, when are you going to toss those sneakers?"

Kendra wasn't shy about her disapproval of some of my fashion choices.

"First of all, they aren't sneakers. They are Chucks. And

second of all, you don't just throw away something because they are a little rough around the edges." My defense would totally hold up in a courtroom.

"Abby, there's a hole wearing in the toe," she shrieked.

I wiggled my big toe, stretching the white rubber to reveal the infamous hole.

"They're my favorite," I claimed simply.

"Then just get a new pair."

Miss Obvious was trying to be helpful, but if she knew what these red shoes symbolized, she would give me a fashion pass.

"I will take your suggestion under careful consideration." Although, I couldn't imagine parting with them. *Ever*.

"You have that interview today, right?" She happily changed the subject.

A car full of teenage boys passed, honking and catcalling Kendra.

"And that is the perfect example of why I don't like dating." Kendra threw her hair behind her shoulder.

The interruption saved me from an uncomfortable conversation that would undoubtedly lead to Wes, so for the moment, I applauded the boys in the car.

The school bell echoed across the parking lot.

"Shoot, we're late," Kendra panicked.

There wasn't time to finish our conversation as we ran separate ways to class.

I CHOSE TO WALK TO the bistro, avoiding the twenty questions from my parents. My dad tried to derail my interview by guising it with my first driving lesson, but he failed to remember I wasn't an impressionable pre-pubescent kid anymore. Plus, I needed the ten blocks to work off my nerves. By second period I had convinced myself to flake on the whole thing, but by lunch I realized my apprehension wasn't because I was afraid to run into Wes, but because he might think I only wanted the job to run into him. At the end of the day, I reminded myself I had applied for the job way before the Hunters came back, with no reason to think they would return. I wanted this job, and considering the other dozen places I applied hadn't called, my options were limited.

I stood outside of the bistro, staring at the sign, studying it like it would be one of the interview questions, stalling as much as I could until I could breathe evenly again. It was like plucking petals off a flower. I want the job, I don't want the job, I want the job, I don't want the job. What petal would be left?

The door opened. "Great, you're here."

Mr. Hunter's voice was kind and his smile captivating. He waved me inside, holding the door open. My shoulders slouched in defeat as I accepted Mr. Hunter's invitation hesitantly.

The restaurant was bustling for a Monday afternoon.

"It's been crazy today. The good weather brings everybody out, and I had a girl call in sick, so I'm going to have to cut the interview short."

He walked me to a table in the back.

"We can reschedule if you need to."

He sat down and motioned for me to do the same.

"Actually, I was going to just say you're hired and see if you could start right now." He laughed.

His laugh was just as enchanting as his smile. I laughed with him and then sat awkwardly when he stopped and didn't say anything else.

"Oh, you were being serious." Panic dispersed through my limbs.

"You don't have to, of course."

Looking around the packed restaurant there was no doubt he needed the help. "Umm, okay. Sure. I can start right now."

"Fantastic." He jumped up, handing me an apron. "If you could just clear tables and refill drinks for now, and then we can set up a training schedule this evening."

I nodded. "Great. Okay. I've got this," I said, feigning confidence. My eyes widened with horror as I scanned unfamiliar territory. Here went nothing.

I called my parents quickly before jumping on the floor to let them know. They seemed fine with it. *I thought*. I told them I would walk home or get a ride from someone.

Fumbling through the late afternoon rush was nothing compared to the dinner rush.

"Excuse me, Miss. Can I get another Coke?"

"Miss, I asked for no onions."

"Can you bring out a kid's plate to keep my baby busy?"

The requests never stopped. One after the other. Watching Mr. Hunter, he hadn't even broken a sweat, floating from table to table, talking with the guests, laughing and smiling as if everything was under control. I, on the other hand, was a sweaty mess with tousled hair falling out of my haphazard topknot.

When the last customer was gone, I fell into a booth and started rolling silverware with another employee who skipped the pleasantries, ignoring me altogether. I only knew her name was Penelope because of Mr. Hunter. I rolled quietly, catching Mr. Hunter out of the corner of my eye counting the register and locking up. Penelope, who had a nose piercing and blue hair and ear buds firmly in place, stood up and walked away with an arm full of rolled silverware without any acknowledgement that I even existed. *Friendly,* I thought sarcastically.

"How was your first day?"

My heart stopped. Wes' words prickled through my body. "F-fine. Good. Great, actually," I said, stumbling on my words. I braved a glance up, immediately regretting it. His long lashes blinked slowly, and his smile melted every bone in my body.

Breathe. In and out. Just act natural.

"Good. I'll see you around." He drifted to his dad across the room.

His words hung in the air like a hovering dragonfly. The energy buzzed around me, making me feel lightheaded, the feeling I always got when Wes was near. Mesmerized by his presence, I watched as he spoke softly with Mr. Hunter. Their bodies were stiff, and their eyes were intensely focused on each other. Something was wrong.

I looked away quickly when both their eyes turned to me, my heart racing. Scooping up the rolled silverware, I passed them with my head down and stuffed the rolls into the podium at the front desk.

"You saved me today," Mr. Hunter said.

I had the strangest feeling he would have been just fine without me.

"No problem. If you don't need anything else, I'll be heading out." I untied my apron and let down my hair, shaking it out gently.

"That'll be it. I have to take care of some things tonight, so can you come in tomorrow after school so we can go over your schedule?"

I couldn't help but look over at Wes who was leaning casually against the podium watching me. Studying me. A drip of nervous sweat ran down the back of my neck.

"I'll come right after school." I smiled nervously.

"Perfect. See you then," he replied.

I reached under the front desk, grabbed my bag, and

walked to the front door, but just as I was reaching for the handle, fingers stretched over my shoulder, grazing my neck and unlocking the door. I peered up and met Wes' radiant eyes. My heart pounded loudly against my chest.

"Are your parents picking you up?" Concern layered his words.

"Uh, no. I'm walking."

His fingers recoiled slowly, brushing across the crook of my neck, dazing me. His touch felt warm and inviting, my neck instinctively extending, exposing it to him.

"It's dark out. I'll drive you," he said softly.

"I've walked home later than this." My argument lacked zest. He had every part of me bursting, begging for more time alone with him, but the other part of me that was still mad, objected. If I didn't get out of here soon, I would be helplessly lying at his feet. "I have to go."

"Wes, we need to go." Urgency was in Mr. Hunter's tone. "She'll be fine."

He seemed almost angry at the thought of Wes driving me home. After a quick look at Mr. Hunter, I said, "See? Even your dad knows I'll be fine." I pushed the door open quickly, welcoming the brisk air breaking the sudden tension. The cool night air awakened my muscles and sharpened my senses again. The exchange between Wes and his dad was unnerving.

Before getting through the parking lot, I allowed myself a glance over my shoulder and caught Wes watching me, his eyes burning fiercely. I tucked my head and turned away, shoving my hands into my pockets and walking the ten blocks briskly, acute to every car, snapping twig, and animal cry around me. I was on high alert thanks to Mr. Hunter's odd behavior. I sped up my pace, sprinting at any break in the silence, and made it home in record time, completely stressed.

That night, I tossed and turned for hours. I knew the probability of seeing Wes at the bistro was high, but I wasn't expecting it to be on my first day. I couldn't shake how he and his dad were acting, secretive and, if I wasn't mistaken, troubled. And then it almost seemed like Mr. Hunter was adamant that Wes not have me in the car with him. The whole situation was off. Who was I kidding? My whole universe had completely fallen off balance.

I WAS NERVOUS ABOUT going to the bistro today, but it was unfounded, because Mr. Hunter acted as though nothing had happened last night. He thanked me for my help and gave me my training schedule. I was working four days a week. I left feeling better and somewhat excited at the prospect of having my own money. No matter what my parents said, it was always uncomfortable asking them for it. A lot of the time I just went without whatever it was I wanted.

Walking up my driveway, I noticed an unfamiliar car

parked in front of the garage. The very same white Jeep I had dog-eared in a car magazine I had left sitting on my desk. I walked by it cautiously as if it might come alive and bite me. When I opened the front door, I was immediately drawn to laughter in the kitchen.

"Abigail, is that you?" my mom called.

"Yeah, Mom." I tossed my bag on the couch, and against every screaming part of my body, entered the kitchen. Around the table sat my mom, my dad, and a young man who looked to be in college. He was handsome with emerald eyes and soft features. A lock of his blond hair fell over his long lashes as he looked up from a glass of water. He brushed it back and smiled, his eyes fixing on mine.

"Abigail, this is Elijah."

My mom introduced the handsome stranger who had me a bit tongue-tied and a strange pull on me that was both dark and mysterious.

"Abby," I corrected my mom.

Elijah stood up and held out his hand. I reached out obediently and placed my hand in his, an unexplainable flash of blackness sucked me in, taking every last bit of oxygen from my lungs. Elijah's eyes remained locked on mine.

"Are you okay, Abby?" He raised an eyebrow.

I pulled back my hand and broke the bond that had me spellbound. I couldn't tell if he was amused or genuinely worried.

"Fine," I answered, trying to disguise the sheer terror that overtook me. I rubbed the dread from my palm.

His eyes studied me, like I was a specimen to dissect.

"Your parents tell me you're interested in buying my car." His voice was smooth.

I looked to my parents for confirmation.

My dad answered, "I saw the magazine in your room."

"You were in my room?" I felt like a mouse claiming cheese from a trap.

"Maybe I should go?" Elijah interjected.

The world had proceeded in slow motion, still dazed from Elijah's touch and betrayed by my dad's intrusion.

"Abigail, isn't that the car you were interested in?" my mom asked, clueless.

I turned to Elijah who hadn't looked at anything but me since I entered the room. "I...I don't have the money right now," I explained to the unwelcomed stranger.

"We already took care of it." My dad stood and shook Elijah's hand. "Thank you, Elijah. I'll drive you home." He paused, then with a gleam in his eyes said, "Actually, Abigail will drive you home."

I was panic-stricken. "What?" My head rapidly went from my dad to Elijah. "I don't have my license." Thoughts of the accident flashed like a disco ball, and my hands started shaking.

My dad laughed loudly, "With me, Abigail. Do you really think I'd let you drive without a license?"

Or with a stranger who could turn out to be the next Jeffrey Dahmer?

A wicked smile crossed Elijah's porcelain skin. "Thank you, but I can call a taxi."

"Nonsense." My dad was suspiciously insistent.

I felt weak. This would be my first time driving since the accident, and now I had two witnesses to the humiliation.

My dad led us outside, and I watched distrustfully as Elijah climbed into the back seat of my new Jeep Cherokee. My dad slid into the passenger seat while I stood paralyzed with fear, tightly gripping the open driver's door as I fought the urge to run back into the house.

"Abigail, the first step to driving is getting in the car and putting on your seat belt."

My cheeks burned with humiliation number one, and I could only imagine how many more there would be. Elijah cracked a smile, but kept very quiet, still observing me intensely.

I tried to block out the accident as I slid into the driver's seat and buckled my seat belt, checking it twice and then a third time to make sure it wouldn't come off in a collision should I be so unlucky.

"It's buckled, Abigail." My dad watched me uneasily, his faith in my driving abilities obviously waning.

I flashed a weak smile and tried to steady my heart. As a distraction, I focused on the surprisingly pristine condition of the interior. The black dashboard shined like a brand new penny, and the smell of the leather seats still lingered. This couldn't be the same car in the ad.

"What year is this again?" I played dumb, gazing in the rearview mirror at Elijah. When he locked eyes with mine, the blood rushed to my head, confusing my train of thought.

"2009," he answered directly.

Even the leather binding of the steering wheel under my fingers felt new.

"It's in remarkable condition." My voice was soft, but there was no mistaking the condescending tone.

"Yes. It mostly sat in my garage."

"Let's get going, Abigail. It was a steal." My dad winked.

I turned the key and listened to the engine roar to life, the soft vibrations settling in my bones.

"This is a 4WD, so you're going to want to leave this lever in 2 High. Not that you'll be off-roading any time soon," my dad teased threateningly.

I chanced another look at Elijah in the back seat. He flashed another smile at my expense, but for the first time since we met, he turned his gaze outside.

I eased out of the driveway, stopping at the bottom to check for any passing cars. "Which way?" I was still on edge, but I was curious where Elijah lived because I surely would have recognized him if he was from Sandpoint.

"Bayview." His eyes connected with mine again in the rearview.

Bayview rivaled the beauty of Sandpoint. It was about

thirty minutes from Sandpoint, around the lake. It hadn't been stripped of the lush forest that wrapped around the lake for strip malls and industrial buildings like Sandpoint. Sure, Sandpoint was nice, but it was like comparing Oahu to Kauai. Bayview was prime real estate for vacation homes owned by very rich people. Very few people lived there year-round.

"How long are you vacationing here for?" I watched for his reaction as I turned toward Highway 95.

"Abigail, you didn't use your turn signal," my dad chastised.

"Sorry," I mumbled, shrugging my shoulders. Humiliation number two. *Thanks, Dad.*

Elijah interrupted, "That's very presumptuous of you, Abby."

His response caught me off guard. I had offended him, and surprisingly I felt guilty for it. I turned onto the highway, remembering my signal this time.

"I'm sorry. I just assumed—"

"Yes, we have established that already," Elijah responded coldly.

I scrunched in my seat, feeling worse. I had hoped my dad would have come to my defense, but he seemed unaffected by Elijah's attitude toward me.

"Abigail, you should concentrate on the road." My dad sat back in his seat, relaxed as if this were a scenic drive around the lake and not his daughter driving for the first time.

The Jeep was quiet for the rest of the trip. I tried to put the radio on, but my dad said it would be a distraction, which was kind of the point. Instead, we treaded in a sea of thick tension.

The traffic was light on the highway, not that there was really any traffic in Idaho. It got busier during commute time, but that just meant reducing speeds to sixty. It was still too early for the night commute.

"Turn left up ahead," Elijah instructed, breaking the silence.

Glancing back again, he was sitting straight up and stiff. *On alert.*

"Am I making you nervous?" I shared a smug smile of my own.

His body relaxed a bit, and a gleam in his eyes ignited. "No, Abby. You could never make me nervous."

My heartbeat gathered speed, flipping at his unexpected response.

"This is the left here." Elijah leaned forward between my dad and me.

He was close enough that I could feel the air he exhaled with his words. It electrified my senses, and it was yet to be determined if the feeling was good or bad, remembering the black hole when we shook hands.

I turned onto a gravel road. *So much for never off-roading,* I giggled to myself. I heard a little chuckle from Elijah in the back seat, sending chills down my spine. I just wanted to get the hell out of here. I was thankful my dad was here.

The driveway was long as we drove up and followed a bend flanked by large, mature trees with turning leaves. Reds, oranges, and yellows led us to a large historic home on the lake. I was awestruck by its size and architectural beauty, and by the time I parked in front, the house had doubled in size.

My dad slid out, leaving Elijah and me alone in the car. My hands stayed firmly planted on the steering wheel, and my eyes fixed out the windshield until he got out.

"You're shaking," he whispered into my ear just before stepping out.

My lungs froze. With two words, he had rendered me defenseless.

He climbed out of the car with very little effort and stood by my dad. They shook hands again.

"Thank you again, Elijah."

"My pleasure, James."

James? Since when were they on a first name basis?

Elijah leaned into the car. "It was a pleasure meeting you as well, Abby." He flashed a mischievous smirk

"Thanks for the car, Elijah," I stammered while quickly thumping my foot. We couldn't get out of here fast enough.

"Eli, please. Elijah is too formal, Abby."

His ability to arouse fear in me was disturbing, but I couldn't deny that I was also inexplicably attracted to him. I played with my lip nervously.

"Goodbye, Elijah." I mustered a little defiance.

"Until we meet again, Abby." Elijah winked dangerously.

He moved aside, and my dad slid back in and shut the door. As I backed up the car, Elijah kept his eyes fixed on mine. Even when I turned the car around, I could still see him in the rearview mirror, *watching me.*

6

AFTER I PULLED INTO OUR DRIVEWAY, I turned to my dad. His motives for purchasing the car weren't lost on me. "Thanks, Dad. I get my first paycheck in two weeks."

"Consider it a belated birthday present. Now you don't have to worry about working." He hopped out of the car.

Quickly unbuckling, I jumped out after him.

"What do you mean? I *want* to work."

He spun around, his laid-back demeanor disappearing.

"But now you don't have to," he challenged, his reaction stern.

Clenching the car keys in my hand, I knew the Jeep was too good to be true. I tossed the keys to him.

"Then I'll buy my own car," I barked, walking past him

into the house. I slammed the front door, cursing under my breath.

"How was your first driving lesson?" My mom popped out of the kitchen, drying a mug, her smile fading when she saw me scowling.

"Like you weren't in on it," I snapped and stormed up the stairs, shutting myself away in my room.

My parents not wanting me to work was ridiculous. They were just trying to keep me away from the Hunters. *From Wes*. Had I gotten a job anywhere else I bet it wouldn't have been an issue. I stomped over to my desk and snatched up the car magazine, flipping it open to the dog-eared page. *Who was Elijah?* There was something mysterious about him, and he seemed overly interested in me. The Hunters were making me paranoid. Before they returned, everything was imperfectly boring, and now everything was perfectly chaotic.

I tossed the magazine into the trash and sat at the window, staring down at my new Jeep. It was my dream car, but driving was still terrifying. After the accident, my parents had me see a therapist to work through the nightmares. She had diagnosed me with PTSD. The accident haunted me and so did those eyes. I knew I couldn't avoid driving forever, but now that it was time, I wasn't sure if I was actually ready.

Kendra jogged up the driveway, her exuberance touching every perfect part of her face as she drooled over my car. She made it hard not to smile. When I opened the window, she looked up.

"Can I lick it?" Her tongue was inches from the door.

"Sure, but I already marked my territory. Just got back from driving it."

"I can't stop touching it," she said as her hands explored every smooth, snow-white surface.

It was uncanny how she always cheered me up.

"Seriously, what are you waiting for? Come down here and show me this thing." She was trying to open the locked door.

"I can't." I looked back at my bedroom door as if my dad would walk in on me and hear the disappointment in my voice. Whatever. It wasn't like we could return it. "I'll be right down."

I tiptoed down the stairs and peeked around the house. My parents were sitting on the back patio, and my car keys were on the entry room console table, taunting me. It was *my* car, after all. Rushing over, I scooped them up and ran out the front door, closing it quietly.

Kendra squealed wildly, jumping up and down.

Laughing, I dangled the keys in front of her. "You are ridiculous."

"And why aren't you more excited? This is your dream car. Hello."

She ran up to me and snatched the keys, running to the car already unlocked by her persistent button pushing. She leapt into the passenger seat.

"Come on, Abby," she whined ecstatically.

Shaking my head, amused by her sheer lack of control, I went around to the driver's side and slid in.

Kendra took an exaggerated whiff. "It smells brand new."

"That's weird, right? It's eight years old." I gripped the steering wheel, remembering the intense feeling Elijah elicited.

"Whoa, Miss Debbie Downer. Don't hate fate." She touched every button within reach.

Maybe she was right. Any normal teenager would be happy to get a car. It suddenly resonated with me how badly I treated both my parents. I was being ungrateful.

"My parents would never buy me a car." She frowned at my lack of enthusiasm.

"I don't know. I guess it just took me by surprise." I leaned back and closed my eyes.

"Most people like surprises, and this is a huge one. Now you can quit that stupid job."

I shot up, somewhat miffed. "Why would I do that?"

"Because you have the car, duh," she said, confused.

"Why does everyone want me to quit my job? Maybe I want to work. Maybe I like it." My patience had worn thin, causing me to unleash my pent-up aggression on my best friend.

"Calm down, Abby. Geesh. You're probably the only teenager in the world that would want to work." She pushed open the door violently.

Great. I had managed to piss off the one person who'd been nothing but a good friend. I grabbed her arm before she was completely out of the car.

"Wait. I'm sorry. That should have been directed at my parents, not you."

The hurt under her lashes faded, and a small smile crept back up. "I'll forgive you under one condition," she said conspiratorially.

I rolled my eyes and feigned begging. "Anything."

She raised an eyebrow, and her eyes gleamed with trouble.

"I CAN'T BELIEVE I LET you talk me into this." My hands were shaking and my heart palpitating as I eased out of the driveway. It was pitch-black because this side of town was absent of streetlamps. The only light guiding us safely came from the crescent moon because I didn't want to turn my headlights on, risking waking my parents.

"What teenager hasn't snuck out and stolen a car? At least it's your own car." She looked over and smiled widely.

She had no idea I had done this before and it resulted in a week's hospital stay, therapy, and two years of haunting nightmares. My parents had done a good job covering up that night, asking the hospital for patient confidentiality, threatening a lawsuit. No one in town knew about the accident.

But wasn't I better now? That was what I repeated over and over again, at least. And it wasn't foggy like that night. In fact, the storms had cleared, and every visible star was blinking brightly.

Kendra connected her phone to the Bluetooth, filling the car with her playlist. My dad said it was an unnecessary distraction, but it was actually very calming.

"So, where are we going?" Nervous excitement brewed inside of me. We had never done something like this, and it was kind of fun being a little rebellious.

"Well, I kind of had an ulterior motive." She sank into her seat and put her bare feet up on the dashboard.

This couldn't be good. "What motive?"

"You'll find out. Head to Sandpoint Beach." She batted her lashes innocently.

"What? Why?" Panic stifled my breathing. I hadn't been there since the accident and wasn't planning on ever going back.

"Look out!" she screamed.

I swerved, nearly missing the curb but correcting quickly. "Don't scream like that. You scared the crap out of me!"

Kendra put her hand over her chest. "Maybe this wasn't such a good idea."

"No, I'm fine." Now I was determined to prove to

myself that I could do this. "What's going on at the beach in the middle of the week?"

"A college party," she said more carefully now.

"And how would you know about a college party, Miss Junior in High School?"

She sat up tall. "Well, I kind of met this guy."

"What? When?" She usually came running to me the second anything slightly interesting happened.

"After the dance on Saturday. I ditched Donny and went to the ice cream shop at the bridge. I was minding my own business when this gorgeous guy sat next to me. He has that whole bad boy vibe and those green eyes. Oh my goodness, I could get lost in them for days…" Her voice trailed off.

"Kendra, does he know you're still in high school?"

"Of course, silly." Her words were completely unconvincing.

"Kendra," I yelled, causing her to jump.

"What?" she whined.

"You have to tell him. You could get him in big trouble." We were underage, so dating older guys posed a huge risk. And keeping a secret in a small town was nearly impossible.

She pouted. "It's so unfair. We are way more mature than most girls in college. Besides, it's not like I would let anything happen."

"That may be true, but you still have to tell him. You can't start something on a throne of lies."

She looked at me as she caught the innuendo, and we shared a laugh as we pulled into the beach parking lot. It was almost full, so I parked in the back where there was still an empty row, not comfortable with my parking yet. Thankfully, I listened to my instincts, because I managed to park across three spots.

We stood at the back of my car, admiring my lack of parking skills.

"How is that even possible?" Kendra pointed to the car.

I bit my bottom lip. Humiliation number three.

"Hello, ladies," a silky voice called behind us, raising every hair on my little five-foot-four body.

Elijah.

I pivoted around slowly, afraid my suspicions would be confirmed. Kendra jumped into Elijah's arms, giving him a hug. A comfortable distance separated me from trouble.

"So we meet again, Abby." His emerald eyes were non-apologetic, entrapping me once again.

"You guys know each other?" Kendra frowned.

Recovering quickly from the weird coincidence, I responded, "Elijah sold my dad this car."

"Eli," his voice said evenly.

"Wow. What a coincidence," Kendra burst out.

"Yeah. Sure is," I mumbled, my instincts screaming foul.

"A happy one, right, Abby?" Elijah winked.

I cracked a fake smile, not responding verbally.

"Shall we, ladies?" He pulled Kendra in close to his side and spun her around, leading her toward the beach. He held his hand out for mine, but I refused, shoving both hands into my pockets instead.

Kendra looked over, her expression begging me to follow. Defeated, I did, because there was no way I was about to leave my best friend alone with him. Every molecule in my body told me he was bad news and not the kind any smart girl should be swooning over.

The beach around the lake was a narrow strand that wrapped around the Sandpoint area and was not much wider than a ski run, so when the weather was good, there was hardly a spot to lay a towel. Right now, it was littered with college kids, lounge chairs, and a bonfire.

"Is this even legal?" Pessimism slipped out of my mouth as we walked down the path through the trees and past the picnic area.

"No," Elijah smiled as he squeezed Kendra, "but I donated a lot to the upkeep of the lake," he said proudly.

Of course, he did. Elijah was keeping secrets, and I was going to unravel them. "What's your last name, Elijah?"

He answered smugly over his shoulder, "Winters."

The unraveling of Elijah Winters.

Without lights above to obscure the breathtaking view, the beauty of the lake was not lost on me. My parents and I used to come here every Fourth of July. Another tradition I had ruined. It was too hard to come back after the accident, but maybe this was what I needed to move forward. Just a little nudge. But then the misty air and familiar pine-fresh scents engulfed me, catapulting me back in time to the most painful memories of my life.

I cemented my feet where the grass met the sand,

paralyzed by my past connection with this place. This was where it all took place. The night I almost died. The night that stole Wes from me. One accident and my life was forever derailed. I couldn't go any farther, so I sat down, hugging my knees to my chest and hoping to pass off as a silent observer.

When Kendra noticed I wasn't following behind, she broke off from Elijah and skipped up to me.

"What are you doing? Come on," Kendra urged, grabbing my hand and trying to pull me up.

"No. I agreed to come, but that doesn't mean I have to actively participate." I yanked my hand from hers.

Shock registered on her face. "What's your deal? You've been weird ever since Wes came back. This whole teen angst thing looks really awful on you."

She kicked up sand as she stormed away. This was our first official fight. She was right, though. Wes' return and voluntary absence from my life had me completely insane. My thoughts were never far from him.

You're obsessed with him.

Kendra blended in around the fire with the college kids. It was so easy for her. She was a social butterfly, whereas my toes couldn't even graze the soft granules of sand only inches away. This wasn't healthy. My palms were sweating just by being here.

The lights of the pier shone brightly in the distance. It wasn't too far away and sitting here was driving me crazy, so I twisted through the trees, the sounds of the party becoming distant. The quiet was soothing.

The bistro was tucked between a row of shops and restaurants just before the pier. The lights inside were visible from where I stood at the far end of the pier. Shadows crossed the windows from inside, and I imagined Mr. Hunter shuffling around, cleaning up and Penelope drowning her sorrows in her playlist as she rolled silverware. It was silly, but I envied her because she was inside there with Wes and I was out here, alone.

The waves rippled softly against the pier, rocking it gently, my body swaying with it. Being *here* didn't seem so bad—so debilitating. I wasn't ready for the beach. Not yet. Every once in a while, laughter would drift from the party, momentarily breaking the peaceful silence.

"Do you feel safe over here all by yourself?"

My body stiffened at Elijah's sudden arrival. Was he asking, or threatening? It was hard to tell. I refused to let him intimidate me, so I firmly planted my elbows on the railing as I admired the glimmer of the moon dancing over the water. "Shouldn't you be with Kendra?"

"No. I believe I'm exactly where I should be."

"Is that right? Is that why you cozied up to my best friend? To get to me?"

"Maybe." His eyes lit up confidently.

"You could have just asked me out." I crossed my arms, feigning courage.

"And what would you have said if I had asked?"

"No," I said firmly.

He chuckled, seemingly unaffected. "Well, then maybe I like your friend."

My heart skipped a terrifying beat as his footsteps creaked under the give of the wood planks, bringing him closer to me. I could see his breath in the chill of the night as he made himself comfortable next to me.

"Do I make you nervous?" He looked over to me.

"A little, honestly," I replied quietly, not turning to meet his gaze. My voice trembled slightly.

He leaned over, sweeping my hair behind my shoulder, his touch trailing euphoric sensations around my neck and shoulder, and whispered into my ear, "I'm not the one you need to be afraid of."

My body stiffened with dread.

Then who do I need to be afraid of?

A chill replaced the warmth of his breath on my neck, and when I braved a glance over, Elijah was gone. I spun around quickly, searching the pier and the trees beyond, but he was nowhere to be found.

Do you feel safe? No, not anymore. I rushed off the pier and back through the trees, flinching at every noise I heard.

"Abby, what happened to you?" Kendra bounced up to me upon my return.

"I went for a walk on the pier."

Concern was evident in her eyes. "You've been gone for over an hour. The pier is less than five minutes away."

How could that be? It felt like I had only been gone for a few minutes. Moments of time had been lost standing on the pier with Elijah.

A wave of nausea hit me suddenly, causing me to grimace.

"Are you feeling okay?"

"Can we go home?"

"Of course. You don't look so good. Elijah disappeared anyway. The jerk." Kendra wrapped her arm in mine.

My legs were wobbly and my mind was hazy, so I gripped her arm tighter to keep from falling. When I glanced up beyond the bonfire, I spotted a pair of eyes fixated on me.

"Is that Ben Hunter?" The boy's hair was jet black just like Ben's, and the eyes seemed familiar even from this far away. My head was starting to pound, and my vision was getting blurry.

"The devastatingly gorgeous guy with black hair and irresistible eyes? Yes, I believe I heard someone call him that. He's one of the twins, right?"

"Yeah." I stumbled a bit, my eyes still on Ben.

"He's weird," Kendra added, holding her grip tighter around me.

My stomach was doing flips.

"I think we're better off without boys." She snickered.

"I think so." My legs suddenly gave out, but before I hit the ground, a pair of arms wrapped around me. I expected to see Kendra above me, but instead, Ben cradled me, my flesh burning under his touch. He handed me over to Kendra quickly and, without a word, went back to the party.

"What was that?" Kendra tracked him, awestruck. "Are you okay, Abby?"

"I really need to lie down," I begged her as all my weight leaned into her.

She hugged me close and helped me as I stumbled through the parking lot.

"You're going to have to drive," I mumbled when we made it to the car.

She took my keys and helped me into the passenger seat and buckled me in. My head sank into the headrest, feeling heavy against the leather. My thoughts swirled with confusion, not understanding what happened on the pier. Elijah's words echoed in my thoughts. Safety had been replaced with fear, no matter how irrational it seemed.

7

I WAS FAIRLY CERTAIN I HAD gotten away with sneaking out. I still couldn't walk by the time we got back to my house, so Kendra dragged me up to my room and tucked me in. She wanted to stay the night, but explaining her sudden presence to my parents was almost as bad as getting caught. For several hours I lay in bed, tossing around the events of the night in my head, over and over again. Elijah made me uneasy, but I was strangely drawn to him. I had always followed the straight and narrow, the black and white. Elijah was gray, and Wes was somewhere in between it all. So, why couldn't I shake them?

Ben, catching me the way he had, wasn't sitting right with me either. I had never officially met Ben or his twin, Zoe. I only knew them in passing, so for Ben to do that was just odd to me. I wasn't even sure he knew Wes and I were friends.

THE CHIRPING OF BIRDS through my open window woke me. It felt as if only moments had passed since I closed my eyes. My body ached, my head was still pounding, and sleep remained heavy in my eyes.

"Abigail, if you don't get ready soon, you'll be late for school," my mom called cheerfully through the door. I grumbled as I rolled out of bed, landing hard and loud.

The door flew open, and my mom rushed to my side.

"Abigail, what's wrong?" She put her hand on my forehead and then on the back of my neck. Her hands felt like ice cubes on my skin.

"Abigail, you're burning up."

"I'm fine, Mom."

"No, you're not. Get back into bed. You're staying home. I'll go get some medicine for your fever."

When she was out of sight, I went into the bathroom, tied my hair up into a knot, and splashed water onto my face. My skin did feel hot. I stared at my face in the mirror, beads of water dripping down, last night's encounter returning vividly.

Do you feel safe? A prickly sensation crawled around inside me, panic consuming me and chipping away at my grip on reality.

"Abigail?"

"I was just using the bathroom." I went back into my room and slid back under the sheets. I swallowed the pills my mom handed me.

"Do you need anything?" she asked.

"No. Just some more sleep."

She tucked the sheets in around me. "Okay. I'll check on you in a bit." She kept the door cracked.

I turned over and stared out the window, still trying to understand Elijah's cryptic message about my safety. For all I knew, *he* was the danger and it was becoming increasingly evident that Elijah was following me, but why?

I stayed in bed for most of the day, listening to my parents come and go as they checked on me several times.

By evening, I was bored out of mind, having finished the English paper that was due tomorrow and trudging through a very, very, very long history chapter.

"Hey, honey. How are you feeling?" My mom checked on me again.

"I'm feeling better. I should be fine to go to school tomorrow," I said, giving her my best award-winning smile to reassure her.

"If you think so." Her voice quivered a bit.

"I'm sure." I stood up and walked to my desk for her benefit, showcasing my sturdy legs.

"Your father and I were going to get a bite to eat. Can I bring you something back?"

She brushed a long golden strand behind her ear. My chestnut locks were courtesy of my dad's genes, and my copper eyes and long lashes came from my mom.

"That would be great. Maybe some chicken noodle soup?"

"Your favorite. We'll be home in about an hour or so."

I watched my parents drive away and then rushed downstairs to jump on my dad's computer. I had been begging for one of my own, but considering I didn't even have a cell phone, it was highly unlikely it would happen before I left for college. I gave up on the cell phone battle rather easily, only having one friend anyway.

Why do you need a cell phone, Peanut?

Peanut was the nickname betrothed on me after I had an allergic reaction to peanuts in preschool. That was a fun day. Now my dad used it as a term of endearment, although how you could make light of a traumatizing day was beyond me.

The computer was already on, so I opened the search engine to search *Elijah Winters*. Typing his name came easy enough, but pressing the *Search* button was a whole different story. I didn't know what I expected to find, but shaky hands and erratic heartbeats accompanied my fleeting moment of courage as my finger pressed *Enter* on the keyboard. My cowardly eyes closed tightly. I counted ten beats of my heart before I peeked one eye open to brave the words on the screen.

Elijah Winters' profiles.

Elijah Winters' photos, phone, email, address.

I clicked on a link, and his address in Bayview popped up with a picture of him in front of his house. There wasn't much else. The fact that I found anything about him at all was a miracle. I guess being rich made him a somebody.

The doorbell chimed, so I closed the tab and ran to answer it. A Sandpoint Bistro takeout bag stared me in the face, held by the dainty-pink polished fingers of my best and only friend.

"You shouldn't have," I teased as I took the bag from her and stepped aside.

"I didn't. It was on your front porch, and it's still warm. How are you feeling?"

She jumped onto the couch, making herself comfortable under the throw blanket. Meanwhile, I was still ten seconds in the past, trying to make sense of the bistro bag that smelled suspiciously like chicken noodle soup.

"It's a takeout bag, Abby, not a boa constrictor." She giggled.

"I didn't order anything." I was holding the bag with my fingertips as far away from myself as possible.

"Is there a name on it?" She flipped on the television and browsed through the channels.

I carried the bag into the kitchen, setting it on the table, unable to take my eyes off of it. There was no way that the contents of this bag could possibly contain chicken noodle soup.

I unfolded the white paper bag and lifted out the container that the bistro packaged soup in. The smell of my favorite soup wafted up to my nose. I peeled off the lid and confirmed that the carrots, celery, chicken, and spiral noodles comprised my favorite chicken noodle soup. My hands were shaky as I put the lid back on that soup, unbelieving that this could be a mere coincidence. Pulling the bag over to put the container back in, I noticed a piece of paper at the bottom. The obvious giver would be Wes, but a part of me was afraid it would be Elijah's name scrolled on it. I unfolded it carefully.

Chicken soup will always soothe the soul. Wes

I let out a huge sigh of relief, although it was still strange.

"What are you doing in there?" Kendra yelled over the television.

I took out two bowls from the cabinet and two spoons and divided the soup.

Kendra was enamored with a reality show when I placed the soup down on the coffee table.

"Sweet! I love their soup. Thanks, Abby."

I handed her the note.

She read it, smiling big enough to scream. "Abby, do you know what this means?"

No, I didn't.

"Don't read so much into it. It's just soup." I sat on the floor in front of the coffee table.

"Your *favorite* soup." She slid off the couch next to me.

I still remembered the first time Wes brought me soup.

"You look awful, Abby."

Wes stood above me as I lay on the couch with a blanket over me. I came home early from school. My sixth grade teacher was convinced I was faking until I threw up on her shoes.

"I brought you your favorite." Wes held up a takeout bag from his dad's bistro.

I started seeing Wes differently that summer. He always fascinated me with his grace, the smoothness of his voice, and the intensity behind his eyes. But now I saw *him*. His auburn hair just long enough to fall over his eyebrows when he laughed, the long lashes that protected his iridescent eyes, the way one side of his mouth curled up when he shared a mischievous thought, and the one thing that affected me the most was how my body came alive whenever he was around. I anticipated the slightest graze when we walked side by side. I knew I was infatuated with him the first day I met him on the swings, but now I was sure I was in love with him and always would be. Wes' absence from my life took a toll on me, and now that he was back, old feelings were resurfacing and I was finding it harder and harder to breathe.

"Abby, are you going to finish that?" Kendra pointed to my half-full bowl of soup. "This place seriously has the best food."

I barely watched the movie Kendra had picked. I didn't even know the name of it. I was too wrapped up with all things Wes that I couldn't think about anything else. At some point, Wes and I were going to have to talk. And not just with broken words and short sentences. No, what we needed were paragraphs. And a lot of them.

"SEATTLE?" KENDRA SLAMMED her locker closed. "That is it. I am staging another intervention. You have been acting so weird ever since Wes came back. Why would you go to Seattle? You need to start talking."

We were headed to the front office for our elective class. She used her power of persuasion and talked the guidance counselor into assigning it to both of us for sixth period.

"And what's with the jacket?"

I hugged my arms around the chocolate leather bomber jacket that my grandpa gave me for my twelfth birthday. He died soon after. It was one of the worst days of my life. We were super close. Closer than my dad and me. I found it hanging in the back of my closet this morning. I used to wear it every day, but I was too small for it, so my mom put it away. It had been years since I wore it. His scent still lingered in between the cracked leather, and it was decorated in war patches, a tribute to his service.

My parents kept his house in Seattle, but it was over five hours away. Getting away from Sandpoint sounded amazing, but there was no way my parents would let me go. There was a train station in the center of town, and I had a little money saved up from babysitting jobs over the summer and my tips from the bistro, so as long as Kendra covered for me I could make it work. It was a crazy idea, but whenever I felt overwhelmed, my grandpa was the one person who could make me feel better. Being in his house again, surrounded by his things, might be just what I needed.

"It was my grandfather's. So, will you cover for me this weekend?" I was looking down at my red Chucks when Kendra grabbed my arm and held me back.

"Ow," I hissed, peering up.

Wes walked through the front door, the backlight illuminating a halo around his frame, and the world froze as it always did when he was around. He raked his hand through his hair, a knowing smile lighting up his eyes when they met mine. He ducked into the office.

"You can start by telling me the truth about you and him," Kendra demanded, looking to where Wes was standing a moment ago. "I've heard the gossip, but I want to hear it from you. What happened?"

"Nothing," I lied.

"Have you even talked to him?"

We stood in the hall just outside the office.

"Only if you count hi and bye." He had said a few more things than that, but I didn't feel like elaborating.

His voice drifted into the hallway. "Thank you, Mrs. McCarthy."

I grabbed Kendra's arm and dragged her behind a row of lockers. The nervous energy filled every cell in my body as footsteps echoed in the hallway and then paused. Both of us held our breath. When the door opened and closed, we both let out a sigh of relief. I peeked around the corner to verify he had left.

"He's gone." I stepped out from our hiding spot.

Kendra smacked my arm. "That hurt."

My nails had dug into her skin, leaving a row of crescent indentations.

"I'm sorry." I frowned apologetically.

"You can't avoid him for long."

No, I couldn't. And really, I didn't want to. The idea that he was staying away from me was unexplainable and hurt like hell.

I MISSED MY SHIFT at the bistro yesterday due to my illness, but I was back to work tonight. Thursday evenings, the bistro had karaoke, which meant for a busy night. After Wes' bold attempt at communication, trepidation covered me like a winter coat.

"Aren't you sweating?" Penelope snickered as she raced away from the front desk with a handful of silverware.

She talks. I was beginning to think she was mute. I stripped two of the layers I was wearing courtesy of the brisk evening.

Once I scanned the restaurant for Wes, satisfied he wasn't around, I stuffed my bag under the front desk and checked my table assignments. I had the front section, farthest away from the stage. I would have to thank Mr. Hunter for that later. I'd been here for karaoke, and aside from the terrible voices that blared through the microphone, the groups seemed to be rowdier closer to the stage.

By the end of the night, I was only wearing a tank top, and I was still sweating. Penelope smirked knowingly from across the room. She either hated me or, frankly, was just socially inept. Maybe it was the blue hair.

When it was my turn to take a break, the crisp night air was beckoning to cool my sticky skin. Slipping out back, I was relieved when the air kissed every exposed part of my body. I closed my eyes, indulging in the noise-free environment, even hearing the lapping of the water just across the pier. The back patio overlooked the lake.

"Did you get the soup?" Wes' voice encircled me, catching my breath in my chest. He was only a foot away from me, his eyes glowing under the soft patio lights. Words escaped me, and my lungs ceased to function. Even my knees weakened. In seconds, I had transformed into a pathetic teenage girl hopelessly in love.

He dipped his head slowly, his eyes peering up, inviting me into his enchanting world, the upturn of his lips teasing me.

"I—How did you know?" A familiar comfort floated between us.

He took a step closer and sank his head in the space between my ear and my shoulder, grazing his lips back and forth, taking in a deep breath. Dizziness swirled around me, my mouth falling open as I took in labored breaths, my hands planted to the wall for support.

"I know everything about you, Abigail Rose," he whispered into my ear as his lips traveled up my neck, his warm breath leaving a trail of goose bumps in its wake. "I know your favorite soup." His nose explored my hair. "I know what shampoo you use."

I was losing myself in him, the will to stay still collapsing.

He continued, "I know that you tie your hair up when you are uncomfortable." One of his hands planted on the wall next to my head, the other glided through my hair, wrapping around locks and tugging lightly. A soft murmur escaped my mouth as his mouth explored my jawline. "I know what I feel when I'm around you."

With that, my paralyzed limbs awoke and my fingers twisted in his hair. His hands cradled my face, pulling my lips to his.

"Wes." A harsh demand reached us from the shadows, pulling us apart. Ben stepped into the light, glaring at his brother, his eyes vicious and his body rigid.

Wes turned to me, regret confronting me for just a moment before he left in the opposite direction of his older sibling. Ben focused his fury on me then, causing me to stumble back into the bistro.

Finishing my shift proved difficult, my thoughts racing between Wes' confession and Ben's obvious and inexplicable rage. My life was quickly spinning out of control, and I wasn't in the driver's seat anymore. I felt Mr. Hunter's eyes on me as I grabbed my bag and ran out to my car where my dad was waiting. He hopped out, taking the passenger seat position. I was surprised when we arrived home. I was on autopilot these days.

"I think you're ready for your test Monday. How do you feel?"

I killed the engine and looked down at the steering wheel, avoiding eye contact.

"Good," I replied with a small smile. How could I concentrate on such mundane things when suddenly I was surrounded by chaos?

"I'm going to miss driving around with you," he confessed and then jumped out of the Jeep. "You coming?"

"Yeah, in a minute."

He looked at me oddly. "Okay."

He shut the door and went inside. I flipped on my iPod playlist and leaned my seat back, closing my eyes, visions of Wes so close to me vividly replaying in my mind. Suddenly, an overwhelming sensation of being watched came over me.

I shot up quickly, startled by Wes standing outside the passenger door. Unforgiving tension passed between us as the seconds turned into minutes until time no longer existed. The storm that had rolled in during my shift had exchanged a light drizzle for an unexpected downpour, soaking Wes, who stood unfazed, studying me.

The click of the handle sent my heart racing for cover as

he slid in, the water rolling off his body and settling into the leather. The cold followed him inside, but as I was reaching to turn the engine on, Wes placed his hand around mine, stopping me, the soft touch reminding me of so many times his hand had touched mine. I sucked in a shallow breath, closing my eyes as the water from his hand dripped onto mine. Only when he pulled it away did I look over, meeting his pained expression.

"What?" I asked quietly.

He twisted his hands tightly on his lap.

"My father told me to stay away from you, but I don't know how to do this." His knuckles turned white as he squeezed them tighter together.

"Do what?" My voice was shaky now.

He shook his head slowly. "Be around you without..." He lifted his head, untangling his hands, and leaned into me. His finger hooked under my chin, holding my gaze to his. I was under his spell once again, entranced by his beauty.

"Without what?" I asked breathlessly.

His eyes reached out and took hold of my soul, absolving pain's past. Then without warning, he dropped his hand and sat back in his seat, securing his hands together once again.

Tears welled in my eyes, the familiar disappointment lingering. "You can't keep doing this to me." My words broke as I choked back humiliation.

"I know," he said regretfully.

"Then, why?" I was begging for answers, pleading for closure before my broken heart was irreparable.

"Because I don't know how to live without you either." He gritted his teeth, the truth setting him free, but also defeating him.

"Then don't," I pleaded. "Don't push me away, Wes. Please." My heart ached.

His iridescent eyes faded, replaced with a terrifying darkness as he pushed my hair away from my neck and leaned into me.

"Your eyes," my voice quaked.

"Are you afraid of me, Abby?" His voice was steady.

I shook my head slowly. "No," I whispered.

He took my wrist roughly in his hand. "Are you afraid now?"

Tears rushed down my cheeks as I shook my head more quickly this time. "No." I was holding onto the trust we had built over the years.

He pulled my face closer to him, his nose gliding over my swollen eyes and dampened cheeks.

"What about now?" he whispered.

"Never." Why was he doing this to me? I felt completely decimated, and it was my fault because I was letting him break me.

His eyes lifted to mine, the onyx melting away to perfect iridescence again. Without warning, he jumped out of the Jeep into the storm and into the forest, his silhouette visible among the trees as lightning flashed across the forest.

I'm not the one you need to be afraid of.

I was stunned into disbelief. Believing in the unbelievable had shifted my sense of stability, forcing me to face all things out of the realm of possibility no longer trapped in the fantasy books of my childhood. The stories ran rampant around me no longer hidden in make believe. They were right in front of me all along. The veil had been lifted. Wes wasn't like me. He wasn't like anyone. He was something else entirely.

8

THE WEEKEND ARRIVED WITHOUT another word from Wes or Elijah. My shift at the bistro didn't start for a few hours, and my homework was finished, so I curled up to the window with a book and tried to forget for just a few hours that my world had been turned upside down and to distract my thoughts from Wes—his smell, his touch, his voice. It was all-consuming and being away from him made me restless.

I read the same paragraph half a dozen times before I finally gave up, tossing the book on my bed. Another storm was rolling in, the threatening clouds foreshadowing a big one. We had more rain in the last few weeks than we had all last year.

I liked the rain. The pitter-patter of it on my window

lulled me to sleep, and the whirring of the wind ignited something exciting and primal deep within me. Today, though, the darkness charging toward Sandpoint scared me, because I now knew that shadows bred hidden dangers. Ones with onyx eyes and devilish grins.

As I descended the stairs, I heard my dad whispering in his office. When I peeked in, he was on the phone and he looked agitated, rubbing his face hard. Before he could see me eavesdropping, I tiptoed around the corner to the front door.

"Abigail, are you ready for work?" my mom called from her knitting chair.

"Yep, but I think Dad is busy, so I can just walk." The thought gave me a mild panic attack.

"I'm ready," my dad announced as he closed his office door.

The dark circles under his eyes were new, and the scruff on his face was growing thicker. I couldn't remember my dad ever looking so disheveled.

Driving to the bistro, I studied him in my peripheral. His laid-back demeanor was replaced with a tapping foot and tense silence.

"Dad, is something bothering you?" I tried my best to keep my eyes on the road.

The tapping ceased.

"No, Peanut. Everything's fine." The exhaustion settling into the creases in his forehead said otherwise.

I had been so wrapped up in my own life that I had

failed to see that things were not fine in the Rose household. There must have been other signs of distress that I missed. I rifled through the last couple of weeks. The only things that stood out were my dad not traveling anymore and the odd moment with him and Mr. Hunter when we had dinner at the bistro.

"You know, I'm not a little girl anymore. I can handle it if things are bad, you know, with you and Mom." I knew I was prying, and I wasn't entirely sure if I wanted to know, but I was worried.

"Your mom and I are better than ever. I'm just working long hours to make up for the loss of clients with the new situation. I promise things are good." He smiled.

Not only was there something wrong, but it was worse than I could have imagined. My dad was an expert liar, and I meant that in a good way. He was the king of elaborate surprises, keeping secrets for weeks and making up cover stories. My mom and I were never the wiser. Today I could see right through him, but I didn't press the issue. I didn't have to. I could tell it was bad, and knowing that the only stability I had left in my life was slipping out from under me was terrifying.

MR. HUNTER WAS A quiet man. He hadn't said much to me since he hired me, but I got the impression he kept me in his line of sight at all times. It should have crept me out, but it felt more like he was watching out for me. It didn't make much sense until the other night, but I was slowly starting to piece things together. Maybe he was afraid for me. That whatever was happening to Wes could possibly hurt me. But then, why move back here?

"I think that table is clean." Penelope smirked.

I had been obsessively rubbing the finish off a table. "Oh." A blush heated my cheeks.

"You okay? You've seemed off all night." Penelope twisted her blue hair around her finger, smacking her gum loudly.

I looked around, confused. "Are you talking to me?" She had essentially ignored me since I started working here.

"No." She spun around and strolled away, planting herself at the table full of silverware and napkins waiting to be rolled.

Well, that went well.

"You can go now." Mr. Hunter was suddenly next to me, his voice kind.

"Are you sure? I can help Penelope with the silverware." Something seemed different about him tonight, but I couldn't place it.

"She's almost done. We'll see you tomorrow." His wider-than-life smile seemed misplaced.

"See you tomorrow then." I untied my apron as I went to grab my bag at the front desk.

The door suddenly crashed open and Ben, Zoe, and Wes all flew in. The twins glanced at me for a second and then walked to the back to join Mr. Hunter. Wes' eyes stayed on me longer, softer and less conflicted than when he left me the other night. My pulse pumped out of rhythm as he drifted slowly by me, his arm grazing mine, and his fingers secretly lingering on mine, the exhilaration reaching parts of me that only he could reach. Once his fingers slid from mine, the connection that bonded us was severed.

Headlights through the glass alerted me to my dad's arrival as he idled out front in the Jeep. Penelope was still smacking her gum, rocking out to her playlist while rolling silverware, and the Hunters were slumped over in a tight circle at the farthest table in the back. There was no reason to be suspicious, but their behavior wasn't normal. Nothing was as it seemed. Not anymore.

MR. HUNTER CLOSED the restaurant for the day, stating a family emergency, so my Sunday would be spent worrying about Wes. As far as I knew, the Hunters were comprised of just the four of them, and a family emergency would mean something had happened to one of them.

I found my mom knitting on the patio in her old lady rocking chair. She hated when I teased her for it. It was a clear autumn day, the sun baking my skin as I stood in front of her. "Knitting another masterpiece?"

"I wish you and your father would leave me and my knitting alone. I mean, what else would I do?"

"Sorry. Where's Dad?"

"He's getting ready to leave for Seattle. He should be back late tonight."

Her hands wrapped the yarn fluidly around a very large and dangerous-looking pin. I was almost afraid to ask what she was making with orange and pink.

"That's cute, I think," I blurted, studying the pile of yarn curiously.

"Don't worry. It's not for you. Cindy's daughter is having a baby girl, so the knitting club thought it would be fun to knit different things for her."

Relief washed over me. "Aw, and I was really looking forward to another one of your lopsided sweaters."

She swatted at me playfully. "You're horrible. Wait until I'm gone. Then you'll appreciate all those lopsided sweaters."

Now I felt kind of bad for teasing her.

"So, what are you up to today?" she asked.

"Well, nothing, unless Dad would let me go with him to Seattle." I could visit grandpa's house without lying. It was a win-win. My mom was staring at me like I had grown a third eye. "What?"

"Nothing. I'm just surprised you would want to spend the day with your dad, that's all. I think he would like that." She flashed an approving smile.

"Cool. I'll go find him." I bounced back into the house, excited now.

I caught up with my dad just as he was heading out the front door. "Hey, Dad, do you think I could come with you to Seattle?" I rocked back and forth on my feet, anticipating his answer.

"I'm just going for business. It's going to be pretty boring, and I won't be home until late. You have school tomorrow."

"That's okay, and Mom said it was okay. Maybe you could just drop me off downtown? I heard Pioneer Square is pretty cool. Lots of shopping and street vendors." I might have been playing up my enthusiasm a bit. "Then we could have dinner together."

He pondered for a moment. "I'm sorry, Peanut. Not this time."

It was hard to hide my disappointment, but once my dad made up his mind, there was no arguing. He shrugged his shoulders and left without another word. I spun around the room, unsure of how to keep myself busy. Wes was plaguing me.

"He said no, I see." My mother stood in the doorway of the patio.

"Yep." I kicked the ground.

"I'm sorry, sweetie. He's been really stressed lately, and I think he was going to stop by Grandpa's house to get it ready."

My ears perked up. "Ready for what?"

"Oh, sweetie, I thought you knew. He's selling it."

My heart broke. The comforts of my childhood lived in that house. They thrived. And now they would be sold to the highest bidder.

My nose stung from the unintended betrayal, and tears fogged my vision. I needed to get out of here. The walls were closing in on me. I snagged my grandpa's jacket off the coat rack and walked out the front door, my head filled with so much sadness. It was an all-consuming pain that I feared would haunt me forever.

I hugged my arms around the jacket and tucked my head, having no idea where I was going or caring. I was angry with my dad for not letting me tag along. Right now, I just really needed my grandpa.

"Abby?"

When I looked up, I came face-to-face with Wes, who was standing on the sidewalk across the street. I was disoriented, not really knowing how long I had been walking for. Looking past him, I realized I had ventured to his house unknowingly.

"What are you doing here?" he asked.

"I…uh…" Embarrassed, I answered, "I don't know."

"Are you okay?" he asked as he crossed the street, stopping just in front of me.

"Are we having a real conversation?" I shifted uncomfortably.

"Don't do that." His voice pleaded.

My heart skipped. "Do what?"

He took both of my shoulders in his hands and squeezed lightly.

"We've never been like this." He rested his forehead on mine. "I can't take it."

I was forgetting how to breathe. "I didn't make it this way, Wes. You are the one who left Sandpoint." I choked back what I really wanted to say. *You left me.*

"I know," he said softly, sliding his hand to the back of my neck now. His pain was evident under his grip.

After a shared silence, he cleared his throat.

"You're still wearing those red Chucks." The tension dissolved for a moment.

My cheeks burned. They were old and dirty, but I couldn't part with them. They reminded me of him. They had survived the accident unscathed.

"What do you remember from that night?" he inquired.

Too much and not enough.

I shrugged my shoulders. "You screaming in pain, me crying, a tree, lots of blood, and…" I wasn't sure how much more I should say, because the next part I wasn't sure about, and I didn't want to come off as completely crazy. I was already unhinged enough.

"And?" Wes held my gaze with a worried intensity.

"And…nothing. Nothing else." I turned away, not knowing if he was believing me. *Hungry, murderous obsidian eyes.*

Ben and Zoe were suddenly across the street, staring at us with their own murderous glare.

"I need to go," Wes said, annoyed.

He traced his finger over my lip, lightly taking my chin in his hand and tilting my head up to him. Everything stopped for us—the birds silenced and the twins forgotten. As he moved in closer, my heart raced and my head pounded, a surge of electricity charging through me. His lips stopped just short of mine.

"Abby," he whispered, filling my lungs with the sweet smell of his breath.

"Uh-huh." Anticipation soared through my veins.

He leaned over farther. "Be careful," he said softly into my ear and then turned quickly, racing to his siblings, leaving me in a state of conflicted bliss.

The Hunter siblings glided back to their house, almost floating. The Hunters had always been pretty private in the community, but I had never noticed how secretive they were. Wes had never invited me to his house, but being so young then, I never really put much thought into it. Now it seemed odd.

I was finally realizing there was so much I didn't know about the Hunters. I didn't care much back then because all I saw was Wes. I didn't see past him, but there was clearly so much more to him. To his family. I wanted to know everything now. I wanted to know why they left so urgently after my accident and why they came back now.

A chill swept through me, so I zipped up my jacket and headed back home. My mother was back to knitting, but inside now because of the chill.

"Kendra called while you were out. Feeling any better?"

"Define better," I replied curtly.

"Look, sweetie, I'm sorry selling your grandpa's house came as a surprise to you, but what are we going to do with it? We never go into the city, and having renters is a lot of work. We just thought it best to let it go. Maybe you'd like to come pack things up?"

Pack things up. Like it was that easy to take someone's life and put it into a securely taped box. "I'd like that. Thanks."

Hiding away in my room seemed like the best thing to do. I watched another storm roll in over the mountains. The smell of my grandpa wafted from his jacket. I couldn't believe I had forgotten about it. He was so proud of it, telling me stories about how he earned each patch, so when he gave it to me I felt like the luckiest girl in the world. Had I known he was dying, it probably would have felt different. The jacket had several pockets. Three on the outside and two on the inside. I explored all of them out of sheer boredom, but when my fingers grazed a key, I was surprised. I dug it out, turning it in my palm. Engraved in the key was an infinity symbol. It was familiar, but I couldn't quite remember why. But I knew this symbol and not from math class.

9

"A BBY? ABBY?" KENDRA'S voiced hissed.

Lifting my head from my desk, I realized I had fallen asleep in class. I had barely slept last night, trying to figure out what was happening with Wes and what that key I found in my grandpa's jacket opened.

Everyone was staring at me. *Everyone.*

"Miss Rose, do you need to go to the nurse?" Mrs. Knight had her hands on her waist, looking less than thrilled with me.

"No." I ducked my head as I slid down in my desk.

She shook her disapproving head and continued the math problem that I could have sworn she was working on before I fell asleep. Either I was only out for a few seconds or this was one of those five-part word problems that never seemed to end and still had a variable in the answer.

I shoved my book and notebook into my bag when the bell rang and strode out with Kendra.

"You were mumbling something about Wes." Kendra laughed, walking close to me in the noisy hallway.

I grumbled, mortified, "How loud?"

"Loud enough." Her amusement smiled back at me.

"You've been demoted from best friend to casual acquaintance." She didn't laugh. "I was kidding, Kendra."

She slammed her books into the locker and switched them out for her next class. "It would be funny if it wasn't true." Hurt pooled in the corners of her ocean blues.

I picked at the corner of my math book anxiously. I had been pretty consumed with work. And Wes. I should have called her back yesterday. "I'm sorry. I've been drowning in schoolwork and the bistro." It wasn't really a lie after all.

"You've always made time for me," she said more forcefully than I'd ever been on the receiving end before, slamming her locker closed.

The hallway was emptying quickly, with students deserting their lockers in favor of their next class. I wasn't sure what to say.

"Nothing? Really?" Disappointed and betrayed, Kendra stormed off.

The second bell rang. I was late for English, again.

IT SEEMED LIKE EVERYONE was avoiding me this week. Kendra barely afforded me a glance, and the only Hunter I saw was Mr. Hunter at the bistro. Penelope even ceased her random comments.

I wrapped up my Saturday night shift and climbed into my Jeep. I passed my driver's test with flying colors, so I was on my own now. My dad was apprehensively proud, and my mom was ecstatic. It would seem that my life had resumed its monotonous routine.

The lights in the bistro turned off, and only the dim parking lights illuminated small circles sporadically around the lot. Employees were required to park in the far corner, and, unfortunately, there were no lights, leaving me in pitch-blackness. Winter was quickly approaching, and the chill had accumulated in my car during my absence. I blasted the heat, revving my engine a couple of times to speed up the warming process. It was only nine, and I didn't really feel like going home yet, but what other choice did I have?

Accepting defeat, I pulled out of the lot and headed down the road to my house. As if the night wasn't creepy enough with the low-lying fog rolling in, each streetlamp burnt out as I passed it, leaving a trail of darkness behind me. Chills shook my body, my instincts telling me to get home faster, so I hit the gas when suddenly a deer ran out into the road in front of me. I slammed on the brakes, the sound of rubber to pavement vibrating in my ears, my heart thumping erratically. The back end of my Jeep fishtailed to the left and right several times, the deer frozen in the middle of the street, its eyes piercing mine, begging for mercy. Narrowly missing the deer, my Jeep skidded off the road down a small incline, bouncing over rocks and pushing through bushes. It came to a stop just before hitting a tree head-on.

My headlights shone on the tree trunk, transporting me into a haunting memory.

"I don't want to drive," I begged, tears falling from my terrified eyes.

Wes screamed in pain, crumpled over in the passenger seat of Ben's car. "You have to," he screamed.

Trembles took over my hands, and panic constricted oxygen to my lungs.

The car was idling in the parking lot at Sandpoint City Beach. My knuckles were white under the incredible grip I had on the steering wheel.

"Drive!" he shouted.

I jumped at the ferocity, throwing the car in reverse and slamming on the gas. The tires spun on the graveled ground, then caught quickly, forcing our bodies forward as the car flew back violently. I was barely fifteen and had never driven a car before.

I slammed on the brakes, threw it in drive, and peeled out of the lot. Wes didn't look good. His face was wet with sweat, and he was grumbling hoarsely.

"Where am I going?" My eyes fixated on the road, squinting through the dense fog.

"Take me home." His voice was raspy and exhausted from the pain.

"Wes, what's happening to you? What's wrong?" I was terrified, and the tears flooding my eyes were blurring my vision further.

"I don't know." His voice was barely audible and just as frightened as mine.

And then his head turned to me. His bright, beautiful eyes of an hour ago were replaced with black blankness that startled me. I jerked the steering wheel to the left too hard, and the car plummeted down a cliff, the headlights bouncing from the ground to the forest ahead. Screams filled the space around us. My screams were quickly replaced by the crunching of metal on metal, folding onto itself. My head jerked to the left, hitting hard on the doorframe and then launching forward onto the airbag. Nausea washed over me, and a haze filled my pounding head. It took me a moment to remember where I was.

"Wes?" I mumbled painfully.

He didn't answer. Adrenaline gave me the strength to turn my neck, shooting pain traveling through my spine. Something wet dripped over my eyes, blurring my vision. Blinking several times, I was able to discern that Wes wasn't in the passenger seat. Dread built, increasing my strength to sit up and survey the car. The windshield was cracked but not shattered, so he didn't fly through it. I looked back to the empty seat and noticed the car door was cracked open.

As wave after wave of pain hit me, I moved slowly to unbuckle *my seat belt, driven to search for Wes. He was in pain before the crash and had to be hurting badly. I was weak and rested my head back on the headrest for a moment and closed my eyes. The thudding of my brain on my scalp intensified, but I needed to find Wes. Forcing my eyes open, I turned my head to my window. My heart stopped as Wes' pair of obsidian eyes bore deeply into mine. I was petrified to breathe, to move, to speak. They held my gaze for so long I thought I might pass out from the pain. Then they blinked, freeing me from an unexplainable grip.*

When the horrific memory faded, I realized I was still in my Jeep, the headlights still illuminating the tree trunk. I patted down my body, looking for injuries, still half trapped in the nightmare of my past. Mild convulsions pulsed through my muscles, and my heart thumped quickly against my chest. Everything was intact except for my sanity. The car looked to be untouched, but I needed to make sure. My parents would never let me drive again if they found I had been in another accident.

You're our baby, Abigail.

I fumbled with the seat buckle as my hands still shook uncontrollably and grabbed the door handle, about to open it when a shadow passed through the headlights. My breath caught in my throat. I wasn't alone.

I'm not the one you need to be afraid of.

I struggled with the door locks, only to find they were already engaged. I needed to get out of here. The engine was still running, so I threw it in reverse, the tires doing nothing to move the car but spin in the mud.

"Come on, come on, come on," I chanted desperately as I revved the engine to no avail.

Not that you'll be off-roading any time soon.

I was never so glad that I had a car with 4WD. I reached down and slid the lever to 4WD Lo, the transmission into reverse, and slowly pressed the gas. I had only practiced it a few times with my mom, since my dad refused not wanting me to be tempted to hit the trails.

"I can do this." The car started to climb the hill. A smile of success praised me, but another shadow racing behind my car pumped the urgency up a notch. I pushed on the gas harder and my Jeep responded, climbing up a little faster and finding the street. I slammed on the brakes, fumbling to get it out of 4WD, but my hands were so shaky it was slowing me down. When I looked up, Wes was standing in front of the car, the headlights giving him the appearance of a glowing angel.

"Wes!" I screamed reflexively.

He disappeared into the forest.

I headed straight to his house, but I lost all courage when I pulled alongside his driveway. The house was on the outskirts of town, in a custom neighborhood. Their house was situated at the end with the forest behind it. The houses in this neighborhood were grand and all very unique, matching their owners' personalities. Wes' house was a traditional cottage with dark gray stone and a bright red door. I had seen one similar in my history book. It was reminiscent of cottages in Ireland. Of course, those were smaller. Their house was by no means small. The Hunters lived on dozens of acres to which Wes and I had happily explored and got lost in more than our fair share.

"Marco!" Wes yelled, his voice bouncing off the trees.

Giggling, I stayed hidden in the trunk of a hollowed-out oak. It was a tight fit for my ten-year-old body.

I leaned far out of the tree. "Polo!" I shouted, hoping the breeze would carry my words far away. It was the summer before sixth grade, and we played tirelessly in these woods.

I tucked my head back in quickly, covering my mouth to keep any hysterical sounds from escaping.

Wes' head popped in less than a minute later, responding with, "Marco," and smiling wide with wild eyes.

"No fair. How do you do that? This was my best hiding spot yet." I pushed myself out of the tree.

"I guess you'll have to find better ones," he taunted as he strolled away.

Our explorations increased in intensity as we matured, giving up silly games for deep conversations about life and death, the stars and planets, love and hate. Those were the days I cherished the most: vulnerable and innocent together, trying to unravel the secrets of our existence. Now I was a stranger in his world, sitting outside of his house like an obsessed ex-girlfriend.

A tap on my window startled me once again. Wes was standing outside with a boyish grin on his face.

"Are you just going to sit there all night? Pretty stalkerish of you." His eyebrows lifted teasingly.

I considered for a moment to just drive away, but we both knew I wouldn't. I was hooked. *I was obsessed.*

I grabbed my jacket from the back seat and swung open the door. After a closer look at Wes, I noticed he was unsteady on his feet, but still presenting pure perfection in his fitted dark denims and black pullover sweater.

"What was that in the forest? You scared the daylights out of me."

He swayed back and forth.

"Are you drunk?" Unbelieving because Wes would never drink. I slipped my arms into my jacket.

"No." He scoffed at the accusation. "Let me take you somewhere." He held out his hand for me.

He had piqued my interest. "Where?" I asked, raising an eyebrow. Mischief was his middle name after all.

"Don't you trust me?"

"You ask me a lot of difficult questions," I replied, still unmoving.

"How is that difficult? You trusted me once upon a time." He shook his extended hand, encouraging me to trust him.

"Once upon a time, you didn't avoid me. Once upon a

time, you didn't jump in my car and say strange things to me. Once upon a time, you didn't scare the hell out of me."

Instantly, I wanted to take it all back after watching his smile fade. I had hurt him.

"I'm sorry," he said sheepishly. "I know I have a lot of explaining to do, and I want to, but you have to come with me. You have to trust in what we had before."

My heart melted. I did trust in us. No matter how many miles apart, oceans between, or years lost, I would always trust him...with my life. The bond we shared was planted beyond logical reasoning. We *felt* each other. We *saw* each other. We didn't need words to tell us we were meant to be together. There was never a choice. He would always be my answer.

I placed my hand in his. "Where to?"

10

W ES GENTLY PULLED ME BESIDE him, squeezing my hand softly, the warmth welcomed and long missed. We walked through the many acres of his property, winding around trees and crossing over small creeks. Sometimes the creeks were too wide, so Wes would wrap his hands around my waist and lift me over, sparking tingly sensations on my bare skin. We explored for a while, silently, letting the energy swirl around us wildly, reconnecting us without words. Every so often our hands would fall away and then intertwine again, magnetically drawn to each other. When our eyes would meet, my heart would flutter.

We made it to a familiar creek bed where we had spent hours skipping rocks and dipping our feet into the water. This was where our deepest of conversations took place.

Wes kicked off his shoes and peeled off his socks, dipping his feet into the crisp water. "It's not that cold," he promised, reading the trepidation in my eyes.

I sat next to him, making my feet bare. I tested the water with the tip of my toe, recoiling quickly. "It's freezing! How are you even able to sit there like that?" I screeched.

His laugh was infectious, luring me into joining him. "Come on." The glimmer in his eyes begged for me to play along.

"Fine, but if I lose a toe or two, it's your fault." I dipped my feet in, the frosty chill cramping my toes, but after several brave moments and deep breaths, my feet warmed to the water. He was holding back laughter while my face contorted painfully during the process. "You're mean, you know?" I hit him playfully on the arm.

"I know." His words were somber as he dipped his head, busily looking for a pebble in the dirt.

I was well aware he wasn't talking about the frosty water. "What happened, Wes? Why did you leave?" *Me.* My heart ached remembering the loss I felt without him.

"It's complicated." He threw the pebble into the creek.

"I assumed, but you promised me answers." I couldn't take my eyes off him. His profile was captivating with the moon glowing aside him.

He threw another pebble, this time skipping it across the creek, finally sinking after five leaps. His tortured expression told me this wasn't an easy conversation for him, and that worried me. Maybe I was looking at this all wrong. Maybe he found someone and he was in love with her and he was just waiting for the right time to confess. My body tensed and my mouth dried up as I braced for the blow.

"I'm…I'm not normal, Abby. I've changed." He took his eyes off the creek and met mine. He looked terrified, and that made my stomach knot even tighter.

"As opposed to abnormal?"

He turned away and searched for another stone, tossing it as far as he could. It made it out of sight down the creek. His forehead creased as he struggled for words. He sighed loudly. "I'm not right for you."

He was breaking my heart all over again, if it had ever mended at all. I ran my fingers over the ground, brushing through the sand, back and forth, trying to keep myself together. "Please, don't say that," I whispered, my words broken as I choked back despair. Being without him when he was miles and miles away was hard, but being in the same town without him was inconceivable.

He picked up another stone and held it out for me. I scooped it out of his hand, sparks flying as our skin touched.

"Ouch." I yanked my hand back.

"Static electricity." His eyes peeked out from under the lock of auburn hair that had fallen.

I shook out my hand and rubbed it lightly. "That was some static. It felt like I got electrocuted." The mood lightened slightly, but the intensity between us remained. There was another long pause. "I…I don't know what to say, Wes." I made circle designs in the dirt and listened to the water trickling over the rocks in the creek bed.

"I bet you have a lot of questions." His eyes branded me. "Start with an easy one. Or I'll start. How about that?" His sideways smile sent butterflies in a flurry to the pit of my stomach.

"Sure." I nodded.

He looked back at the creek, his beauty radiant.

"Did you get hurt?" he asked.

My chest tightened. I wanted to say, "Of course, I got hurt. You decimated me." But I didn't.

"In the accident just now. Did you get hurt?" Concern was evident in his slumped shoulders and sad eyes.

"No." I shook my head. "Scared mostly."

"Good." He released a reassuring breath, looking back at the creek.

I sucked in a nervous breath. "Wes?"

He turned to me again, his hold on me penetrating every cell in my body.

"How were you there tonight?" I swallowed hard, anticipating an unexplainable response.

"I was walking to the bistro to meet my dad, and I saw you lose control. I wanted to make sure you were okay."

His answer was so normal.

"So, it was a coincidence?"

"Yes."

There was a part of me that wanted to believe him, but another part of me knew there was more to it. Why would he be in the woods, and why would he be walking when he had a car? A very expensive one.

"Then why did you run away?"

"I was afraid. I didn't know what I would say to you."

He took another pebble and tossed it, this time leaping only once before it sank. The fog was getting thicker, and the chill was settling into my bones and rubbing my arms didn't seem to be working.

"You're cold." He pulled his black sweater over his head, his undershirt catching and revealing how much he had matured physically these last two years. It also revealed a large scar across his left side just above his hipbone. He handed me the sweater while he fixed his shirt. I turned away quickly, embarrassed, and peeled off my jacket, throwing his sweater on and then putting my jacket back on. His lemongrass scent overwhelmed me.

"Thank you," I whispered shyly.

He leaned over and untucked my hair that had caught underneath my clothes, his fingers grazing my neck, sending dizzying sensations down my back.

"This is nice." His lips curled up slightly, and his eyes begged for another chance.

Opening up to him was harder than I thought it would be. I had gone over this moment so many times and had already failed once when he was at my house. If I didn't get out what I needed to, it would drive me insane.

"You look troubled." His finger glided down my

cheekbone and slid under my chin, momentarily pausing two years of questions while I succumbed to his enchantment. I lifted my eyes to his and gathered all the courage I could.

"I missed you," I whispered, barely audible from my quivering lips. A single drop of heartbreak fell from my lashes, landing on his finger.

He moved in, slowly resting his forehead on mine. "I'm sorry," he whispered, too, his pain matching mine. "I'm never going to leave you again."

I inhaled his words, taking them deep inside my soul. "I believe you," I responded, placing my hand on his cheek, our carefully intertwined lives transferring between us: the innocence of friendship, the pain of the accident, the heartbreak that followed after, and love reuniting.

"There are so many things I want to tell you and show you. I want to make you understand that I didn't leave because I didn't love you. I left because I *do* love you."

His eyes raised and his hand slid off my chin back up to my cheek. His lips were close to mine, grazing lightly across and back, my heart fluttering and my skin tingling. *This* was the moment I had dreamt about time and time again, never believing it would come true.

"Why me?" I asked breathlessly.

"Because you're extraordinary."

His fingers wrapped around the back of my neck, holding tightly, as he breathed in deeply, my breathing matching his.

In and out. In and out.

We were floating in a momentary time of unadulterated bliss. The moment just before the first kiss. The kiss that would never be forgotten.

"I want to kiss you, Abigail Rose. I live in torture every moment that passes that I don't."

"Then why don't you?" Our voices remained quiet, as if we disturbed anything around us it would break the pull between us.

His eyes burned with a primal desire. A desire for me. "Because I can't. I'm sorry." He slid his hand from my neck, leaving me with a tormented apology.

It was apparent he wanted this as much as me. I just didn't know what was keeping him from it. His body shifted away from me and back to the creek. The moment lost.

"Why, Wes? Is it your dad? Your brother and sister?" I paused and then peeked up. "Someone else?"

"There will never be anyone else." He threw a large rock. It landed hard in the water, creating a big splash, spraying us lightly. "We need to go. Your parents will be worried."

He held his hand out and I took it, allowing him to help me to my feet. He held onto it protectively as we made our way back to my car. He opened my door like the gentleman he is, and I slid in obediently.

"When will I see you again?" I was worried I wouldn't.

"Soon," he answered, his crooked smile comforting me.

He shut my door, and as I drove away, I watched him in the rearview mirror. It was odd leaving happy and afraid. Our time together posed more questions, but the way he made me feel...the things he said to me...I finally had the most important question answered. He loved me. I wasn't some crazy-obsessed girl like Natalie had taunted me with for years. He confirmed what I had believed to be there all along. He said things were complicated, and how things went tonight, I knew they were more than complicated. I just didn't know how much more. A new kind of euphoria swirled around me, giving me confidence that no matter what Wes told me, it would never break what we had. Never break us.

The elation faded quickly when I drove up to my house and a cop car was parked in my spot. Either something happened, or something was about to happen. I shuffled to the front door apprehensively. On the other side awaited scolding, worry, and a good chance of being grounded. Maybe I should just turn around and go back to Wes', but the door flew open. So much for an escape.

"Abigail." My mom wrapped her arms around me, squeezing me tightly. "We were so worried. Where have you been?"

Peering over her shoulder, my dad's exhausted eyes stared back. Officer Gates closed the notebook he had been writing in, and to my surprise, Kendra was sitting on the couch. Officer Gates was my dad's best friend from high school.

"If everything's okay here, I'm going to get going," Officer Gates said kindly.

"Yes, thank you, Jake." My dad shook his hand.

"Ma'am." Officer Gates dipped his hat as he slid past us, closing the door behind him.

"Abigail, do you mind telling us where you have been for the past two hours?" My dad's voice was stern.

Two hours?

"I…" I looked over to Kendra, knowing that her presence meant I didn't have an alibi. "I…I was with Wes." If I could have dug a deep hole to hide in, I would have. The dead silence was worse than a shouting match. The lines around my dad's eyes creased deeply with his scowl, and the shadows under my mom's eyes darkened ten shades of worry.

"Kendra, you can go now. Thank you for coming." My dad kept his voice even, but his eyes told a very different story. A hell-hath-no-fury story.

Kendra jumped up. "Actually, I told my parents I was staying here tonight. They are out with friends."

"Oh, well, James, we can't let her go home then." My mom's maternal instincts kicked in.

"No, I guess not. We'll talk about this tomorrow. Both of you go on then."

Kendra raced over and grabbed my hand. "Thanks, Mr. and Mrs. Rose." She dragged me up the stairs, giggling softly as she pulled me into my bedroom and closed the door.

"Okay, spill."

I pulled off my jacket and tossed it over my desk chair.

"Is that Wes'?" Kendra pointed to his sweater that I failed to give back to him.

Slightly embarrassed, I admitted to it. "Yes, but it's not what you think."

"Then what is it?" She bounced excitedly on my bed.

"Shhh. You're going to give my parents an aneurysm." I couldn't give away anything if I truly didn't know anything. "There's nothing to tell. I went to his house to talk, and that's what we did."

She frowned in disappointment.

"Sorry we aren't more exciting," I teased. "Are your parents really gone for the night?"

"Yes, but the other part was a fib." She winked. "I figured your parents couldn't go off on you if I were here."

I sat in my chair and spun around in slow circles. "Thanks." Kendra was pretty upset with me before, and I was glad it was over.

"Did he tell you why he left after the accident?" She rolled onto her stomach, ready for all the juicy details.

"No." I pouted. "To be honest, we didn't talk all that much. It was more about us being together again. It's hard to explain." How did you put into words the undeniable chemistry Wes and I had? It was like watching a movie of your favorite book, all the details that made you love the story lost in translation.

"Is he as weird as his brother? I ran into Ben again at the bistro. He has bad boy brooding mastered."

I stopped spinning. "No way! You're into Ben, aren't you?"

She jumped to her knees, posing shock. "What? No. Eww."

I stifled a laugh. "You are. Wow." I spun myself around again.

Kendra flung herself back onto the bed. "Fine. He's gorgeous. The bad boy look works on him."

"This is too much." I giggled.

"Best friends and their brothers. What couldn't be more perfect than that?" she asked the ceiling as she lay flat on her back, daydreaming.

I could think of a few things. I tore off my shoes and pants and got into my favorite black sweats.

"You look like a ninja."

I guess I kind of did look like a ninja since I was still wearing Wes' black sweater. "Maybe I am." I winked.

"I'm thinking your coordination would debunk that theory." She rolled off the bed. "Can I borrow some sweats?"

"Yeah."

While she rummaged through my drawers, I pulled Wes' sweater up to my nose, inhaling traces of tonight. It was one perfectly crafted moment, and I hoped for many more.

Kendra fell asleep instantly, sleeping like a dead body. I, on the other hand, couldn't sleep, my insides bursting with every recollection of Wes' touch. There was no denying our connection. It was unparalleled. What did he mean about not being normal? I couldn't even begin to imagine what he was trying to not tell me.

THE MORNING SUN poured a huge dose of reality over me. My parents were ready to discuss last night. I feared them taking my Jeep away at the very least. Grounding me to my room seemed a little juvenile at this point. Kendra was an early riser, her clothes still in a pile on the floor, telling me she was still around, something I would definitely owe her for. My parents wouldn't kill me in front of a witness.

"Abby, you awake yet?" Kendra stood in the doorway.

"Yeah." I sat up in bed, stretching my arms. "Is breakfast ready?"

"Yep. Your mom made French toast."

"That's surprising. I'll be down in a minute." I pondered everything that had happened last night. I used to tell Kendra everything, but there was so much going on and I wasn't sure where to start.

I pulled out my topknot and brushed through the tangles, put on a happy face, and hoped I wasn't grounded for life.

"Morning, sweetie. I made your favorite." My mom's eyes sparkled as I entered the kitchen.

This was the weirdest punishment ever. I shot Kendra a questioning look and she shrugged in mild amusement. My dad sat at the table reading the paper.

His eyes peered over. "Sleep well, Abigail?"

"Uh, yeah. I guess."

All those hours watching *The Twilight Zone* had prepared me for this exact moment. I could even hear the theme song in my head. I had definitely entered a warped reality.

"Good." His eyes hid back behind the newspaper.

My mom placed full plates of French toast in front of us.

"Everything looks spectacular," Kendra raved.

"Thanks, Mom." I exchanged looks with my equally dumbfounded friend.

We ate quietly, the sipping of orange juice and mouthwatering bites filling the void. When we finished, Kendra helped me clear the dishes. "We'll clean up, Mom."

"Sounds good. James, would you like to have another cup of coffee on the patio with me?" She poured two fresh cups.

"I would love to." He stood up, leaving the newspaper on the table. I trailed them as they left the kitchen, waiting for the back door to shut.

"What was that?" Kendra laughed.

"I have no idea. That is *not* how I imagined this morning going." Something was clearly up with my parents, and it terrified me.

"Well, indulge while you can. I'm sure it won't last." Kendra handed me a pan from the stove.

"No, I'm sure it won't."

After we finished cleaning up, Kendra went upstairs

to take a shower. My dad locked himself in the office, and my mom knitted on the patio under the protection of the patio cover as the drizzle from a new storm glistened on the blades of grass.

"Hey, Mom. Can we talk?" I sat in the rocker next to her.

"Sure, hun. What's up?" She looked up, not missing a knitting beat.

"About last night—"

"It's okay, Abigail," she cut me off. "Wes came by early this morning and explained everything."

I widened my eyes, astonished. "He did what?"

"Yes, and it was really sweet of him to care that much about your safety."

I was still lost. "Yeah, it was." I played along without knowing the rules of the game yet.

"You don't have to be afraid to tell us these things. Accidents happen. I mean, really, Abigail. We wouldn't be mad at you."

The accident. He told her. "I was just really upset about it and nothing happened to the car, so I didn't want to worry you guys."

"It was nice that he helped you get it out of that ditch. What spooked you so much?"

"A deer."

"Those darn things. They are so cute, but they wreak such havoc. I'm just glad you're okay. So is your dad."

"So, I'm not grounded then?" I was still bracing for the ultimate blow.

"No, Abigail. Don't be ridiculous. In fact, your dad has finally agreed to get you a cell phone. Just one of those pre-paid ones, so you can call us in an emergency. You were lucky Wes was driving by when he did."

"Yes, lucky." A coincidence. I feigned a smile. "Okay. Well, thanks for not being upset with me. I'm going to go take a shower." This was shaping up to be an odd day.

A FTER I DROPPED KENDRA off at her house, my intention was to go to Wes', but the other night on the pier, with Elijah, was still spinning in my head. I didn't even know him, so going to his house was probably one of the dumbest ideas I've ever had, but I needed to know why he felt I was in danger, especially after last night's peculiar encounter with Wes. If Elijah was going to hurt me, he had every chance on the pier. We were alone and hanging over a large body of water. Accidents happened. I shuttered at the thought of how easily something *could* have happened, but I was trusting my instincts and right now they were telling me Elijah wasn't a threat.

Thirty minutes later, my Jeep was bouncing on the gravel road that led to Elijah's house in Bayview. Adrenaline pumped through my veins as I parked. This was crazy. I should turn around and go home. I looked around, seriously considering it, but I didn't. It didn't look like anyone was home anyway, so being brave was a little bit easier.

"It's now or never."

I took a deep breath, killed the engine, and stepped into the rain. I dashed to the front porch and peeked into the sidelights. A flicker of light danced behind the frosted glass. It could have been a fire, but it was hard to tell. I raised my hand to knock, but then dropped it. Maybe it was smarter to walk around the house first and see what I was getting myself into. I zipped up my grandpa's jacket and ducked my head to shield it from the downpour as I stomped my way through the muddy gravel to the other windows. Curtains were pulled closed, obstructing my view, but I caught a strong aroma wafting around the house, so someone was definitely home. Instead of going back to the front door to knock, I ventured around to the back of the house.

The view from the back of the house was stunning. The lake rippled under the pressure of the raindrops, the waves catching glimmers of light from lit houses.

"Can I help you?"

Hairs on my neck rose. I was scared to take a breath. I turned slowly to face Elijah. He was standing on the back patio, wearing an apron and holding a ladle. I was at a loss for words. I expected to see glaring eyes and possibly a knife in his hand. Was that—I took a deep breath. Chili?

"You can stand in the rain, or you're welcome to come in. I need to get back to the stove, though."

We all had choices, but not all of them were good. This was going down as a bad one. A very bad one, but I stepped onto the patio anyway, shaking off the water on my jacket and ringing out my hair.

"I think it's going to take a little more than that to get you dry. Come on." He moved aside for me.

Nervously, I shuffled sideways, keeping my eyes on him. His lips rose in a smug grin, followed by a chuckle as I moved past him. Once I was inside, he closed the door and headed to the stove, stirring the pot. He lifted the ladle to his lips and took a taste.

"Mmm. Perfect. Would you like to try?" He held the ladle out for me.

"No. I'm good." What in the world was going on?

His crooked smile was mischievously seductive. He put the ladle down and closed in on me. My body began to tremble, and I flinched when he slid behind me, his body close enough for strands of loose hair to shift on my shoulder.

"Let me put your jacket in the dryer," he offered softly, his voice carrying from closely behind my neck. I sucked in a deep breath as he slid off my jacket, disappearing quickly with it, giving me a moment to regain my composure. I wasn't sure if I was scared or something else entirely. Elijah still hadn't reappeared, so I strolled over to the stove to check out the chili. My stomach grumbled loudly. It had been hours since Mom's French toast.

I spun around and scanned the room. His house was remarkable. The kitchen was gorgeous with antiqued white cabinets and traditional farm-style appliances. It was an open floor plan so the kitchen spilled into the living space, which was absent of personal touches. Aside from a portrait that hung over the fireplace, the room looked cold.

"You look like you're taking inventory," Elijah observed as he walked back into the room.

"Should I be, so if I go missing I can leave clues behind?" Half of me was teasing, and the other half was taking mental notes.

"Like a trail of breadcrumbs. I like it. I have cornbread. Would that work?" He pulled a pan of cornbread out of the oven.

"It should." I played along. "That's a lot of food. Are you expecting guests?"

He looked over his shoulder while stirring the chili with an arched eyebrow and a coy smile. "No. Just me. And you now."

There was no question that Elijah was gorgeous, his green eyes striking against his tanned skin, and blond hair that fell over his lashes much like Wes' style.

"That's very presumptuous of you." He used his own words as a weapon. "I can't stay." My blushing cheeks betrayed me.

He turned the stove off and spun around. "Why are you here, Abby?"

His voice was even and inviting, entrancing. I cleared my throat. "On the pier you gave me a cryptic warning."

"Ah, I see. And I bet you would like to know who I was talking about." His posture remained relaxed, easy.

"And you're going to tell me?" I asked, unconvinced.

"Sure. Why not? Over chili and cornbread, though. I hate eating alone. Deal?" His eyes glimmered.

"Umm…sure. I guess." Such a bad choice. No one knew I was here. No one even knew I had left town, and here I was eating lunch with a virtual stranger.

"Great. It'll give your jacket time to dry." He winked and turned back to the stove to scoop chili into bowls.

I sat at the butcher-block kitchen table and picked at my fingers nervously, second-guessing every decision I had made since Wes came back that led me to sitting in a complete stranger's house.

Elijah put a large bowl of chili and a piece of cornbread in front of me.

"This smells amazing." I inhaled the aromas of green chilis and garlic deeply. I was becoming oddly comfortable around Elijah.

"Thank you," he said as he climbed over the bench across from me.

I followed the spoonful of chili to his lips and then quickly looked away when I realized what I was doing.

"You're staring." He smiled.

Humiliation burned my cheeks. I quickly scooped up some chili and shoved it into my mouth. My eyes watered immediately, the temperature burning the inside of my mouth. I fanned at my lips wildly.

"It's hot," he warned too late.

"Water," my raspy voice begged.

Elijah glided to the sink, filled a cup of water, and slid it across the table. I washed down the chili quickly, only finding relief after finishing off the glass.

"Why didn't that burn you?" I asked, carefully blowing on the next spoonful.

"You shouldn't have assumed it wasn't hot." He took another mouthful of chili.

"My mistake." He was intriguing.

"We all make mistakes. Just make sure you learn from them." He bit into his square of cornbread. "The cornbread is delicious. You should try some."

I took a little bite. "Elijah, who were you warning me about? Wes?"

"Eli, please." He flashed another seductive smile.

"Are you avoiding my question, Elijah?"

"Maybe." He pointed his clean spoon at me.

"Fine. Then tell me about yourself. How did you come about meeting Kendra?"

"At the ice cream shop," he said simply.

"Okay, but there's more to it or else you wouldn't have found me on the pier. You met Kendra on purpose to get to me. But why? What is it about me that you are fascinated by?"

"Fascinated?" His smile was radiating. "Might I remind you that you came to my house? Maybe *you* are the one fascinated with *me*?" He downed a glass of water and pushed his food aside, crossing his arms on the table and leaning toward me.

"Are you serious right now?"

He chuckled. "My interest is not of my doing, I assure you."

"Okay then, whose doing would it be?"

He sighed apprehensively. "I am repaying a debt."

It was a mistake coming here. Fear collected with the millions of questions that pummeled me.

His smug smile faded. "I'm sorry. I don't mean to scare you."

"What debt?" I was almost afraid to ask.

"A very large one. Call me your guardian angel, if you will. I was assigned to make sure nothing bad happens to you."

"Why on earth would I need protection?" This was absurd.

"Really? Don't you think you're being pretty naïve?"

I got up from the table and paced in front of the fire. "Naïve of what? The only thing I might be naïve about is coming here and thinking you weren't a serial killer. And now you're telling me that you're my guardian angel or something because you owe someone a debt. Don't you think you're sounding just a little bit crazy?"

"I'm not going to hurt you, Abby." He stood up.

"Why is it so hot in here?" I flailed my arm quickly in front of my face. Panic was rising in my chest.

"Just try to calm down and I'll explain."

I escaped to the patio, welcoming the spray from the rain.

Elijah followed. "Why don't you sit down?"

I obeyed, sitting in a wicker rocker.

"I come from The Order of the Crest."

"The what?"

"The Order of the Crest," he repeated. "It's a powerful organization that prides itself on privacy and protecting the innocent. You have recently acquired friends that have raised concern, so they sent me to assess the situation."

My heart was aching. He was talking about the Hunters. About Wes.

"A promise made a long time ago has me here for other reasons."

"You're not making any sense."

"The Hunters aren't what you think they are."

Nausea rolled through me. "You mean who, right? Not *what*?"

"They're dangerous, Abby. All of them, including Wes."

I stood up, shaking my head in disbelief. "And someone sent you to protect me? From Wes? I've known him almost my whole life. I think I would know if there was something wrong with him."

"But how well do you really know him *now*?"

He was alluding to the two years he was gone. All the things that seemed different about Wes suddenly consumed me. His eyes, his physique, his behavior. "I just can't believe he would hurt me," I replied weakly.

Elijah kneeled in front of me, capturing my wrists, leaving me no option but to look at him. "Abby, you need to understand you're a part of a world far beyond your imagination. You will always be in danger."

"But why?" I pleaded for more answers. "I'm just an ordinary girl."

"You're anything but ordinary, Abby." His words trailed off as he stood up. "You need to stay away from Wes. From all the Hunters. I promised I would keep you safe, but you have to trust me." His desperate eyes bore deep into mine.

"I have to go." I felt weak and defeated. I had just found Wes again, and now Elijah was saying my life depended on staying away from him. I raced into the downpour, slipping in a puddle of mud and crashing to the ground, skinning my knees. My heart was breaking all over again. I couldn't imagine a life without Wes in it. I had tried, and I felt nothing. I was lost and empty.

"I'm sorry." Elijah's voice shouted over the storm.

Pulling myself up, I ran to my car, fumbling to get the key in the ignition, failing as they slipped from my fingers to the floor. My body finally succumbed to the revelation.

This wasn't happening. This couldn't be real.

I pounded my palms against the steering wheel until they ached and then slumped over, feeling the world fall from beneath my feet once again. It was hard driving home. I wasn't even sure if that was where I needed to be. I needed to be with Wes. I needed to hear from him that this was all a big misunderstanding. I went to his house and pounded on the door, but after several minutes passed with no answer, I gave up and drove home.

It was almost two, and I was scheduled to work tonight. I could ask Mr. Hunter where Wes was and then get the answers I needed.

Having talked myself down from near hysterics, I pulled into my driveway. My mom's car was gone, and I was hoping that meant my parents were both gone.

It was still raining hard when I ran into the house. "Mom? Dad?"

Silence.

I left my muddy shoes out front and carefully tiptoed up the stairs, trying to keep the mud from slipping off of me. I headed straight for the bathroom. My chestnut hair was plastered to my skin, and my mascara bled into the dark circles forming under my eyes. The worst part was I didn't recognize the person staring back. She was hollowed and broken.

I piled my clothes in a corner and got into the shower, soaking in the last few days. *Nightmares.*

I had a little more clarity, washing away most of the

doubt that Elijah had planted in me. It didn't matter what Elijah told me or what he thought Wes was. I knew Wes better than anyone, and he would never hurt me. If I were in danger, *Wes* would protect me. I didn't need Elijah for that.

My car was a muddy disaster, so I headed out to clean it. I didn't expect to see Wes standing next to it, but I was glad just the same.

"We have to stop meeting like this," I teased solemnly from the overhang of my patio.

Headlights shone on the driveway, making Wes flinch.

"It's probably just my parents. You don't have to go," I pleaded.

"It's not," he growled and then raced into the woods.

An unfamiliar blue sedan parked behind my Jeep, and Elijah stepped out.

"You forgot your jacket at my house." He held it out as he approached the front porch. He looked over his shoulder into the woods where Wes had gone.

"Thanks." I snatched it. "You can leave now."

He flashed a hurt glance, and then without a word, headed back to his car.

I yelled at him, "I don't want you protecting me. I don't need it."

He paused for a moment but kept walking to his car without acknowledgement.

"He won't hurt me." My voice lost power. "He couldn't." I waited, hoping Wes would come back after Elijah left, but he didn't.

12

WHEN I GOT TO THE BISTRO for my shift, I was relieved to see Wes floating around the tables, laughing and chatting with the customers. Mr. Hunter was pouring drinks at the bar, and Ben and Zoe were sitting at a table in the back, watching a game on TV. The music flowing out of the speakers was cheery, and the mood of the restaurant was upbeat. Penelope even said hi to me. Things suddenly didn't seem so bad.

I tucked my bag under the register and smiled all the way to the table where Wes was refilling glasses like a completely normal human being. Nothing abnormal about him. "I'll take that." I touched his hand lightly as I took the pitcher from him, transferring a familiar energy between us.

"Thanks." His fingertips grazed my waist as he sidled between me and the table behind us.

As the night went on, I stole as many glances at Wes as I could, blushing when he caught me, and admiring him when he didn't. At the end of the night, Penelope didn't plant herself at the table to roll silverware. Instead, she grabbed her purse and rushed out, looking somewhat stressed.

"Where is she going in such a hurry?" I asked Wes who was cleaning off a table nearby.

"Not sure. She said she got an urgent phone call. Gives me a chance to introduce you to my siblings since you haven't officially met yet."

All this time and his siblings never gave me the time of day. It was a little bit weird, but now the pressure seemed insurmountable and dread filled my fingers, dropping the salt shaker from them and shattering salt all over the floor.

"I'm so sorry." I swept my hands around the salt, gathering it into piles, but Wes' hand caught my wrist.

"Leave it." He locked his eyes with mine intensely, rubbing my wrist gently.

"But I—" Looking down, the salt had disappeared. "Where...what..." I searched the area frantically. I was losing my mind.

Wes pulled me up by my elbows, watching me carefully. "Don't freak out, okay?"

I nodded nervously and followed as he led me to his family.

"Ben and Zoe, this is Abigail. Abigail, these are my siblings."

I always thought it eccentric how he referred to his brother and sister as siblings. No one spoke like that.

Ben stepped forward, his jet-black hair slicked back, defining the contours of his thin cheekbones, sharp nose, and narrow jaw. In all the years I had known the twins, I had never been close enough to get a good look. It was clear now that all four of them shared the same iridescent eyes.

"Hi, Abigail. It's nice to meet you. We have heard many things about you over the years." Ben winked sincerely. He bent over and kissed my hand, then stepped back.

My body flushed with embarrassment. What had Wes told his family about me?

Zoe glided forward, her hips shifting gracefully and her blonde hair flowing freely, curls bouncing around her shoulders. The only similarities the twins shared were their eyes.

"I'm sorry we haven't met until now." Her simple smile showcased a dimple on her right cheek. She had soft cheekbones hidden under a round face and a ski slope nose that offset her full pink lips. She was magnificent up close.

"Me, too." My voice cracked slightly. Wes squeezed my hand reassuringly.

Zoe bowed her head and backed up next to Ben. Their light skin glowed brightly under the fluorescent lights.

"And you already know my father, William." Wes tipped his head to him.

I nodded affirmation. I was so nervous it was hard to formulate words.

"Some things have recently been brought to our attention, and we thought it was time to discuss them," Mr. Hunter said authoritatively.

My eyes darted from one pair of eyes to the next, landing on Wes' last. He wore an expression of regret, as though he was sorry, almost like he was trying to protect me from this.

"What things?" I questioned, working hard to keep an even voice.

Ben spoke up, "Knowing will put you in danger. I just want that to be clear before you agree to this."

Wes' jaw tightened. "She's already in danger. That's why we're here."

What sounded like a low growl escaped Ben's lips.

"Enough," Mr. Hunter threatened. "Wes is right, but we may be getting ahead of ourselves. We are more than capable of containing Elijah."

Elijah? My legs buckled. Wes caught me before I hit the floor and sat me carefully in a chair.

"See, she's not ready," Ben argued.

Zoe sat next to me, sliding over a glass of water. "Hydrate. It will help." Her voice was so motherly.

"You're white as a ghost." Wes' worried eyes focused on me.

I took a sip of water, the chill on my throat taking away the dryness that accompanied my collapse. "I'm fine."

"She's too fragile," Ben hissed.

Abby has always been a bit fragile.

"I'm *not fragile*," I spat vehemently.

"If we really believed you were too fragile, we wouldn't have brought you here." Zoe patted my hand.

Her encouragement was comforting.

Mr. Hunter leaned against the bar. "As you can see, we aren't exactly normal."

I didn't respond. Instead, I slid my finger around the rim of the glass and remembered when Wes told me he wasn't normal.

"And you're not safe around us." Mr. Hunter's words came out slow and calculated. *Careful.*

I stopped circling the rim of the glass while all eyes studied me, waiting for my reaction. "What do you mean?"

"This is wrong." Ben knocked over a chair and stomped a few feet away, causing me to jump.

Wes bolted up and confronted Ben. "What is your problem?"

Mr. Hunter jumped between them and glared from one set of eyes to the other. The boys backed down without a word.

Wes took my shaking hands. "Don't let him scare you. He's just being a jerk."

I bit the inside of my lip and nodded, repeating to myself, *I'm not fragile.*

"Wes," Mr. Hunter pressed urgently.

"We need to talk about the night of the accident. Is that okay?"

I nodded again.

"The night of the accident I was sick," Wes began.

"Yes, I remember." The memory vivid.

"I scared you, and you lost control of the car."

"Yes." The thumping of my heart pounded in my ears, time slowing down as Wes recounted that night.

"There was a lot of blood. Your blood. My blood."

Crimson splatters were on the windshield and pooled on the seats.

I nodded.

Wes' eyes fell in shame, the next part difficult for him to admit. "I tried to *kill you* that night." His face winced in pain.

I swallowed hard. "What?" My voice weakened.

Wes looked over to his father who nodded, giving him permission to go on. "Something was happening to me, and I lost control." He took a deep breath and rubbed my hands methodically. "Elijah was there. *He* saved your life."

The world began to spin and breathing became difficult. "What?" My eyes were wet with tears.

"Can we have a moment alone?" Wes looked to his family.

"Of course," Mr. Hunter replied.

I shot up before anyone had a chance to move. "I think I need some fresh air," I whispered, scared to look up again.

"I'll go with you." He wrapped his arm around my waist and pulled me alongside. The whispers among the twins and Mr. Hunter started up immediately behind us.

Wes walked me down the back steps to the pier and we stood silently against the railing overlooking the lake, the cool air prickling the sweat that had accumulated on my body inside the bistro. I closed my eyes, trying to focus on the soft ripples of the water.

"Better?" Wes' voice was soothing.

"Yes." My shoulders relaxed, and my breathing became easier.

"You must have a lot of questions."

"A few."

Wes took my hand in his. "I'm not a mortal, Abby."

A surprised breath escaped me, the dizziness returning.

I'm not the one you need to be afraid of.

Wes is not what you think he is. He's dangerous.

"I…I'm not sure what to say."

"The night of the accident—that's when I turned." He leaned on the rail of the bridge, digging his fingers into the wood, splintering off pieces as he spoke.

"I don't understand." I put a comforting hand over his.

"I had been fighting the change for years, but that night I couldn't anymore and all that blood summoned this primal urge to kill. I lost control."

"What stopped you?" My lips quivered. I was so close to death that night.

"Elijah." His voice faded, and his eyes wandered to some far off place. "I was staring hungrily at you through the window. It was just you and me, and then he was there." His voice relieved.

"If he saved me, then what made you hate him so much?"

"When I found out he was with The Order of the Crest. That makes him a dangerous enemy. Everyone in The Order has an agenda. He was there for a reason. I just don't know what it is yet, but I'll find out before you are pulled into this any deeper."

"Why does it have to be a bad thing? Maybe he just feels the need to protect me because he saved me that night. He said he was here to protect me."

"Abby, please don't ever let your guard down with him." He grabbed my shoulders urgently. "I'm so sorry. I'm sorry I came back here and put you in the middle of a war." He brushed his finger down my cheekbone to my lips. I pushed into his touch, wanting more. "I tried to stay away. For your sake. William took us far into the Appalachian Mountains, teaching me how to restrain my primal urges and training me how to fight. But he was also keeping me away from you."

"Then why did you come back?" I whispered desperately.

He removed his finger from my cheek, allowing the cloud to lift. "The Order of the Crest hunted us down. They told us we had violated our agreement because I had exposed myself to you. That's when I figured out that Elijah was one of them because no one else knew the truth about that night, aside from my family. William forged a deal to keep me alive, but we know how The Order works. It's swift and merciless and we couldn't be sure you were safe.

That's why Elijah is here, Abby. Despite what he did for you in the past and despite what he has told you. He's here to kill you."

My thoughts were all over the place—the accident, Wes, the bounty on my life. "But I'm just an ordinary girl. I'm Abigail Rose. A simple girl from a small town." I shook my head.

He took both of my hands. "You're anything but ordinary, Abby. We can't trust him. I'm sorry."

"But if that was the case, if he were truly here to kill me, then why hasn't he?"

"I don't know." He pulled me into his chest, hugging me protectively.

"What did it feel like that night? When you were changing. You looked like you were in so much pain."

"It's hard to explain."

"Can you try?"

He squeezed me tightly. "There are purebred immortals that are turned by another immortal, and then there are hybrids, albeit rare. It happens when an immortal and mortal conceive, but that kind of union is forbidden, so having a child wouldn't be ideal. Most immortals find humans inferior, but my dad fell in love with my mom and he described her as an immortal would describe a True Mate."

"So, what you're saying is you aren't a purebred? You're a hybrid?"

"Yes. That's why I age the same as you."

"And that night…"

"I became immortal. Every bone in my body felt like it was breaking, and every muscle felt like it was being stretched from my tendons." His voice darkened. "And my veins felt like they were boiling, but the worst was the thirst for blood and the hallucinations that followed."

"Hallucinations?"

Wes looked away shamefully. "I thought I killed you that night. Let's leave it at that." The pain was evident with the cracking in his voice, tears surfacing in his eyes.

"I'm sorry." I touched his face, feeling the coldness for the first time.

"You don't have anything to be sorry for. This isn't your fault. Don't ever be sorry with me, Abby. I'm here now, and I'm never leaving you again. We won't let anyone hurt you. You're family." He pulled me in close.

Family. My mother's worrisome eyes flashed before me. My heart clenched at the thought of putting them in danger. "What about my parents?"

"There are a lot of things we need to figure out, but we will, and we will do it together," he assured me. His embrace tightened one last time, comforting me, before he let go and took my hand in his.

We walked hand in hand back inside the bistro. Zoe jumped out of her seat, expectantly gleaming from ear to ear while Ben stood close to Mr. Hunter, arms crossed defiantly.

"How are you feeling, Abigail?" Mr. Hunter prodded.

"Still processing," I responded honestly. The existence of

immortals was going to take a little more than five minutes to digest.

"You look puzzled," Mr. Hunter observed.

My eyes traveled from each of theirs, trying to figure out the answer for myself. Pale skin, unusual eyes that turned black when enraged, and unparalleled beauty.

"Are you...vampires?" They immediately started laughing in unison, making me feel like an idiot.

Wes choked back his laughter and spoke first, "Vampires are a gross exaggeration of immortality, but the myths aren't completely off base. With immortality come longevity, strength, and other...gifts. Our bodies survive much like humans. We don't want to suck your blood or grow fangs, and we prefer our meat cooked." He winked.

Zoe added, "And some of us like the company of mortals." She smiled innocently.

"Do you have any more questions?" Mr. Hunter asked.

They all stared cautiously at me, making me feel very uncomfortable.

"I promise we won't laugh, right?" Mr. Hunter warned the others.

"Right," Zoe agreed.

"Whatever." Ben shrugged.

Wes squeezed my hand. I took a deep breath and exhaled my question. "How long have you all been...living?" They exchanged glances again as if they had the ability to talk without speaking. *Maybe they did.*

Mr. Hunter answered, "I have lived the longest. You

could equate it to four lifetimes. I found Zoe and Ben two lifetimes ago. They are both on their third lifetime. Wes is the youngest, as you know. This is his first lifetime."

Doing the math was easy, but mind-altering. "So, Ben and Zoe aren't your children?"

Mr. Hunter glanced to Zoe who answered.

"No, Abby. That's just our human story. Really, it's ridiculous anyone believes it. Ben and I look nothing alike. Ben is my True Mate. He saved me." Her smile beamed with adoration, returned with a wink by Ben.

"What is a True Mate?"

Zoe continued, "All immortals have one. Before you find them you feel empty, like a whole chunk of your soul is missing. You live as an immortal, but never feel satisfied. Immortals without a True Mate are dangerous. They have nothing to lose, so they go on binges."

"Binges?" My stomach knotted.

"Killing sprees," Ben cut in. "That's why The Order was created. To apprehend immortals."

The word *apprehend* made me shiver.

"If humans knew immortals existed, there would be chaos, so The Order keeps us a secret."

"Why wouldn't they just kill you?" They laughed again, but stopped quickly when Mr. Hunter glared at them.

"We aren't that easy to kill, Abby. In fact, it's damn impossible, but we believe they have found ways because we have heard of some of our kind disappearing." Mr. Hunter's voice tapered off solemnly.

"The Order claims to want peace between our kind." Ben scoffed.

"But you don't believe that?" I looked around at their disapproving expressions.

"No, we don't. We think they are stalling until they are confident they can kill us all."

Envisioning a world without Wes was horrifying.

"There are rules, Abby, and no one wants to die, so both sides follow them. For now, at least." Mr. Hunter stood in front of me. "Elijah is a threat. And The Order's interest in you is because of your interest in Wes. They are watching us, so they have a valid reason for apprehending us."

"What's keeping them from just taking you?"

"Strength in numbers. Immortals don't live alone. We all have families. We are just a few of many dozens in our family. They would be starting a war."

Now I was starting to panic. "The Order has that much power? You're immortal."

"The Order is powerful. They have proven that over the decades, which is why immortals agreed to abide by a set of terms. Not all immortals are bad, and most just want to be left alone."

"We aren't going to give Elijah or The Order a reason to react," Wes said as he brushed his fingers through my hair.

Mr. Hunter addressed everyone, "We just need to act like everything is normal and not raise suspicions. Once they see we aren't a threat to you or anyone else, this will all blow over. I'll keep a watchful eye on Elijah. Wes, you try to stay as close to Abigail as possible, starting by taking her home so her parents don't worry. It's getting late."

"I'll follow you home," Wes said softly.

Zoe gave me a hug while Ben and Mr. Hunter bowed their heads. The whole drive home one thing nagged me—who was Wes' True Mate?

WES FOLLOWED CLOSELY behind as promised. He was at my car door before I had a chance to open it with his hand held out. We stood by the car, unmoving.

"I should go in before my dad sees you." I settled up against the Jeep as he shut my door.

He leaned in close and asked, "Are you going to be okay?"

"I think so." I smiled shyly, my heart always fluttering when he was around.

"You're taking this a lot better than expected." He twirled his finger around a lock of my hair.

"Did you always know that you would be an immortal?"

"Yes."

His hand brushed the exposed skin between my neck and shoulder, taking the breath from my lungs. He leaned in closer, taking my lock of hair and inhaling deeply.

"I love the way you smell, Abigail Rose."

My chest rose deeply, and I stood very still, anticipating

our first kiss, but it was quickly interrupted when the porch light flickered on.

Wes released my hair and whispered quickly, "I'll see you soon."

"Uh-huh." I nodded.

"Abigail?" My dad's voice interrupted.

"Coming." I raised on my tiptoes and kissed Wes on the cheek and then sprinted to the house, my heart still racing.

"Was that Wes?" My dad held the door open for me.

"Yeah. He just wanted to make sure I got home safe." I avoided eye contact.

"I think it's about time you had him over for dinner. Invite him tomorrow."

"He might be busy, but I'll ask him."

Tonight, my dreams wouldn't be filled with nightmares of the past. Instead, they would be replaced with impossibilities for the future.

13

*A*CT NORMAL.

Kendra, with her sparkling eyes and a bigger-than-life smile, ran to my car and jumped in.

"You're in a good mood. You do know it's Monday, right? There are thousands of memes to commemorate the not-so-joyous beginning to the week."

"So I'm happy on a Monday. Sue me." She applied her lipstick in the visor mirror. "What did you do this weekend besides work? This job is really getting in the way of our relationship." She smacked her lips together, showcasing a bright red sheen.

"I'll talk to Mr. Hunter. Maybe I can get Friday or Saturday nights off." I cringed when Kendra squealed wildly as I turned into the school.

"Do you think he'll give you this Friday off? Natalie is having a get-together, and I'm on the prowl for a date to the Winter Wonderland dance. I need my wing girl." She winked.

Focusing on Kendra was difficult this morning because my thoughts were heavy on last night.

"Abby?" Kendra was staring at me with a questioning look.

"Sorry."

"Are you okay?"

"Yeah, I'm fine. You know Natalie is the bane of my existence, right?"

"It's a means to an end. She has the best parties, and we don't have to talk to her. Come on. I can't do this without you."

The first bell rang. Grabbing our bags, we crossed the parking lot quickly.

"Fine. I'll go with you, but would you mind if I brought Wes?"

"So, you're like a thing now?" We rushed to our lockers, switching out books and being careful of our voices because classmates surrounded us.

"Yeah, kind of," I said with an embarrassed grimace.

"Ooh, so, you think he would set me up with Ben?" The romantic possibility brightened her eyes.

"He's actually taken, and it's pretty serious." I bit my bottom lip, anticipating her disappointment. Zoe and Ben had been together for over two hundred years, so being serious didn't quite cover it.

"Darn it, but I would've been surprised if he wasn't taken. He's dark, mysterious, and gorgeous. So the manhunt is still on for Friday then." She slammed her locker and bounced away, her white curls bouncing along with her.

A party was so trivial at this point, but Mr. Hunter instructed us to act normal, and I had already been distant with Kendra. If anything, going to this party would buy me a little time alone with Wes without sending up red flags.

Getting through the day proved difficult, so I was grateful when school finally ended. I made it to my car before Kendra and was shocked to see Elijah leaning up against it casually as if we were friends, arms crossed and sporting a confident grin. I wasn't ready for this. Last night, I had found out he had saved me. What could I say? *Thank you* just didn't seem adequate. But he was dishonest with me, and that hurt, so I straightened up and confronted him, my eyes burning with angry tears.

"You lied to me." I nudged him out of the way and opened the driver's door.

"About what exactly?" He slammed the door closed.

"Get out of my way," I demanded, tears starting to fall down my cheeks. The revelations were catching up with me, and the panic I had been holding back was surfacing.

"What did they tell you? That you should be afraid of me?" His voice pleaded.

"Shouldn't I be?" I glared at him angrily.

"I told you the truth. I'm not here to hurt you, Abby."

"I need to go," I choked out. I barely knew Elijah, but I felt connected to him now, and his betrayal stung.

He let go of the door and stepped back, watching me with confusion in his eyes.

Before I closed the door on him, I paused. "You should have told me, Elijah." I shook my head sadly. "You should have told me," I mumbled. I slammed the door and turned the engine on, avoiding his gaze and sniffling back more tears. I wanted so bad to hate him, but I couldn't because he had saved my life, and how do you hate someone so selfless? When I looked up, Elijah was gone, and Kendra was running across the parking lot. I wiped my face quickly and overly compensated by waving wildly with a big smile.

She jumped into the car. "Sorry. I had to drop off a paper for English."

"It's okay," I said way too enthusiastically.

Kendra looked at me strangely. "You're acting weird." She buckled her seat belt.

So much for acting normal.

After dropping Kendra off, I drove to Wes' house. I tried to shake my confrontation with Elijah, but it just kept replaying in my head, and it hurt like hell. I turned the corner to his house when, out of nowhere, he jumped in front of my car. I slammed on the brakes just in time.

"What are you doing? Are you crazy? I could have hit you!" I screamed hysterically through the windshield.

He raced to my side and yanked the door open, his eyes

as black as night and lips pursed tightly. "Where have you been?"

I looked at my clock. It had only been twenty minutes since school let out. "School, and then I had to drop Kendra off." I purposely omitted the part about Elijah.

The black receded from his irises, and the iridescence returned, his shoulders relaxing, too. "I forgot about Kendra."

"Yeah. Sorry. I didn't mean to worry you."

He pulled me out and into his arms. "I was a couple of minutes late getting to the school, so I went to your house, and when I didn't see your car there, I went a little crazy," he admitted, hugging me tighter now.

"I can see that. You're crushing me," I choked out.

He released me and swept his hand down the side of my face longingly. "Please, don't scare me like that again."

I shook my head. "I won't." I thought for a moment. "Do your eyes always do that when you're upset?"

His sideways grin returned. "Yes." His fingers caressed my cheek.

"So, my dad wants you to come to dinner tonight."

"Now that's surprising." His hand dropped, and his eyebrows raised curiously.

I grumbled, "I know. He saw us last night, and now I'm sure he wants to drill you and try to intimidate you."

Wes laughed. "I think we both know we don't have to worry about that, now do we?" He winked. "I'd love to hang with dear old Dad and Mum."

I hit him playfully on the chest, feeling the real strength that accompanied his immortality. He caught my wrist and brought it to his mouth, pausing only to flash his most devilish grin, then he kissed the skin that protected my pulse. I could feel the coolness of his lips pass over my skin, eliciting a low groan from my breath. Embarrassed, I pulled my wrist away.

"I like that sound on you." He nuzzled his nose in my neck.

"Wes, stop." I giggled.

He met my gaze coyly. "Probably wise. I wouldn't want you to die laughing. You're fragile, after all."

"I'm *not* fragile." He had struck that nerve again.

He took my shoulders in his hands. "Yes, you are, Abby. You can get sick. You can get hurt. You can die. I worry every second you aren't with me."

I let my clenching fists relax. "I'm sorry. It's just after you left town, I came undone and everyone has been holding it over me, saying just how fragile I am." I kicked the gravel around with the toe of my Chucks.

Wes' grip on my shoulders tightened. "Abby, you are anything but weak. You're the strongest person I know. You survived a horrific accident, and when I told you that my family and I were immortal, you barely flinched. Your strength doesn't lie within the confines of your skin. It's here," he placed his hand on my heart," and it's here," his other hand cupped my head, his begging eyes bringing down my defenses.

"I love you, Wes." My stomach dropped, and my hands trembled. What if he didn't say it back? Even worse, what if he didn't love me?

He kissed my forehead and hugged me again. "I love you, too, Abigail Rose. I love you, too."

He rocked me gently until the sun fell behind the trees and twilight was upon us, and then he drove with me to my house, never letting go of my hand. I cherished every moment we were alone, even if we could only express our feelings with simple touches and gestures. It was enough, our connection running deeper than superficial layers.

"So, my dad can be kind of…difficult." I was prepping him for an interesting dinner that could end as a huge debacle.

He swung my hand gently as we walked up to the house without a care in the world. "I can do difficult. I promise." He kissed me on the corner of my lip.

The front door was the only thing separating *us* from *them*. So many wonderful aromas washed over us as soon as we entered the house. I observed my mom flying across the kitchen and taking several sips of red wine. Actually, it was more like several gulps, and she was frantically rearranging silverware on the table.

"Hey, Peanut."

I about jumped out of my skin, dropping my hand from Wes', when my dad appeared out of the living room.

"Wes, glad you could make it." My dad stood tall and proud.

"Thank you for inviting me." Wes politely held out his hand.

My dad kept his firmly in his pockets. This was going just swimmingly so far. Wes only shrugged it off with a smile.

"You're here," my mom squealed. She put her glass of wine down and hugged me tightly. "Well, come on in. Dinner's ready."

Her greeting was warmer than my dad's. We followed my parents into the kitchen where my mom had prepared enough food to feed the whole neighborhood. On the counter, there were a large salad, biscuits, broccoli, mashed potatoes, and T-bone steaks still sizzling.

"Sit." She pulled me down into my chair.

My dad took his seat next to me. "Your mom's a little nervous," he said under his breath.

I chuckled quietly to myself.

"Are you going to sit, boy?" My dad's voice rose suddenly.

Wes was standing behind his chair next to mine.

"If you don't mind, sir, I'd like to wait until all the ladies are seated."

The tension was already rising. My dad would either take this as a show of disrespect or that Wes was just showing good manners.

"Oh, don't be silly." My mom waved her hand. "It's a buffet. Grab your plates and fill them up." My mom downed the rest of her glass of wine.

The four of us shuffled quietly down the line, putting food on our plates. As promised, Wes waited until my mom and I were seated before he took his seat. A few bites in, my mom broke the silence.

"So, Wes, are you back at Sandpoint High?"

"No, ma'am. My father has someone coming to the house to homeschool us. We fell behind during our travels."

I was transfixed by how easy Wes could lie to my parents.

"Oh, that's right. I heard something about that. Where did you travel to?"

My dad ate while my mom performed the first part of the interrogation. Roles were definitely switched.

"All over, but we settled in the Appalachian Mountains for a good amount of time. My dad rented a cabin there, and we spent a lot of time hunting." Wes cut his steak carefully and placed a bite into his mouth. "The steak is delicious, Mrs. Rose."

She giggled appreciatively. "Call me Lucinda."

My dad grunted in disapproval.

"How are your sister and brother, Ben and…I can never remember your sister's name," my mom asked, snapping her fingers.

"Zoe. Ben and Zoe. They're great. They are getting back on track to graduating with their class."

"That's splendid. It was always hard for me to believe they were twins, being how different they look and all. Sweet kids." Mom moved on from wine in favor of water and took a long, uncomfortable sip.

My dad continued to eat silently while Wes calmly answered my mom's questions. Something wasn't right. My gut was telling me that my parents had an ulterior agenda. By the end of dessert, I knew everything about Wes and his family from the time he moved here in third grade to his travels across the world. The one subject my mom didn't encroach on was Wes' mother. Although I really wanted to know what happened to her, it wasn't dinner conversation. My dad said three things throughout the whole thing: *thank you*, *no thanks*, and *decaf*.

"Sorry if I prodded too much," my mom said politely. We were all standing at the front door to show Wes out. "This is just the first time Abigail has brought a boy home or even mentioned a boy…" My mom shifted uncomfortably from one hip to the other.

"Absolutely, Lucinda. I'm an open book."

It was subtle, but my dad turned his head slightly at Wes' comment. Did he not believe Wes?

"Okay, well, I'm going to drive him home now." I was pushing Wes out the door as I said this.

"Thank you again for having me." Wes bowed his head.

My mother waved nervously, and my dad stood unmoving and unaffected.

"I'll be back in a little bit," I promised.

"Not too late. You have school tomorrow," my dad warned.

I responded with a grin and shut the front door. We had survived.

"I'm not sure if I would call that a success. Your dad didn't seem to like me." Wes held my hand as I drove him home, his thumb rubbing circles in my palm.

It *was* out of character how quiet he was. Normally, he did all the talking and my mom stayed quiet when we had company.

"I'm not really sure what to make of it. He's been really stressed about work, so I'm sure it's just that. Meeting his daughter's boyfriend ranks a little lower on the priority scale."

"Boyfriend?"

I could feel Wes staring at me through the dark. I rolled down my window, suddenly feeling very hot and claustrophobic from my unexpected confession.

"Yeah, you know. Boy and friend. Boyfriend." I played it off.

He laughed. "I like being your boy…friend." He kissed my hand.

"You do?" I asked sheepishly, still mortified as I pulled into his driveway and parked.

"Why do you question how I feel about you? If my words don't convince you, then how you feel when we are together should. We are connected, Abby, like nothing I have ever felt." He watched me closely.

"I felt it from the second I met you," I admitted shyly, bowing my head and biting my lip.

He raised my chin, rubbing it lightly. "Me, too."

One side of his mouth curled up slowly as he pulled my

chin closer to him. His nose circled mine gently and then brushed over to my cheekbone, his lips so close to mine I could almost taste him. I reached over and grabbed the back of his neck, not wanting him to pull away this time. *Not letting him.* His ragged breath matched mine as our willpower was ebbing quickly. His lips passed over my jawline to my neck just below my earlobe, kissing me softly. His body was tense under my grip, and our chests rose and fell in unison.

"Kiss me," I whispered.

He released a pained grunt, forcing himself off of me. "I—we can't, Abby."

My desperation was only increasing by the second. "Why? And don't say it's because I'm fragile, or I might punch you in the mouth with my delicate little fist." I waved it in front of him pathetically.

He grabbed it, holding back laughter. "It's not that, Abby. It's me. I've never dealt with this before. I need to make sure it's safe."

I flung my head back on the headrest and sighed loudly in obvious frustration. "*This*," I waved between the two of us, "is really, really hard."

"I know. For me, too." He paused for a moment before saying, "I should go." He jumped out of the car. "I'm going to be away this week with my father, so you'll probably spot Ben or Zoe hanging around."

I didn't even try to hide my disappointment. "Really?"

"I'll be back Friday. Go straight home and lock your

doors. No more sleeping with the window open."

"How—?"

He winked, making me flush.

"Sweet dreams, Abby."

14

Wes was gone this week, so I wasn't in a rush to get out of bed. The sun was blinding, the forecast showing mild weather for the next few days, so I buried my head back under the sheets. Maybe I could just stay under here until Friday.

"Good morning, sunshine." Kendra's chipper voice pierced through the solitude.

"Go away," I grumbled.

"I brought you coffee."

She was enticing my caffeine-crazed side. I peeked one eye out from the covers to confirm she was telling the truth. She waved two cups of coffee from the local coffee shop.

I drew the covers back and sat up. "What time did you wake up?" How could she appear so flawless at—I looked over at my clock—at seven in the morning. "No, seriously, when did you wake up?"

She giggled, sitting on the bed with me. The coffee was still hot enough to burn my hands.

"I got it extra hot."

I took a careful sip and stared at her, waiting for an answer.

She rolled her eyes, "Fine. I had a before-school date."

"A what? Is that even a thing?"

"It is now," she answered with a glimmer in her eye.

"All right, fess up. Yesterday you were desperate for me to be your wing girl at Natalie's party so you could find a Winter Wonderland date. What's changed?" I took another sip, enamored by her response.

She took a sip and then another, avoiding eye contact. She was stalling. "You're not going to like it." She took a sip of her coffee.

"Try me."

"Okay, but you have to pinky promise you won't freak out on me." She held out her pinky.

"Are we in first grade again?" My hands were still firmly on my coffee.

She shook her pinky and pursed her lips.

Shrugging, I held out my pinky and wrapped it with hers. "You're ridiculous."

A second later, she beamed, "I was with Elijah."

Oh, no she didn't. No, seriously. Pinky promises couldn't

have jurisdiction here. I bit my lip so hard it made my eyes water.

"You're mad." Her smile disappeared, and her eyes widened.

I held onto my lip with my teeth and grunted, "Uh-uh."

"You're lying," she pressed.

I nodded while still holding onto my lip. Pinky promise, after all. "Mm-hmm."

"Are you going to drink your blood or your coffee?" She bit out, disappointed.

I finally let go, the metallic liquid from my lip overpowering the coffee aftertaste. I took another quick sip. "I pinky promised, but if you want the truth, you'd have to let me out of it."

She stood up. "No way. You keep your little promise. So much for a supportive best friend. You don't have to like who I date. What if I don't like Wes?" She stomped around the room.

"You don't like Wes?"

"That's not the point. Of course, I like Wes, because *you* like him. See? Good best friend." She pointed at herself.

The lines of being a good friend were blurred when it came to Elijah. He was using her to get close to me, but I couldn't tell her that, so I sighed and played along.

"I'm sorry, Kendra. You're right. I'm being unfair." I peeled my sheets off and jumped out of bed, racing around to get ready.

"What's the rush?" Kendra watched me quizzically.

"I totally forgot I have a makeup exam in math today. I was supposed to take it before school." I ran into the bathroom and brushed the mess that was my hair.

"School doesn't start for another hour."

"Can you walk today? That way you don't have to sit around waiting for first period." I shoved a toothbrush into my mouth.

"Sure," she replied, perplexed.

"I'm sorry. I'll drop you off at home so you don't have to walk."

Kendra huffed as she got out of the car, and I felt really bad since she brought me coffee, but what Elijah was doing was wrong. I planned on storming up to his front door and telling him to back off. I sped down the street, but didn't make it any further because Zoe jumped in front of my car. I slammed on my brakes and yelled, "Again? Seriously? What is with you guys?"

Zoe sidled to my window and knocked nonchalantly.

"Going somewhere?" She smiled obnoxiously.

I rolled down the window. "I was, but then this really large animal jumped in front of my car," I informed her sarcastically.

She pouted. "I hope not that large."

I lay my forehead on the steering wheel. "You're not going to let me leave, are you?" I peeked to the side.

"Sure, I am. But I want to go with you," she said exuberantly.

Why was everybody so cheery this early in the morning?

"It'll be a girls' day." Her hair bounced with her around the front of my Jeep to the passenger door.

She hopped in before I could answer. "Ooohhh, leather." She ogled my interior, touching everything. "This is a nice car, Abby."

"Glad you approve." I smirked.

"So, where are we going?" She fidgeted excitedly, opening the center console, turning on the radio, and playing with the car windows.

"Are you about done?"

She giggled sheepishly. "Sorry. I just haven't hung out with another girl in a while. So, where are we going?"

Where was I going? I couldn't tell her I was headed to Elijah's. She wouldn't believe the lie I told Kendra since I was headed in the opposite direction of school, so I blurted out, "Shopping. I was going to Spokane to find a dress for the Winter Wonderland dance." Anybody who knew me would call me on the lie because I hated dances.

She bounced even higher, squealing, "Really? You didn't strike me as the fashion type." I ignored her jab. "So fun. What about your parents, though? Do they know you're skipping school?"

"Are you really asking me if I have permission from my parents? I'm seventeen."

"Okay, but don't mention me when you get caught." She put on her seat belt and sat with her hands on her lap. "Well, what are you waiting for?"

What did I get myself into?

"Can I ask you something?" I clenched the steering wheel as I drove to the highway.

"You can ask me anything, Abby. You're part of the family now." Her pale skin was even more radiant in the sunlight.

"Do you know much about Elijah?"

"Oh, a serious question." She frowned.

"Sorry, I just—"

She shushed me with her hand. "It's fine. You're curious. If you weren't, I'd be worried. I mean, you just found out your boyfriend is immortal. That's kind of a big deal. Ask away."

"It's just hard to believe that someone who saved me would come back later to kill me. That seems strange, right?"

"We don't really know all that much about him, which is why we are being so cautious. Plus, anyone with The Order of the Crest is not to be taken lightly. William and Wes are out trying to find out as much as they can without raising red flags." She played with the radio.

"They are?"

"He didn't tell you?"

I shook my head.

"Oh," her voice dropped, "he probably didn't want me telling you then. Oops." She searched through the radio stations.

"I have a few playlists on my iPod." I handed it to her.

"Oh, goodie. I was just about to pull out my phone, but we can give yours a listen." She scrolled through rapidly, her face contorting in disgust, surprise, and apology.

"What?" I spat, offended.

"Your playlists are interesting, Abby. I really like the one labeled *studying*." She giggled.

"Give it to me." I put my hand out for my iPod.

"I'm only teasing."

I hadn't mentioned my run-ins with Elijah to anyone yet. I was conflicted. I knew if I told them, they would freak out and I really needed to know why he was in the woods that night.

"Zoe?" I looked over. Her eyes were closed, and she was tapping her fingers to the music.

They perked open. "Yes?"

My nerves trembled. "You mentioned how lost immortals were before they found their True Mates, and it had me thinking about Wes and…"

"And you're wondering if you could possibly be his True Mate."

"I guess. Yes."

She replied sympathetically, "Honestly, I don't know. He's so new."

An uneasy feeling swirled in my stomach. "What was it like before you met Ben?"

The life drained from her eyes. "It's hard to put into words. Much like what I said before. I had no purpose. No reason to not act on my impulses. The Order of the Crest was already assembled, and I knew of their punishments, but I didn't care. Dying didn't seem so bad after the things I had done," she said solemnly as she peered out the window. "The worst part was, I didn't know there was a better life. That there was someone out there meant for me. Someone that would make me a better person. I was abandoned after I was turned and didn't run into many immortals. I was afraid for a very long time, so I hid."

My heart broke for her. "How did you know when you met Ben that he was your True Mate?"

Zoe's eyes brightened. "I came across this small village about fifty years into my immortality. It was on a Norwegian Island in between the Arctic Ocean and the Norwegian Sea. It was like nothing I had ever come across before. All the houses were built the same, out of wood slats, peaked roofs, and bright colors. There was snow on most of the island, and polar bears mostly inhabited it. They were beautiful and so mesmerizing. I spent a whole day watching a family of them. The way they navigated ice islands and swam gracefully from one place to the next reminded me so much of myself. It made me wonder if humans looked at me with the same fascination. Before Ben, I was ashamed of what I was. I hated who I had become, and my human memories still tortured me. I couldn't let go of that life."

She bowed her head shamefully. "Holding onto the past had made me merciless. I was bitter because I wanted it back." Revulsion seethed between her teeth as she spoke, "I followed the family of bears to the village, ready to kill anyone in my path, and that's when an enchanting scent overwhelmed me. It was a familiar scent of eucalyptus trees from my human childhood. It entrapped me in this painful thirst, leading me deeper into the village. I tracked it to the last house on the edge of the village. I peered through a window that flickered with dancing flames, the eucalyptus burning my nose as it invaded every cell in my body. Then I saw him. He was tall, his hair black as night, and when he turned to the window, his eyes paralyzed me. They were the same as mine. He floated to the window, placing his hands on the glass. I placed mine over his, and the connection was made. Our connection is as strong today as it was that day. He gave me purpose," she beamed.

Her story was breathtakingly beautiful, but it also raised so many doubts about Wes and me. I had never felt a connection like the one Wes and I shared, but I also hadn't experienced the void that Zoe had. I couldn't imagine going fifty years feeling as lonely as she described.

"I don't think I could have survived," I admitted.

"As an immortal, you don't have much of a choice. Death doesn't come easy for us." She sifted through her purse, pulling out a subtly pink lipstick and applying it carefully.

Wes had mentioned the same thing—that immortals didn't die easily, but The Order had found a way. Or so they suspected.

It only took us an hour to get to the mall, and the parking lot was deserted. "I guess it's a little early for shopping." I turned to her and feigned an innocent smile.

"I knew you weren't really going dress shopping, Abby." Her words were gentle.

"You did? Then why did you let me drive all the way out here?"

"Because I like you and I wanted to get to know you," she replied genuinely.

After I dropped Zoe off at home, I headed to school. I was grateful for Zoe's intervention, because I wasn't thinking this morning. If Elijah was a threat, I needed to be more careful.

When I got home that afternoon, my dad was waiting for me.

"Abigail, can you join me in the kitchen, please?"

He was sitting in the kitchen, drinking a cup of coffee. My first thought was the school called him about my tardy, but he didn't seem upset. "Hey, Dad." Trying to act normal, I grabbed a banana and a glass of water and leaned on the counter casually.

"How was school?" He took a sip of his coffee.

"It was school," I said carefully, trying to figure if the school called. I only missed part of first period.

"How's the Jeep running?"

I sighed in relief. I was in the clear. "Good. I love it. I get paid Friday, so I'll be able to start paying you back."

"I already told you it was a gift," he said, defeated.

My chest became tight. Something was wrong.

He rubbed his face hard and mumbled, "Your mother should be discussing this with you."

Oh no. It was one of *those* conversations. "Dad, please don't. I already know about boys." I was mortified.

"It's not what you think. I assume you know *that* by now, but it is about Wes. I have a bad feeling about him. Normally, I would trust your judgment." He straightened his back, sitting tall.

"Then trust me." I tossed the banana onto the counter, annoyed. "I have to do my homework before work."

"Hey, Peanut?"

He caught me before I reached the stairs. I spun around. "Yeah?"

He sighed. "If you trust him, then I will trust you."

My dad sounded as tired as he looked these days. His hair was a little grayer, and the hallowed black circles around his eyes were more defined.

"Thanks, Dad." I headed back up the stairs with a bad feeling in the pit of my stomach. Something wasn't right, and I knew my dad wouldn't tell me the truth, so I needed to find a good time to talk to my mom when he wasn't around.

It was a quiet night at the bistro. Mr. Hunter and Wes were gone, so Ben was filling in. He mainly stayed behind the bar, serving drinks. He didn't seem to be comfortable around a lot of people. Penelope latched onto him near the end of the evening. It was disgusting how she was drooling over him and in front of Zoe. And since when did she laugh? She barely ever cracked a smile.

"You okay, Abby?"

Zoe startled me, and I dropped the tray of dirty glasses

I was carrying to the kitchen.

"I'm so sorry, Abby. I didn't mean to scare you." Zoe helped sweep the glass onto the tray. "I'd do my salt trick from the other night, but that might freak out the customers." She winked.

"Yeah, probably not the best idea." I peered up at the bar and was relieved to see Penelope had moved on.

"Why are you so jumpy?" Zoe asked, concerned. "Did something happen?"

"No, I was just thinking about my dad." We stood up, the last of the customers ignoring us again.

"Is he okay?" She grabbed my arm for support.

"No. Yes. I don't know. He just looks really tired lately. I'm just a little worried." She followed me to the back where I emptied the tray of glass into the trash.

"Did you ask him about it?"

"No, he wouldn't tell me even if there was something wrong. I'm hoping my mom will."

"That sounds like a good plan." She smiled approvingly.

"I should get back on the floor. Thanks for helping me clean up." I rushed back to the floor, looking for Penelope. She was helping a customer at the register, her scowl firmly intact again. Zoe made her way to the bar with Ben. I envied them. When they were together, they emitted this soft glow. Their connection was undeniable.

Penelope fixed her eyes on Ben and Zoe when she was finished with the customer. She was acting so weird today. She turned my way with violent disdain. It was slightly unnerving.

"Hey, do you guys know much about Penelope?" I sat with Zoe, who was watching Ben adoringly as he wiped down the bar. It was almost closing time, so the bistro was clearing out.

"Not too much. She started right when we moved back. Why?" Zoe cracked an amused grin.

"You'd be able to tell if she was with The Order, right?" I pressed.

"Abby, you're being paranoid," Zoe said reassuringly.

"So, you think I'm just overreacting?"

They both turned to me and said, "Yes," simultaneously.

Zoe took my hand. "Answer me this. Would you have thought something different about Penelope before we had the immortals-live-on-this-Earth talk?"

I felt kind of silly now that she put it that way. "No, I guess not. You would be a good mom."

Ben and Zoe exchanged a knowing look.

"I'm sorry. I said something wrong, didn't I?" I buried my head in my hands.

"No, not at all." Zoe comforted me.

Peering between my fingers, I asked, "Really?"

"Yes." She chuckled, looking over to Ben. "Having each other is enough. You should go. You have school tomorrow. We'll finish cleaning up."

"Are you sure?" I climbed off the stool, tugging at my shirt to smooth out the wrinkles and running my fingers through my hair to untangle the knots from my bun.

"We clean fast." Ben winked.

"Right. Immortals. Thanks. See you Saturday. I still have Friday off, right?"

"Yes, I'm going to fill in. It'll be fun." Zoe and Ben exchanged conspiratorial glances.

"Oh, brother." I rolled my eyes playfully. "Night."

By the time I got home, my mom had gone to sleep and my dad was nowhere in sight. They always waited up for me. Things were changing. I just didn't understand why they were changing at home.

15

MY WEEK WENT BY IMPOSSIBLY slow waiting for Wes to return. Luckily, I only had to sit through a few more hours of school and then he would be home.

"Are you excited for the party tonight?" Kendra asked as she took a bite of her sandwich.

My eyes darted from my plate of barely touched salad up to Kendra. I had completely forgotten about the party.

"You forgot, didn't you?" She rolled her eyes. "Figures."

"What's that supposed to mean?" I snapped defensively.

"As if I even need to say it." She dropped the rest of her sandwich onto her plate.

"Sorry. I've just been—"

"Busy, I know," she cut me off.

My absence was definitely not going unnoticed. "I

might have forgotten, but I'm still going. That should count for something, right?"

Her pout faded. "Fine, but you better not ask to leave early."

"Are you still bringing Elijah?"

"Yes."

I frowned disapprovingly.

"Don't," she said before I could say anything. "You pinky promised to be a good friend. At least try to like him," she begged.

"Look, we don't know anything about Elijah, except that he's in college and lives in a nice house in Bayview. We don't know if it's his or his parents'. Does he even *have* parents?" I took a bite of my salad.

"Really? That's your case? Abby, everyone has parents. *He* has parents."

I turned my head toward the center of the room and clashed gazes with Natalie and her clique. Natalie liked to be the center of attention, so she and her clique always sat in the middle of the cafeteria. "Why is Natalie staring at us?" I chewed on my plastic fork.

"Because she's envious of the beauty radiating from our table." Kendra glowered.

"Did she see you talking to one of her boyfriends again?" Natalie was a real piece of work, and it took until eighth grade for me to see her true colors. "She's coming over," I hissed.

Natalie swung her hips as she passed by the football

players, blowing them a kiss, and stopped in front of our table with a couple of her lackeys standing a few feet behind her.

"Hi, girls," she sneered, peeling back her red stained lips to reveal her bright white teeth.

"What do you want, Natalie?" I sat up straight.

"I'm sure you heard about my party tonight at the lake house." She focused on her nail polish rather than us.

"Maybe." Kendra's snotty retort made me proud.

"Good. Well, I hope you're coming. You wouldn't want to miss it. It's the biggest party of the year." Her hazel eyes glared at us.

"We might be," Kendra lied.

We had planned on going all week.

"Great. See you tonight. Eight o'clock." She strolled out of the cafeteria.

I leaned in close to Kendra. "Why does she care if we go tonight?"

One of Natalie's followers bent down. "Because the football team refused to go if Kendra wasn't there." She giggled and then caught up with Natalie and her group.

We both looked over at the rambunctious table of boys and shared a winning laugh.

"Something tells me you won't have a problem finding a date for the Winter Wonderland dance."

"What makes you think I'm still looking?" She raised her eyebrow, testing me.

"You know my feelings on the subject, so my lips are

sealed." I zipped my fingers across my lips.

Last period dragged on forever. Wes was meeting me after school, and I was dying to see him. As soon as the bell rang, I raced to my car, but Wes wasn't there. I scanned the street, hoping he was just late, but I didn't see him or his car anywhere.

"Expecting someone?" Kendra walked up behind me.

"I was hoping Wes was home from his trip, but I guess not." We climbed into the Jeep.

"Do you want me to come over? I can help you get ready for the party."

Even after blowing her off for work and Wes, she was still my best friend. "Thanks, but I'll be fine." I pulled up to her house a couple of minutes later.

"See you at eight?" Kendra asked before closing the door.

"Yeah. Eight." I smiled feebly.

She shut the door and ran to her house, performing a little leap and blowing me a kiss. I wasn't looking forward to being in a car with Elijah again, but at least this way Kendra wouldn't be alone with him.

I swung by Wes' house on the way home, but no one seemed to be there. I was disappointed, but I was also getting worried.

"Mom?" I called.

"Yeah, sweetie?" She appeared from the kitchen, wiping her hands on a dishtowel and adorning a knitting needle in her hair.

"Really?" I chortled and pointed to my hair, mocking the needle.

She searched for it absentmindedly and pulled it out, her hair falling over her shoulders. "I forgot I put it there."

"Is Dad home?" I set my book bag onto the floor.

"No."

"Cool, because I was wondering if I could talk to you."

"Sure. Can I knit while we talk? I was just heading back out."

"Yeah." I followed her to the patio, eyeing the large pile of blue

bonnets on the ground.

"Something you want to tell me?" I asked, pointing to the pile.

"Oh." She laughed. "The hospital asked our knitting club if we would make them for the newborns."

"Good, because I was ready to have you committed."

He fingers moved hypnotically as she picked up where she left off. "So, what's up?"

I sat in the rocker next to her. "Why did you start knitting?"

"Well, when you started going to school full time, and with your father gone all the time, I got bored. I thought about getting a job, but your dad earned enough money. I took up gardening, but that only filled a few days a season. Then one day when we were visiting Grandpa in Seattle, we took the bus and I became fascinated by this little old lady who was knitting in the front seat. You were about five or six then. Do you remember?"

It was hard to forget because it was my first time on a bus. "I do." The memory became vivid again.

"When we were downtown, I popped into some of the knitting shops, and the rest is history."

Until my mom mentioned the old woman, I had completely forgotten about her. When we were getting off the bus, she gave me a charm for a bracelet, and that was where I remembered the infinity symbol from. It was an infinity charm. I kept it in a musical jewelry box that my mother had given me.

"Abigail?" My mom had stopped knitting and was staring at me. "Where'd you go?"

I had dazed off remembering that day. "Nowhere. I'm here." I smiled.

"As much as I love talking about knitting, I doubt that's what you wanted to talk about."

"Is everything okay with Dad? He seems really worn out lately." I picked the polish off my nails nervously and bounced my foot.

"He has seemed a little tired, hasn't he?"

I was happy she was open to talking about this. "Yeah, I've never seen him with circles under his eyes. I thought being home meant he was slowing down."

She rocked in sync with the knitting needles. "Unfortunately, it's the opposite. He's had to work longer hours to keep up what he was doing before, but he loves being home, Abby. He wants to be here for you." She stopped knitting for a moment to pat my hand.

"So, it's my fault?"

"What? No, Abby. He's fine. Things are fine. Don't worry so much."

"Where is he today?"

"He had another meeting in Seattle. He won't be back until tomorrow night. Do you have any fun plans this weekend?"

"There's a party at Natalie's tonight, but that's pretty much it." It didn't even occur to me to ask her permission to go. "Is that okay?"

"Of course, honey. Just be back by eleven."

Heading back in, I paused to listen to my mom humming a tune from my childhood. It was the same one from my music box. My mom had boxed up all of my stuff when we redecorated my room when I hit the tween stage, but the memory of the old woman sparked an interest in seeing that charm again. It couldn't possibly be related to my grandpa's key.

The attic access was at the end of the hall in front of my room, and that was where all my old stuff from my room was stored. I yanked hard on the pull cord, and the collapsible ladder unfolded. I flipped on the light when I got to the top of the attic and located my boxes stacked together in a corner.

I dragged the box marked *Keepsakes* over to the light and

ripped off the tape. The music box was wrapped in paper safely on top. I unrolled it carefully and held it up. It was just as I remembered, and it still played music, the ballerina spinning with the melody. The infinity charm sparkled among other trinkets.

"Abigail, Kendra's on the phone," my mom yelled from below. I scooped up the charm and squeezed it in the palm of my hand, taking the music box down with me, too.

"Abigail, what are you doing?"

"I heard you humming, and it made me want to dig this up."

"I think it's great. My mother gave it to me." She smiled. "The phone is in your dad's office."

"Okay, thanks." I dropped the music box off in my room and ran down to the office.

"Hey, Ken, what's up?"

"I can't go tonight. I got food poisoning or something. I'm sorry." She sounded miserable.

"If it makes you feel any better, I didn't really want to go anyway."

"I knew it. I gotta go. I'll see you Monday." She hung up quickly.

I was more than okay with not going tonight. I felt bad she was sick, but it wasn't like I was looking forward to a night with Natalie and her crew. *Or Elijah*. As tempting as it was to hop in my Jeep and drive to Wes' again, I refrained. Instead, I climbed under a blanket and curled up at my window seat. Another storm was due to roll in tonight or tomorrow, and the chill was already seeping through my windowpane. I pulled the infinity charm out of my pocket and held it in one hand while the other held my grandpa's key. The symbol was unique with one half filled in, the same on the charm and the key. It was too unique to be a coincidence, but what connection could my grandpa's key have to a charm that a complete stranger gave me when I was six?

A tap on my window drew my attention. For a moment, I thought it was just the wind brushing a tree branch against my window, but then a louder tap followed. I squinted through the glass, twilight fading into darkness, but there was still just enough light to make out Wes standing by my car. Excitement overwhelmed me. I stuffed the key and charm into my pocket and raced down the stairs.

"Bye, Mom," I yelled.

"Have fun, honey." She had moved into the sitting room to knit.

I quickly put on my grandpa's bomber jacket and rushed outside straight into Wes' arms, pushing him back a step.

"I missed you, too." He laughed, digging his nose into my hair and inhaling deeply.

The wind whipped around us.

"Did you know you smell like oranges?" He gleamed from his revelation.

"I did not know that, but we do have an orange grove out back. You have a scent, too." I looked up into his eyes, transfixed by his beauty.

"And what is it?"

"Lemongrass," I beamed.

"Well, at least it's something masculine." He winked and squeezed me in tight against his chest again. "Can I take you somewhere?"

I nodded excitedly.

"I'll drive," he said as he interlaced his fingers with mine and led me to his gray convertible, opening the door for me before hopping into the driver's side. The engine was still running, and the heat blasted from the vents.

"I was afraid you forgot about me," I nervously admitted, biting my lip.

"I could never forget you." He reached over and took my hand in his.

I didn't care where we went. He was back, and we were alone.

"What did you do while I was gone?" His curious eyes turned to me briefly.

"Waited." My answer not carrying an ounce of shame.

"Me, too." He lifted my hand and kissed it softly.

I was a bit surprised when he pulled into the bistro parking lot. I opened my mouth to ask him what we were doing here, but he quickly put his index finger on my lips.

"Trust me," he said mischievously.

"Okay." I nodded. Excitement was building as we walked hand in hand behind the bistro to the pier.

"I was worried the wind would ruin my plans, but it looks like it's cooperating for the time being."

"The calm before the storm." I pointed to the dark clouds rolling in.

"It should hold off for a few more hours. Come on." He tugged me lightly to the pier. The end of the pier was lively with neon lights and people perusing the few shops there were, but where Wes and I stood it was peaceful.

I wanted to live in this moment forever with just Wes, the water, and the infinite stars.

"Don't move." He climbed over the railing and made his way down to the water.

"What are you doing?" It was so dark I couldn't see where he went. "Wes?" I hissed frantically.

Then the tip of a rowboat floated out from under the deck with Wes balancing in it. He held up two paddles and a large grin.

"You scared me half to death."

"Immortal, remember? Come on. Climb down."

He held the boat steady while I climbed over the railing and dropped down into it. It was just big enough for the two of us.

"Where did you get this?" I held my hand out for one of the paddles.

"It's ours. Well, technically, it's my dad's." His eyes gleamed.

Once we paddled out into the lake, Wes took a blanket and laid it out on the bottom of the boat. There was just enough room for us to lie side by side, watching the slowly spinning world above us.

"This is stunning." I was enamored with the glorious beauty of the sky.

"It's only that way because you're here." Wes turned to me, our faces only inches apart because of the tight space.

"Do you want to talk about what you did this week?"

He reached over and brushed my hair behind my back, lightly grazing my neck.

"Not really." His fingers gripped the back of my neck softly as he moved closer to me. "Have you ever been kissed, Abby?"

My body was trembling as I shook my head. Words had completely failed me.

"Good." He smiled crookedly and then pressed his lips against mine.

The coolness sank into me, taking every last breath from me, my mind spinning with the boat, fully engulfed in the numbing sensation taking over my lips. I pressed my lips on his harder, wrapping both my arms around his neck and pushing him close to my chest. I had waited so long for this, but then the rocking of the boat became a wave of nausea in my head and it began to pound. I felt weak.

"Abby? Look at me. Abby?" Wes suddenly begged.

His voice became distant as the fog in my head thickened. Wes' cold hands on my cheeks reminded me for a brief moment where I was. I focused on his eyes just long enough to see the fear they emitted.

"Abby, what's wrong?"

"I don't know. I'm sorry." My voice was barely a whisper. "I think I'm seasick."

He laughed lightly, brushing an apologetic hand down my cheek. "Then I should probably get you off this boat." He kissed my forehead gently and then paddled us back to the pier.

My head still felt fuzzy, and my body was covered in sweat, but I was more coherent when we reached the pier and also more than mortified. Maybe I *was* fragile.

Wes tied the boat to the pier. "You made it." He helped me up onto the pier.

"I'm cold." My body shivered. He snatched the blanket from the boat and wrapped it around me, holding me tightly to his side. "I'm really tired. Can you take me home?" I was getting weaker by the second.

I fell asleep in the car, and when I woke briefly in the middle of the night, I discovered I was in my bed. Alone.

16

My DOOR WAS CRACKED OPEN, and the faint whispers of my parents down the hall slipped around me

"I'm worried, James." My mom's voice cracked.

"You did the right thing calling me," my dad replied.

My dad knocked softly on my door. "Peanut? Are you awake?"

I turned on my side to face him. "Yeah, I'm awake."

"Your mom told me Wes brought you home sick last night. She said you couldn't even walk. What happened?"

For all my parents knew, I went to that party with Wes and probably assumed I drank myself into a coma. That was definitely better than the truth. I wasn't sure they would react too well to me being alone with Wes on a boat in the middle of the lake.

"Yeah, I think I got food poisoning or something. Kendra has it, too."

"That's what your mom said. She talked to Kendra's mom this morning. Probably the same thing." His eyes raised, daring me to tell him otherwise.

"I'm sorry I worried you guys. Wes was great, though. I'm glad he was there." I yawned dramatically, hoping he would get the hint.

"Are you hungry? It's almost two."

"No, I'm okay. Just tired. But can you call Mr. Hunter at the bistro and let him know I won't be able to make it tonight?"

"I was going to suggest that. Perhaps a few days off?"

It was more a request than a question, and when he did that, I couldn't argue. "Sure, Dad. A few days off would probably be good. I'm going to go back to sleep now."

"Glad you're feeling better. I'll wake you for dinner. Sleep tight, Peanut." His smile was strained as he closed the door.

I needed to see Wes. I *wanted* to see him. Last night was mortifying. Maybe I could convince my parents to at least let him drop by. After taking a shower, I went downstairs to eat. My stomach was grumbling painfully.

"You're up." My mom jumped up from the couch. "Let me fix you something. What do you think your stomach can handle?"

"Thanks, Mom. I think my stomach is good now." I was ravenous.

"You sure you're not running a fever?" She put her hand on my forehead. "You look better." She smiled.

"I feel much better."

"I'll heat up some soup."

I didn't see my dad anywhere. "Is Dad mad that he had to come home early?"

"What? No. Abby, stop worrying so much about your dad. You'd be surprised how strong he is." She placed the bowl of soup onto the table. "Now sit and eat."

"Is this from the bistro?"

"Yes. Your dad picked it up for you."

"Where is he?"

"Since he left early from Seattle, he had to go back to finish his business there. He'll be back tomorrow. He wouldn't leave unless he knew you were better." She squeezed my shoulder.

"I feel a hundred times better. I just needed some rest. I was actually thinking of running over to Wes' to let him know I was better. He's probably worried."

"Oh. Are you sure you're up to driving? I don't mind driving you. Or maybe you could just call him?"

"Really, Mom, I'm all better. And the soup is really helping."

"Just don't be too long. I think you should take it easy the rest of the weekend. And don't tell your dad I let you out of my sight."

"Thanks. I won't." I took a few more bites and then tossed the rest into the sink.

I sat in the driveway for a few minutes while the inside of my car heated up. It was freezing outside. A tap on my window startled me, causing me to jam my knee into the dashboard. Elijah smiled back at me, so I rolled down the window.

"Cold?"

I rubbed my bruised knee. "Ow, seriously. You can't do that."

"Can I sit with you?"

"I guess." I considered saying no, but with all the questions surrounding, well, everything, I knew I couldn't turn him away.

He slipped into the passenger seat. "It's a hundred degrees in here, Abby." He reached for the thermostat knob, but I swatted his hand away.

"Don't." I pointed my finger at his face. "The max temperature is eighty-six, so you're wrong." I protected it with my hand. "What are you doing here, Elijah?" I was beginning to think having a car was a bad idea. It attracted too many surprise visits.

"We need to talk," he said seriously.

"Why? How can I be sure that anything you tell me is the truth?"

"I should have told you the other night." Regret darkened his mood.

"Saving my life is kind of a huge thing to leave out."

He sighed deeply. "The deal was for me to maintain no contact, but then…things changed."

"The deal. So, if you are here to protect me, then why is everyone worried you're going to hurt me?"

"Drive and I can show you."

"And now I am supposed to trust you?"

"Yes, because you want to know what I know."

I hated how right he was. I put the car in reverse and drove out onto the street.

"Where are we going?" *Please don't say his house.*

"If I say my place, are you going to freak out?"

My palms were sweating nervously. Or maybe it was the eighty-six degrees in the car. Either way, I just made another really bad choice. I knew the Hunters felt he was dangerous, but my grandpa always told me I had great instincts, and right now they weren't screaming serial killer. He scared the hell out of me, but he saved my life once, and I owed it to myself to find out why.

"Your place it is." My stomach flipped anxiously. "We have a long drive, so you could start talking now." I watched his reaction from my peripheral.

He looked out the window. "You won't believe me. I need to show you." His voice was soft.

Why did he care so much? Why did anybody care at all? I was just a small-town girl. I dared a sideways glance over to him. When I met Elijah, I was strangely attracted to him. And it wasn't because he was heartbreakingly handsome either. It was something else. Seeing him now, staring out into the storm, his fist opening and closing just enough to see his knuckles flex and then relax, I realized he was nervous, too. *Vulnerable*. The other times he was poised. *Confident*. Something had changed recently. Something was wrong. Was he afraid *for* me?

My focus went back to the road in front of me. Large raindrops hit the windshield, bursting and spreading like spider webs. The rain was light at first, but strengthened as we exited the highway into Bayview.

Elijah had drifted his gaze back to the road ahead, too, but his stare was distant. It was making me nervous again, and the tension was building exponentially. The sound of the gravel driveway under my tires crunched loudly.

Before I turned off the car, I faced him. "Should I be scared?"

His eyes locked with mine, a sort of sadness swirling in his sea of green. "Of me? No."

"But of someone else?" I persisted.

"You already know the answer to that."

He took my hand and put it on his chest, our eyes fixed on each other.

"Do you feel that?" he asked.

"Your heartbeat? Yes."

"I have one, and you have one. Your parents have one. The Hunters don't, Abby. They don't have a heartbeat or a soul. They aren't human. They don't feel the way we do, and they certainly don't care like us. Now, ask me again if you should be scared."

I was stunned into disbelief. How had I not noticed Wes didn't have a heartbeat?

"Ask me, Abby. Should you be scared?" he repeated.

"Should I be scared?"

"Yes, you should be very scared."

Thunder suddenly shook the car, breaking the tension.

He released my hand from his chest slowly. "Follow me."

We raced in the front door, soaking wet even from the short distance. After the Hunters revealed what they were, I wondered if Elijah was, too, but when he raked his fingers through his hair, I noticed how human he was. *Imperfect.*

Inside, Elijah came to my side and helped pull off my wet jacket. His fingers tingled the back of my neck, and I had to close my eyes and suck in a slow breath to keep from whimpering.

"Tea or coffee?" he asked as he hung up my jacket.

"Huh?" I asked in my stupor.

"Do you prefer tea or coffee? Or are you a hot cocoa girl?"

"Oh." I tugged my long sleeves down over my hands uneasily. "Hot cocoa. Thanks," I shyly responded as I directed my attention away from him, trying to regain my composure.

I followed him into the kitchen. A fire was blazing in the fireplace, so I sat in the sofa chair next to it, trying to get dry. I tried to distract myself from Elijah, but I was failing miserably. He pulled his soaked sweatshirt over his head, taking his undershirt with it, giving me a peek of his muscular lower back. I looked away quickly when he turned toward me, ashamed at the heat that rushed through me.

He put a teapot on the stove and walked over, taking a seat across from me. He leaned over his knees, his fingers tugging at each other. His vulnerability was dangerously attractive.

As if he read my thoughts, he asked, "Your boyfriend isn't going to bust in here, is he?"

I chuckled lightly. "He doesn't know I'm here, so I highly doubt it."

His eyebrows pulled in tight, making his expression serious, and he looked at me, determined. "You underestimate him. Don't."

"You want me to be afraid of him." It wasn't a question.

"Not just of him. Of all of them." His head dropped.

"The Hunters?"

He shook his head slowly and then lifted his gaze. "No, Abby. *All* of them."

I shivered. How many were there? "You brought me here to show me something. What is it?" I was starting to question coming here.

The teapot whistled before he could answer. He got up and busily prepared the hot cocoa. My crossed leg kicked up and down nervously as I waited impatiently for answers.

He came back with two mugs. "This should warm you up."

"Thanks." Three marshmallows floated on top. "Marshmallows?" My eyebrow arched playfully.

"Don't judge," he said as he took a sip. "It's hot just like the chili was, so consider yourself warned." He winked.

This wasn't supposed to be comfortable and easy, but it was.

I blew on the steaming cocoa. "Why three marshmallows?" I asked curiously.

"Because two isn't as much fun." He smiled coyly.

Because three makes a triangle, I thought. *And trouble.*

"If you're not immortal, then what are you?"

He peeked up through his lashes with a look worth melting for. "Why do I have to be anything other than mortal?"

"For you to owe someone a favor that is in the realm of keeping someone safe from immortals, you must be pretty extraordinary." I raised a curious eyebrow. He was hiding something, and I was determined to find out what.

"I'll take that as a compliment." He took a sip of his cocoa.

"That wasn't an answer."

"Was there a question in there?"

I didn't know how he managed it, but he seemed to make me smile…a lot. "This is good." I raised the mug.

"Thanks." He paused and then continued, "There are some extraordinary mortals in the world, Abby. Extraordinary enough to handle immortals on some levels."

"And are you telling me you're one of them?"

He drank more of his hot cocoa, his eyes narrowing as if he were deciding whether he should tell me his deep, dark secret.

"Yes," he said simply.

A quiet gasp escaped my lips. I thought there could be a chance, but somehow it still seemed so unbelievable, but nothing was out of the realm of possibilities, especially since immortals had jumped out of the pages of fiction and surrounded us.

"Don't be so small-minded, Abby. If immortals can exist, don't you think it plausible that others could, too? That mortals have evolved with gifts to protect themselves from immortals?"

I was mind blown. There were humans with gifts. "Small-minded? That's pretty rude." Here we were, sitting by a fire in a gorgeous house on the lake, sipping hot cocoa, but instead of discussing standard things like the weather, we were debating about what kinds of things existed in the world.

"I don't mean to demean you, but it's utterly ridiculous that you believe in immortals, but you haven't considered other possibilities."

I scrunched my face at his bluntness. He had me, though. "In my defense, I've only known about immortals for a week!" I leaned over, getting closer to him. "So then tell me. Educate me, Elijah."

His demeanor went dark, and his eyes fell. My heart instantly ached. My instincts were telling me he was about to divulge something bad.

"An immortal attacked my mom and me when I was six. My mom tried to protect me, but he was strong. She used her body as a shield, and I can still remember how her racing pulse felt against my neck, and her hands," he looked down at his own hands, "they were shaking so hard against my body. She was so scared and begged for mercy. To spare *me*." He cleared his throat. "She sacrificed herself." He blinked hard and long, staving off tears and then continued, "He grabbed her from me, but I didn't want to let go, so I held firmly to her wrist. That's when I felt it for the first time. A surge of energy traveled between us. Like a charge of electricity. I was only six and hurting, so I didn't think much of it."

His eyes looked into the distant past, far from the living room we occupied. "He ripped her from me, and then she was gone. I heard her screams for a few seconds until they faded completely." He stood up and walked to the mantel, putting his mug down, and rested his forehead on his arms.

I wanted to go to him. To comfort him, but I waited, giving him a moment.

"My father found me curled up in the corner of their bedroom. Seeing my father crumble the way he did was almost as hard as watching my mother being taken. He called the police, but they couldn't do much. My mother and that thing disappeared without a trace. My father couldn't accept that she was gone, and since no one else was helping us find her, we packed up and went on our own search. We didn't have any leads for several years, and then we met someone one day. He listened to my story and brought us to The Order of the Crest. When I told them about the surge of energy I felt with my mom, they said they would help us find her if we would join The Order." He stopped again, taking a deep breath and straightening up.

"Did they? Find her, I mean?" I was completely immersed in his memory and having a hard time keeping it together myself.

"Yes, but it was too late." He grabbed the mug and carried it to the kitchen sink. "Be lucky you just found out about immortals. Monsters became real for me

when I was eight." He stayed at the sink, unmoving, looking broken all over again.

I wanted to offer some sort of relief, so I went over and just barely touched his shoulder, afraid he would recoil. When he didn't, I caressed his shoulder with my thumb, just enough to let him know I was listening and that I cared. He turned into me and wrapped his arms tightly around me and cried softly in the crook of my neck, breaking every damn piece of me. The man I was supposed to be fearful of, who was supposed to protect me, needed me, too.

17

IT WAS HARD TO SEE ELIJAH like that. It would be hard to see anyone go through what he had. He retreated upstairs to shower and to take a moment for himself. The thought of him sending me home after his confession weighed on me because I didn't want him to. This overwhelming feeling of needing to be near him was consuming me. We had shared something so ugly and yet so beautiful at the same time. He had let me in. He trusted me. I owed him the same.

When he came back downstairs, he looked refreshed. His hair was wet, slicked back with some strands escaping around his face, and the gleam in his eyes had begun to return.

"Sorry about that before." He brushed off our moment.

"Don't be." I shook my head. "I feel honored you shared that with me."

He had a seat on the couch, and I had a strong urge to sit next to him, but I kept my distance. I was unsure where we stood as far as our friendship went, and things were getting more and more complicated, and lines were blurring quickly.

"I've never told anyone," he admitted as he rested an elbow on his knee and brushed his hands over his face, looking emotionally exhausted.

No wonder he broke down. "That's a lot to carry around for…" It dawned on me that I had no idea what his age was. "How old are you, Elijah?"

"Twenty."

Wow. He was only a few years older than me and had already gone through so much. I couldn't imagine. "What do you do for The Order?"

"My father was trained for missions to apprehend rogue immortals."

There was that word again. *Apprehend*. It gave me the chills not knowing exactly how The Order defined that.

"He was obsessed after what they did to my mother, but no matter how many he brought in or how strong he appeared, he still mourned my mother. Until the day he died."

I slid my hand over my mouth, trying to stop the tears. The tragedies just kept coming.

"I was too young for missions, but they taught me about my gift. The surge of energy wasn't just an adrenaline rush. I spent the better part of my youth learning how to use it. They said I was a tracker, and I wasn't the only one, although I've never met any others."

"Can you track anyone?" *Was he tracking me?*

"Yes, if I've been in physical contact with them."

I sat back in my chair, chewing on my hand. "The accident…" I trailed off, not sure how to finish my thought.

"Yes." He nodded apologetically. He was sharing a secret, and I could tell it was killing him for having it.

"I felt something when we shook hands in my kitchen." I rubbed the palm of my hand, remembering the black hole sensation that had nearly scared me to death. It was inexplicable at the time, but now I understood.

"Now that we have…connected, you'll always feel something when we touch. I've heard sometimes it's just a shock, but other times it's been…" he stared intensely at my reaction, "more."

More was right. Every time he touched me, it was a euphoric rush of tingles all over my body. Except when we met. That was disturbing.

"Are you all right? Your cheeks are turning red."

"Yeah…I…uhh…it's hot in here. Are you hot?" I waved my face wildly. This was so embarrassing.

"Let me get you a glass of water."

My eyes were glued to him as he passed by me to the kitchen. It could have just been wonderment that he was…extraordinary, but the way he made me feel, it was intoxicating.

"Here." He smiled as he handed me the glass.

"Thanks." I guzzled it down, and he laughed in mild amusement.

"What?" I smirked.

"Nothing." He brushed it off.

I placed the glass on the end table and asked, "Do you feel it, too? When you touch me?"

He rubbed the back of his neck uncomfortably. "Yeah."

Okay, this was getting uncomfortable. Good uncomfortable, but uncomfortable nonetheless.

"You should know that when I pulled you from the accident, I had already been watching you for a while. I was instructed to keep my distance until it was necessary. Nobody planned on the accident, and I couldn't just watch you be mauled by that thing," he spat fiercely. "That night I had no choice but to interject. My job was to keep you safe, and that's what I did, but…"

His pause had me waiting on the edge of my seat.

"Over that year before the accident…" he searched for the right words, "you were so young, but I became captivated by you."

My skin pebbled. He was admitting to stalking me, and instead of being frightened, I was excited. I couldn't explore this with him any further. It felt wrong.

"How old were you when you were assigned to me?"

"Seventeen. You were technically my first assignment. I

had a few trial runs, but you were the first where I was on my own."

"That's a pretty big responsibility for someone who was barely legal."

"Yes." A haunting sadness overtook him. "That night changed me. *You* changed me. My objective became less about a responsibility and more about a commitment. I didn't want to be on the outside looking in anymore. I wanted to *know* you."

I fixed my eyes on the floor. "Why didn't you then?" I was uncomfortably comfortable with our conversation.

"Become a part of your life?"

I nodded apprehensively.

"That wasn't the assignment. It's complicated, Abby. I was asked to watch you, not interact with you. And I highly respect the person who requested me."

Tension built as the confession hung thickly between us. "I shouldn't have said that." He stood up, shaking his head in disbelief. "This isn't about me or how I feel about you." He rubbed his face hard, the stress eating at him. "What I tell you has to stay between us, Abby. You can't tell the Hunters."

I braced myself and nodded for him to continue.

"You are extraordinary, too."

My eyes widened. "Like I have an extraordinary gift?" He nodded. "That's impossible. You're insane." I laughed nervously and paced frantically.

Elijah stood in front of me, putting both hands on my

shoulders and looking hard into my eyes. His touch radiated through my body. "Think about it, Abby. You know when things don't feel right. You can sense it."

"Lots of people have great instincts," I challenged.

"Yes, but do you ever question yours? Do you ever feel conflicted about them?"

I shook my head. "No." And I hadn't. Not once were my instincts wrong. "Is that not normal?"

He grinned. "No. Not unless you're Spiderman."

I rubbed my face, exhausted from the rapid-fire revelations. This was all way too much, and I was totally buying into it. Because you know why? Because my instincts were telling me to.

"The Order of the Crest wants you. They seek out Specials so they can train them to join The Order."

"So, we are called Specials now? I don't understand. Let's say for a second that I play along with this. How would they even know about me?"

His hands dropped from my shoulders. "*That* I need to show you," he said darkly. He left the room, and my stomach tightened. My heart filled with terror when I heard the front door open and then close. I couldn't stop my hands from trembling. Maybe my instincts were wrong this time. I took a few steps to the back door, but it was too late. Elijah returned, and I wasn't ready for who he brought with him.

"Dad?" I looked back and forth between them, confused. "No, no. This can't be happening." A wave of nausea hit me like a ton of bricks. I clutched my stomach, bending over, wishing for an escape. Elijah's debt was to my father, but worse yet, my father had been betraying me. It stung. Bad. I couldn't keep the tears from racing down my cheeks.

"Abigail, please." My dad ran to my side and tried to comfort me.

"Don't." I waved him away. "I can't."

He stumbled back. "You have to listen to me."

"No, I don't." My voice cracked. I did have to listen, but right now, I needed to sit. White spots were dancing in front of me, and the dizziness was thick in my head. I fell into the chair, placing my head between my knees, sobbing, trying to block out the whispers between them. "How could you keep this from me?" I gritted through my teeth. I peeked up and the regretful expression that had taken hold of my dad almost made me falter. Almost.

"Please, just listen to what I have to say before you draw any conclusions."

"Too late. They've been drawn." As painful as this was and no matter how angry I was, he was my dad and this was my life. Elijah, Wes, immortals, Specials. It was my reality now.

He sat across from me, leaning over his knees with his hands tightly clasped together, the skin on his dry knuckles splitting. The silence was deafening. "I am a member of The Order of the Crest."

The oxygen had been punched from my chest. "What?"

"So was your grandfather."

He watched my pained expression deepen. My grandpa

and I were so close. He told me everything. So I thought.

"And so was his father. Our commitment to The Order goes back four generations. I wanted it to end with me. I didn't want my daughter involved in this. I wanted you to have a normal life."

I cackled. "Normal? You mean blind. You wanted to keep me blind."

"Yes." His head dropped shamefully. "But I knew when Wes returned, it was only a matter of time that you found out. I knew how close you two were."

My eyes darted up. He knew about Wes. "So, you knew about Wes? For how long?"

"The Order has always known about the Hunters, but Wes was an enigma. We didn't know about hybrids. When William took a human as his wife, it drew a line with The Order. It was an act of war, whether he meant it to be or not. He tried to plead his case, but after they found out about Wes…"

"Oh, no." I threw my hand over my mouth. "They *killed* her?" My breaths shortened, only adding to the fog in my head. My father and Elijah exchanged a knowing glance. "But she is human," I whined. "How could they do that?"

He sucked in a deep breath. "That's why I called Elijah. I didn't know what they would do if they found out about you and Wes. They are capable of anything, Abby. There are days I think they aren't any better than the immortals."

"Think? They aren't." Elijah's story ran parallel to Wes', and it made my stomach turn. "So, now what?"

My father tried to rub years of stress from his face. "We leave," he mumbled, his heart thick with remorse.

"What? No." I shook my head. "I can't. School…" The tears flowed again. "Kendra…Mom?" *Mom.* "Does she know?"

He shook his head. His betrayal was for us both.

"The Order knows about your gift. They've been wanting to recruit you, but now with Wes in the picture, I don't know if we can trust their intentions."

How could the world possibly spin out of control and explode into a million pieces, only to come back together all wrong? "How did they find out about my gift?" My voice cracked.

Pain filled his eyes. "Your grandfather." I sucked in a shocked gasp. "He was so proud and wanted you to be a part of The Order. He was determined, Abigail, even though I vehemently disapproved. That's why our relationship soured. He went behind my back and told them about you. I was trying to keep you from all of this."

"Wouldn't they have recruited me anyway?" Everyone before me had been a member of The Order.

"I had pleaded with them to spare you. When they refused, I made a deal with them."

He was in so much turmoil. It was so hard to see him like this. My father, the pillar of confidence and strength, was falling apart before my eyes.

"What deal, Dad? What did you promise them?"

A tear fell from his eye, and I knew it was bad. Not just bad, but tragic.

"I promised them my firstborn son."

"But you didn't…" No, no, no. Oh my God, no. I couldn't breathe. The world was closing in on me. "Please tell me you didn't." He looked away. "You couldn't. Right, Dad? It's not possible!" I shouted through broken words and a bleeding heart.

"I thought," he cleared his throat, "I thought I could stay emotionally detached…"

By the surprised look on Elijah's face, I knew he didn't know. I had a brother. Somewhere. It was something I had always wanted. My only wish.

He continued, "I was so angry with your grandfather, Abigail. I hated him. Everything I had sacrificed to keep you safe… When he got sick, I didn't visit. I wanted him to die alone for what he did." He shook his head sadly. "I can never forgive him, Abby. Never. I lost my son." He choked back the tears. "You lost your brother."

I was still crying, and I was biting my fist so hard, I had punctured the skin. It was so hard to digest what he was telling me. All the facts were jumbled together, not making sense.

My father crawled out of the chair and over to the bottom of my feet. He took my face in his hands, his red eyes locking with my own. "I will do whatever it takes to protect you. Say the word, and I will hide you from The

Order and the immortals. I will take you and your mother far away from all of this." He was desperate, teetering between forgiveness and tragedy.

My eyes burned, and my heart ached. There was only one thing on my mind. "I have a brother?" I asked painfully.

He nodded. "Yes, Abigail. You have a brother," he confirmed.

It was a sliver of sunlight on a stormy day. A light at the end of a dark tunnel. My wish, in its messed up way, had come true.

"I want to meet him," I announced, wiping my runny nose.

My father stood up. "It's not that easy. He doesn't know about you or even me for that matter. I handed him over right after he was born." His voice darkened. "He doesn't know about us."

I immediately thought of Elijah and how tragic it was for him to grow up without a mother and then without a father.

"Why, Elijah?" There had to be a connection. There had to be a pretty damn good reason for Elijah to come here behind The Order's back. I looked over to Elijah, who was leaning on the wall with his arms across his chest, watching us restlessly.

"When I went to The Order to ask for a tracker, Elijah came forward. He felt he owed it to me. Elijah's father and I were partners within The Order. We had promised each other if anything happened to either one of us, we would watch over the other's family. One night, we were ambushed by a group of immortals we had been following. Blane was killed." He looked over at Elijah. "I kept my promise. Elijah was only thirteen and still needed guidance. The Order let me look over his training."

A revelation hit me. "That's why you were always gone."

"Yes, I was with Elijah. I was relieved when he came forward. It gave me the opportunity to watch over both of you and not have to be so absent anymore. They agreed. It also allowed me to control the information that went back to The Order. Elijah only reported back what I told him to. It was bad enough they knew about your gift. I couldn't let them find out you were running with immortals," he said, disgusted.

"I love him," I whispered, barely audible.

"I know you care for him, Abigail. I tried to keep you two apart when you were younger because I knew what the other Hunters were, but it was a lost cause. You always managed to find your way back to him. I wanted to believe in your instincts, but I also knew he could be immortal, too, and just being around them puts your life in danger." He paused. "Is he, Abigail? Is he immortal?"

I was surprised he didn't know the answer to that and debated whether I should tell him after all the secrets he had kept from me. For committing my brother to a life of slavery, but in the end, I knew my father would do anything for me. He proved that by giving away his own child to keep me safe. "He's a hybrid," I said softly.

"That's what I was afraid of. The Order had its suspicions, but they haven't been able to confirm it. He's been hiding it well."

"Are you going to tell them?" Panic was rising. If they were willing to kill a mortal, I was terrified what lengths they would go to, to kill Wes.

"No, they don't take kindly to immortal evolution. There's no telling what they would do to him or those that know about him."

Chills ran down my spine.

"When the Hunters relocated here years ago, I developed a relationship with William. The Order assigned me to keep close tabs on them. They were afraid of what William would do after they took his wife. They didn't know about Wes at first. Not until I reported it."

My eyes widened with fury.

"Before you get upset with me, you have to understand, that was my job. I didn't know you two would become close or that it would endanger your life. It was a monumental mistake. I see that now, but I can't take it back. I can't change what I did, but I can control what happens."

Everything was splattered on a wall painted with tears, betrayal, and blood. Lives had been taken, and trust had been lost. Where did we go from here? The room was quiet, only the crackling of the fire making its presence known.

My father sighed deeply. "No one knows who The

Order is, and no one can ever know. It'll put everyone's lives in danger, including your mother's. Do you understand, Abigail? You can't tell the Hunters."

What he was asking me to do—what I knew I had to do—killed me. Lying to Wes seemed inconceivable, but fear was a strong motivator. I could never put my mother's life at risk. "I understand," I said, my voice trembling. I buried my face in my hands, trying to block out the last horrible hour of my life.

"I'm sorry, Abigail. I feel like I've failed you."

"You haven't failed me, but I'm not sure if I can ever completely forgive you."

"I understand. The Order isn't happy with me for hiding your gift. They are going back on our deal. They want you. No more negotiations."

It was a death sentence. My father's plan had backfired, and now he would be losing both his children to The Order, but what if… "I'll go," I announced bravely.

"What?" Elijah pushed off the wall, looking stupefied. My father put his hand up to silence him.

"Why?" he prodded.

"My brother is with them." It was good enough for me. I didn't know how, but I was going to take him back.

"Abby, he doesn't even know we exist, and he's not a little kid. He's thirteen now. All he's known is that life."

"So, what? You just want me to forget he exists? To give up on him? He's our family. He needs us." I was baffled that

Dad wasn't fighting harder for him. "You said it yourself. Your deal is broken. That's on both sides."

He thought long and hard, pacing. He knew I was right. "Infiltrating The Order is impossible, but if you were invited…"

"She would blend in as just another recruit," Elijah finished.

The wheels were spinning, and plots were being built.

"What have the Hunters told you about themselves? About immortals?" my father asked urgently.

"Why?" I was afraid to tell him too much about them. When it came to the Hunters, I didn't trust him or Elijah.

"We might need them, if things…" He stopped abruptly.

"I'm sorry if this is out of line, but are you seriously considering this?" Elijah addressed my father.

"What choice do I have? You know The Order. They will yank her from her bed if she doesn't turn herself in. It's inevitable, but we have an advantage here, Elijah. And if it means I could get my son back, I'm willing to trust in Abby's strength."

Elijah stepped closer to me. "Abby, what you're volunteering to do is dangerous. It won't be easy."

"He's right. The training is rigorous, and they have spies everywhere. They will be watching you very carefully."

"You said it yourself. I don't really have much of a choice. They are coming for me either way."

"You always have a choice. We could still leave." My father rubbed my arm.

"No, I want to do this. I want to help bring my brother home."

"I'm going, too," Elijah announced.

"What?" my dad inquired. "You would do that? You'll be sacrificing your freedom if you go back."

Elijah's selflessness knew no bounds.

"I know."

"All right. Then you go together." My dad held out his hand, and Elijah took it. "Thank you."

Elijah nodded his head humbly.

"I need to see Wes," I confessed.

My dad's shoulders slumped. "He's a monster, Abby. All of them are. They are murderers."

"They aren't all murderers." I defended the Hunters. "Wes would never hurt me. Neither would the others."

"You don't know what they are capable of. You haven't seen what I have seen. What Elijah has seen." He raised his voice. "They ripped his mother to pieces."

A pin could drop and echo off the walls with how silent the room became. My eyes darted to Elijah remorsefully.

"I'm sorry, Elijah. I didn't—" my dad apologized.

"Don't. It's fine. She needs to know the truth about them. She needs to see for herself."

I couldn't shake the image of his mother being pulled apart. It was nauseating.

"We don't have much time, Abigail. If you don't go, they will come and get you. It would be better if you went on your own. It would make them trust you more."

My dad was right. If I went kicking and screaming, they would never trust me, and I needed them to. That was the only way I was going to find my brother. It hurt like hell to leave Wes, but if it meant I could bring my brother home, it was worth it.

"Just give me until tomorrow night. I need to say goodbye to him. You owe me that much." Those words cut my dad deeply, but it was the truth. His debt to me would never be fully paid, but this was a start.

"Tomorrow night, but that's it," my dad agreed apprehensively.

Elijah kept quiet.

"We should get home. Your mom is going to worry."

"Okay."

"Thank you again, Elijah," my dad said proudly.

"You're welcome," he replied simply.

"I'll be in touch tomorrow night," my dad informed him as he ushered me toward the front door.

I peeked over my shoulder, stealing a last glance at Elijah. He smiled, but it was fraught with turmoil.

I stopped by the car door. "Can I ask you a question?"

"Anything."

"Does Mom know? I mean, she couldn't have given up her son easily."

His expression darkened. "She thinks he was stillborn. We had a funeral for him. It was just us. You were only four at the time, and we didn't want to expose you to that."

"Why don't I remember any of this? I think I would

remember Mom being pregnant. It was all I ever wanted."

He came over to my side of the car and took my shoulders in his hands. "You'll never forgive me if I tell you."

"You have to tell me everything, Dad. I'm going in there completely vulnerable. I need to know what I'm facing."

"There are other Specials. Some can move objects with their minds. Others move faster than a car. And then there are those who can wipe your memory."

I shook my head, unbelieving. "You had them take my memories? How could you do that?"

"I'm sorry."

"I know. I've heard that a lot tonight." I yanked my shoulders free and got into my Jeep.

He shrugged and got into his car. The pain that was brewing in me was so completely blinding I didn't know how to breathe. I gripped the steering wheel hard, willing the pain into it. To free me of it, but nothing was going to save me. Not from the betrayal. I looked over, and Elijah was watching me. He put up his hand and waved sympathetically. What my dad did was disgusting, and I wondered how much of it Elijah knew.

18

CLUTCHING THE SHEETS IN MY fingers, I waited until the quiet settled throughout the house. A ping on my window broke the silence. Peeling back my sheets, I raced to the window and saw Wes below. My heart ached. This would likely be the last time I saw him. I branded the image of him in my head, standing there, eyes glimmering and a mischievous grin.

I snatched up my grandpa's jacket and tiptoed down the stairs, my heart pounding nervously as I passed my parents' closed bedroom door. I was tempted to leave them a note, feeling guilty if they woke and discovered I wasn't home, but I didn't.

"Hey." I smiled nervously as I approached Wes. Trying to steady my heart was harder than I imagined. I didn't want him to suspect anything, but I was a horrible liar.

He looked at me strangely. "Hey, yourself." He stepped into me, grazing his nose and lips along the crook of my neck, inhaling deeply as he always did. I sucked in a breath, my neck tensing.

"I missed you," he whispered close to my ear, still nuzzling in my hair. "I was worried."

My fingers crawled up the back of his neck, entangling in his hair, gripping tight. Every time we touched, I was on the precipice of his world and mine, teetering on the border, ready to cross, but not knowing to which side.

"I missed you, too," I replied softly, stretching my neck, inviting him in. He kissed it lightly then pulled away, studying me closely.

"You were with *him*." Blackness was swirling in his eyes.

"It's not what you think. He commandeered me when I was on my way to see you." I paused. "That didn't come out right." I tried to take back what I said, but it was too late. Wes' hands tightened around my arms, the darkness consuming him.

"He what?" His lips peeled from his teeth as he hissed.

I grabbed his cheeks and forced him to look at me. To stay with me. "I'm fine. Look, I'm not harmed. It's not what you think. He just wanted to talk. He's not going to hurt me. I promise. He really is here to help me."

"I don't trust him, Abby. And I think it's a mistake you do."

I let go and tugged at the cuffs of my long sleeves, pulling them over my hands anxiously. "Can we go somewhere, please?" I was torn between a promise of silence and honor to tell him the truth. It was making me physically sick.

He leveled down, his eyes returning to their magnificent beauty. "Of course." He pulled me in close, comforting me and then leading me to his car at the bottom of the driveway.

"When do you need to be back?" he asked blankly as he started the convertible.

"Sunrise."

"You look upset," he observed.

I shifted my glance his way. "It's been a long day," was all I could say.

He placed his free hand on mine, my body instantly relaxing.

"I know just the place." He smiled.

I was grateful when he turned away from the lake. I didn't need to add to the list of bad things associated with it and saying goodbye was going to be monumentally bad. We drove up into the hills where large estates sprinkled the hillsides situated on large acres of land. They had the most magnificent view of the lake. My dad and I hiked up here once, but I hadn't been back since.

There was a well-traveled dirt road that led up one of the hills to the site of a fire where a house had been lost. Only the bottom half of the brick fireplace remained intact.

"Wow, what happened here?"

"It burned down just after we moved here. William helped save the family that lived in it."

Picturing Mr. Hunter doing something so human made all of this that much more difficult. Immortals were painted so ugly, not only by my father and Elijah, but also in every fairy tale I had ever read. Yet couldn't humans be just as ugly, if not worse? They murdered, cheated, lied, and bullied. Monsters burrowed within humans, too.

He took my hand in his as we walked carefully over the rubble. "The view here is the best in the valley." He smiled.

Had it not been for the fireplace it would have been hard to decipher there was a home here at all. It was a peculiar and eerie site that spooked me.

"What are you thinking about?" he inquired.

I hadn't realized I had stopped to admire the fireplace for so long. "The three little pigs," I said blankly.

He laughed. "As in 'I'll blow your house down'?"

I laughed with him because it was utterly ridiculous. "Yes. The brick house was the only one that stayed up when the wolf huffed and puffed. This brick fireplace is very symbolic, don't you think?"

"I see your point." He smiled for a moment, admiring the fireplace as I saw it.

He nudged me eagerly through the rubble to the back. It was overridden with waist-high weeds. Beyond the weeds, miles of stars compelled me. I had stepped into Van Gogh's *Starry Night*. It was breathtaking.

"This way." His eyes lit up as he led me to the cliff where a metal park bench overlooked the cliff's edge.

"How did this get here?" It was out of place to see

among the ruins. The white paint coating was chipping off the bench, showing the years of wear from the Idaho storms.

"I found it out front, but thought this was a more fitting place for it." He walked around and sat down, his eyes pleading for me to sit next to him.

Without hesitation, I snuggled into his body, his arm wrapping around my shoulders naturally. He leaned over and kissed my forehead. Everything Wes did made it impossible to see him as a monster. He was still the Wes from before the accident. *My Wes.* I could never see him any differently.

"It's like finding a needle in a haystack. I mean, I know there are a lot of beautiful views from up here in the valley, but this is a magnificent, unobstructed view of the whole city. And we're high enough that the city lights don't obscure the view of the stars," Wes shared.

I was just as amazed. "I can't believe something so magnificent exists."

Wes' thumb caressed my hand gently, his eyes peering over his lashes. "I can."

He was adoring me, and it made my stomach flip. His free hand slid down my cheek, his thumb following my lips from one end to the other, my heart skipping with each shallow breath I took. We pulled in closer, our legs overlapping and fingers tangled in each other's hair. His breathing became as erratic as mine as I nuzzled into his neck this time, kissing him softly, wanting so much to feel his lips on mine again. *Yearning. Needing.* He gripped the back of my neck, only making me want him more, knowing he was losing as much control as me. *So very human.*

We both pulled back, resting our foreheads together, catching our breath.

"I love you, Abby. With everything I was and with everything I have become. Nothing will ever change that."

It was killing me to keep secrets from him. I waited for so long to be here with Wes. To have him back in my life. The universe had brought us back together, only to unfairly rip us apart again, but I couldn't stay knowing I had a younger brother out in the world somewhere thinking he didn't have a family. Being raised to hate the very thing I loved.

Tears betrayed me as Wes caught some with a quick swipe of his fingers.

"Why are you upset?" His hands cupped my face gently. Concern flooded his eyes.

"Nothing. I'm sorry. It's just been a really long day," I lied.

He leaned over and kissed my wet cheeks. "I'll never leave you again. I promise."

All I could do was nod because he wouldn't be the one leaving. I rested my head on his shoulder, and watched the twinkling sky. Every once in a while a shooting star would fly across the sky, its tail blazing fiercely and then fading.

"Did you know that shooting stars are actually meteors?"

"I did." I smiled. "Knowing the truth kind of takes the magic out of it, though. When I was little, I wished on as many stars as I could."

"What were your wishes?"

"There was only one." My voiced cracked remembering how I would clasp my little hands together tightly, squeeze my eyes shut, and picture my wish coming true.

He looked down at me. "Really? All those stars and you only wished for one thing?"

I nodded, trying hard not to cry. I pressed my head a little closer to his chest, noticing for the first time that Wes' chest didn't beat with life, just a steady rising and falling as his lungs took in air.

"I don't have one," he answered before I asked. "It was weird at first. It's nice feeling a pulse again." He rubbed his thumb over the pulse on my wrist.

"So, before the final change, you were human?"

"Yes. Immortal, too, but still human." He hugged me tighter, lifting my legs over his knees.

It was hard not to think about tomorrow. To think about not being in his arms again, but I was here now and I savored every touch of his body, every word he uttered, and every memory we created.

"What was your wish?" he asked.

Hesitantly, I softly revealed my wish. "For a brother or sister." It hurt saying it aloud. "I begged my parents every day until I was twelve. I stopped asking after my grandpa died."

"I know it's not the same thing, but you have Ben and Zoe now, and they are the best siblings anyone could ask for."

Why did this have to be so hard? Words stuck in my chest. There was nothing I could say to change the future. I was exhausted, so I laid my head on Wes' chest and closed my eyes.

"Abby," Wes whispered.

I blinked, my eyes heavy with sleep.

"Abby, it's almost sunrise."

I peeled my eyes open urgently. The sky was glowing dimly like embers in a dying fire, and the morning dew had layered on my face and clothes.

"I need to get you home." He tried to stand, but I pulled him back down. "Aren't you worried your parents will discover you're missing?"

"I don't care." This might be the last time I saw him, so no, I didn't care if my parents knew I had been out all night. My dad might be mad, but he would understand. He would have to.

Pinks and oranges filled the sky. The colors mixed with a thin layer of cumulus clouds left over from the last storm, creating a rainbow of clouds that took on an iridescence.

"It's stunning, Wes. The clouds look like your eyes." I looked between the two, comparing. The similarity was uncanny. "I've never seen anything like it." I was wonderstruck.

"You know it's very rare to witness an event such as that. Small water droplets or ice crystals in the clouds scatter the light from the sun, causing an effect similar to that of oil in water puddles. But the droplets or ice crystals have to be of similar size, and the cloud has to be paper thin to cause the iridescent glow."

"Wow. Maybe it's good luck." I wanted it to be a sign that everything was going to be okay. That things would work out the way they should. That Wes and I would be able to be together one day, the forbidden curse broken. I nuzzled my head into the crook of his neck and watched the swirling of the iridescent clouds. "What color were your mom's eyes?" He never talked about his mom.

"Green." He smiled. "And even in photographs they were piercing."

I wondered if Wes knew the truth surrounding his mother's death. "How did she die?" I asked carefully.

"She didn't survive childbirth," he said plainly, but he was lying. He knew how she died, and I could only imagine the hatred he had for The Order and anyone associated with it. It made me fear for my father's life.

"How did your dad live so long without a True Mate? I mean, I thought immortals were…"

"Unruly?" he asked before I could find the right word. "He found ways to control himself. He isolated himself from the world for almost a whole lifetime. When he found my mom, he said it was like finding peace in the middle of a war. He doesn't talk about her much. I think it's too painful, but he loved her more than anything."

"I'm sorry," I said, picturing The Order sweeping in and killing his mom in cold blood. Did they do it in front of William or at least spare him that horror?

"I believe you're my True Mate, Abby."

"Wes—" I needed to tell him. This wasn't fair.

"You don't have to say anything. I just wanted you to know. Your stake in this relationship is much higher than mine."

Was it really, though? William has had to endure a life without his True Mate all because he fell in love with a mortal, possibly watching her murdered. Who was investing more risk was unclear.

"I should take you home now." I didn't stop him this time.

"Thank you, Wes."

"For what?" he asked curiously.

"For this." I pointed to our view. "And for sharing everything you did."

"Like I told your mom, I'm an open book, Abby. I have nothing to hide." He turned and started toward the car.

He was an immortal and had nothing to hide, and I was mortal and had everything to conceal. The serenity of the night dripped off of me as I walked to the car, all of it stripped by the time we reached my house.

19

I FIGURED SNEAKING BACK into my room at this point would be pointless, so instead, I sat on the back porch and reviewed the last twenty-four hours of my life. Shortly after, I heard someone in the kitchen. Today was quite possibly the last time I would see my mom for a while, and it hurt to think about.

The sliding door creaked open, and the smell of fresh coffee wafted around me.

"How long have you been up?" my mom's cheery voice asked.

"I couldn't sleep much. I watched the sunrise." I played with my fingers, hating that today would be all about lying.

"I haven't done that in a very long time. We should do it together next weekend." She sat in her rocker next to me.

Looking over, I admired her dainty fingers looping around her mug. "I'd like that."

We both stared out over the valley of hills behind our house. It faced the sunrise, and since we were the highest house on our street, we had a view of the untouched land that made its way to the lake. Unfortunately, we were too far back to see the rippling waters of Lake Pend Oreille.

"I really liked Wes. He seems to care about you quite a bit. It's nice that after all this time and after the accident, you two reconnected the way you did. It must be fate." She took a sip of her steaming cup of coffee and smiled at me with a twinkle in her eye.

"Yeah. He's been a good friend." My heart pounded slowly to match my somber mood.

"Your dad went running this morning. He didn't sleep very well last night either. I think the stress is really getting to him. I worry. He's not as young as he used to be." She shared with me.

She was being so open. It wasn't like her. Now that I was getting older, she was confiding in me as more of a friend than a daughter. "I worry about him, too, but he's strong. He always has been. And he loves you."

"He's been a good husband," she agreed. "I wish that for you one day. A good husband and a family. Graduation first," she joked.

A soft giggle escaped me, lightening my mood for just a fleeting second, but then my next words would haunt me. "That sounds good." It all seemed out of the realm of possibility now.

The slider opened again, and my dad joined us. "What are my two favorite girls up to?" His mood seemed lighter today, the confession to me probably attributing to it.

"Your little girl watched the sunrise this morning. I was just telling her how we should all watch it together next weekend. The weather is supposed to be nice."

My dad looked over at me with a knowing glance. "That sounds nice. I'm going to hop in the shower." He leaned down and kissed my mom and then came to me and kissed my forehead—an unsolicited show of affection neither one of us was used to. I was still upset with him, but I couldn't show it in front of my mom. It would just instigate more questions. "I want to take my girls to breakfast, so get ready." He smiled widely and went back into the house.

"He's in a good mood today." My mom giggled.

I kept quiet. My dad knew today was possibly our last day together as a family, so maybe today I would just try to enjoy the day with them.

"I'm going to take a quick shower, too."

"Okay, sweetie."

As I passed by her chair, I placed my hand on her shoulder and squeezed lightly. "I love you, Mom."

She put her hand over mine. "I love you, too."

Today was about internal strength. Staying strong for my mom and giving her this last good memory of us as a simple family spending a Sunday together. That was all today needed to be about.

My dad chose to avoid the bistro, which confused my mom since it used to be our traditional spot, but I helped him sideline the conversation.

"I heard Eggs and Place was really good, Mom. It can be our new spot." I smiled from the back seat of their car, my dad's eyes meeting mine with approval. The last thing he wanted was to be around the Hunters. I looked away, staring at the trees outside blurring as we drove by. The day was clear, and the temperature was in the high sixties. Perfect for a Sunday out with the family. Perfect if heartbreak wasn't looming.

Eggs and Place was only a few doors down from the bistro, and it overlooked the lake. We sat out on the patio in full view of all the shops at the pier. I could see the bistro bustling down the way. Penelope was serving tables, her hair a bright pink now. It caught me off guard when her head lifted from the guest she was talking to and made direct eye contact with me as if she knew I was watching her. Something wasn't right with her. I felt it from day one, but I ignored it. Maybe ignoring her wasn't the smartest thing.

"Honey, will you order me an orange juice? I'm going to use the ladies' room." My mom scooted out of her chair.

"Of course," my dad answered, carefree.

When she was out of earshot, I leaned over the table and

whispered, "There's someone who works at the bistro that isn't sitting right with me."

"Who?" His full attention was on me.

"That girl with the pink painted hair that works there, Penelope. I've always had a weird vibe about her, and just now she was on the patio and looked straight at me like she knew we were here."

My dad was seated facing the water, so he could look sideways inconspicuously. "Pink hair?"

"Yeah."

We both straightened up when my mom came back to the table.

"What are you two whispering about?" she asked, genuinely interested.

"Whether I should dye my hair pink," I replied playfully.

"You better not. Honey, please tell her not to ruin her beautiful head of hair."

He laughed. "Peanut, don't punk out on us."

It was nice to share a laugh with my parents. The rest of breakfast was filled with light conversation and funny stories. We walked down the pier after breakfast and got ice cream and then sat on the beach for a bit.

I dug my toes into the warm, dry sand just beyond the water's reach, laughing as my parents acted like teenagers again—my dad chasing my mom into the water, lifting her up and spinning her around. That was what true love looked like. *Easy. Fun.* I was surprised how comfortable I was being here on the beach. Leaving my mom overshadowed the sense of dread this place once gave me.

"Hey." The sun shone brightly in my eyes, obstructing the view of my best friend. She stepped in front of it, bathing me in shadows and holding her sandals in her hand.

"Hey." I smiled. This was a nice treat. I wasn't looking forward to disappearing without seeing Kendra. "What brings you down here?"

"I guess my parents had the same idea. We just finished lunch at the bistro."

Was it lunch already? The time was flying by.

"Your parents seem happy." She laughed as she watched them frolicking in the water.

"They do, don't they?" I wanted this life for them. For us. *For me.* And before monsters became real, it could have been possible. Now it was just a fantasy.

"How are you feeling?" She sat next to me.

"Better. And you?"

"So much better. Although I never heard from Elijah. You were right about him. Just another jerk."

I put my arm around her shoulders. "Good thing there's a ton of fish in the sea."

She placed her head on my shoulder. "Good thing. How are you and Wes?"

"Figuring things out." I was trying to keep my bag of lies as small as possible.

"Yeah, that relationship seems complicated. Take it slow, and I'm sure it'll be great."

Kendra was ever the optimist. She was my sun in the perpetual darkness. "I believe that for you, too, Ken. Once they get past the blinding beauty," I teased.

"Stop. You're beautiful, too. We are a couple of beautiful babes inside and out." She looked back to the water. "Your parents are seriously adorable."

"They really are." Seeing them this way made my decision a little easier, knowing that they had each other and wouldn't be alone when I left, because either way I needed to go. My brother needed me.

Looking over Kendra's shoulder, I caught sight of a familiar face. "Is your brother home?"

She looked back at him, too, as he approached with his shoes in his hands. "Oh, yeah. He told my parents it was fall break, but I have a feeling he just missed someone." She winked at me. "Studying abroad the past year must have been torture on his pour little heart."

I turned back to the ocean, biting my lip. "It's not like that, Kendra. It never was."

"That's not what he thinks," she sang quietly as he fell upon us.

"Mom and Dad are ready to go."

I shielded my eyes from the sun as I faced Jack. "Hey, Jack," I said politely. I really didn't need this right now.

"Hey, Abs. You look good." His honesty was refreshing and a little bit embarrassing in front of his little sister.

"Thanks." The awkward silence hung in the air.

Thankfully, Kendra stood up. "Eww. That's our cue to

go." She laughed as she brushed off the sand from her capris, grabbing Jack's arm. "I'll call you tonight." She waved.

"See you later, Abby." Jack dipped his head, smiling admiringly.

"Bye." I waved.

Jack hung out with Kendra and me a lot when I was over, so naturally we became friends, too. He was only three years older and was always a lot of fun to be around. It was last year before he left for college that he decided to declare his affection for me. I wasn't sure how I felt about it. I had never really gotten over Wes, and I had never seen Jack in that way. Before he drove away to college, he kissed me on the cheek. It was uncomfortable to say the least. Especially because his whole family was watching. He called me a few times while he was gone, but I never called him back. I felt bad, but in my eyes I was doing him a favor. And now I knew I had helped him dodge a huge bullet. My life was a train wreck.

Of course, before I looked away at my two friends leaving, Penelope was watching me again. I was officially creeped out.

We grabbed hot dogs on the pier before we headed back home. I knew time was running out, and I wanted to talk to Wes about Penelope. My parents were in the kitchen when I raced down the stairs, grabbed my car keys off the key ring, and tried to slide out unnoticed.

"Abigail." My father leaned on the threshold to the

kitchen with his arms crossed. "Where do you think you are going?"

"I have to say goodbye, Dad. I might not see them again."

He stepped into the foyer, lowering his voice. "Fine." He wrapped his arms around me and hugged me tightly, caressing my hair. "I'm so sorry, Abigail. It's my job to protect you from heartbreak. I am so very sorry."

"I know," I responded and then turned and left, my breath trapped in my throat as I made my last drive to Wes' house.

It wasn't fair to leave without telling him the whole truth. He deserved to know. He had to know. As I turned the corner up Wes' street, Penelope was standing in the middle of the road. I slammed on the brakes, my heart racing and panic taking over. What was she doing? I could run her over with my car, but there was no way I could kill someone. I pulled over and got out of my car. "What are you doing, Penelope?" I snapped.

As casual as could be, she sidled up to me, smiling. "You know why I'm here, Abigail." She looked up at the Hunter's house. "We couldn't very well have you spilling all of our secrets to them."

"The Order?" I had my suspicions that might be what it was.

"Who else? Don't tell me you thought I was one of them." She looked to the Hunter's house, disgusted.

I put on my best poker face. "I was just coming to say goodbye to them. I'm leaving town with my dad on a trip."

"That's very sweet and all, but the fact that you are knowingly in love with an immortal makes me sick. But you'll understand soon enough. You'll hate them as much as the rest of us."

"You don't know them," I hissed vehemently.

"All I need to know is they are immortals. That's enough for me."

Hatred poured from Penelope. She wasn't much older than me, so to know that kind of anger made me feel sorry for her.

"So, now what? Are you going to hurt me? Drag me to The Order? You're a little late for that because I was already on my way." She stepped closer. "Have you ever heard of personal space?" I snapped.

"Maybe I'm not bringing you to The Order."

Shock shook my body. I looked from her to Wes' house and back, unbelieving what I was hearing. Was she kidnapping me? Trying to kill me? Did she know about my gift? I searched the ground for something to use as a weapon. I thought about screaming. Wes would probably hear me. I even thought about running, but to where?

Penelope watched as my thoughts spun out of control, ready to launch if I made a move in the wrong direction. Her fingers opened and closed into fists, and her knees were bent and ready to chase me. My heart shredded as I looked back up to Wes' house, considering my chances of making it there before her.

"Back off, Penelope." Elijah stepped from the tree line.

Penelope glared violently and then took off quickly.

"Are you okay?" Elijah rushed to my side.

"Yeah. What was that all about?" My hands were still shaking.

"I don't know, but Penelope is bad news. Trust me on that."

"Why did you come here?" Looking at Elijah after last night was hard. Different. He had been hiding so many secrets, but he was also carrying a tragic burden. Ultimately, he was a part of the reason I was leaving, and it made me want to hate him just the same.

"We couldn't risk you telling them about us."

"But my dad knew I was coming. He gave me permission," I pleaded softly.

"He was afraid you would lose it in front of your mother if he said no, so he sent me. I made your dad a promise to watch over you, and I owe him for taking care of me after my dad was killed." He held his hand out for mine.

"So, this is for my dad?" I challenged him, but his reaction told me it was something more. He cared for me. I'm not sure how deeply or in what capacity, but he cared whether I lived or died, and nothing I would say to him now would convince him to let me go. I took his hand apprehensively.

A branch snapped, echoing down the street.

"Let's go." He directed me to the passenger's seat and then practically dove into the driver's seat. I wanted to say something, but he was on high alert, scanning our surroundings. He floored the gas, and we went flying forward, tires screeching as we hugged a corner. We hit the highway in half the time, never losing speed.

"What's going on?" I held onto the side of my seat, petrified by the speed in which we were traveling.

"Penelope went rogue from The Order. How do you know her?"

"She works at the bistro."

"So she's been watching you." He shook his head. "I'm glad I got there when I did."

"Why would she want me?" The thought that I was possibly moments from death made me tremble again.

"I honestly have no idea, but I'm going to find out."

My town whirred by as we headed for the interstate. "I didn't get to say goodbye." I wiped away my tears.

"I'm sorry, Abby. I really am. And what your father did…giving away your brother…you have to know that it couldn't have been easy on him."

I didn't respond. I couldn't. It was too much to think about.

"I'm here for you, in whatever capacity you need. I'm your friend, and I won't let anything happen to you. I promise." His hand fell on my thigh, and I let it stay because comfort in any form was the only thing that was going to get me through this.

20

"WHERE ARE YOU TAKING ME?" The silence had been unbearable, but my mind was muddled and I needed sleep. We had been driving for several hours, and it was dark outside. I wondered what excuse my dad gave my mom about my sudden disappearance.

"Somewhere your dad felt you would be the safest." Elijah's voice was troubled.

"This is nuts. You know that, right?" I stared at him incredulously.

"I haven't experienced anything that slightly resembles ordinary in a very long time, Abby. This is just another day in a world of chaos."

It made me think about his mother's kidnapping. I tried to remember what I was doing when I was six. Probably playing with dolls and dressing up with my friends without a worry in the world that monsters lived under my bed. *Or just outside my window.* How does a child even process something like that? Having his mother ripped from his arms was bad enough and then to discover it was by an immortal.

"I feel like we could have been friends if things were different." I meant it, too. He was honest and compassionate. He didn't hide behind walls and haunting memories.

"If things were different, the odds are we would have never met."

Shadows moved across his face as headlights from oncoming traffic passed by, highlighting dark circles under his eyes that seemed to have appeared overnight. Working for The Order didn't seem easy by any stretch of the imagination, especially this assignment in particular. *Me.*

"Can I ask you something?" His eyes veered from the road ahead for a moment to take in my response.

"Sure," I replied. My anger had subsided, and exhaustion was fast setting in. My body relaxed against the leather seat, and my eyes closed.

"What was it like with your father?"

I rolled my head in his direction remorsefully. "I'm sorry about your father, Elijah. Being alone at the age of thirteen must have been hard."

His shoulders tensed and his fingers tightened around the steering wheel, a sign of how uncomfortable this was for him. "It was, but James did a lot for me. Had he not stepped in, I would just be a nameless face working for The Order."

An image of my brother popped in my head. A nameless follower. That was what he was. My bloodshot eyes focused on the road ahead again, the glow of the headlights breaking through the blackness of the night as if it were nothing. My grandpa used to tell me that no matter how dark it was, all you had to do was shine a light and it would overpower the darkness. Of course, I was nine and he was talking about putting a nightlight in my bedroom, but the more I thought about it, it applied to many things. Like now, for instance.

"It was quiet," I said, suddenly fidgeting with my fingers, remembering how empty the house felt when my dad was gone. "Growing up with my dad. He was gone a lot. I used to resent him for it, but I understand now."

Elijah's shoulders rose as he inhaled deeply. "Abby, he was a good man. He *is* a good man. He talked about you all the time…" His voice trailed off.

"What?" I pressed him. He almost seemed embarrassed.

"Nothing." He blew it off.

Elijah was tough. Almost unbreakable. *Almost.* It was funny how amongst all the millions of questions I had regarding The Order, missions, and my dad, the ones I wanted to ask the most were about Elijah himself.

We passed a highway sign. "Are we going to Seattle?"

"Yes."

My dad had spent a lot of time in Seattle recently. He knew this was coming. We were going to my grandpa's house. All of the good memories were going to be tarnished.

It was disheartening. *Nothing was safe anymore.* It made me wonder how many happy memories I would have left. Looking over at Elijah again, I knew it wouldn't be long. He was haunted by his violent past, and that overshadowed every good memory he had made with his mom and dad. Maybe darkness could be stronger than light if enough time passed without redemption.

Once we exited the freeway and took a few turns, I wasn't surprised when we pulled up to my grandpa's house. The porch light was on, but the rest of the house was dark.

"I should have known." I shook my head, feeling utterly stupid for believing that they were selling it. My mom probably had no idea either.

Elijah opened the garage and pulled in, closing it behind us.

"My parents told me we were selling it. Is my dad here?"

"Not yet. He has to take care of things with your mom. He'll be here tomorrow."

It was after midnight, and all I really wanted to do was sleep, but my adrenaline was still running on full. Stepping out of the car was like stepping into my past, becoming my grandpa's little girl again, carefree and invincible.

My pink ballet flats hit the garage floor and I raced into the house, my long pigtails flying behind me, excited to see my papa.

"Where's my little Abigail?" My papa's voice bellowed from the kitchen.

When I got around the corner, he was on bended knee with his arms outstretched. I jumped into them, knocking him to the floor, laughter surrounding us.

"You're getting so big, Abby." He chuckled. "How old are you now?"

He knew, but he asked every time I visited. "Nine, Papa." I rolled my eyes playfully.

"If you don't slow down, soon you'll be bigger than me."

"Abby, are you okay?" Elijah was waiting at the garage entrance to the house.

I still had one foot in the car and one foot on the floor, my pink flats replaced by worn-out red Chucks. "Yeah." I brushed off the memory.

"Your dad brought you some clothes and I believe a new pair of shoes." He pointed to my exposed toe.

"Great. He thought of everything." I stepped out of the car, passing Elijah as he held the door open. The house managed to trap my grandpa's signature scent. It was both comforting and overwhelming all at the same time. I slid my hand across the counter, closing my eyes and taking a moment to remember the kindness in every crease of his face. His eyes always lit up for me.

"You were close to him," Elijah said as he came up behind me.

"In some ways I was closer to him than my dad." I spun around and took in the kitchen and the family room that were separated by a half wall. Everything looked exactly the same. My dad didn't change or move anything.

"How so?" He stood uncomfortably in the threshold from the hallway.

"My grandpa was always present when I was here. Nothing else mattered. The phone would ring, and he would ignore it. And he always had things planned for us." I smiled. "He even indulged in a pedicure with me once." I stifled the memory. "I can't speak to his character as a father or a member of The Order, but I can, without a doubt, tell you he was the perfect grandpa." Elijah's hand fell on my shoulder, but instead of accepting it, I stepped away. "Make yourself comfortable. He would have wanted that." I retreated quickly out of the kitchen to the back of the house where my room was. Lights illuminated my childhood sanctuary. Looking around, the memories flooded me, so sweet yet so bitter now. I missed my grandpa so much, and this room, the way it was designed was so important to him. He wanted to make sure I felt comfortable here and that my space was my own.

Whatever you want, Abigail. If you want butterflies on the wall and pink ruffles, I'll buy it. This is your *room.*

He brought me to several cute boutiques in town, but I had bypassed all of them for an antique store. Everything in this room had a mysterious history. Even the comforter was a vintage French provincial pattern from the fifties. A light green metal pedal table served as a nightstand, and atop sat a vintage pink phone with a tall stand and circular dial. I asked for the windows to stay bare because I wanted to see into the backyard, so we picked sheer curtains instead of blinds. Looking at the walls always made me giggle even to this day. My grandpa thought it would be fun to grab a palette of colors and just paint whatever. In the end, we wore more paint than the walls, but it became a perfectly imperfect abstract painting by us.

I walked over to where we signed our names in the corner.

Every artist must sign their work.

I brushed my fingers over his name. *Papa Rose.*

"Your things are on the chair."

Startled, I spun around to face Elijah. He was lurking in the doorway. "I meant it when I said to make yourself comfortable. The guest room—"

"Is across the hall. I know."

He hadn't stopped studying me since we got here. As if I might break. *Fragile.* Maybe I would break, but not now. Not like this. "Goodnight, Elijah," I said evenly and without indignation.

"Goodnight, Abigail."

I followed him to the doorway and closed the door. Inside the bag of belongings my dad had left were a pair of black army-style boots. A far cry from my red Chucks. I admit it was time to retire them, but it felt like accepting defeat. Like I had to give up my past in order to survive my future. These shoes had beautiful and tragic stories hidden deep within their soles. I could never truly let them go, just like I could never truly forget Wes Hunter.

I pulled them off and tucked them underneath my bed, out of sight but never out of mind. There were several changes of clothes in the duffel. It was obvious I wouldn't be going home again any time soon, so all I had from there were the red Chucks and the infinity charm and my grandpa's key that were still tucked safe and secure in my pocket. I pulled them out and studied them carefully.

Life is infinite. My grandpa's voice filled my head. I remembered the day he set me on his lap to watch a meteor show. He pointed to all the stars and told me how life was as infinite as the universe. It never ended because energy couldn't be destroyed and we were all composed of energy. It was a nice thought, and it especially comforted me after he died, believing he was still somewhere in the universe. Now, though, I wasn't sure what he really meant by that. Was he just talking about immortals? I wished I could ask him. Things would be so much easier.

I pulled out one of the red Chucks and tucked the charm and key into the toe and scooted it back underneath the bed. Tomorrow I would have to find what that key opened. Not tonight, though. I was too tired.

It was still dark when I awoke. The antique clock hanging on my wall read just past five in the morning. At least I slept for a few hours. The guest room door was closed, so I tiptoed into the kitchen to make tea. The cabinets had been freshly stocked with all of my favorites, including an assortment of chai. I had to search the cabinets to find the teapot. In the process, I located the pots, mixing bowls, silverware, and mugs. The only thing I ever cared to find when I was younger was hidden in the refrigerator dairy drawer. When I swung the fridge door open, I was pleasantly surprised to see the drawer stocked with dark chocolate bars. It was my favorite treat, and my grandpa always made sure to have them when I visited. I took one out, coveting it.

"Chocolate for breakfast. I like it."

The bar flew out of my hand and crashed to the floor, breaking into several pieces. "Elijah. Seriously. I'm getting you a cowbell."

He bent down and picked up the bar, studying it. "Aw, the great debate. Dark or milk chocolate."

Snatching it out of his hands, I scoffed. "There's no debate. Dark." I flung it into the trash. "Why are you up so early?"

"I never went to sleep."

"How noble. Afraid I'd sneak off?" Making myself busy, I set up my cup of tea.

"I hope we're passed that." He stood in the doorway.

"Okay, look, Elijah. You have to relax. You're making me even more nervous than I already am. Sit or something. Just don't hover in any more doorways." I took out another mug. "Tea?"

"Sure." He chuckled as he sat down at the table. "Better?"

"I am going to ignore that you are completely patronizing me and just say yes. Better."

I joined Elijah at the table with the tea a few minutes later.

"So, when do you get to sleep? Because you look like hell."

"When your father gets here." He rubbed his eyes.

The silence was nice as we sat through the sunrise, drinking our tea. I wasn't sure how much else we had to share. I could be bitter that he stole half of my dad's time, but then that would be selfish. If anything, I felt the exact opposite. I was glad he had somebody. "What's it like working for The Order?"

"Exhausting," he bellowed.

"I can see that." I snickered. "What else?"

"Lonely."

He never held back. "Don't you have a partner?"

He shook his head. "No. I wanted to work alone. That was my only stipulation. I don't know what I would do if I were responsible for someone else and they died. I don't know how your dad did it."

He had a valid point. A partner was not only a physical liability, but also an emotional one. "But you said you were going to watch over me?" I was bordering on vulnerable territory.

"Yes, I did. And I meant it," he said proudly.

"Because you owe my dad?" By pressing him, I was hoping to reveal more than he was leading on.

"Yes." He hesitated.

It was just a spilt second, but that was long enough.

He pushed back from the table. "I think I will go lie down. Don't run away. Your dad might kill me if you do."

He disappeared into the hall. "I wouldn't think of it," I said under my breath.

Elijah had started a fire in the fireplace, so I sauntered over to the couch, pulling my grandpa's old throw blanket over me, and watched the embers pop and crackle. The heat it emitted warmed my cheeks as I rested my eyes once again.

"WHERE IS SHE?"

Was I dreaming? My mom's voice filled my head. It was so much harder to open my eyes this time.

"On the couch," Elijah answered.

My head was pounding. "Mom?" My voice croaked.

"Abigail." A soft, cool hand wrapped in mine while another brushed hair from my cheeks sticky from the heat. "Sweetie, are you feeling okay?" Her voice was alert and concerned.

I was really having a hard time snapping out of my daze. I felt drunk. With heavy arms, I pulled myself up and rubbed my face hard. It wasn't helping much. What I needed was a shower. "I'm fine. Confused, but good."

My dad stood to the side of the couch, and I imagined Elijah was behind me somewhere.

"James, she looks sick. Is she sick?"

"Lucinda, calm down. She said she's fine."

For my mom's sake, I squeezed her hand and smiled.

"Mom, I just need a shower. Then we can talk."

I stood up, but it took every last bit of strength to not fall over. "See, I'm up. Just give me a few minutes." As gracefully as I could, I made my way to the bathroom, locking it behind me. The shower helped me emerge from the thick haze.

All eyes were on me when I came back. Fresh-faced and awake, I sat on the couch next to my mother. I wasn't sure what she was told, so I kept quiet. My dad was sitting in a chair reading the morning paper as if everything was normal. Elijah stood next to the front window, staring out. I had entered the Twilight Zone once again.

"Your father told me about Wes," my mom started.

I glanced at my dad who lowered the newspaper and winked. A wink. What did that mean? What did he tell her? I was panicking.

"Oh, he did?"

She rubbed my knee. "First love is hard to get over, honey. Trust me. We have all been there, but running away isn't the answer."

"Run—right. Yeah, I know. I just needed to get away from Sandpoint for a few days." My dad was spinning an interesting tale. One that put Wes on the chopping block, of course. "He's a good guy, Mom, really. We just need some space."

"I'm just glad you're staying so levelheaded. When your father told me you ran away to Grandpa's house, I was a bit surprised. We haven't been here in years. And look at it. It's just the same."

Secrets. Lies. Betrayal. But it was for the better good. Or was it?

"Yeah, I was surprised, too."

"Well, if you're feeling better, we should get you home." She patted my leg and stood up.

My dad put down the newspaper. "Actually, I thought it would be fun for us to stay here for a few days. I've lost so much time with my little girl over the years, and the timing couldn't be better."

"What about school?" She seemed skeptical. "And I have that knitter's retreat this week."

I watched the exchange between them.

"Oh, that's right. I guess it'll be just the two of us then." He smiled over to me.

"Not to be rude, but what is the boy who sold us the Jeep doing here?" my mother asked.

My dad and I exchanged blank looks.

"Oh, uh, Elijah and I started hanging out, and I asked him to come with me. I was scared driving here by myself." I kept my body still. *Please believe me. Please.*

"I'm not sure if I should be grateful you weren't alone or upset you were alone with an older boy in Grandpa's house." She looked to my dad.

"I will talk to her about it." He tilted his head at me sternly.

I needed out of this suffocating web. "I'm going to get

some fresh air." I couldn't get out back fast enough. Elijah followed behind. "You don't have to watch me like a circling hawk."

"I needed an excuse to vacate that train wreck in there. I can't imagine how hard it is on him to have to lie to her."

"Try being on the receiving end."

The backyard was still thriving. The lot was small, being just outside of the main drag, but my grandpa had done so much with it. In the back corner, he had built a playhouse just for me, equipped with a swing and slide. He painted it bright aqua with pink doors. It looked more like a dollhouse than a typical wooden structure. I spent so many hours playing make-believe in there. And then there were the fairy village and pond in the other corner. The rest of the yard was grass and trees and colorful flowers.

And he made it all for me.

"This place. It hurts my heart." I hugged my arms around my body.

Elijah put his arm around me and pulled me into his side. "Life isn't easy, Abby. Whether you're mortal or immortal, death follows you everywhere."

We sat on the white porch swing, rocking quietly, waiting for the calm to end and the storm to begin.

21

"Bye, Mom. Have fun." I hugged her tightly. There was no telling when I would see her again.

"I will. I love getting together with the girls."

I laughed. "Oh, Mom. You're an elderly woman trapped in a thirty-five-year-old body."

She laughed, too. "I love you, sweetie. I'll see you next weekend. Have fun with your father."

She kissed my cheek, and then Dad walked her to the car. I watched from the doorway as he helped her in the passenger seat, still in love. I waved from the porch as my mom drove away, a piece of me going with her. My dad walked back over and put his arm around my shoulders.

"Now what?" My body was stiff, not completely forgiving him for all the lies.

"We go to The Order."

My mom honked at the corner as she turned and disappeared. She was oblivious to the monsters in the dark and the liars right in front of her.

"Isn't it hard to lie to her?" I waved back.

"You have no idea," he mumbled, ducking his head shamefully and going back inside.

Elijah was staring out the front window again, and my dad sat on the couch, staring mindlessly into the fire. If his remorse wasn't so evident, I would probably hate him, but this was hurting him just as much as me.

I joined him, putting my head on his shoulder. "I need to know everything, Dad. I can't go into this blind."

"It's hard to believe how much you've grown up. If I didn't know better, I would think you were much older than your seventeen years."

"I suddenly had to grow up fast," I replied somberly.

"Yeah. I guess so." He sighed deeply. "The Order isn't all bad, Abigail, or else I wouldn't let you go. The Order has kept humans safe for a very long time. I'm sorry for assuming that all immortals are dangerous. It's just hard to believe otherwise after what I've seen."

"You're referring to the Hunters?" I asked with a weak, victorious smile. I couldn't imagine what my dad had been through.

"Yes. I can see that Wes means a lot to you."

The fire crackled loudly, drawing our attention. We used to spend a lot of time right here. Mainly myself on the floor, playing or reading because my grandpa didn't own a television. He didn't believe in technology that stripped society of quality time with their families. It never really bothered me not having one. It was why my dad never gave me a cell phone. Not until recently, at least, and I hadn't even used it. I had forgotten all about, leaving it on my desk at home.

"Do you have a gift, Dad?" He smiled widely, a sparkle in his eye. "What?" My eyebrow raised curiously.

"How do you think I was able to keep so many secrets from you?"

It had never dawned on me. I just thought he was a really good liar. And apparently he was. Supernaturally.

"No one can detect when I'm being dishonest. It has become invaluable in keeping your gift hidden. Until my father, that is."

The bitterness was fading a bit, replaced by guilt.

"These seem like odd gifts, don't you think? I mean, when I think of gifts, I think of flying or transporting. Something a little more spectacular."

He squeezed me close. "It's the subtle things that go unnoticed and prove to be the most effective. Your intuition will save your life, Abigail. You just have to learn how to trust it."

"Can you teach me?"

"I'm certainly going to try." His voice was comforting and calm. "There are twelve of us that run The Order. The rest work for us, going on missions and upholding our decisions."

"Has anyone ever left The Order?"

"No one leaves The Order, Abigail. There are too many secrets. We have kept human gifts a secret for over two hundred years. That's why your grandfather bought this place. To hide away. He just wanted peace in his last years. They consider it a retirement, but you still have to check in, and they still keep tabs on you to make sure you keep the oath."

"So, it's a lifetime commitment, and those born of Order members don't have a choice? That's pretty rigid."

"It's no different than royalty blood, Abigail, and The Order is much more important than royalty. We have to protect The Order. No matter what the cost."

I stood up, uneasy now. A few weeks ago, I was worrying about my homework and avoiding dances. Now, I was talking about the fate of my future, fighting rogue immortals in a secret society. Pacing and chewing on my fingers obsessively, I tried to picture the world at war. Humans against immortals.

"The Order wants to maintain peace, and to do that, they have to maintain control of the immortals. It's the only thing that will keep the world from imploding with violence."

"If you truly believe in The Order, then why wouldn't you gladly groom me for my rightful place within it?"

"Because it's dangerous. I told you that. The immortals have been trying for years to disband The Order so they can live as they please. You're my baby, Peanut. I didn't want to throw you in the crosshairs of a never-ending war."

Protection or not, I was a part of the war now.

"We don't have much more time like this, so I'd like to enjoy it. Want to play solitaire?" my dad asked.

Elijah had retreated to his room and my dad dug out two decks of cards. We played double solitaire, but I was understandably distracted. I was quickly realizing that transparency was out of the question. I knew I would be asking a ton more questions and, if I was lucky, getting back a few answers.

"Why do you go on missions if you have others to do it for you?"

"Some missions require more attention."

"Will I be going on missions?"

"You will attend training, but I will do my best to keep you from being assigned to anything too dangerous, but everyone in The Order is required to do their part."

I looked up from the rows of cards. The Hunters crossed my mind. "Is it like Kung Fu fighting?" I teased.

He raised an amused smirk. "Kung Fu fighting?"

I giggled. "Come on, Dad. I'm making a joke. It doesn't have to be all doom and gloom."

He shook his head with a smile. "No, it doesn't."

"Do you think you'll ever tell Mom?" I finished the row of clubs.

"The only way to keep her safe is not to, but maybe one day when we are old and gray." He winked.

My relationship with my father was layered with deception, love, and complications, but I was confident that he would always have my back, and he would do anything to protect my mom from this madness.

"I can't believe you'll be eighteen next year."

"Yeah," I said, unbelieving myself. "Instead of dancing at my senior prom, I'll be dropkicking a beast that I used to think only existed in books and movies." I completed the row of hearts. "Better catch up, Dad. I'm beating you."

"It's a relief not having to lie to you anymore, Peanut. Not that I wouldn't trade anything to have you hidden still, but I've felt very alone in all this since your grandpa died."

I was seeing another side to my dad. A sensitive side. *Exposed.* It wasn't something I was accustomed to seeing. He was always so strong and self-assured. I reached over and caught his hand before he grabbed another card. "You're not alone, Dad. You never were. You've had Elijah, and now me."

"I'm so proud of who you have become, Abigail Rose."

"Me, too." I paused for a moment. "Hey, Dad?"

"Yeah?"

"What makes you think we're safe here? How did Grandpa keep it a secret?"

"He placed the deed under your grandmother's maiden name, and he had a small cabin in Bayview that served as his place of residence according to The Order. When the dementia started to set in, he moved here permanently, falling off the grid. I was able to convince The Order he was of no use to them anymore, and they agreed. They left him alone, and he was able to go in peace."

"I don't remember him having dementia."

"Good. He wouldn't want you to."

Grandpa Rose was always so vibrant, but he did become more forgetful near the end. He left himself reminder post-it notes all over the house. I thought it was a silly game, but now I understood.

"I'm sorry about Wes. I know you had strong feelings for him." He gathered up his row of spades and hearts.

"*Have,* Dad. I *have* strong feelings for him. Present tense." This was where things got tricky. As much as I knew tangling with an immortal was dangerous, I also knew what my heart felt. I wasn't going to be able to just give Wes up so easily, but I also wouldn't turn my back on my dad. I would find a way to have them both in my life.

"Elijah's a good guy." His eyes lowered.

"Are you trying to set me up?"

He feigned a cough. "Not now, of course, but maybe in a year when you're eighteen."

"Dad, please do me a favor and don't meddle in my love life. It's just weird."

He smiled widely as he closed his clubs and diamonds, leaving me blindsided. "I won. Want to play again?"

I was stupefied. I was ahead a moment ago. "You distracted me," I whined.

"First rule when challenging an opponent—never get distracted." He shuffled his deck proudly.

It was nice to see he wasn't letting me win anymore. "I think I'll get some fresh air."

The fog was drifting in, making the air thick in my throat. It was a little past nine, and the bustling of the city was still echoing down the residential streets. Seattle was lively until the bars closed. When I was younger, I had a hard time sleeping here on the weekends because downtown seemed to spill into all the surrounding neighborhoods. People were loud and drunk. My grandpa could have set up a second residence anywhere. Why would he do it here?

Elijah joined me on the front porch. "How are you holding up?" he asked.

I sat down on the porch step and hugged my knees to my chest. "I don't know. Lying to my mom's face tonight certainly didn't help things."

He sat next to me. "She'll be okay, Abby. She'll be safe, and we'll make sure she knows that you are, too."

"More lies upon lies."

He put his arm around my shoulders, which suddenly felt different since my dad mentioned us in a romantic way. I had felt attracted to Elijah since we first met, but had never thought of him that way. Not really, anyway.

"Are you ready to be an official member of The Order?"

"As ready as I can be." I picked at my jeans. "When do we leave?"

"Now," my father interjected. He was standing in the doorway behind us. He was unsettled.

"What's wrong?" Elijah jumped up.

"I just got off the phone with The Order. They want her there by morning. They heard about Penelope."

Elijah helped me to my feet. "So, this is really happening then?" My heart sputtered nervously.

"Look at it as an adventure." My dad smiled.

"Kung Fu fighting," I teased. Elijah looked at both of us, confused.

My dad retreated to my grandpa's room, Elijah to the guest room, and myself to my room. We were packing quickly and traveling to who knows where.

I grabbed the duffel of clothes my dad had brought and reached under the bed for my disheveled red Chucks, my fingers not finding them, so I crouched down and peered under, but they were gone. I knew I put them there, I thought, completely confused as I sat back on my knees. My door closed quietly behind me and, when I looked over my shoulder, Wes was standing with my Chucks dangling from his fingers.

"Looking for these?" He grinned.

"Wes," I nearly squealed loud enough to alert my dad and Elijah. I launched into his arms, hugging him tightly and never wanting to let him go.

"So, this was a kidnapping?" He pushed my head into his chest gently.

"Kind of. I mean, yes and no." I inhaled the lemongrass scent that followed him everywhere. "How did you find me?"

"Your mom."

"You shouldn't be here."

He pulled me away from him, cupping my face in his

hands and locking his eyes on mine. "How could I not be here? Do you know how worried I've been? I thought they—I thought you were—"

I put my hands over his. "I'm fine. See? I'm in one piece."

"Thankfully. What happened?"

I locked my bedroom door.

"So much, Wes. I don't have time to tell you everything, but Elijah saved me. I was on my way to see you yesterday afternoon when Penelope tried to kidnap me. She went rogue from The Order of the Crest. Elijah intercepted and brought me here to hide."

"Abby, we can protect you better than Elijah and your dad. We're immortal, remember?"

The deceit stung. He had no idea what was really going on, and I couldn't tell him the whole truth.

"You have to go, Wes." My words were as broken as my heart, the tears threatening their own betrayal. A knock on the door was followed by Elijah's voice.

"Abby? Are you okay?"

The doorknob rattled. "I just need a moment. I'll be out in a second." Fear flowed through my veins, my heart raced, and my throat was bone dry.

"Sure. We'll meet you at the car."

When his footsteps faded, I turned back to Wes, his stare ripping my strength apart.

"It sounds like you're going somewhere voluntarily." His stance stiffened, and his fists tightened into balls.

It was clear that we had gotten under each other's skin,

digging our nails in deeply so no one could tear us apart, but while our love was strong enough, the universe was once again working against us. I nodded my head sadly.

"Were you even going to say goodbye?"

"I tried yesterday, and then I left my phone at home. They haven't let me out of their sight for more than a few minutes. Wes, you have to believe me when I say I'm doing what's best for you. For us."

"How can anything be better if we aren't together?" His body deflated in defeat as he stepped into me, wrapping me in his arms again. "Abby, I love you."

With so many secrets I was keeping, I had to give him one. "My father is an Order member."

"What?" He looked down at me. "The Order is dangerous, Abby." Recognition filled his betrayed eyes. "So, you're going with him? To The Order?"

The stench of my betrayal overwhelmed even me.

"I don't have a choice, Wes. It's in my blood. Order royalty. If I don't go, they might go after my dad. And my mom. I can't risk their lives. I was born into this life. I have to go." I was begging for forgiveness and pleading for him to understand, but I still couldn't tell him the main reason I was going—to find my brother.

He bent over and kissed my lips softly, his cold mouth on mine enveloped me, the tingles lingering as he pulled away. He brushed his hand along my cheek, my body leaning into it instinctively.

"The Order is corrupted, Abby. Be careful. Don't trust

anyone. Don't ever let down your guard with them. Ever."

"I won't." Tears were spilling over now.

"If you need me, you know where to find me." He leaned down and kissed the top of my head.

"I love you, Wes."

"I love you, too, Abby." He hopped out the open window.

I was barely holding it together, and when I spun around face-to-face with the red Chucks that bound us together, I came undone. Crumbling to the floor, I latched onto my knees and rocked back and forth. I could very well be making the biggest mistake of my life, and my only salvation just jumped out of my life.

22

DRIVING AWAY FROM MY grandpa's house felt like an ending to a beginning that never had a chance to flourish. I had gotten my wish to say goodbye to Wes, but I didn't get the closure I needed, and it felt like Wes gave up on me so easily. He didn't even try to convince me to run off with him. It made me question whether our connection could survive the separation.

"You're quiet." My dad was driving, but for whatever reason, Elijah decided to sit in the back with me. We were headed to the airport, but I didn't know exactly where we were going.

"Still processing things," I responded softly.

"It's a lot. I know."

"Did your father join The Order because of what happened to your mother?"

"Yes, but The Order failed us." His anger was palpable in this small space.

"How so?"

"They had been tracking the immortal who took her, but they didn't act fast enough. My dad joined The Order to ensure that didn't happen again. It's the reason I'm helping you."

It made sense. What bigger motivation than retribution for a loved one's death? "The Hunters aren't dangerous, Elijah. They've proven that. And Wes—"

"You love him. I know. It just doesn't make sense to me. Why love a monster when you can love—"

"Elijah, don't. Please. I can't control my feelings any more than my place in The Order. I'm sorry." I didn't know how his sentence would have finished, whether he was talking about humans in general or if he was about to confess something more. I was trying to stay strong. Trying to accept my fate without tears, but it was hard. I had mourned Wes for over two years, only to have a few weeks with him, and then have him ripped from my life again. I had no idea what to expect with The Order, and that was terrifying.

"You're a million miles away," Elijah acknowledged.

"More like light years." I leaned my head back on the headrest and closed my eyes. I didn't want to talk anymore.

I didn't want to think anymore. If I could stop feeling, I would shut that off, too.

It was nearly midnight when we arrived at the Tacoma International Airport. As we parked the car in the airport garage, my stomach knotted. My dad handed me my bag from the trunk and then looked down at my feet.

"What happened to the new boots I bought you?"

I patted my duffel. "They're in here."

"Is there a reason you chose shoes with holes over brand new ones?"

"I'm not ready to give away all the old."

He nodded in understanding.

My body was stiff, and every bone felt broken. The slightest movement of my fingers released shooting pains up my arms, and opening my eyes was a challenge. When I finally succeeded, I was met with sterile brightness.

"Peanut." My dad's encouraging voice penetrated the dull pounding in my head. His fingers caressed my hand soothingly.

"Dad?" I was disoriented, but memories of the accident quickly flooded me. "Where's Wes? Is he okay?" I tried to sit up, but I was met with an agonizing pain in my stomach. My dad pushed my shoulders back down onto the bed.

"You can't move, Peanut. You need to rest and give your body time to heal."

He was skating around my question. "Dad, is Wes okay?"

He brushed my hair back and smiled. "He's just fine, Peanut. Now, rest."

My mom appeared around the curtain, holding clothes in her hand and my red Chucks on top. They still looked new, surviving the accident unscathed, unlike myself.

I tossed the duffel over my shoulder and followed Elijah and my dad through the deserted parking garage, our footsteps echoing loudly off the cold concrete walls. It felt like a mausoleum in here with the air still damp from the most recent rain. The airport was just as deserted as the garage and painfully bright. Exhaustion was setting in, and I could barely walk. We didn't have bags to check, so we went straight through security to our gate, choosing three seats along the window. My dad sat in the middle, creating much needed space between Elijah and me.

We still had thirty minutes before boarding, but I couldn't keep my eyes open any longer, so I curled over three empty seats close by and closed my eyes. They started whispering immediately, but I was within earshot.

"How do you think this is going to go?" Elijah's voice was full of concern.

"The only way it can go. She'll pledge her allegiance to The Order, then she'll join the training facility." Sorrow overwhelmed my dad's words.

"It'll be a long time before you see her again," Elijah reminded him.

"I know, but she's determined. Nothing is going to stop her from finding her brother. And at least there, I know she'll be safe."

I felt the connected seats shift. Peeking an eye open, I watched as my dad walked to the window overlooking the sea of parked planes, staring out the glass.

I slid off my makeshift cot and stretched. "I'm going to use the bathroom. I'll be right back." Elijah stood up abruptly, and I looked at him strangely. "I can find my own way. I'm a big girl."

"I was just going to tell you it's around the corner," he retorted.

"Oh," I replied, somewhat embarrassed. "Great. I'll be back."

My dad glanced over his shoulder in acknowledgement and then turned back to the window.

In all my seventeen years, I had never been in an airport. I had always imagined crowds of people, screaming children, and business people working busily on their laptops. What I didn't expect was a deserted wing and the only sign of life being the janitor dumping out the trashcans. It definitely took the magic out of my daydreams.

All the stall doors were unoccupied. I didn't really have to use the bathroom. I just needed a moment to myself. I stood at one of the many sinks that lined the wall, staring at my reflection, but not really looking. Instead, I was seeing the future in my terrified eyes. The shadows under my eyes that weren't there last week were defined, and my chestnut locks were in desperate need of a brush.

A click of a stall door startled me. I had thought the bathroom was empty. I leaned over the sink and rinsed the sleep from my face. When I looked up, Penelope was standing behind me.

"Hello again." A dark smile crossed her face, and her eyes became as cold as ice.

Her hand covered my mouth before I could scream, and my lungs burned like fire. I choked violently for breaths and fought against her hold, but my muscles were weakening and I was beginning to feel dizzy.

"Shh, my friend," Penelope's voice whispered as she caressed the top of my head.

THERE WERE MOMENTS in between sleep and wake and dreams and reality when things didn't seem quite right. That was where I was. Lost in the confusion, wondering where I was and what had happened. Opening my eyes was similar to struggling against the harsh ocean current. I knew I was alive, or at least I thought I was, but I was paralyzed. My mind had rebooted before anything else, and it was horrifying. The pungent smell that had brought me into my deep slumber still lingered on my clothes, or maybe it was just embedded in my brain. Either way, it still surrounded me.

"Your eyelids do this weird twitchy thing when you're asleep. I hope it was a pleasant dream."

Penelope's wretched voice violated my ears. I wanted so badly to spit on her, but I couldn't move.

"Don't bother. The poison is still running its course through your veins, but don't fret, my friend, you'll walk again." She cackled to herself.

I was finally able to pry open my eyes. My vision was blurry, but I could see Penelope standing next to me.

"Oh goody, you can see me now." She leaned over my face and smiled. "You look positively frightened. I'm not going to hurt you, Abigail Rose. I need you alive."

Her smirk incited a thousand questions.

"I'll be back in a bit. You should be back to normal by then. And don't try to run. I'm faster."

The door closed, and deafening silence filled the room. As the poison dissipated, it was replaced with itchy tingles all over my skin. Sitting up was somewhat difficult, but not impossible. Looking around, it appeared as though I was in a guest bedroom in a house. The room was plain with factory white walls, a dresser, and gray sheets. I knew it was stupid to think the door would be unlocked or unguarded, but I had to try. I jiggled the knob and was surprised it wasn't locked, but as suspected, Penelope was waiting in view, sitting on a couch. It was a small apartment or townhouse from the looks of it.

"I could have climbed out the window." I was still unstable on my feet, using the wall for balance.

"And fall to your death. We are three stories up." She

kicked her leg up and down that was crossed casually over the other.

"Fine. Whatever. Why am I here?" I fell onto a chair next to the couch, surveying my surroundings for an escape. There were a few windows on the exterior walls and a slider leading to a balcony. I discerned we were in a corner unit, and since there weren't any stairs I deduced we were in some sort of apartment complex, which meant thin walls. I could scream and hope to garner our neighbor's attention.

"Like what you see? Let me help with your future failed escape plan. No one lives next door or below, and there are no ways to climb down the balcony." Her smile was smug.

"You thought of everything." I smirked back.

"It's nothing personal. Well, it is. You just got stuck in the middle." She stood up and walked to the kitchen. "Water?"

My throat was so dry I could drink a lake. "Please."

She filled a glass and handed it to me, and I chugged it down quickly. "Thanks," I said, wiping my mouth.

"When I found out about the existence of The Order, I was more than willing to sign up."

She lounged back on the couch.

"How old are you?" While I was scared out of my mind, I wanted to find out as much information about her as possible.

"Twenty-three."

"How did you find out about The Order? I thought it was a big secret?"

"My brother was turned by an immortal." Disgust dripped from her words.

"I'm sorry."

"So am I."

"Where is he now?"

"Dead," she said matter-of-factly. "Forever dead. Not undead dead."

Somehow I didn't think offering my condolences was going to make an impact. "I don't know what I would do if I lost someone I cared for."

"Yeah, well, the pain never ceases." She took out a dagger from her waistband and started carving into the coffee table.

"Is this your place?"

"It was my brother's."

I guess that explained the monochromatic simplicity and lack of personal touches.

"Where are your parents?"

"You ask a lot of questions." She was still busily carving.

"Not much else to do." Had I not known Penelope before her taking me against my will, I probably would have refrained from talking.

After a few silent moments, she stood up and walked to the balcony slider. Glancing at the front door, I noticed several deadbolts but also a reverse doorknob, so you needed a key to open it. I wondered if her brother had done that or if she did when she planned my kidnapping.

"Can I use the bathroom?"

"You don't have to ask," she snapped without turning to me.

When I got up, I got a good look at the carving. It was an infinity sign. The same as the charm and key still tucked in my pocket. It couldn't be a coincidence. The symbol meant something. When I got back from the bathroom, Penelope was back on the couch, staring at her carving in a daze.

"What does that mean?" I asked carefully.

"You've never seen an infinity sign?" She scoffed.

"I know what it is, but it must mean something more to you if you're carving it into a perfectly good table."

She jammed the point of the dagger into the table, causing me to jump. "It's the mark of immortality."

She removed the dagger and went to the other bedroom, slamming the door. She was obviously certain that escape was impossible. I leaned down and traced the carving. How was the old lady who gave me the charm connected to all of this? Maybe she was an immortal, but that didn't explain her giving it to me. How would she know I was connected to The Order and immortals?

I watched the closed bedroom door for a good five minutes before tiptoeing into the kitchen, opening the drawers quietly, hoping to find a sharp object. She might be stronger than me, but the element of surprise was even more dangerous. After all, everybody thought I was fragile, so no one would expect the scrawny seventeen year old to brand a weapon and fight back.

"You won't find anything in there." I looked up, taken by complete surprise. "I cleared the apartment after he died." She leaned on the hallway threshold without a care in the world that I was looking for something to kill her with. Either she was grossly underestimating my will to live or blindly overconfident.

"What was he like?" If I was going to get out of this alive, I needed to switch gears.

"Irreplaceable." She looked to the floor. "After our parents were killed in a house fire, we were sent into the foster care system. I was nine, and he was thirteen. They kept us together because we were siblings. He looked after me because our caretakers weren't exactly parental material. When he turned eighteen, he got a construction job and officially adopted me. Six months later, he disappeared for a few days. He came back immortal, barely holding it together. He left to protect me and said he would be back for me when he could control his rage. He never came back."

"How do you know he's dead and not just out there still trying to control himself?" I wondered if she knew about the True Mate craze.

"A few years ago, I tracked his whereabouts. We made a lot of unique friends in foster care, and they helped me. My brother protected all the younger kids and was loved by everyone. He didn't deserve what he got. Anyway, I was led to The Order. They told me he was dead and took pity on me, or should I say, took advantage of me. When they discovered I had a special gift, they sent me to their training facility and promised me the world. I was a beggar before I found them, so they fed on my poverty, giving me a place to live, food to eat. I even made friends at the facility. At first, it all seemed too good to be true, but it grew on me."

Knowing someone as crazy as Penelope had a gift rose the hairs on the back of my neck. I wondered what it was. "Then why betray them? It sounds like they were pretty good to you."

"They made a lot of promises they didn't keep. Assigning me to you, a fragile high school student was the last straw. Then I saw my brother's maker in Sandpoint."

The world stood still for a blinding moment.

"I found a picture of Zander's maker stuffed between the mattress and box spring in his bedroom. I didn't know what it meant or who he was, but the first night I got to Sandpoint, I saw the same person in that photograph at the beach. He was swimming in the lake. It was foggy, though, so I went to get a closer look, and that's when I saw the mark. That's when I knew. It was a Hunter."

"But you can't be sure. You're only speculating." I wondered which one she thought it was.

"Oh, I'm sure." Her anger was increasing.

I crossed my arms, frustrated. "Why did you choose me to be your revenge pawn? What do I have to do with all this?"

"The immortals you call friends are responsible for turning my brother, and The Order is responsible for killing him. Enough reason for you?" Her stare could kill, and her words cut me deep. She was out for blood, and I was now certain my days were numbered.

I retreated to my bedroom of captivity. It was hard to imagine one of the Hunters turning someone. It was forbidden and would cost them their life if The Order found out. I refused to believe it. Zander must have provoked the Hunters. There was no way they would risk their lives to change him. Either way, it didn't change my circumstances. Penelope was distraught, and she would stop at nothing to avenge her brother's death.

I lay back on the bed, my body confused by the short intervals of rejuvenation. One minute I was wide-awake and the next I could fall asleep walking. If I had any sort of a fighting chance, I needed to rest. I needed to plot. I just needed to get out of here.

T HE BEDROOM DOOR SLAMMED open, the abrupt interruption jogging me from sleep.

"Rise and shine." Penelope cackled. "It's time to see your boyfriends." Her lips curved condescendingly.

I rubbed my face, still acclimating to being awakened suddenly.

"I'd apologize for scaring you, but I'm not."

She grabbed my arm forcefully and pulled me up. Her mood had darkened, my fear of her officially growing. She pulled me into the living area, grabbed her dagger, and continued pulling me out of the apartment. The position of the sun told me it was probably around nine in the morning, and by the looks of the scenery, we were still somewhere around the lake. It made sense that Zander would live near

Sandpoint. The Hunters moved here nine years ago, which would be around the same time Zander was turned, but it was still unbelievable that one of them would do that. Wes had described the transition from human to immortal, and it sounded awful for both involved. There was more to the story, and if I could figure it out, then maybe Penelope would stop all this.

"Get in," she snapped.

She drove a newer model Mazda Miata. I slid in and got my leg out of the way just before she slammed the door closed. She revved the engine and swung out of the apartment complex. Daring a glance over, I could see her jaw clenching. I needed to get her talking again.

"Fancy car." I smoothed my hand along the pristine dashboard, pretending to admire it.

"I have friends, too," she answered smartly.

I shuddered to think what friends she kept. Working at the bistro would definitely not pay for this. Of course, now I knew that was just a ruse so she could keep tabs on us.

"Where are we going?"

"To a remote location for a little family reunion." She chuckled lowly, sending chills down my spine.

Her dagger was within reach, tucked into her belt, but judging from the other night when she tried to grab me before Elijah showed up, she was fast. I wondered if speed was her gift.

"What's your gift?" she asked me abruptly, as if reading my thoughts.

"What makes you think I have one?"

She picked up speed on the freeway. Traffic was light in between rush hours, but there were still enough cars on the road to alert how fast we were going.

"Don't play games with me. The Order doesn't want just anybody. I've only ever brought back Specials."

I sank in my seat, not exactly sure how much I should tell her. I didn't want to tell her anything, but she was angry, and who knew what she would do if I pushed her too far?

"It's stupid." I tried to blow it off.

"No gift is worthless."

I chewed on my finger nervously. "I have good instincts."

"That's a pretty impressive gift," she admired.

"How so?"

"Instincts are primal. Ancestral. Ingrained in your DNA. Most people are too self-centered to connect with their instincts, and those that aren't usually ignore them because they are selfish. But if someone were able to harness their instincts—to become one with their true nature and tap into their ancestry—their power is limitless. You're not just a Special, Abigail. You're a Chosen, which makes you invaluable."

My stomach turned. I had just given her more ammunition. How could I be such an idiot? *So much for great instincts.* "What's the difference?" I pressed for more information. She was the first person to go into detail.

"A huge difference. There can only be one Chosen at a time. When one dies, another one is born. It's mystical. It lies dormant in the Chosen until it's time."

"Time for what? I'm not going to become Buffy, am I?" I joked, but I was also terrified.

"Did you tell your immortal boyfriend about your gift?" She looked over, smirking proudly.

"No," I admitted apprehensively.

"It's best you don't. For your sake, anyway."

My stomach was knotting tighter and tighter with each second that passed. If I were a Chosen, then why wouldn't my dad tell me? Or even Elijah? And I guess the more important question was, how did being a Chosen change my fate with Wes? I leaned into the window, craving privacy as the suffocating space closed in on me. "Why would you tell me about being a Chosen?"

"Why not? It in no way affects me or changes the predicament you're in. Plus, you haven't been trained, and you have no idea how to wield your power yet. You're just a fragile human girl. But I have to admit. I'm a little jealous."

I turned to her, shocked. How could someone so deadly be jealous of me? "But you move so fast, and Elijah was even afraid of you."

She laughed loudly. "Oh, he was? Good." Her smile could reach the sky. "Elijah is pretty amazing in battle, too." She winked.

My body heat rose with envy. "How do you know Elijah?"

"He didn't tell you? I guess you aren't as close as I

thought. We were at the training facility together. We became *close*."

Gross.

"I had hoped we would be partners after our training, but he requested to work alone." Her voice filled with disappointment, which gave me a small taste of satisfaction. He volunteered to work with me and gave Penelope the boot.

"What do you hope to accomplish with all this, Penelope? You said it yourself; your brother is gone. Nothing can bring him back."

Her fingers tightened around the steering wheel, and she floored the gas. We sped up considerably on a deserted stretch of highway.

"And for that, all the guilty parties will pay."

"And somehow you think they are just going to risk their own lives for me?"

"I know they will for three reasons. One, a father would do anything to save his little girl. Two, Wes loves you, and three, you're a Chosen."

In one breath she had just threatened the lives of two of my loved ones. "How could you think of condemning someone else to the same kind of loss that you have experienced?

She might have been considering what I said, but it passed quickly. "It's nothing personal." She cranked the music up to deafening decibels, signaling the end of our exchange. We were surrounded by long stretches of farmland and then nothingness and then farmland again. We had been driving for a few hours, and I was famished. I was relieved when we pulled into a roadside gas station with a mini mart.

"Stay here," she demanded, locking the doors and initiating the alarm.

I slammed my head back on the headrest and clenched my stomach. I needed food. A few minutes later, Penelope approached the car with a large plastic bag, hopefully full of food.

She tossed the bag onto my lap. "Take what you want. Just leave me the bar."

She shut the door again. While she attended to the gas pump, I peeked inside the bag, happy to see a plethora of junk food, as well as a warmly wrapped hot dog. I grabbed it and inhaled it quickly. As Penelope slid back into the car, I was downing a large soda. A look of repulsion stared back at me.

"Dude, if you were hungry, you could've said something." She shook her head. "Hand me my bar and a water."

I dug them out and handed them over. She popped open the water and tore the wrapper off the protein bar. "We're almost there."

I immediately lost my appetite. A half hour later, we pulled off the road and made our way to one of the many large farmhouses we had passed. It was massive, painted bright white with yellow trim.

"Was this your brother's, too?" I asked.

"Close. This is where I grew up. The house that was nearly lost to the fire. My grandmother had it rebuilt with the insurance money before she died. The deed was left to my brother. Neither one of us could stomach coming back here, though. This is the first time I've been back."

It was infuriating that one minute she could make me loathe her, and the next pity her. "Penelope, this isn't going to end well. You know that, right?" I said sheepishly.

"I do, and since I don't have anything else to live for, I don't really care." She opened her door. "Now, get out."

The dagger was still firmly in place on her belt, and I was still clueless as to how to get out of this, especially now that we entered the land of nowhere to run. I was either going to have to impair her ability to walk or kill her. The only problem was I didn't want to hurt her. I wanted to help her. She was a victim of circumstance and still in mourning. It felt wrong to convict her because of that.

She unlocked the front door and pushed me inside, dragging me by my arm down to the finished basement. It was a little dusty, but looked newly constructed. The only furnishing was a mattress on the floor.

"I'm going to rest up. We have a big day tomorrow. I'll bring you food later. There's a bathroom behind that door." She stomped back up the stairs, closed the door, and locked it. It could have been worse, I guess.

The windows were sealed shut, and the bathroom was at least stocked with soap and toilet paper. There wasn't even a towel to dry my hands. With nothing else to do, I lay down on the mattress and sighed loudly. I was going to die of boredom. I remembered the charm and key in my pocket, so I dug them out, examining them again, trying to figure out what the key could possibly open.

I jumped up when I heard the front door slam and ran to the window facing the driveway, listening carefully. An engine roared to life and then faded. *She left.* My heart kicked into high gear as I ran up the basement stairs and forcefully jiggled the knob. Putting all my weight into the door, I pounded against it with my shoulder, barely causing it to vibrate. It was solid. There was no way I was going to be able to knock it down, and I had missed Picking Locks 101. Screaming loudly in frustration, I went back to the window and looked around for anything to break it. There was nothing except my elbow. I raised it hesitantly, knowing the pain it would cause, squinted my eyes, and sucked in a deep breath as I braced myself for the blow, but I couldn't do it. I dropped my arm and lay back down on the mattress, deflated. I imagined Wes coming to my rescue, even hearing his voice whisper my name, but as time passed so did my hope.

Fear returned as the front door slammed once again, my heart jumping with it. The basement door flung open. "You can come up to eat," Penelope yelled.

The smell of greasy hamburgers and fries wafted down

the stairs. I had barely eaten since my grandpa's house. The fact she was feeding me at all was a good sign. I was trying to remain cautiously optimistic.

I scaled the steps slowly and peeked through the door before entering. The kitchen table was in sight, an unwrapped burger and container full of fries placed at one seat. Penelope was sitting across from it, inhaling her food quietly. She didn't even look up when I walked up and sat. I was afraid to agitate her. Even the crinkle of the wrapper made me cringe.

I ate my burger slowly, buying more time out of the basement, taking in my new surroundings as much as I could. When Penelope grabbed for her water, I noticed a tattoo on her wrist. I didn't know how I missed it before. It looked like a combination of the infinity sign and the yin and yang symbol. One end was shaded dark and the other translucent.

"What does your tattoo mean?"

She turned her wrist over and ran her thumb across it. "It's the crest for The Order. The shape is the infinity symbol of immortality, and the shading represents the dark and light. Both bring balance."

"Why the immortality symbol?"

"Because humans and immortals are infinitely bound. It's a reminder of the infinite threat immortals pose to human kind. You're branded when you complete the training and become an official member of The Order." She scoffed. "I was so proud the day I got this. I wanted every immortal to pay for what they did to my brother. I didn't want justice. I wanted revenge. I believed being a part of The Order would make it possible, but then I found out they were just as vile as immortals." She paused. "You see this scar?" She pointed to a diagonal raised scar across the crest. "I wanted to cut it off my skin. I hated The Order that much, but then crossing it off seemed more symbolic and serves as a reminder of what my new mission is."

"And what's that?" I was almost afraid to ask.

"To take down both."

Her confidence was astounding. She might be capable of taking out a few, but to think she could take down two completely different worlds seemed pretty unrealistic, especially now that she had blown her cover. She had completely lost it, and finding a way to escape was the only way I was going to survive.

After dinner, she ushered me back down to the basement with a towel and toiletries. "Shower if you want," she said just before locking me in.

The only light came from the bathroom, so I left it on for the duration of the night. Once I was sure that Penelope was asleep, I shoved the towel and a rolled up sheet under the throw blanket, hoping if she peeked down she would assume it was me. I rushed to the window and tried to open it. It took a few tries, but it finally shifted under the pressure and slid open. I jumped up into the window well, closed the window quietly, and climbed up the ladder, peeking my head into the yard. The rocks on the ground glistened under the moonlight, lighting the path I would take. I crouched to the window to make sure there were no signs of movement and then stood up, my heart beating out of my chest and my legs wobbly from adrenaline.

It was now or never.

24

TIPTOEING ACROSS THE GRAVEL yard, I was frantically looking around for danger, but the night was dead silent. We were in the middle of nowhere, but Penelope had come home with fast food and it was still warm, so it had to be somewhat close by. I had never walked more than a couple of miles, but I was in good shape, so I could probably jog most of it.

When I was a good distance from the house, I picked up my pace to a steady jog, the loud crunching of the gravel under my shoes escalating my nervous energy. It took several minutes to get to the main road, and I knew it was at least a mile to the highway. I didn't remember seeing anything other than farmhouses vastly spread apart as we drove here, but I wasn't giving up. I needed to get as far away from Penelope as possible. I quickened my pace to a sprint, sweat beading on my forehead and my chest burning after a few minutes. I was cursing myself for not joining the track team last year.

I was about a hundred yards from the edge of the highway when I heard Penelope's angry voice break through the quiet. For a second I froze and then searched frantically for a place to hide. If I kept running to the highway, she would see me. I was flanked on both sides by tall forests of weeds, so I tore off a piece of my shirt and tossed it on the weeds to the left and then took off running to the right. Maybe it would fool her long enough to give me a better lead. I ran low and quietly, trying not to agitate the weeds too much. What if she caught me? Would I fight or give up?

My feet were aching and my shins were burning, and I was losing stamina quickly. My nerves were shot, and I hadn't heard a peep from Penelope again. Suddenly, I heard weeds rustle close by. I dove down into the cover of the weeds and tried to steady my breath and listen to where the rustling was coming from. A hand suddenly wrapped tightly around my mouth, suffocating me with fear. I struggled violently until a whisper paralyzed me.

"Shh! It's me. Elijah."

He spun me around to face him. His green eyes met mine, and I wrapped my arms around his neck, my body collapsing into his. "How did you find me?"

"I tracked you. I'm sorry it took me so long, but I'm here now."

I pulled away. "Where's my dad?"

"With The Order council. We parted at the airport. I tried to call him, but there's no service out here."

"Elijah, Penelope's hunting me."

"I know. We need to keep moving. My car is about a mile down the road."

He peeked up, listening, and then motioned for me to stand with him. "Let's go," he whispered.

"Let's not." Penelope stood maybe ten yards in front of us.

Elijah pushed me behind him protectively. "Penelope, it doesn't have to be this way."

"Yes, it does." She took a few steps in our direction.

"What could possibly make you go rogue like this?"

Elijah had no idea. I was surprised Penelope hadn't told him, considering her insinuation that they had been close.

"Zander was everything to me, Eli," she bellowed unstably.

Elijah was like a brick wall in front of me. I could hide behind him completely unnoticed with his stocky frame in comparison to my thin one.

"And that's why you joined The Order, Pen. To right the wrongs, but Abigail has nothing to do with this."

I was waiting for the bomb to drop.

"The Order is corrupt, Eli. They aren't what you think." She held up her wrist, flashing the tattoo. "*This* isn't what you thought."

I wondered for just a moment where Elijah's tattoo was.

"You aren't making any sense. Why would you think The Order is corrupt?"

In a flash, she had pulled out her dagger and flung it at Elijah. She caught us both off guard, and it struck Elijah in the chest. I screamed so loud the world within miles could hear. He grabbed the dagger, stunned, and stumbled back into my arms. I fell to the ground with the weight of him on me as he landed on my lap, his eyes wide and focused on me.

"No, no, no. Elijah." My hands were shaking violently as I stroked his cheek, one of my tears falling just below his eye.

"I'm sorry, Abby," he choked out, trickles of blood spewing from his mouth.

My chest tightened with unfathomable grief as I continued to soothe him. His eyes became heavy. "Stay with me, Elijah. Please. I need you. Don't go." I cried hard, arching over and resting my forehead on his. His skin was hot and sweaty. I shot my head up and glared at Penelope. "How could you? You loved him!"

She walked over and looked down at Elijah, finally answering his question. "Because they killed my brother." She leaned over and pulled the dagger forcefully out of his chest, blood pouring out of the open wound. Instinctively, I placed both hands over it to stop the flow.

A loud noise alerted Penelope and me. She spun the dagger in her hand and held it out, ready to attack again.

"Don't go anywhere," she spat out as she disappeared into the thicket of weeds.

I refocused my attention on Elijah. His eyes were still cracked open, but his body was limp. "Elijah, you have to hold on. I think someone is here. We'll get you help, but you have to be strong."

His hand slowly reached up, touching my cheek, and he managed a small smile. "Be brave."

I didn't know if he was telling me to be brave or finishing my plea for him to live. "Yes, be brave." I smiled through tears and a pain I had never experienced before. It felt like someone had ripped my heart from my chest and crushed it. His fingers gripped my cheek, and he pulled me in closer. I leaned down, positioning my ear close to his lips.

He whispered, "I love you, Abigail Rose. I have from the first time I touched you, carrying you in my arms the day of the accident."

His confession stung because deep down I knew in some way I had fallen for Elijah, too. I shifted my lips over his and leaned down, kissing them lightly at first, but then he used the last of his strength to wrap his arm around my neck and push harder into my own wordless confession. The infinity charm flashed in my thoughts. I couldn't explain why, but my instincts were telling me it served a purpose more than hanging from a bracelet.

I pulled away, the last of Elijah's strength gone, his arm falling onto his chest and his eyes closing. It was impossibly hard to scoot out from under him, but the charm was in my pocket. I finally slid him off and dug it out. It was so nondescript in my palm, but something told me it was so much more.

I wasn't sure what to do with it, so I placed it on the wound and waited. It felt like hours as I watched Elijah's chest barely rise and fall. Nothing happened, though. Fear of losing him coursed through my body, squeezing the life out of my soul. I shook my head, disbelieving that Elijah could die. His chest stopped moving.

"No, Elijah. Please," I begged helplessly, squeezing his hand and the other softly planted on the charm on his chest. I was only a girl, and there was nothing I could do to save him, except be here for him. Just like he was always there for me. He wouldn't die alone.

"Abigail." Wes' voice rang in my ears, full of sorrow and pity.

I peered over my wet lashes. "He's gone." Saying it aloud somehow crushed me even more. The permanence was out there for all to hear.

Ben, Zoe, and William flew to Wes' side, quickly followed by my dad.

"Penelope," I sobbed.

"She won't be a threat anymore. She's with The Order."

After everything that she had done to me, taken from me, I still felt sorry for her. I couldn't imagine her time with The Order would be pleasant.

Wes kneeled down beside Elijah and me. I was covered in blood.

"Are you hurt?" Wes asked carefully.

"No." I choked back my pain.

"Abby, I can save him. His heart still beats."

I locked knowing eyes with him, but I knew I couldn't decide that fate for Elijah. It would be a decision made from selfishness. Immortals had murdered his parents. His despise for them ran deep. To become one would be condemning him to something that, in his mind, was worse than death.

I shook my head. "I can't do that to him." As painful as it was to admit, I had to let him go.

Seconds later, the field was lit up like a collision of planets. The ground shook as feet stomped over to us. At least a dozen men and women dressed head-to-toe in black aimed guns at us.

"Nobody move," one of the women demanded.

My widened eyes met Wes' again. "Run," I whispered urgently.

Wes looked over to his family, and with a nod they disappeared into the weeds, half of the gun-wielding people chasing after them.

"Stand down!" my dad shouted over the chaos.

He approached the woman who appeared to be in charge of the group and yanked the gun out of her hand. She stared at him, stunned. He flashed something on his side, and she nodded in understanding, backing off.

"Sir, is that Elijah Winters?" She stood at attention.

My dad came to my side, pulling me up to my feet.

"I can't leave him, Dad. We can't let him die alone."

He pulled me into him and held my head to his chest, rocking me slowly. "We won't." He looked over his shoulder. "Take him to the infirmary. Quickly."

Several approached Elijah and picked him up carefully, carrying his limp body through the weeds. I buried my head back into my dad's chest and sobbed uncontrollably. A gunshot broke through the night.

"Dad, you can't let them hurt the Hunters." I looked up to him for understanding.

"It's out of my hands, Abby. They are immortals, and we are The Order. It's predator against prey. We can't change the natural order of the universe, and I can't defy The Order. Let's just hope they were faster."

His eyes were remorseful. He didn't want them caught, because he knew how it would hurt me. Because he loved me that much that he would let me love my immortal friends.

TIME PASSED IN A BLUR, traveling from the field, to a black car, to an airplane, to an unknown bed. I was numb, the events proving to be too much for me.

Abby has always been a bit fragile.

Those words once stung, but now they rang true. It only took a trial beyond my control to admit it to myself. I *was* fragile.

Judging from the matching green bedspread, curtains, and pillow shams, I was in a hotel room. A sliver of light filtered between the drawn curtains. Even after sleep, I was beyond exhausted from the events, and the pit in my stomach remained. Elijah was most likely dead, and Wes was gone. I was rescued, but I never felt more alone.

Voices on the other side of the door lured me out of bed. I had been changed into my favorite sweats from home. My legs were sore, making it difficult to walk just from the bed to the door. As I got closer, I recognized the voices. I yanked it open, relief stretching from ear to ear.

"Mom, you're here." I forced my legs to move quicker as I closed the distance and fell into her arms.

"Of course, I am, sweetie. I'll always be here." She stroked my head lovingly.

She and my dad had been sitting on the couch, talking.

I looked over her shoulder to my dad, confused.

"I told her everything, Peanut. I had to after what happened to you."

I released from her embrace, more worried than relieved. "But I thought that was against The Order rules?"

"It is, which is why they can never know."

I nodded, understanding.

"I changed you into your pajamas, and I brought more stuff from home," my mom said cheerfully.

I expected my mother to be...different after finding out we were battling a secret war, but she was the same mom I left a few short days ago. "You are taking everything well." My crooked smile was unsure.

"I'm sure I'm handling it just as well as you, Abby. It's a lot to wrap my head around, but it won't help any of us to fight the truth. You're my baby." She took my hand and then looked at my dad. "And you're the love of my life." She took his hand with her other. She was sandwiched between us. "I will do whatever it takes to keep our family together."

My dad appeared a thousand pounds lighter, having ended the lie that weighed him down since he had met my mom.

She stood up. "I should go."

Alarmed, I jumped up, blocking her way. "Why? Where are you going?"

She looked to my dad.

"We have to be careful. We are too close to The Order's headquarters. She needs to go home and act as though everything's normal."

"But she just got here," I whined. The glances they shared made me uneasy. "What?"

"I've been here for three days," she answered.

I looked quickly between them, trying to process how I could have possibly slept for that long. "How?"

"The Order gave you a sedative. You were in shock. They wanted to give your mind and body time to recover."

My mental state had been delicate, but I didn't realize it

was that bad. "What about Elijah and Wes?"

"Let's walk your mother out, and then I'll tell you everything I know."

He slid his hand on my mom's back, leading her to the door. She picked up her duffel bag and purse and gave my dad a kiss.

"Come here, sweetie." She waved me over.

This time I held her, squeezing tightly. "I'll see you soon, right?"

She pulled away and brushed unruly strands from my face. "Of course. I love you, Abigail. Stay safe."

She kissed me on the cheek, and after several more goodbyes, she hopped into a rental car and drove off. That was when I got a better look at where we were. We were at an inn somewhere in the woods, the pavement freshly layered with rain, the clouds still threatening more.

It was difficult seeing her leave after everything I went through, especially because I wasn't sure I'd ever see her again. "I'm not going to see her for a long time, am I?" I was still in the door opening, staring after her car as it drove out of sight.

His hand landed on my shoulder. "No."

I knew why, but it was still hard. I needed her. "Did you tell her about my brother? Her son?"

"No." His head dropped shamefully. "This isn't the time. Come inside," my dad urged.

I closed the door, putting the locks securely in place, and turned to him. "Is Wes okay?"

"Yes. They all are. The Specials weren't fast enough for them."

"And Elijah?" I was still hanging onto a sliver of hope.

My dad's eyes dropped. "I don't know. The Order isn't talking, but he didn't have a heartbeat when they left."

My heart just kept breaking. He died because of me.

"I'm sorry, Peanut. He meant a lot to me, too."

"Dad, you revealed yourself to the woman in the field. I thought no one was supposed to know who you and the other council members were?"

"No one does, except for that elite group of Specials. They know everything. In fact, they probably know more than we do. It's their job."

I remembered the fear in the Special's eyes when my dad told her to stand down. As if she saw death staring back.

"I'm never going to see Wes again either, am I?" I didn't even have to ask. I knew it was the truth.

"Never say never, Peanut."

"So, what now?" I was living somewhere in between a nightmare and another life.

"We continue where we left off. Nothing has changed."

Yet everything had. My heart felt vacant, waiting for something to fill it again, only I didn't know what could possibly fill this kind of void.

"When do we go?"

"The Order would like you as soon as you're awake and ready."

I bit my lip, wondering if I should tell him what Penelope

had revealed about me. Maybe he already knew.

"What's bothering you?"

"When I was with Penelope, I told her about my gift. She said it was rare and that I wasn't a Special." His eyebrow raised curiously. I continued, "She said I was a Chosen?"

His face dropped slightly. "Did she now?" He paced a few steps, combing his fingers through his hair. "There's so much for you to learn before that. You can't become what you are until you've learned how. You need The Order for that. The Kung Fu fighting." He threw me a smile.

"So, it's true then?" I was taken aback.

"Yes, it can be. We are counting on it. We are at a huge disadvantage without a Chosen."

"But you tried to keep me from all of this. If you needed me so bad for this war, then why would you risk that?"

He took my shoulders in his hands. "Because, Abigail, none of this matters if you're dead. I've told you that over and over. I will do anything to keep you safe, which is why I will be your official partner when your training is complete."

"You will?" A part of me was happy to hear that, but it was also a reminder that Elijah could be gone. He was supposed to be my sidekick.

"What's going to happen to Penelope?" In one moment she had turned my world upside down and shook the life force out of it.

"The Order has her. She'll be handled properly."

"They won't kill her, will they?"

My dad looked at me, revolted. "No, Abigail. We aren't killers. We ensure the safety of humans and bring justice to those who deserve it. We aren't out for the slaughter."

"Not for humans, at least." I wiggled from his grip.

"Abigail, immortals aren't alive. They don't have a heart, and their souls left their bodies as soon as their hearts stopped beating."

"But they love and laugh and fear. What is more human than that?"

His eyelids dropped, sorrow and regret looking up through his lashes. "I'm sorry, Abby. That's just not how it works."

There wasn't much more to say on the subject. "I didn't even get to say goodbye," I mumbled sadly. Wes had left the field so quickly.

"I know, and for that I'm truly sorry." He walked toward the second bedroom. "We leave in an hour."

I had an hour to embrace my new life. A life without Elijah or Wes and with a whole bunch of people I'd never met.

25

I COULDN'T STOP FIDGETING ON the drive to The Order's headquarters. I was queasy, and my lip was swollen from chewing on it so much.

"You okay, Peanut?"

My dad was staring at my stretched out shirtsleeves that my hands had been working on for the past hour. I interlocked my fingers to stop them from causing any more damage.

"No." I sniffled, looking out the window.

"I know it's a lot, but you'll adjust quickly. I did."

I had never asked him about his experience. A part of me was worried I would drudge up bad memories for him with Grandpa and Elijah's dad.

"Dad?" I paused.

"Yeah?"

"What's it like?" I was picturing a concrete structure surrounded by barbed wire, much like a prison. Not sure if it was to keep people out or to keep people in.

"Believe it or not, much like being on an extended vacation."

I looked at him, surprised. "Really?"

"For the most part. Don't get me wrong. It's hard work, too. Most of your days are spent training, which is exhausting, but The Order has taken great care into making your experience tranquil. A lot of The Order training is based on Zen ideas."

"It doesn't sound as horrible as I imagined." I smiled, thankful.

"It's even better in person. You'll never want to leave. Integrating back into the real world after spending a year there was not any easy transition," he admitted openly.

His honesty curbed my nerves a bit, but knowing I would be confined for a year without any possibility to communicate with Wes or my parents was breaking me.

"We have a stop to make before The Order. There's one last thing I'd like to do for you."

My heart jumped excitedly. My dad always had the best surprises, and I could definitely use a pick-me-up right now. He pulled off the highway in a cute little suburban town, surrounded by mature, bushy trees in every fall color imaginable. It felt like we had stepped back into the past when life was simpler, houses smaller, and kids could safely play on the streets as they were doing now. A soccer ball raced in front of the car followed by a little guy. He waved with a huge smile on his face as he retrieved it and ran back onto the sidewalk where a group of kids his age were playing soccer on the large lawn in front of a house.

"Why are we here?" I was beguiled by the serenity. I rolled down my window, taking in the warm, fresh air.

"You'll see," he said mischievously.

Leaving behind the town, we wound through a thick forest of deep green cedar trees and open road. Thirty minutes later, we pulled into the Roosevelt Grove of Ancient Cedars. I was awestruck by the massive nature of these trees and immediately jumped out of the car and ran to the informational sign. The trees dated back two to three thousand years and were over 150 feet tall, and the trunks were as wide as twelve feet in diameter, the sign read. My dad caught up to me.

"You've always wanted to bring me here," I said nostalgically. My grandpa had taken him here every year as a little boy.

"I wanted to continue the tradition, but then Elijah needed me, and there just wasn't enough time. My dad and I stopped coming here the year I entered The Order. I wished that we would have come back, but it never happened." His memory was fraught with regret. He draped his arm around my shoulders.

"Time for a new tradition," I exclaimed.

"I think so. I brought waters, lunch, and snacks." He

patted a large hiking backpack.

"What about The Order?" I followed him to the trailhead marked Granite Falls.

"They've been waiting long enough. They can wait a little longer." He turned around and winked.

The weather was perfect. The sun was shining, but there was a light, cool breeze and plenty of shade from the trees. My red Chucks kicked up dust, rifling butterflies nearby. We had the trail all to ourselves. As we walked up the steep incline, wildflowers sprinkled the forest floor, boasting an array of pinks, yellows, blues, and whites. The waterfall echoed off the tree trunks, escalating my excitement. I had never seen a waterfall in person. We were close now.

My dad bent over to tie his shoe. "Go on ahead. I'll be there in a second."

I danced up the last of the trail and froze. At the edge of the waterfall, standing between two trees, stood Wes. My heart palpitated with unhinged excitement, happy tears falling down my cheeks. I turned back to my dad who had caught up.

"Dad, I—" There were no words to thank him for the grandest gesture a father could make for his daughter.

"The way you are with him," he pointed toward Wes, "the way you look at him is exactly how I look at your mother. And he looks at you the same. I don't agree with it. This goes beyond the overprotective father, but I can't deny you someone that you love, human or not."

I jumped into his arms, squeezing him as hard as my little arms could. "Thank you, Daddy."

"There is no limit to my love for you. I want you to be happy, and if I can give you this moment, then I am honored."

I snuggled into his chest a little longer until he pulled me away.

"Now, go. I'll be back at sunset." He handed me the backpack and then headed back down the trail.

I put it on the ground and spun on my heels, but Wes was gone. I frowned until a pair of arms wrapped around my waist, lemongrass electrifying my senses.

"I never want to let you go again," he whispered.

There were so many things I would miss. Wes' cool breath on my skin was on top of that list. I closed my eyes and branded this moment into my heart.

"Then don't," I replied in a feeble voice.

He rested his chin on my shoulder. "It's otherworldly, isn't it?"

"Breathtaking." I placed my hands on his, lifting them up, tucking under and spinning to face him, falling perfectly into his arms. "I'm glad you're safe."

"Ditto." He hugged me intensely. "And Elijah?"

I couldn't even form the words as a lump stuck in my throat, so I just shook my head.

"I'm sorry, Abby." He nuzzled into my hair. "I know he had become a friend to you."

"Are you really, though? I mean, you didn't hide your

dislike for him, and you assumed he was going to kill me, and yet he was the one to save me." I didn't mean to be so abrupt, but he showed nothing but hate for Elijah until he was hurt.

Wes put his hands on my shoulders and pushed me away so he could look at me. "That doesn't mean I would wish death upon him. You misunderstood my displeasure."

"How so?"

"I didn't like or trust him around *you*. Outside of that, his affairs meant nothing to me. I would have saved him had you given me permission."

It was true. He had offered to turn him, but I declined, not being able to choose someone else's fate. My heart ached deeply in his absence, though, and I believed it always would.

"Come with me." He pulled my backpack over his shoulders and took my hand gingerly, his crooked smile melting my insides.

We climbed down an unmarked, rocky path alongside the thundering waterfall, the mist cooling my cheeks from the bright rays of the sun. There was no sense trying to talk over it, so we walked silently, enjoying the tranquility. I followed him as he veered off to the right, leaving the waterfall behind and leading us deeper into the forest. The massive trunks of cedar trees were covered in bright green moss, and the ground was covered with more wildflowers. I felt like I had stepped right into a fairyland forest.

"This is gorgeous." My eyes studied everything in sight,

including Wes who was only a few steps ahead. He moved fluidly across the rocky terrain while I had to be more careful, not wanting to fall.

We came upon a beautiful arched wood bridge with support railings that stretched across a large stream supplied by the waterfall.

"This reminds me of all our adventures around my house." He squeezed my hand gently and pulled me over the bridge, stopping in the middle, enveloping me within his arms.

"It's so unreal in person. I never imagined beauty this great."

"I have," he said as he turned to me, catching a lock of hair and placing it behind my ear. He held my ear between his thumb and index finger, massaging it gently, making my cheeks hot and my knees weak. One touch was all I needed to be reminded of the love that could never be broken no matter how far apart or how much time passed.

"It's not fair," I mumbled as I leaned into his touch, closing my eyes and imagining a forever future with him. Like this.

As we stood in the middle of a fairy tale, I wondered if he would kiss me again.

"What are you thinking about?" He leaned on the rail, his full attention on me.

I blushed, dipping my head slightly as my heart raced. His finger hooked my chin, lifting it up. We shared a moment, the forest silencing for us. An eternity could have drifted by, and I wouldn't have cared, because I was suspended in time with the one person I wanted to spend my forever with.

His finger pulled my lips closer to his. His lips were soft on mine as they kissed slowly and released. He did this several times, each touch just a little more intense than the next. He gripped the back of my neck and rested his forehead on mine.

"I love you, Abigail..." He paused.

"But?" My throat dried as fear slithered up my spine.

"I don't know if I can be this for you. I'm afraid."

He caught me off guard. "Afraid?"

"Of losing you," he admitted.

I took a step back and stared into his wounded eyes. "I have to go, Wes, but that doesn't mean you're going to lose me. Nothing they say will ever make me turn my back on you."

"Not because of that, Abby." He shook his head.

I didn't understand at first, but then it dawned on me. My heart cracked, and my soul ripped. "Because you're immortal and I'm not."

He nodded, his whole body distraught from the raw truth that he would outlive me.

I grabbed his face hard. "You can't do that, Wes. You can't think like that. Not now. Not like this. All that matters is now. Do you understand?" I was half-crying and half-shouting because he was trying to pull away even though he promised he wouldn't.

He took me into his arms, rocking me protectively.

"You've put me under your spell, Abigail Rose, and I never want it to be broken. Thinking about the years passing without you is maddening."

Everything he said were fears I had possessed, but instead of fighting the inevitable, I chose to embrace it, and I needed him to do the same.

"I know your life is infinite, and mine is finite, but I'd rather die now than live a lifetime without you."

"You're extraordinary, Abby. Everything about you."

The sun was falling too quickly. I wasn't ready to let Wes go. I had been struggling to tell him the truth about my brother, about being a Chosen, but I feared what he would think of me then.

We crossed the bridge, making our own trail into the forest beyond. Watching Wes hook his hand around tree branches and swing under was breathtaking, like watching a bird nosedive from the sky and pull up effortlessly in one fell swoop. His shirt would lift just a little each time, showing the definition of his muscles beneath.

"Penelope mentioned immortals were marked."

He turned to face me, still walking backward. "We are."

I was expecting him to sound ashamed, but he boasted proudly.

"Where is it?"

He stopped abruptly under the cover of flowering vines hanging from the tall cedar above. He lifted his shirt slowly, exposing his chest and the infinity symbol. It was tattooed over his right peck. I approached him carefully, drawn to him. He stood unmoving as I reached out my hand slowly.

"May I?" I asked permission to touch it.

My fingertips traced it gracefully, Wes' body twitching under my touch.

"Are my hands cold?" I asked quietly.

"The opposite," he teased.

"Right." My hands would feel warm on his cool skin.

I stepped away, and he released his shirt, hiding the symbol once again.

"The sun is setting soon, and we have a long walk back."

"I know," I mumbled sadly.

"You didn't eat. Are you hungry?" He pulled the backpack from his shoulders.

"No." How could I possibly eat right now?

He slid the backpack back on. His fingers slid down to my hand and fluidly interlocked with mine. We silently walked back to the bridge, stopping in the middle again. I rubbed the railing of the bridge. Our bridge now.

Wes pulled out a pocketknife and carved the infinity symbol into the wood, placing an *A* in one circle and a *W* in the other.

"Forever," I whispered as I traced the carving and then placed my hand on his shirt over his mark.

The walk back up the waterfall was emotionally exhausting because every step brought us closer to saying goodbye. The cliff edge came into sight, and my dad was standing at the top waiting for us. Before we were in earshot of him, I turned to Wes.

"Promise me you'll meet me here in exactly one year. On the bridge." My eyes searched his for the answer. "Promise me, Wes."

"Of course, I will, Abby. I will be counting down the days."

I leaned over and kissed him urgently, a tear mixing with our lips, sealing the fate of our last kiss.

He wiped the tear from my cheek.

"I can't believe this is it." I shook my head in disbelief. "We didn't even get a chance," I whined softly.

"We will, " Wes declared, confident.

"Abigail," my dad called down to us.

Wes put the backpack over my shoulders. "This is where I leave you." He brushed his thumb along my cheek.

"I love you," I whisper-cried, wrapping my hand tightly around his head.

"I love you, too."

He pried my hand from him and kissed it, lingering for a moment, and then dropped it and climbed back down the ravine. I looked up to my dad and then back down, but Wes was already gone, leaving a gaping hole in my chest. I climbed the rest of the rocks sobbing uncontrollably. My father held me the whole way back to the car, buckling me in and reclining my seat. He blared the music, giving me as much privacy as possible while my body drained of every last shred of happiness. I didn't know what was worse, crippling fear or debilitating sadness.

26

THE THUMPING OF THE CAR woke me. I put my seat up and looked around. We were driving through another forest, the cedars replaced with Douglas firs.

"Good nap?" my dad asked carefully.

"Yeah. Where are we?"

"Washington. Colville National Forest, to be exact."

"Another hiking adventure?" If only. My heart dipped in my chest thinking about Wes. I knew it was possible that I was merely infatuated with him, being so young, but it hurt just the same.

"Afraid not, Peanut." He looked over remorsefully.

"I didn't figure as much." The road was unmarked, but looked to be heavily traveled over the years. It curved around mountains, teetering on narrow cliffs, finally dropping us off into a valley that was covered in miles of lush greenery. There was so much beauty in the world, and I had only seen a tiny fraction of it. I hoped one day to change that.

The road ended suddenly, right in front of a lake. I looked around, confused. "I hate to break it to you, Dad, but there's nothing here."

He laughed loudly. "You didn't actually think The Order would be assessable by road, did you?"

I sank back in my seat. "I guess not. So you lied when you said no more hiking."

"This is more like a short walk." He winked and then got out of the car.

I grabbed my duffel from the back of the car and slung it over my shoulder, grateful it wasn't too heavy because I hadn't planned on walking through a forest. I had to give credit to my dad, though. We weren't even there yet, and I already felt like I was in paradise. As we followed the lake, laughter became louder. Once we got around a mountain-sized boulder, I saw a group of boys and girls that looked to be close to my age, playing a game of volleyball in the water. I stopped to watch for a moment, the carefree nature of the moment drawing me in.

"They belong to The Order," my dad informed me.

I was surprised, to say the least. Again, I had imagined hard running paths and structured activities. This looked anything but rigid. They actually looked like they were having fun.

"Starting to see why it was so hard for me to leave?"

Yeah, I mentally replied.

As we continued, a massive compound came into view, and it wasn't concrete walls and barbed wire. It was a large white stucco building behind a matching white stucco wall with at least a fifteen-foot-tall, ornate black wrought iron gate. It opened automatically upon our arrival. I looked up and saw a surveillance camera pointing toward us. Two armed guards dressed in black, much like the Elite unit that came to my rescue, stood on either side of the gate. They nodded as we passed by.

"This is the main building. There are more spread out over a hundred acres."

The tall stucco wall expanded out of sight. The grounds in front of the building were expertly manicured with flower planters and water fountains. Kids were strewn about the green lawns, reading under shade trees, while others were grouped together playing music or doing yoga.

"Is this what college looks like?"

My dad laughed again. "Yes, it kind of does."

We followed the flat rock path to a set of large, inviting glass doors to the building. Butterflies scattered throughout my stomach.

"Ready, Peanut?"

"No turning back now." I giggled nervously.

He swung open the doors, waiting for me to pass. A radiant redheaded woman, who looked to be in her sixties, popped her head up from a counter that expanded almost the whole width of the room. It was more sterile inside, but camouflaged with perfectly placed pots complete with tall ornamental trees and flowers.

"James," she shouted wildly as she bounced around the counter with her arms wide.

A huge smile covered my dad's face as he opened his arms to her. "Polly, it's been too long."

She stepped away from his hug and hit him playfully on the chest. "Yes, it has." She set her eyes on me. "And is this Abigail? Oh, my word, she has gotten so big."

Confused as to when we might have met, I forced a smile and replied with my hand out politely, "Hi. I am, indeed, Abigail."

She took my hand in both of hers and shook it as wildly as she had jumped into my dad's arms. Her touch seemed oddly familiar, but I couldn't place it.

"It's so good to finally meet you. Your father showed me pictures of you when you were this big." She put an arm up to my waist. "And look at you now." She wiped a tear from her eye.

This woman was completely off her rocker. I wondered if she knew I was a Chosen. That title weighed on me. What if everyone knew? Would I be scrutinized like a freak by the other kids, or be put on an impossible pedestal? One that I would constantly worry about falling off of? Both sounded equally lonely.

I rocked on my heels uncomfortably.

"We are so happy to have you here." She studied me for

a few more moments and then perked up again. "Well then, let's get started with the tour."

Her dress flats clicked on the marble floor as her long, flowy skirt wrapped around her ankles. We followed casually behind, my worn-out holey red Chucks horribly out of place. I was already feeling self-conscious, and we hadn't even left the front office.

"James, how is that cute little wife of yours?"

My father fell in stride with her as I fell further behind, my feet feeling heavier as we approached another door. This was where I would be living for the next year, and soon my dad would be gone, and I would be left with Positive Polly. I guess it could be worse.

Polly pushed through the doors, giving me my first glance at my new home. All one hundred acres of it. We were at the top, looking down into a vast valley, white stucco buildings sprinkled across the green hills, people everywhere.

"You came at a good time. It's leisure time," she said cheerfully.

I flashed an unsure sideways smile as we followed the path to another white building.

"This is where you will be staying."

The building was marked with the number one.

"All the buildings in the middle are numbered. You move through them numerically throughout your stay."

I looked over at my dad questioningly.

"It's a great system, Peanut. You learn something new in

each building and move on once you've mastered it."

I looked down at all the buildings with renewed anxiety. "How many buildings are there?"

Polly laughed. "Only twelve master buildings. The rest are for recreational purposes."

"Aww," I said sarcastically under my breath. This was nuts.

We went inside building one. It was more sterile than the main building, free of anything. There was a set of elevators in the middle of the room, which was peculiar since this was a one-story building. On either side were two doors that led somewhere else.

We went to the left.

"Girl dorms are on the left, and boys are on the right." She smiled. "Everything else is co-ed."

Fabulous. I thought it curious how nothing was locked. "Everything seems very open."

"The facility is highly secure on the outside, and we would never let anyone in that we felt would compromise the safety of the facility or its guests."

She made it sound like a resort, which I guess from an outsider looking in it could very well be one. A very exclusive one. We passed many doors, all painted red, and stopped at the last one.

"You're very lucky, my dear. The corner room has windows on both sides."

Lucky is not the word I would have used to describe my current situation.

She drew open the door and stepped aside. "I'll wait out here." She waved us in.

My dad walked around the barren room, smiling like a fraternity boy.

"What?" I tossed my duffel onto the twin bed covered in white sheets.

"This was my room in this building."

"Fitting since I'm following in your footsteps, after all."

He walked over to the corner windows. "You have a perfect view of the sunset from here. This was always my favorite building. Being on top of the hill, looking down on everything."

I dropped onto the bed. "You think it would be the opposite."

"What?"

"Most climb up the ladder to success."

He nodded. "Good point."

I stared down at my fingers, picking at them obsessively. My dad sat next to me.

"This isn't a bad thing. I know I made it sound like it at first, but at least here you'll learn how to defend yourself from the Penelopes of the world."

"And the Wes'," I said what he wouldn't.

"I didn't say that."

"You didn't have to." I stood up. "Do you think I'll run into my brother here?"

"Doubtful. He would have gone through the program when he was nine."

"That's pretty young. I mean, where would he go after that?"

"I'm not sure. They didn't want me to maintain a connection with him, fearing it would cloud my judgment. I have to assume they had an Order family foster him."

Things were just not adding up. If they knew I was a Chosen, why would they just trade me for my brother? Unless...

"They thought he was a Chosen, didn't they?"

My dad stood still and seemingly unaffected. "Yes. There's never been a female Chosen, so when it was predicted that your generation of Roses would be the next, they naturally assumed it was your brother."

"Predicted by whom?"

"A Special. Her family has been locating Chosens for over two hundred years. We should get back to Polly."

I could hear the guilt in his voice. Would he have made the same choice had he known I was the Chosen? Handed me over instead of my brother? My life could have been so different.

As we left my new sleeping quarters, I was grateful to see a lock on the doorknob. It was keyless, so I couldn't lock it when I wasn't here, but knowing I could have some sense of privacy in my own space was comforting. We walked back down the hallway, a door swinging open just as we passed. A girl much younger than me with jet-black hair and stark green eyes peered at us shyly, tucking her head down. She was wearing a white terry cloth robe and white flip-flops.

"Jasmine," Polly exclaimed, surprised. "Shouldn't you be at the pool?"

"Oh, yes. I forgot s—something," she stuttered.

"Well, since you're here. This is Abigail Rose. She just arrived."

Jasmine's eyes widened admiringly at the mention of my name, sinking my heart into my stomach. Everyone *did* know.

"It's nice to meet you." I smiled, trying to disguise my own discomfort.

She smiled back and then raced passed us out the door.

"Jasmine just joined us last week. She's the youngest recruit we have had in a long time." She looked to my dad.

Was she referring to my brother or Elijah? "How old is she?" I inquired.

"Thirteen," Polly said proudly.

"She's just a little girl." I shook my head.

"Yes, well, circumstances aren't always as ideal as yours, Miss Rose. You'll need to remember to mind your manners if you want to make friends."

Polly packed a punch, after all. *Ideal?* I'd hate to find out what she considered to be not ideal, because my circumstances were less than stellar.

"We have a few more stops before we say goodbye to your father."

We pressed on, passing by buildings two, three, and four, and entering an unmarked one off to the right, several eyes outside watching us curiously. One pair belonging to Jasmine who was entering a smaller building that must have been the pool.

"That was strange."

"What, my dear?" Polly looked back at me.

"Nothing," I mumbled, afraid of another verbal lashing.

My dad leaned down and whispered, "This is a forbidden building. That's what elicited all the stares. No one goes in here."

"Then why are we?"

"I'm not sure," he replied honestly, which only made me more nervous.

The only thing in the forbidden building was a large elevator, which meant we were going underground since all the buildings were one story.

Polly pressed the only unmarked button, and the doors opened immediately. "After you," she said, holding open the doors.

I stepped inside, but she put her hand out, stopping my dad.

"Not us. We aren't permitted."

I opened my mouth to come to my dad's defense, but he shook his head and winked.

"It's okay, Peanut. I'll see you later."

Polly let the doors close, my whole body losing weightlessness within the lonely confines of the four steel walls around me. There were no buttons to press, but the elevator started descending anyhow. I held onto my dad's reassuring wink. He knew what was down here and would never let me be put in danger's way. I closed my eyes and counted down slowly from ten, concentrating on steadying my breaths. I was beginning to calm down when the elevator stopped and the doors opened.

I came face-to-face with a medical professional in head-to-toe blue scrubs and a white face mask.

"This way, Miss Rose." The woman turned and proceeded down the white hall.

I followed her without a word. She stopped in front of a door marked with the symbol for a woman.

"Please, go in and put on the scrubs. I will wait here."

Now I was officially freaking out. They brought me down here to run tests on me because I was a Chosen. Maybe they didn't really believe it. I knew I didn't.

The bathroom was small and plain. The blue scrubs, booties, and a face mask sat atop a small table in the corner.

I grabbed the scrubs and slid them on over my clothes and shoes. I tucked all my loose strands into the hair cap and put the white fabric face mask over my face. Looking in the mirror, I was as unidentifiable as the woman standing outside waiting for me. A mild panic attack tightened my chest and labored my breathing. Gripping the sink and squeezing my eyes shut, I counted back from ten. After a few deep breaths and a terrifying glance at my reflection,

I opened the door. As promised, the woman was waiting patiently.

"Please refrain from removing any part of your uniform. It's imperative to the health of the patients."

Patients? My pulse quickened. My confusion continued to deepen until we stopped in front of a window and the person on the other side turned to me. Our eyes locked and my breath caught.

"Ho—How is this possible?" I whispered to myself. The realm of possibilities had just blown wide open and swallowed me whole.

"You may go in," the woman said.

I opened the door and approached the bed cautiously. Emerald greens stared back at me, full of vitality. Elijah reached his hand out to my trembling fingers.

"Elijah, I—" I bit my lip, trying to keep it together. "I thought you were—"

"Dead?" the woman's voice finished. "He was."

My eyes followed her as she walked around the bed, positioning herself opposite of me. She seemed nonthreatening before, but now she seemed lethal.

"Are you implying something?" My anger rose as she stole away what should have been a very redeeming moment.

"Do we have to do this now?" Elijah struggled between painful breaths, his face crumpling with the effort.

"Yes, we do," the woman said tartly.

I took Elijah's hand and squeezed it lightly. His eyes begged for forgiveness.

"And why do you think I would have answers if you don't? I am going out on a limb here, but I assume you're a little more versed in otherworldly things than me."

Elijah stifled a laugh. She looked unamused as she walked to a drawer, pulled out a wooden box, and brought it to my side.

"Open it," she challenged, holding it out in both of her hands.

I pulled up the top, and resting atop a red velvet pillow was my infinity charm. I had completely forgotten about it amongst all the chaos.

"My charm. You found it." I reached inside to take it, but she snapped the top closed, almost taking off a few fingertips in the process.

"It's now the property of The Order."

"How do you figure?" My body was heating up.

"Magical objects are forbidden. Since you are new and haven't been introduced to the rules, we are going to let it slide." She lifted up her index finger. "One chance. No more."

Her voice wasn't mean; it was dangerous.

"Ow," Elijah called out.

I looked down at our interlocked hands and realized I was the one causing him discomfort. I loosened my grip quickly.

"I'm sorry. I'm sorry." I stepped in closer to the bed.

"There will be a tribunal hearing tomorrow. Be prepared to supply us with the facts." She looked over to Elijah. "You have ten minutes," she said and then left the room.

"Tribunal hearing?" I was worried.

"Don't worry, Abby. It's not as scary as it sounds, and Miranda's bark is way worse than her bite."

"If it's all the same, I'd rather not find out for myself." I stared out the door, scared she would reappear magically.

"Hey." Elijah shook my hand gently to regain my attention.

"Hey." I smiled warmly. *Elijah was alive.*

"You look tired, Abs." His forehead creased with worry.

"You should look in the mirror." I laughed playfully. "It's been a rough week."

"That it has," he agreed.

"How, Elijah? How are you here? I watched you die, in my arms." The memory flooded back and I shuddered, because for just a split second, I considered having Wes turn him.

"Your charm, Abby. Your charm saved me."

"I had no idea." I shook my head. This was crazy. It was just a charm a little old lady gave me.

"I can see that. You look as surprised as the rest of us."

A thought shot through me like a murderous arrow. "Elijah, you aren't immortal, are you? The charm is the sign of immortality." I was talking fast.

"Abby, calm down. No, I'm not immortal. I promise. Give me your hand."

The panic was choking the life out of me as I reached for his hand again, having dropped it only seconds ago. He took it and pulled me close to his side, making me lean over to reach his chest. He pulled down the sheet, exposing his upper body that was clearly unaffected by his injuries. Blushing, I let him take my hand and place it on his chest. His heartbeat was strong as it pounded against my palm.

The unexpected intimacy had me a little weak and a lot confused. My eyes fixed on his as the beats under my hand pumped regularly, sharing more than just friendship, although lopsided. I could never feel for him what he had admitted feeling for me, but today it was stronger than it had ever been. I pulled my hand away shyly.

"When can I bust you out of this place?" I changed the subject.

He smiled knowingly. "Tomorrow."

My heart fluttered. "Then, if they allow me to, I'll be outside waiting for you."

"Sounds good," he agreed.

His face looked suddenly troubled as he scrubbed his hand across it.

"What is it?"

"I need to tell you something."

"Okay." I gripped my hands around the side rails of his bed.

"Zander's alive, and they have him here."

Penelope's whole purpose the last few years was to get retribution for his murder, and he was here the whole time. Right under her nose.

"Where?"

"There's a building where they keep unruly immortals." He studied me. "You look surprised?"

"I had just assumed immortals were disposed of if they stepped out of line."

"Only ones that are a lost cause. The Order isn't a mob, Abby. Would the world be better off without immortals? Yes, but we also recognize cold-blooded murder when we see it. We aren't about that. We try to rehabilitate, and if that fails..." He trailed off.

"I get it." I was getting a better understanding of The Order, which was somewhat comforting.

"Time's up." Miranda reappeared out of nowhere.

I leaned over and lay on Elijah's chest, mimicking a hug the best I could. He wrapped his arm around my back and squeezed, whispering into my ear so only I could hear, "Be careful at the tribunal. Don't say too much."

He kissed my cheek as I pulled away, searching his eyes for more answers, but he had returned to a smile. I watched him as I walked out of the room with the woman named Miranda. When he was out of sight, I stood tall, restoring the brave front that would help me survive the next year of my life training with The Order of the Crest.

27

WHEN THE ELEVATOR DOOR OPENED, my dad was waiting. I couldn't contain my joy as I bounced to him.

"He's alive, Dad. Elijah's alive." I jumped into his open arms.

He squeezed me tightly and whispered, "I know."

I pulled away quickly, unsure if I should be happy or angry.

"What do you mean you knew? How could you—" He slapped his hand over my mouth and glared at me urgently and then looked to the corner of the room where there was a camera. I nodded, letting him know I understood. He let go and wrapped his arm around my shoulders, pulling me outside.

"Where's Polly?" I shielded my eyes from the sun.

"She had to go back to the main building. Let's take a walk."

He led me down the path between buildings and then off the path around a very large and tall Douglas fir. My dad sat down at the base of the trunk facing away from the facility down into the valley.

"What are we doing here?" I sat next to him.

"There are cameras everywhere. Inside and out. During my time here, I discovered this was a dead zone for surveillance. The only dead zone. We can talk openly here. Just keep it to a low hum." He winked.

"Why would it matter that you knew he was alive?"

"It doesn't in the grand scheme of things, but it could make members suspicious of who is feeding me information."

"I get that, but you saw how much I was hurting?"

He hugged me into his side. "And I hated it, but I took solace knowing you wouldn't be in pain for long. It was just too big of a risk. I'm sorry, Peanut."

I played with my laces. "I know."

"Sometimes lying is a necessary evil to keep our loved ones safe."

"Do you know about the charm and the tribunal meeting?"

"I just learned of it. Unfortunately, I was the last to know. The council runs on an eighty percent majority vote, which equates to ten of the twelve members. They had enough to move forward without me. Polly filled me in."

"Doesn't that make you angry?"

He sighed. "Yes and no. I knew how The Order worked when I accepted my council position. If it were another member, I would have done as they had."

"What's going to happen?" I tapped my foot nervously.

"It's intimidating only because all the council members will be there, including me, only we'll be shrouded in darkness to keep our identities hidden. You will be asked a series of questions, you'll answer them, and then be excused."

I knew my dad wouldn't lie to me, so I felt better about it. "I don't know anything about the charm, so I'm not sure how much help I'll be."

"Where did you get it? I don't remember us buying it for you?"

"Remember when we visited Grandpa when I was six, and Mom took me on the bus through downtown? It was my first time on a bus."

"Of course, I remember. You were so excited when you told me."

"What I didn't tell you was that an older lady who was knitting on the bus stopped me just after Mom got off the bus and put it in my hand. She was so sweet and insisted I have it. I was so little I didn't think anything of it. I tucked it in my pocket and forgot about it until we got home that night. I put it in my jewelry box and that was it."

He leaned forward, resting his arms on his knees. "Huh. That's odd."

"Had I thought anything of it I would have told you sooner."

"I know, but what made you put it on Elijah's chest, and why on earth did you have it with you?"

I was trying to remember why I had dug it out. "It's funny, but I'm not sure why I retrieved it or why I held onto it for all these years. Mom and I were talking about why she started knitting, and it was because of the old lady on the bus. Then I remembered the charm and felt a strong urge to find it. I kept it with me after that." I looked at my palm, remembering the charm and that day. "I knew the symbol was for infinity and the mark of immortality, so grasping at my last shred of hope, I placed it on Elijah's chest. I wanted to believe it would heal him, but I had no idea it actually would."

"If I have learned one thing over the years, it's that there are no coincidences. That woman was put in your path to give you that charm." He scratched at his chin, trying to solve a puzzle with too many missing pieces.

"By whom?" I was so perplexed.

"I don't know, but I'm going to find out. Let's keep this between us. Don't lie at the tribunal if they ask you directly, but skate around it if you can."

"Okay. Do you think they'll ever give it back to me?"

"No, I'm sorry. We've never seen a magical object that can bring someone back from the dead. They won't let it get into the hands of anyone."

"Except the council," I corrected.

"Not even us. It will be locked up after the tribunal tomorrow with all of the council members present, and it will take all of us to retrieve it. We have many fail-safes to prevent things getting into the wrong hands, including council members."

"I feel like everything's moving so fast. A few weeks ago, I was sitting in English class reading Greek mythology, and now I'm here living it." I picked at the hole in my shoe.

"I would hardly call this Greek mythology." He chortled.

"Close enough."

"Yeah, I guess so. I have to go soon, but I'm not leaving the facility until after the tribunal."

"Which building will you be in?"

He stood up and held out his hand to me. I grabbed it, and he swooped me up to my feet.

"I can't tell you, but at least I'll be here for your first night."

I flashed a sympathetic smile for his sake, but the comfort that brought couldn't possibly erase the surmounting fear of my new surroundings. He walked me back to building one, stopping inside the lobby.

"This is you." He gave me a big hug, and if I wasn't mistaken, he choked back tears.

"Glad Mom packed me a few books." My room was empty. No television or stereo.

He laughed loudly. "Trust me when I say after tonight you will be begging for boredom." Now that was a horrifying thought. "Sleep well, Peanut. I'll see you in the morning."

"Night, Dad." The sun hadn't even set yet, but the grounds were clearing. It must be close to dinner, and I was starving.

My dad waited for me to go through the door, and when it closed, a little part of my heart was chipped away. I knew he would be here tomorrow, but then I wouldn't see him or my mom again until the year was up. It almost seemed cruel, but he had told me that distractions were dangerous, and this would allow for 100 percent of my attention to be on the training. I wondered if Elijah would be around for long. *That wouldn't pose as a distraction at all*, I thought sarcastically.

The hallway was quiet until Jasmine's door opened again.

"Hi," she said softly with her eyes on my chin, her silky black strands falling over her shoulders, contrasting her head-to-toe white shirt and pants. They sure liked monochromatic colors here.

"Hey." I stopped and stood awkwardly.

"Do you need someone to show you the dinner hall?" She sounded deflated.

"Yeah, that would be great, considering I'm starving and no one told me where to go."

Her eyes gleamed. "Really? Okay." She closed her door, and we walked back down the hall and outside. She stared at the ground as she led me up the path to the main building.

"I like your shoes," she said honestly.

"Thanks." Her shoes were bright white. "So, what's with the outfit?"

"It's our uniform in building one. You'll find yours in the dresser."

Great. If I wanted a uniform, I would have gone to a private school. I guess I should be grateful it wasn't green plaid.

We walked through large double doors in the back of the main building and were immediately hit with delicious smells. My mouth salivated. Had my eyes been closed, I would have assumed we were the first to arrive, but they weren't closed, and we were most definitely not the first here. All eyes were on me, and I thought I had stumbled into a bag of Skittles, only they were perfectly sorted by color in rainbow order. Kids dressed in white were on the far left. The next table over were dressed in gray, followed by brown, red, orange, yellow, green, blue, turquoise, purple, pink, and black. It was one of the oddest sights. Twilight Zone worthy for sure.

"You'll get used to it," Jasmine whispered.

"What? Everyone staring at me, or the taste of rainbow displayed before me?"

"Welcome." A young man wearing black down to his shoes with red hair stood in front of me. He was tallish with light blue eyes, freckles, and a deep smile. He stood tall and confident.

"Thank you." I looked around uncomfortably, but at

least all the eyes had gone about their business, ignoring me for now.

"Splendid, I see you've met Jasmine. I trust she will show you the ropes. There are only three rules in the dining hall: no talking, eat, and then leave. This is not recreation time. Any questions?" He smiled proudly.

"Nope." I shook my head once.

"Great. Welcome again," he said as he strolled to his table.

Jasmine nudged my shoulder and cocked her head to the buffet line at the front of the hall. She was almost as tall as me, so the only thing giving away her youthfulness was her full cheeks and innocent eyes. Those wouldn't last long. Innocence in a world of immortals was contradictory. I wondered how much she knew about immortals.

There were only a few kids left in line, and we were at the end. There was a miraculous spread of foods from around the world—Italian, Spanish, American, Indian, Chinese, salads, soups, fruit, and breads. The only thing absent was any type of sugar. I would have to ask Jasmine about that later.

As I grabbed a plate and started to fill it, I could feel the eyes on me again. Was my food choice really that interesting? I kept my eyes on my plate, grabbed a pre-made glass of water, the only beverage option, and followed Jasmine to the white table.

Kids finished quickly, clearing their plates and stacking them neatly in the corner of the room. I had barely dug in when the dining hall had practically emptied. I could see why they wanted to get out of here. Eating in complete silence surrounded by at least a hundred people was beyond confining and attributed to my loss in appetite. Jasmine noticed, darting eyes on me and then my food. She was demanding me to eat, and I did, because for her to look that concerned over malnutrition must have meant I needed it.

I cleaned my plate and downed my water, finishing at the same time as Jasmine. We were the last two people to leave the dining hall, and as soon as we stepped out the doors, the lights turned off automatically. We were definitely being watched.

I sweated nervously throughout that whole dining experience, so the cooler air on my sticky skin was inviting.

"So, that was weird," I stated calmly.

"You get used to it. Once someone explained the reasoning to me, I was good with it." Jasmine shyly raised a half-smile.

"And what would that be?"

"It's all about discipline here. They offer many opportunities to be social. In fact, the only time you can't talk is during meals and skills instruction."

That was somewhat reassuring. The sun was setting, but I wasn't tired. I had slept for three days before coming here and had a lot of energy to shed. "Do we have to go to sleep now?"

She giggled. "No. They have movies in that building over there," she said as she pointed to the first building on the perimeter to the left, "and games in the next building down. You can also swim or run the track."

The track ran along the perimeter behind all the buildings.

"All the buildings on the perimeter are for recreation. The twelve buildings in the middle are sleeping quarters and skills training. By color, of course. Everything shuts down at ten. Curfew."

Jasmine seemed genuinely happy telling me everything.

"Who do you hang out with?" I inquired.

"No one. You're the first."

I wasn't entirely surprised, sensing the introvert in her, but it irritated me. This was supposed to be a community. A support system. How could anyone feel safe if they felt like no one had their back?

"Well, I'm honored."

Her eyes lit up. It was a light I used to emit, but I wasn't sure if that would ever return. And because of that, I would swear my life on keeping hers burning bright. She wasn't alone anymore. I would have her back.

"I'm pretty tired, but I'd be happy to show you the rec areas, if you'd like." She yawned widely.

"I'm good, Jasmine. I heard this place is exhausting. I'll see you in the morning."

"Okay, night." She skipped back to our building.

Until I explored every inch of this place, I would be on edge. I walked back to my room, finding two drawers full of white clothes and two pairs of white shoes in the closet. I pitched my clothes into my duffel tucked away in the closet and put my red Chucks carefully on one of the shelves. I outfitted myself as just another white clothed kid in the crowd and took to the track, twilight upon me now. The track below my feet lit up, immediately lighting the way in the dark. *They must have known how clumsy I could be,* I joked to myself. I hated running. I didn't mind walking around Sandpoint, but a pace faster than that was always very unappealing to me. Mainly because the lack of oxygen made me panic. Why would someone purposely make themselves suffocate?

Thanks to the watch that I had found on my dresser, I knew it was nearly eight. I had noticed everyone wearing the same one in the dining hall. It stood out like a sore thumb because it was the only thing that wasn't color-coded. It was silver.

I thought I was alone on the track until a boy in blue with a hood over his head zoomed passed me without a word. His stride was perfect. I used to watch the track and field team practice after school when I was considering trying out, and they all had that same fluid movement. The front foot striking just below the knee, the arms bent at a ninety-degree angle with loose fists, and the back foot pushing off the ground effortlessly. It was breathtaking and something I knew I could never accomplish, so I didn't even try.

The boy was down the hill and out of sight in no time. I continued with my walking pace, checking out each building as I passed. The first building on the perimeter was the one Jasmine pointed to. The walls shook as an action movie of some sort pounded inside. I couldn't see if anyone was actually in there, and I didn't want to stop to investigate.

I reached the next building within a couple of minutes. Everything really was pretty spread apart. The lights were bright inside, and I could see several bodies moving around a pool table, laughter seeping out the open door. I was tempted to see what other games were in there, but I didn't. One night to myself wasn't too much to ask. I had a year of socializing ahead.

I descended the hill to the next building. The lights were on, but it looked and sounded empty, but still I was curious. None of the buildings were marked except for the twelve in the middle. *Skills training*. I wasn't looking forward to my first day, which I assumed would be tomorrow. I walked up to the doors of the building and pressed my face against the glass. I couldn't see anything or anyone.

"The door's unlocked."

I jumped, grabbing my chest and spinning to face the boy in blue. I sucked in a few quick breaths that I had lost.

"I didn't mean to scare you." His voice was familiar, but his hood was shrouding his face.

"How did you get back here so fast?" I had only been walking for maybe fifteen minutes. This place was huge, so if the track stretched around the perimeter, there was no possible way he could have made it all the way around. He must have taken a shortcut.

"I'm a very fast runner."

He peeled back the hood, and I lost my balance. "J—Jack?"

"In the flesh." He winked.

His incessant flirting never ceased. Not even here in the last place I ever thought I would see Kendra's big brother.

"I know you're surprised to see me, but I hope happy, too?"

I still hadn't caught my breath from him scaring me, and this on top of it was wrecking any hope for redemption.

"How can I be happy to see you here? Do your parents know? Kendra?"

"Of course not, Abby."

I was a little bit relieved, knowing that Kendra hadn't been lying to me all those years. "How are you here, Jack?"

"They recruited me when I went abroad."

"Wow. Did you know about me when you returned?"

"Yes. That's why they sent me. They were afraid that Penelope was compromised, so I was sent to strictly observe. I'm sorry I couldn't help you when she took you."

What was happening? Kendra's brother was a member of The Order? I didn't even know what to think anymore. No one seemed to be who they said they were.

"Do you run?"

I realized I hadn't said anything. I chuckled. "No."

"Why not? It's fun. Freeing."

"Only if you mean free to fall on your face. I'm not the most graceful person on the planet."

He laughed. "Yes, I do remember that. That'll change. You'll be all kinds of graceful when they are done with you."

My eyebrows drew down while I contemplated that.

"You're thinking," he observed.

"Yeah? Aren't most people when they aren't speaking?" I didn't mean for it to come out snidely. "I'm sorry. That came out rude."

"It was kind of refreshing. Manners are a huge thing here, so a little sarcasm is appreciated, and yours is always welcome. I miss hanging out with you."

Oh no, this couldn't be real. Jack has had a crush on me forever, and now he was here with me. As flattering as it was, I had enough to deal with at the moment.

"Anyway," he walked backward while speaking, "I'll see you around." He raised a lopsided smile that revealed one of his dimples.

I lifted my hand. "Bye." I waved awkwardly.

When he was out of sight again, I decided to head back to my room even though I still had over an hour before curfew. I didn't want to risk running into Jack again. I needed to process him being here before I said anything stupid.

My building was quiet, and I found it eerie that I hadn't run into anyone else. Were people purposely avoiding me? That seemed a little paranoid until a girl opened her bedroom door and then closed it quickly when she saw me. I was tempted to knock on her door to see what her problem was, but it wasn't worth the effort. Instead, I stopped in front of Jasmine's door, pressing my ear to it. It was silent, so I just kept walking to my room.

Once inside, I locked the door. With how dull my new surroundings were, I didn't see it taking long to fall asleep. I put on pajamas and grabbed a book from my duffel and crawled into bed. The sheets were crisp and probably hospital issued with how uncomfortable they were. I was in the middle of reading *Grimm's Fairy Tales* before all this started. My mom must have seen it on my nightstand. It didn't seem like an ideal genre, all things considered, but maybe it was just what I needed to get my mind off things. *Maybe.*

28

MY CHEST TIGHTENED, AND MY fingers clenched the white sheets as I awoke in my new strange place. I pulled the sheets up close to my chin, waiting for the tremors to pass. The sun was just rising, casting unfamiliar shadows around the room. Deep down I knew I was safe. My door was locked, and I was in a lockdown facility that bred warriors. There wasn't anywhere else in the world that could possibly be more secure, but still my heart raced. And it didn't help when the alarm on my watch blared loudly.

I snatched it up quickly, but my shaky hands dropped it immediately, the alarm still going strong. The alarm that I had not set. I rolled out of bed to recover it, pressing all the buttons frantically to get it to stop. When it stopped, I sat back against the bed. How could I function this early?

Moments later, doors slamming echoed through the hall. I crawled to my door and peeked out. Several white clothed bodies exited the hall quietly. I recognized Jasmine's jet-black hair immediately. "Jasmine," I hissed.

She looked over her shoulder and smiled. "Abigail." She headed back to me. "You're not dressed yet. And why are you sitting on the floor?"

I stood up quickly. "My watch went nuts."

She laughed. "That's the morning alarm. You really should hurry and get dressed." She looked down at her watch. "Lineup is in three minutes, and you don't want to be late. Trust me."

Spoken like someone with shamed experience.

"Okay. Go. I don't want you to be late on my account."

She raced out the door. In a flurry, I threw on my white clothes, socks, and shoes, and fixed the knot my hair had fallen out of overnight. Vanity must have been unacceptable, because I hadn't seen a mirror since I got here except for in the infirmary bathroom. I ran across the hall with my toothbrush and quickly brushed my teeth in the bathroom. I ran back to my room, tossed the toothbrush onto my dresser, and ran out the door. I silently cursed myself for not grabbing the sweatshirt, as the chill bit at my skin. I rubbed my arms for warmth and then raced over to where the line of white clothed kids stood straight and still. I stepped in line next to Jasmine.

"You just made it." She turned to give me a quick smile.

When I looked up, I saw a rainbow of colors all the way

down the hill. Each set of kids standing tall with their hands by their sides. They all stood in a horizontal line on the side of their building.

I did as the others, not knowing what to expect. Jack walked out from the cover of our building, only he wasn't wearing blue. He was wearing black. He held his poker face as he made eye contact with me on his way down the line, inspecting everyone. I was thoroughly confused.

He walked back to the center. No one breathed. Or at least it seemed that way. I could hear a pin drop.

"Abigail Rose," he called.

I didn't know what to do. "Umm, yeah?"

A wave of movement traveled down the line of kids.

Jasmine whispered through the side of her mouth, "You're supposed to just step forward."

"Oh." I stepped forward. "Sorry."

Jack walked over and stood in front of me. As hard as he was trying to keep his poker face, I could see a shimmer of humor in his eyes.

"You're to report to the main building."

"Okay." I stood unmoving.

"Now, Miss Rose."

"Oh." I bounced. When I looked down the line, the kids were stifling giggles. "See you later then, I guess?" I saluted Jack and then jogged up the path to the main building. I stole a quick glance back and caught Jack watching me with an amused expression. This was going to make for one interesting year.

As soon as I reached the doors to the building, I slowed down to a snail's pace, my courage depleting. I tried to remember that my dad would be at the tribunal meeting even if I couldn't see him. I wouldn't be alone. *I can do this.* I took in a deep breath and pulled open the door. Polly greeted me enthusiastically.

"Abigail, you made it, and you're just in time."

She made it sound like I was going to a bake off. I wished. Sampling desserts would have been way better than this.

I smiled condescendingly. "Yep, I'm here."

She made her way around the counter and started walking to the door opposite the one we went through to get to the infirmary. She stopped at the door and turned to me.

"Well, come on. We don't want to keep them waiting."

This was it. It felt like I was on trial for a murder I didn't commit. I focused on Polly's long, flowy skirt. Today it was a dark blue with a bright floral pattern.

There was an elevator just like on the other side of the room. She pushed the button, humming softly. Normally, I would have welcomed the distraction, but what she hummed stalled my heart. It was the song from my jewelry box, and she hummed it exactly like my mom.

"Where did you hear that song?" My voice was cracking.

The elevator door opened. "Good luck." She winked, leaving my question hanging, unanswered and unacknowledged.

I stepped inside, and the doors closed immediately.

Polly's eyes fixated on me until the doors swallowed me. There weren't any numbers to tell me how far I was descending, but it was definitely farther down than the infirmary. I was relieved when it finally stopped, and I was met with Elijah's green eyes when the doors opened.

"Elijah," I squealed and jumped into his arms, sinking into the comfort of his presence, the stress melting away. His body shook as he laughed and hugged me back. "What are you doing here?"

"I was the one you raised from the dead." He flashed his heartwarming smile again.

I snuggled my head into his chest. He smelled like a hint of freshly washed skin and light musk. "Is this really happening?"

He rubbed my back gently and rested his cheek on my head. "I'm here, Abby. I told you I would never leave you, and I meant it."

His unconditional devotion to me was awe-inspiring. My dad was a great judge of character and had helped raise Elijah into an extraordinary young man.

"We need to get going, but I won't leave your side." He took my face in his hands. "We're in this together."

His hands slid down, interlacing one with mine and leading me down a narrow white hallway. "You look good in white," he teased.

"Wait until you see me in red," I joked.

"I'm looking forward to it." He squeezed my hand.

Was he hinting at being here during my training? I

hoped so. I would wish upon every star that flew across the sky if it meant I wouldn't be here alone.

The hallway spilled into one giant space. There was a spotlight in the middle of the room while darkness flowed out into the perimeter, making it impossible to see how large the room actually was.

"Step forward." I heard my dad's voice call from the center.

Elijah and I did as instructed, still holding hands, my heart beating fiercely against my chest. Once we were in the circle, low lights lit the rest of the room. I could make out twelve figures hidden within the shadows. They were raised on a balcony above us.

"This is an informal tribunal meeting for informational gathering purposes only. Do you understand?"

I nodded. "Yes."

"Yes," Elijah said confidently.

A woman's voice spoke up from the left, "Abigail Rose, do you deny saving Elijah's life?"

The voice sounded a lot like Miranda's voice from the infirmary. "No."

Keep it short and simple. Don't give away too much.

To the right, a man's voice asked the next question, "Where did you find the charm that saved Elijah's life?"

I focused on steadying my heart. "On a bus." Elijah caressed the top of my hand with his thumb, a show of support.

And yet a different voice tossed out the next question. "When?"

I searched the darkness, trying to ascertain where to speak. "When I was six. I can't remember exactly when, though."

"It was July," my dad interrupted.

I was grateful for his intervention.

"Go on," the same man who had asked the question pressed my dad.

"It was our first visit to Seattle and her first bus ride. She was with her mother."

The room went silent. Were they questioning my dad's truthfulness? My palm within Elijah's was sweating.

"Abigail, did you have reason to believe prior to Elijah's resurrection that the charm held any magical properties?"

Each council member was sharing in the questioning. It gave me a chance to bank their voices if I ever came face-to-face with one of them. I now knew my dad and Miranda were members, although I wouldn't recognize Miranda by face since she was completely shrouded by her scrubs.

"No."

"So, then what made you place it on Elijah's wound?"

That was a great question. One I couldn't answer definitively. "I…I don't know. Instinct, I guess."

Several gasps came from the balcony and then hurried inaudible whispers.

"What's happening?" I turned to Elijah.

"I don't know." Concern plagued him.

A shuffling sound from the floor off to the far right garnered mine and Elijah's attention. Another spotlight popped on, encapsulating Penelope with shackles around her wrists and ankles. She looked disheveled and dazed. She barely even glanced our way.

"What is she doing here?" my father shouted venomously. "This is not a trial."

I was startled at the harshness in his voice. I had never heard him that way.

"Sit down, James. We didn't need your vote. It was unanimous amongst the rest."

What was unanimous? I squeezed Elijah's hand hard, fearing the worst. If they went behind my dad's back, it had to be bad.

"I demand to know what is going on," Elijah said boldly as he took me into his arms protectively.

I couldn't peel my eyes from Penelope. I actually felt bad for her.

"You don't demand the council," Miranda's voice snapped.

"Enough," another council member boomed.

The room went silent again until Penelope laughed wildly.

"Silence!" My dad's voice broke through the darkness. "While I don't approve, let's get on with it."

The line of questioning continued.

"Is this the woman who kidnapped you?"

"Yes."

"Did you see the woman in question throw the fatal dagger at Elijah?"

"Yes."

"Did you know the woman in question before you were kidnapped?"

"Yes."

"How?"

I was fairly certain they knew the answers to all these questions. "At Sandpoint Bistro. We both worked there."

"Were you friends?"

"No. We barely said more than three words to each other." Elijah squeezed me gently. I turned to him, hoping this would end soon. I locked my eyes on Elijah's.

"Mr. Winters?"

"Yes," Elijah responded.

A sigh of relief washed over me when the tables turned, but it was of little comfort because it was at the expense of someone I had recently become very close to.

Penelope was barely able to stand at this point. She had weakened in the short days she was apprehended, but she stood unmoving. *Obedient.* What were they doing to her?

"Is the woman in question guilty of your murder?"

He chuckled. "If she were, I wouldn't be standing here."

Miranda's voice challenged him. "On the contrary. When you were brought here, you were deceased. All your body functions had shut down, and you registered no brain activity."

"Semantics. I'm here, aren't I?"

I didn't know what was happening, but Elijah's body language had shifted from relaxed to agitated, and his grip on me was tense. I wished that my dad would speak up again, but he didn't. We were being baited. I could feel it.

"Mr. Winters, how would you sentence the woman in question?"

What? I looked to Penelope and back at Elijah. Penelope seemed unaffected by the sudden turn of events, and Elijah looked angry. He was holding his breath, and his face was turning a dark shade of red.

"I wouldn't. I'm alive. She's done me no harm."

For Elijah to be defending Penelope meant that something unfathomable would come of her if he had demanded justice. Penelope managed a curious glance our way.

"Miss Rose?"

The hairs on the back of my neck stood on end. They were looking to place blame on someone other than the council for whatever fate they had planned for Penelope.

"Miss Rose, how would you sentence the woman in question?"

I was surprised at how angry I was getting. After all, Penelope did kidnap me and kill Elijah. She was far from innocent, but I also knew she was a victim of her own tortured existence, thinking her only connection to the world was murdered by The Order. Only he wasn't, and she had no idea. She needed to know.

"Miss Rose?" a council member spoke loudly and impatiently.

"Her name is Penelope, and I won't be your scapegoat for her conviction. She believes her brother's murder is on your hands and did what many others would do in her position. She sought answers." My voice was shaky and fueled with adrenaline.

"She sought vengeance," Miranda spat.

"Retribution," I countered.

Penelope stayed quiet as her fate was being argued in front of her.

"She's guilty of treason," another member said matter-of-factly.

"What century are we in? Treason? Really? Why don't you tell her the truth?" I yelled defiantly.

The room was silent again. I looked over at Penelope's confused expression.

"Go on. Tell her about her brother."

"That will be enough, Miss Rose." The voices were beginning to blend as my anger guided my quest for resolution.

"She deserves the truth. Had she known Zander was still alive, she would never have come after me, and Elijah wouldn't have been hurt." A thought caught in my throat. *An instinct.* What if Penelope was the scapegoat? What if they wanted Elijah dead and I had spoiled their plan?

An agonizing wail came from Penelope who had collapsed.

"I think we're done here," my dad finally spoke up.

Elijah pulled me out of the spotlight, dragging me out of the room as I watched Penelope's reality be ripped to shreds as she lay on the cold floor, alone.

Elijah whispered, "We can't help her, Abs. I'm sorry."

My heart broke for her. Even after all she had done, I knew I was capable of going to such lengths to avenge a loved one's death. Everyone was. It wasn't fair that she was pushed to the edge under false pretenses, and now that the veil was lifted, she had to live with the consequences of her actions. She had to find a way to forgive herself.

I yanked my hand from Elijah's and stepped back into the room.

"I forgive you, Penelope."

She lifted her head, searching for me in the darkness. I went back to the spotlight so she could see me. Tears filled her eyes as she made eye contact, and then the room went black. A hand grabbed mine and pulled me into the bright hallway.

"Abby, what are you doing?" my dad seethed. "You're putting your life in danger."

"Am I, Dad? I am a Chosen, after all," I said sarcastically.

"Don't do this, Abigail. They are on your side, but if you push them…" He stopped.

"What, Dad? Finish what you were going to say." I couldn't shake the fury that was building within me.

He sighed apologetically. "Abigail, I know what they did in there didn't seem fair, but Penelope is not an innocent.

She essentially murdered Elijah, and her intentions with you weren't much better. I understand she may have chosen a different path if she had known her brother was alive, but maybe not, because if she had known, then she would have also known he was here. In captivity."

I tried to find a way to argue, but I couldn't. She probably wouldn't have done anything differently, but there was still that small possibility, and I saw whom she was when I was with her. She wasn't just some crazy sociopath. She was hurting.

"I won't condemn her, Dad. And neither will Elijah."

He placed his hands on my shoulder and rubbed them lightly. "I know, and you two have made me very proud."

"What will they do to her?"

"Keep her here."

Elijah was observing quietly a few feet away.

"For how long?" She looked like she was on death's door already.

"Forever. They'll try rehabilitation, but it's doubtful they'll ever trust her again, and that makes her a liability."

The thought sank in slowly like feet trapped in quicksand. I ran through all the moments that would define the rest of her life. A prisoner with a life sentence and no chance of parole.

"That's awful."

"It is, but she understood what the consequences were when she joined The Order if she betrayed them. She could have walked away just like she could have chosen not to kidnap you. The life as a member of The Order of the Crest is a choice, Abigail. I know it doesn't seem like it, and it might be under a stronghold, but if you really wanted out, they would let you, although you'll always be watched in some way or another."

I shook my head. "No, I don't believe it. Not with me, at least. Not if they really believe I am a Chosen for this generation. I never had a choice, and I think we both know that."

And my dad did. That was why he was trying to keep my gift a secret. But the secret was out because of my grandpa, and my fate was paved down a path unchosen.

"I'm sorry," I said, regretting my tone. This was the last time I would see my dad for a year, and I didn't want him to leave like this.

"No, I am. I should have seen this coming. At the very least, I should have prepared you for all the possible scenarios."

"Are they going to punish me?"

"I don't think so. This is a big change for you. They may be council members, but they're also human. They have families and feelings. Desperate times call for desperate measures."

Elijah interjected, "We should take this conversation somewhere else."

"Probably a good idea."

Desperate times?

Silence fell between us as we took the elevator up and

out to the main lobby. Polly was nowhere to be found, thankfully. I didn't think any of us could take her level of enthusiasm right now, but then just as we were exiting the building, Polly's voice stopped us.

"James?" Her voice was serious and monotone.

"I'll be right back," he assured me.

I watched as Polly and my dad stood close, whispering. Reading his expression, he wasn't happy and neither was Polly, although she seemed to feel bad for being the messenger of what had to have been bad news. Then she hugged him, my dad comforting her rather than the other way around, and sauntered back to us. Polly wiped her cheeks and then took her post behind the counter again.

"What was that all about?" I asked nervously.

"Let's go to the tree."

He took my elbow and led me out gently. We walked down the path between the buildings and stood at the tree without surveillance.

"So?" Elijah said before I could.

"They are taking a vote to remove me from my seat on the council."

"What?" I shouted. "That's not fair."

"Abigail, calm down. They're pissed how the tribunal went. They wanted answers, and they didn't get any. They are blaming me."

"I answered all of their questions."

"Yes, but all of those they knew. They needed them on

record. They wanted more answers about the charm, like who gave it to you."

"But I didn't know the old woman. I can't even remember what she looked like. The memory is a blur."

"They also wanted to see Penelope punished, but they can't if you two won't convict her. Bottom line is, they're mad, but they'll get over it. I am close with many of the council members, and I doubt they'll turn their back on me. Honestly, at another time I would have welcomed this, but now that you're here, I will make sure my position is secured. Don't worry."

But I was worried. I was terrified. If they expelled my father from The Order, I would be alone.

"When are they voting?" Elijah asked.

"Now."

My stomach hurt, butterflies traveling up to my throat. My dad wrapped me up close to him and rocked me. "They're going to be watching you very closely this year. They suspect you're a Chosen, but they want proof."

"And what if I'm not?"

"Then I'll be glad."

I looked up at his scruffy chin, confused. "Why?"

"Being a Chosen puts a bigger target on your back. You'll be more powerful than anyone here, and I don't mean strength. You'll be wise." He tapped my forehead.

"What happened to the last Chosen? Penelope said there's only one at a time."

He shared a knowing glance with Elijah, making my stomach flip. *He was dead.*

Polly surprised us. "It's time." She forced a weak smile. "Thanks, Polly."

My dad grabbed my arms with conviction burning in his eyes. "No matter what happens, I will not leave you. I know all their secrets. And Elijah will be here with you." He hugged me again. "I love you, Peanut."

"I love you, too."

He released me and then held out his hand to Elijah and shook it vigorously. "Take care of her."

"You have my word," Elijah promised.

He smiled bravely one last time before he made his way up the path to the main lobby where Polly stood out front, waiting.

"It'll be okay, Abby."

Elijah put his arm around my shoulders, holding me close to his side. Everything wasn't going to be fine and I knew that, because that was what my instincts were telling me, and I was listening intently.

29

I REFUSED TO GO BACK TO MY building. Instead, I paced in the lobby of the main building, waiting for my dad to reappear. Time passed so slowly that one minute felt like ten. I asked Elijah what time it was every few minutes, and while I would have lost my mind if someone did that to me, he would answer patiently each time. What could be taking so long? They had been in there for over an hour, and Polly had abandoned her post.

When the click of the door opening finally echoed in the lobby, my heart sank as I saw Polly's face. Tears rolled down her face. She was followed closely by Jack, who was dressed in all black still. *An Elite member.* Then my dad came into view, followed by another Elite member dressed in black. I ran up to them.

"Dad? What's happening?" Panic filled my voice. His apologetic eyes said it all. "No. They can't do this." I passed Polly, but Jack stopped me.

"Step aside," he said coldly.

"No," I refused and punched him in the gut. He was unfazed by my weak attempt.

A pair of hands grabbed ahold of my arms from behind and held me back. I glanced over my shoulder, surprised Elijah was the one holding me. "Let go," I screamed as tears rolled down my face and my heart pounded in my ears.

"Stand down," Jack commanded.

I felt like I barely knew him anymore. The Jack I grew up with would never have betrayed me like this. "Dad?" If hearts could shatter, mine would.

"I'm sorry, Peanut." He shook his head, defeated.

"How could they do this?" I fought against Elijah's hold. "Let go of me." Yanking only made his grip tighten. Polly was holding the doors as Jack led my father out. I refused to let my dad leave like this. I bent down and bit Elijah's hand hard, breaking his skin. The pain forced him to let go, and I ran toward my dad. Jack tried to stop me again, but this time I crouched under his arm and punched him where it hurts. He crumpled briefly, giving me a chance to hop into my dad's arms before the other Elite member could interfere.

"Please, don't leave me here, Dad. Take me with you. I can't do this without you." He held me tightly.

"Remember everything I told you and trust no one.

Stay close to Elijah." His voice lowered. "Find your brother. Bring him home."

Jack's arms wrapped around my waist, tugging me violently. I tried to keep my hold around my dad's neck, but he reached up and pulled my fingers away.

"There's no sense in fighting, Peanut."

He released my grip on him. "I love you." Jack grabbed ahold of me. "I'll see you soon," he said as he walked out, Jack restraining me against his chest. When my dad was gone, I wiggled violently in Jack's arms.

"Let her go," Elijah commanded, coming face-to-face with him.

"Yes, sir."

Jack let go, and I fell to the floor, my strength weakened and my will broken. They left me crying on the floor. To mourn for my dad. But what they didn't know was the vengeance Penelope had felt was now boiling in my blood. The Order would regret shaming my dad. I would train hard, and if I were a Chosen, I would make them pay.

Elijah crouched next to me, scooping me in his arms and lifting me up. My head fell on his chest, and I closed my eyes. I was completely drained, and all I wanted to do was sleep.

A memory infiltrated my sadness.

"Hold on, Abigail. I'm getting you to help." Elijah's voice was desperate.

My body hurt all over, and those horrifying iridescent eyes were branded in my mind. I looked up to my rescuer, a stranger, but one who knew my name. Shaggy blond hair covered his ear, and his face was tight with concern as he raced forward. He glanced down for just a second, his bright green eyes captivating me before I blacked out.

The sun was hot on my skin as Elijah carried me from the building. I shifted in his arms when he balanced me to open doors, and then I heard a voice I didn't recognize.

"Hey, you can't be in here. Girls only."

Elijah ignored her and then opened another door. I finally cracked my eyes open when he put me down on my bed, kneeling in front of me so he was eye level. I watched his green eyes reflect my pain as he carefully pushed strands of hair off my face, his thumb rubbing my temple gently.

"I'm here, Abby."

My chest crumpled as tears surfaced. "You tried to keep me from saying goodbye," I gritted through my teeth angrily.

"If I didn't, they would have, and I'm their commander. If The Order is going to let me keep my position, I have to show I'm still in control. I'm sorry, but I can't risk them voting me off the island, too." He smirked.

I allowed a small smile for his attempt at cheering me up. "Why would they do that?"

"It was a power play. If they control your father's fate, they assume they control yours. Like your dad said, they are desperate for answers and control. Ever since the last Chosen was murdered, they have lost control of the immortals."

Nausea rose with a new kind of terror. *I was a target.*

Elijah continued, "More and more are rebelling, and humans are either being killed or turned. There is a war brewing, Abigail, and they need to know if you're the new Chosen, and if you are, they have to secure your allegiance."

"By kicking my dad off the council? That's a way to guarantee my rebellion." I scoffed venomously.

"They are afraid he will let his love for you cloud your mission. I don't agree with how they went about it, but I can't argue their logic. Not if it means your safety is in jeopardy."

His hand slid down my cheek and hooked my chin, his thumb caressing my cheek now, sensations numbing the pain, and desperation begging for comfort no matter what form it came in and no matter who projected it.

"My dad would never put me in danger."

"Not on purpose, but an unconditional love such as that makes people do crazy things."

"And what about you?" I locked my hazel eyes with his sea of green. I knew he cared for me. How deep it went I wasn't entirely sure of, but it was there, and it was strong. I could feel it flow through his touch.

"For now, that will remain our little secret," he whispered, leaning in.

His lips hovered in front of mine, waiting. Waiting for permission? Waiting for me? My emotional state was frenzied, and my loneliness was insurmountable. I needed to feel something else even for just this one time. I pressed against his lips, entangling my fingers in his hair, pulling him tight to me. He pressed back and took my cheeks in his hands, lifting me up to a sitting position, his passion helping me lose myself in the moment. His lips were warm, his touch causing my heart to flutter and raising goose bumps on my arms.

My guilt finally pushed me away from him. "I love Wes," I said simply, needing to reinforce it even though my actions were proving the opposite.

"And I love you," he said truthfully. "Quite a predicament." He smiled as he brushed his hand over my cheek.

"Yes, quite." Moments like this conflicted my heart and made me question my choices, but Wes had always been my forever, and nothing would change that. "So, what do we do?"

"*We* go about business as usual. Use that anger as fuel to become what you're destined to be, Abigail. Extraordinary."

I teased, "I thought I already was?"

He stood up. "I'll make sure you have a free pass today, but tomorrow you have to be on your game. They won't let you lose control. This place is about proving to yourself that you can make a difference. You have nothing to prove to them."

"Thanks, Elijah. I don't think I would survive this without you here."

"The feeling's mutual."

He took my hand and placed something cold and smooth in my palm. It was the infinity charm.

"How—" I couldn't believe what I was holding.

"Stealth is only one of several things you will master here." He smiled mischievously.

"But they'll know it's missing." I shuddered to think what they would do to Elijah if they found out.

"I replaced it with a fake. They'll never know." He paused. "That charm belongs to you, and I believe it's only worth a damn if *you* have it. I don't believe in coincidences, so if that was meant to keep you safe, I'm not taking any chances."

I squeezed my palm shut around it. "Elijah, thank you."

"Keep it hidden, Abby. Don't leave it where they can find it. They search these rooms all the time."

"I won't."

"I have to go, but if you need anything, let me know."

I jumped off the bed and wrapped my arms around his neck, inhaling a deep breath and relishing in the comfort he offered unconditionally. He wrapped his arms around my waist and lifted me up.

"You know we can't do this out there, right?" he joked as he put me back down.

I laughed lightly. "I know."

"I'll see you later, Abs." He kissed my forehead and left.

I locked the door immediately, staring at the charm. Where was I going to hide it? I looked around the room for a spot, but there were only a dresser and a nightstand. They would surely search those. I heaved open the closet door, my dirty and worn red Chucks staring back at me. They would never touch those. I pulled them out and sat on the floor. The fabric inside one of the shoes was lifting, making the perfect hiding place for the charm. I lifted the fabric and slid the charm all the way underneath to the toe where I had hidden my grandpa's key. The fabric was still a little sticky from the glue, so I pressed the fabric down hard, concealing and securing the charm. They would never find it there.

I put the shoes back on the shelf and closed the closet door. I slid under the sheets. Today I would rest, but tomorrow I would train. This was going to be the longest year of my life, but I would come out on the other side stronger, wiser, and back in the arms of Wes.

I stared out the window and watched the stores pass by, my little, six-year-old fingers splayed on the glass excitedly. I had never been on a bus before. I bounced in my seat, free from a seat belt.

"Sweetie, sit down, please."

I was sitting up on my knees so I could see everything. I slid back down, kicking my legs excitedly as they hung well above the bus floor.

The bus stopped, and my mom stood up, holding her hand out for mine. "This is our stop."

I took it eagerly, jumping off the seat and hugging to her side tightly as we waited for other riders to pass by. When it was our turn, my mom pushed me behind her to navigate the narrow walkway. The older woman who was knitting behind the driver's seat during the ride smiled widely, stopping me as my mom and I waited in line to get off the bus.

"Aren't you a pretty thing?" she said as she put her knitting down on her lap.

"Thank you." I giggled. Her eyes were a crystal blue, and her cheeks were rosy, some wrinkles settling into her face.

She dug her hand into the pocket of her dress and held out a closed fist to me.

"Can I see your hand, dear?"

I trusted her kind eyes, so I put out my hand. She flipped it over and placed a charm in my palm. Her hands felt cool and soft.

"For me?" My little heart was happy at the unexpected gift.

"For you," she confirmed. "Keep it safe, for you never know when you'll need it."

I stared at the shiny, round metal. "Thank you."

My mom moved forward. "I have to go."

The woman clenched both of my hands tightly, her mood shifting from carefree to intense. "Life is infinite," she said passionately.

"Come on, Abigail," my mom summoned.

I smiled uncomfortably, and then the woman released my hands. "Until we meet again, Abigail." She winked.

I sat up in bed, my heart racing and my whole body shaking. Polly was the old woman on the bus.

Here's a sneak peek at
MIDNIGHT WINTERS,
the highly anticipated sequel to *Midnight Rose*.

ELIJAH

ER SADNESS COULD FILL A hundred buckets and still overflow, seeping into the hollows of my heart. That kiss, as desperate as it was, loosened The Order's noose around my neck, but also solidified the suffocating darkness I would travel to free myself from the hell that has been my life ever since Abigail Rose fell into my arms. When I had turned from the closed door that shrouded her pain in secrecy, a young girl with jet black hair peered at me with an odd look. I thought she looked familiar, but it was hard to remember all the recruits. They had become an army of faceless warriors, but this one pierced me with accusatory eyes. Did she know what I was guilty of? What I was? Impossible. She was just a kid sucked into an endless battle at the wrong time. I felt sorry for her. For all of them. They signed on thinking they had a chance. That they were fighting for the greater good, but those lines had crossed, tangled, and intertwined so many times that the path had been all but erased and there were no absolutes anymore. Good or bad. Wrong or right. They floated in between here and there and swirled with doubt, confusing me. What side would I land on?

I slammed my fist into the punching bag again, feeling the satisfaction vibrate under my skin, sweat dripping off my skin like a fresh downpour. That kiss flashed between impacts, her translucent hazel eyes punching back, each time crashing against my soul.

Lies upon lies, the truth so hard to see anymore. And that kiss making it harder. She was supposed to be just an assignment. A repaid debt and then back into hiding, but I dug my grave deeper instead and the fall into it would be infinite. All my regrets would descend beside me, taunting me, telling me I should have turned away when I had a chance. Now I would end up like Penelope in the end. The noose pulled taut until I broke. Choose my life over hers. And I knew what I would do. It's what chained me to The Order once again. To protect her. To die for her if it came to that.

The bag swayed with another punch.

I unwrapped my hands, my knuckles still cracking under the pressure of my anger. Abigail was on to something with Penelope and her brother, but I knew the truth. I knew why

Penelope wanted me dead. I was the reason her brother was in that prison. I had tracked him for The Order. I took pleasure in it. Every single one of those monsters bore the face of the one that had taken my mother. I would have killed them all if I could, but The Order liked to collect them and I knew better than to ask questions. Only The Order had lied to me. Zander wasn't just any monster. I could feel it. He was different, but it was too late. He was immortal.

The hot water felt good on my sore muscles as I washed off in the locker room. I had been training hard since Abigail decided to come here. I knew I would need to be in prime shape if either of us stood a chance. I cranked up the heat, leaning into the shower wall as it stung my skin, hundreds of needles puncturing the sensitivity I had developed from Abigail. My love for her might just be my undoing.

I needed to make a formal request to be Abby's partner and I needed to play it smart. Carefully craft every word I spoke. They could deny me because of our connection, which we made apparent at the tribunal. But if I could make them see that as an asset rather than a hindrance, then they might favor me by her side knowing I would do anything to protect her. Everything hinges on Abigail's abilities. I remembered studying the prophecies of the Visionary when I was a Potential, and it mentioned that there would be one that would be above all others. A person who would encompass everything and everyone. A true weapon against immortals. No one suspected it would be a girl. In history past, Chosens had all been males. Strong and agile.

DANI HART

From what I had seen of Abigail, she was off balance and frail. The Order still questioned if she truly was a Chosen, and they would go to extreme lengths to prove it without a doubt. Knowing what tests she would undergo, made my muscles tighten. I could protect her out there, but not in here. We were at the mercy of The Order's discretion. If Abigail was not the Chosen, she wouldn't survive what The Order had in store for her. Only the Chosen could endure the final trial. For The Order's sake, she better be the Chosen or my wrath would bring an end to their empire.

I slipped out of my building, a temporary housing unit for members between missions, tucked at the bottom of the hill behind building twelve. It was unmarked and, therefore, off limits to anyone else. It was one of the very few buildings using fingerprint technology, and only when you were expected would your fingerprint be active. It was almost curfew for the recruits, so it was dark and quiet on the grounds. Jack was running the track just as he seemed to do every night. Jack was itching to go on missions, but I knew he didn't have what it took to be in the field. The Order had recruited him because of his connection to Abigail, not because he garnered any gifts. He was smart, and The Order planned on him training him as a field doctor. No actual combat. Just a man in waiting should one of us fall.

Jogging up the hill, I entered the main building where a new receptionist had replaced Polly. Tawny was younger and very pretty, but didn't exude the warmth that Polly had. I was angry that The Order had removed Polly after

Abigail's father had been exiled. I tried to plead for her, but in the end, they knew she could be a liability around Abigail because of her connection to the Rose family.

"Mr. Winters, they are ready." Tawny stood up and smiled demurely.

"Thanks," I gruffed, ignoring her subtle advance.

As we approached the door that sealed Penelope's fate at the tribunal, my fists clenched. I had always hated The Order, but being back in this room would push me to my limits.

Tawny pressed her thumbprint on the keypad and held the door open as I passed through. Her perfume made me nauseous, and only after she closed the door did I inhale. The elevator chimed, and I stepped in, counting the seconds it took to get to the basement. I wanted to memorize every damn inch of this place.

I walked the infamous hall, noting there were no rooms to explore. There were two vents in the hallway, and the return was by the elevator. The crawl space would be small, but Abigail could fit. My fingers twitched looking for Abigail's hand as I stepped into the tribunal room, taken aback by the sudden wave of disappointment that rushed through me at her absence. I rubbed the emptiness from my hand and walked into the spotlight.

"Good evening, Mr. Winters," One of the silhouettes off to the right announced.

I tried to memorize the cadence and pitch of each word he spoke, picturing a stocky man in his fifties. They didn't know my gift stretched into sound waves. James kept it between us as he trained me relentlessly on it. Soundwaves reverberated around the source, making an outline of colors. The details were absent, such as clothing, but the shapes pulsed vividly.

"What matter is so urgent that you needed an immediate presence?" The man asked curtly.

His eyebrows fell inward. His voice had stayed even, but his body language told a different story. He was annoyed. "I'd like to request that I partner with Abigail as she goes through the buildings." Silence was followed by hushed whispers.

"And why is that?" a plump older woman asked.

"I know her weaknesses better than anyone. I can help break her of them."

"But you care for her," another woman, young and petite, commented.

I continued to catalog each council member carefully. "I have been tracking Abigail for three years now. I know everything there is to know about her. Her enemies. Her friends. I can make her stronger."

Silence again and then more whispers.

"Do you think you have the ability to make her hate the one thing she loves most?"

The question rubbed like coarse sandpaper against my chest. *Wes.* He is what they wanted most. For her to hate him and his family, because then they knew she was capable of destroying all of the non-humans if she had a good enough reason to. If her heart turned against them.

"Without a doubt," I answered confidently.

More whispers. This time, I followed the soundwaves around the balcony, each shape manifesting dimly. None of them stood out physically, except for one man. He was taller than the rest and thin. I could pick him out of a crowd.

"We have voted, and your request has been granted, under one condition."

I gnashed my teeth together. Another debt to be paid, but wasn't Abigail worth it?

"You must bring in Wes Hunter, immediately."

A low rumble hummed in my chest, and the cracks on my knuckles bled as I squeezed my fists closed. Abigail would hate me if she ever found out. She would never forgive me. And that's exactly what The Order wanted. They wanted her to hate us both, so she wouldn't hesitate when they asked her to choose them above all else.

"Mr. Winters?" The stocky, older council member who started the tribunal pressed.

"Fine," I bit out and then left.

I stormed out of the elevator, full of rage. My eyes were burning, and my head felt as if it were going to explode. I knew it wouldn't be easy. I knew they would want something in return, but this? How the hell was I going to do this without earning Abigail's undying hatred for a lifetime? A very long lifetime. I forced the door to the lobby open with so much force the hinge buckled and Tawny flew under the counter. I snickered. She wouldn't last a week here.

Red glistened on the dew-slicked roof tops, the moon full of the blood of my victims. I wondered if it would rupture like a balloon filled beyond its capacity. My work would never be done. Not until the world was rid of the murderous filth that littered our streets and preyed on our kind. They were here because of fools dabbling in dark magic centuries ago. And now their numbers were greater, and pure humans were on the brink of extinction. I believed in what The Order was trying to do. I even believed in their methods, although I would have preferred killing immortals and supernaturals rather than locking them up, but something had shifted within The Order. I left because of it, and now here I was again, supporting a cause that had been distorted, finding myself at their mercy again.

Jack was heading my way as I stomped to the armory. Maybe he would sense my mood and—

"You look like you're in a mood," Jack said as he slowed his jog next to me.

"And you have horrible survival instincts," I grumbled.

"You headed to the armory?"

I ignored him, my patience waning, but he followed close behind. I scanned my thumbprint at the door of the armory and pushed it open when the lock released. When Jack tried to follow me in, I pushed my hand into his chest. "Where do you think you're going?"

"Aww, come on, Elijah. I've never been in there," he whined like a pathetic teenager.

"Because you don't belong in there. Now, go," I seethed.

He studied me for a moment and backed up a few steps. "You're going on a mission, aren't you?"

"Why else would I be here?" Jack was getting tiresome.

"Take me with you."

I threw my head back, releasing an epic laugh and then stopped abruptly and responded, "No."

"Why? I've been through all the training, and I was good enough for them to make me a commander."

"You babysit recruits. That hardly qualifies you for battle." I crossed my arms in annoyance.

"That stereotype is exactly why I need to go with you. To prove I'm capable. I'm a Potential for the Elite program, and this would look good."

I had seen Jack fight in the final trial against an immortal, but they had been imprisoned and half-starved. Hardly a real challenge. If I brought him with me, he could be killed but, really, what did I care? "Fine, but you have to do everything I say, without question."

Jack's eyes lit up.

"And lose the smile. You won't need that where we're going."

The door slammed shut behind us, the LED's flickering on ahead as we walked down a long hallway and turning off behind us.

"That's not creepy or anything," Jack said, untrusting.

"If someone were to get past our security, it would ensure we still have the advantage in the dark." I shuddered at the thought. If our enemies were to find a way in here we would all be dead. This is where the safe was that housed magical objects collected over the centuries, including Abigail's charm that had brought me back from the dead. Only, the safe contained a fake charm now since I switched it out to return the original to Abigail. The armory had many failsafe's, so it was doubtful anything would survive this hallway, but nothing was out of the realm of possibility. Luckily, I knew where every trap was set.

We just passed the wall of fire, which was found to be the most effective when dealing with ninety percent of the non-humans, and all humans. The other ten percent would surely be killed by the ceiling of blades directly above us now. The only supernaturals that could possibly survive those things were the ones with the ability to transport. Humans had mislabeled them as ghosts because of the transparency they present right before transporting, but they were just another form of evil that had evolved over the years.

The last obstacle was an unbreakable fiberglass wall that would seal them in this hallway, so they could be captured. It was automatically engaged upon the door opening by someone without clearance. Nothing could transport through the lead lined buildings and not just because they were lead. The building buzzed with some sort of universal energy. The Order wouldn't admit that it was magic since that went against our code, but they had done a lot of things in recent years that crossed the line. We were barreling down a path that wasn't much better than those we fought against.

I scanned us through two more doors, bypassing the usual weapons of guns, arrows, and knives. I went straight for the Elite weapons assembled by weaponry and engineer specialists. The same ones that the Elites were brandishing the night they had come for Abigail. They were armed and ready to take down anything that got in their way, only the Hunters had managed to escape, something that was damn near impossible against an Elite. Wes had offered to save me that night and I feared he would have. That he would change me into what I hated the most, but Abigail was the one who had saved me. She understood me. She put what I would want before herself. And the thought that Wes had the ability to care enough about her to save his enemy had confused me. It caused me to second guess my years of blinding hatred and perpetual unhappiness. Now, I had to capture Wes, virtually sentencing him to a life of torture. I wasn't sure how I felt about it.

I snatched up a device that looked similar to a Taser gun, only much more dangerous. Non-humans weren't affected by electrical impulses, so this had been fashioned to inject them with a serum temporarily shutting down their seemingly human functions, giving us enough time to apprehend them. It had been what Penelope used on Abigail when she kidnapped her. It was thought to kill humans, so the fact that Penelope was brazen enough to use it on her was infuriating, but it also proved she knew all along that Abigail was a Chosen. *The* Chosen. And the only way she could possibly know that was if the council had told her.

"Dude, don't point that thing at me." Jack put his hands up defensively and moved out of range as I checked the Taser.

"Relax. It's not loaded." I opened a box that contained the miniscule needles filled with serum, gathered a handful, and secured them in a little pouch, tossing them into a large army backpack.

"Those are the backpacks the Elites carry. Are you an Elite?" Jack looked stunned.

I scoffed, but didn't answer. I was beyond an Elite. There wasn't a name for what I was. No other human was as strong or as smart as me. The Order tested my abilities in the trials to the point where I was damn near death. James finally stepped in when they wouldn't listen to my father. The pain still pulsed through my veins, a permanent scar on my childhood. I wanted to make them pay for what they had put me through, but in the end, I understood this battle was bigger than me. Bigger than an orphaned boy with no hopes or dreams. They had given me a purpose and, although my faith in it had faded, it made me what I was today. A weapon. And until Abigail, a well-guarded one. No emotions, no pain. But then I had seen those honey-dipped eyes, and my walls crumbled.

Here's a sneak peek at
MIDNIGHT WINTERS,
the highly anticipated sequel to Midnight Rose.

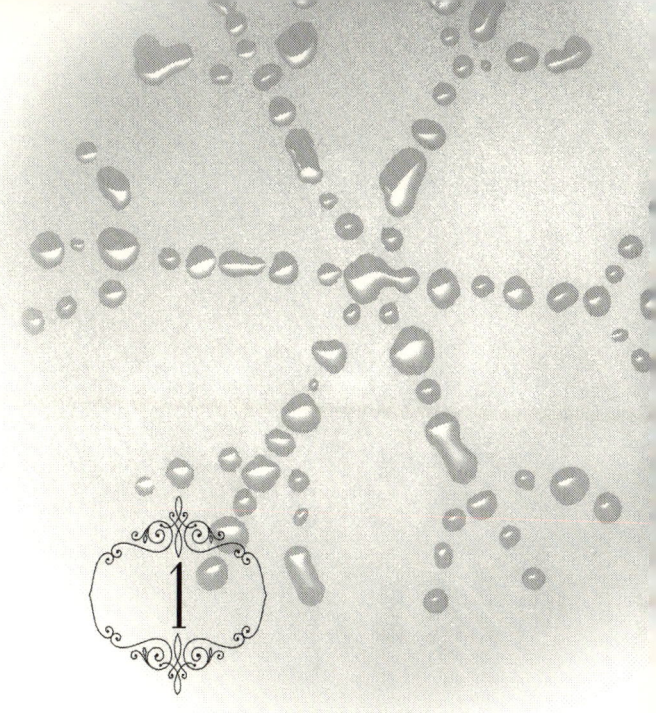

1

ELIJAH

Her sadness could fill a hundred buckets and still overflow, seeping into the hollows of my heart. That kiss, as desperate as it was, loosened The Order's noose around my neck, but also solidified the suffocating darkness I would travel to free myself from the hell that had been my life ever since Abigail Rose fell into my arms. When I had turned from the closed door that shrouded her pain in secrecy, a young girl with jet-black hair peered at me with an odd look. I thought her name was Jasmine, but it was hard to remember all the recruits. They had become an army of faceless warriors, but this one pierced me with accusatory eyes. Did she know what I was guilty of? What I was? Impossible. She was just a kid sucked into an endless battle at the wrong time. I felt sorry for her. For all of them. They signed on thinking they had a chance. That they were fighting for the greater good, but those lines had crossed, tangled, and intertwined so many times that the path had been all but erased and there were no absolutes anymore. Good or bad. Wrong or right. They floated in between here and there and swirled with doubt, confusing me. What side would I land on?

I slammed my fist into the punching bag again, feeling the satisfaction vibrate under my skin, sweat dripping off my skin like a fresh downpour. That kiss flashed between impacts, her eyes a fountain of maple from the trunk of its source pouring into me, flooding my soul.

Lies upon lies, the truth so hard to see anymore. And that kiss making it harder. She was supposed to be just an assignment. A repaid debt and then back into hiding, but I dug my grave deeper instead and the fall into it would be infinite and I would see all my regrets descending beside me, taunting me and whispering to me that I should have turned away when I had a chance. Now I would end up like Penelope in the end. The noose pulled taut until I broke. Choose my life over hers. And I knew what I would do. It's what chained me to The Order once again. To protect her. To die for her if it came to that.

The bag swayed with another punch.

I unwrapped the protective gauze around my hands, my knuckles still cracked under the pressure of my anger.

Abigail was on to something with Penelope and her brother, but I knew the truth. I knew why Penelope wanted me dead. I was the reason her brother was in that prison. I had tracked him for The Order. I took pleasure in it. Every single one of those monsters bore the face of the one that had taken my mother. I would have killed them all if I could, but The Order liked to collect them, and I knew better than to ask questions. Only The Order had lied to me. Zander wasn't just any monster. I could feel it. He was different, but it was too late. He had been changed.

The hot water felt good on my sore muscles as I washed off in the locker room shower. I had been training hard since Abigail decided to come to The Order training facility. I knew I would need to be in prime shape if either of us stood a chance. I cranked up the heat, leaning into the shower wall as it stung my skin, hundreds of needles puncturing the sensitivity I had developed because of Abigail, my love for her pushing the needles deeper into the marrow of my bones, siphoning the cancerous cells that split and grew into a forest of hatred after my mother was taken from my arms.

Abigail will be tested beyond her limits here, and I have already heard the venomous distrust of the recruits. She will have no allies. No friends. Getting permission from the council to be her partner, a shadow, is imperative. I made my formal request to the council and they accepted to meet with me tonight, but that wasn't the hard part. They could deny me because of our connection, which we made apparent at the tribunal, so every word and sentence I spoke needed to be carefully crafted. If I could make them see that our connection was an asset rather than a hindrance, then they might favor me by her side knowing I would do anything to protect her. Everything The Order had been planning hinged on Abigail's abilities. I remembered studying the prophecies of the Visionary when I was a Potential, and it mentioned that there would be one that would be above all others. A person who would encompass everything and everyone. A true weapon against immortals. No one suspected it would be a girl. In history past, Chosens had all been males. Strong and agile. From what I had seen of Abigail, she was off balance and frail. The Order still questioned if she truly was a Chosen, and they would go to extreme lengths to prove it without a doubt. Knowing what tests she would undergo made the tendons lasso around my muscles, playing a game of tug-of-war. I was able to protect her outside of these walls, but not in here. Everyone was at the mercy of The Order's discretion. If Abigail was not The Chosen, she wouldn't survive what The Order had in store for her. Only The Chosen could endure those tests. For The Order's sake, she better come out the other side of this unscathed or my wrath would bring an end to their empire.

I slipped out of my building, a temporary housing unit for members between missions, tucked at the bottom of the hill behind Building Twelve. It was unmarked and, therefore, off limits to anyone else. It was one of the very few buildings using fingerprint technology, and only when you were expected would your fingerprint be active. It was almost curfew for the recruits, so it was dark and quiet on the grounds. Jack was running the track just as he seemed to do every night. He was itching to go on missions, but I knew he didn't have what it took to be in one-on-one combat. The Order had recruited him because of his connection to Abigail, not because he garnered any gifts. He was smart, and The Order planned on training him as a field doctor.

Jogging up the hill to the main building helped expend the nervous energy stifling my concentration, only to tense up again when met by Polly's replacement upon entering the building. Tawny was younger and pretty, but didn't exude the warmth that Polly had. I was angry that The Order had removed Polly after Abigail's father was dragged out. I tried to plead for her, but in the end, they knew she could be a liability around Abigail. She had known too much and had become too close to James over the years.

"Mr. Winters, they are ready." Tawny stood up and smiled demurely.

"Thanks," I gruffed, ignoring her not so subtle advance.

As we approached the door that sealed Penelope's fate at the tribunal, my fists clenched. I had learned to hate The Order, and being back in this room would push me to my limits.

Tawny pressed her thumbprint on the keypad and held the door open as I passed through. Her perfume-drenched body made me nauseous, and only after she closed the door, leaving me alone in front of the elevator, did I dare to inhale. The elevator chimed, and I stepped in.

I walked the infamous hall again, only alone this time, noting there were no doors leading to other rooms. Just blank white walls, two vents, and a large return. The crawl space would be too small for me, but Abigail could fit. My fingers twitched on cue reaching for the memory of Abigail's hand as I stepped into the tribunal room and into the spotlight at the center.

"Good evening, Mr. Winters," one of the silhouettes off to the right announced.

I tried to memorize the cadence and pitch of each word he spoke, picturing a stocky man in his fifties. They didn't know my gift stretched into sound waves. James kept it between us as he trained me relentlessly on it. Sound waves reverberated around the source, making an outline of colors. The details were absent, such as clothing, but the shapes pulsed vividly.

"What matter is so urgent that you needed an immediate presence?" the man asked curtly. His eyebrows fell inward and his voice had stayed even, but his body language told a different story. He was annoyed.

"I'd like to request that I partner with Abigail as she goes through the buildings." Silence was followed by hushed whispers.

"And why is that?" a plump older woman asked.

"I know her weaknesses better than anyone. I can help break her of them."

"But you care for her." A comment from another woman,

young and petite. I continued to catalog each council member carefully.

"I have been tracking Abigail for three years now. I know everything there is to know about her. Her enemies. Her friends. I can make her stronger."

Silence again and then more whispers.

"Do you think you have the ability to make her hate the one thing she loves most?"

The question rubbed like coarse sandpaper against my chest. *Wes*. He is what they wanted most. For her to hate him and his family, because then they knew she was capable of destroying all of the immortals if she had a good enough reason to, but only if her heart turned against them.

"Without a doubt," I answered confidently.

More whispers. This time, I followed the sound waves around the balcony, each shape manifesting dimly. None of them stood out physically, except for one man. He was tall and burly. I could definitely pick him out of a crowd.

"We have voted, and your request has been granted, under one condition."

I gnashed my teeth together. Another debt to be paid, but wasn't Abigail worth it?

"You must bring in Wes Hunter immediately."

A low rumble hummed in my lungs, and the cracks on my knuckles bled as I squeezed my fists closed. Abigail would hate me if she ever found out. She would never forgive me. And that's exactly what The Order wanted.

They wanted her to hate us both, so she wouldn't hesitate when they asked her to choose them above all else.

"Mr. Winters?" the tall, older council member who started the tribunal pressed.

"Fine," I bit out and then left, storming out of the elevator, my insides raging with insuppressible fury. The intensity of their request blurred the world, and the fists of a hundred men pounded against my skull. I knew it wouldn't be easy. I knew they would want something in return, but this? How the hell was I going to do this without earning Abigail's undying hatred for a lifetime? A very long lifetime. I shoved the door to the lobby open with so much force the hinge buckled and Tawny flew under the counter. I snickered. She wouldn't last a week here.

Red glistened on the dew-slicked rooftops, the moon full of the blood of my victims, reminding me that I was a murderer, a beast groomed to kill other beasts. I wondered if the moon would rupture like a balloon filled beyond its capacity. What was one more? My work would never be done. Not until the world was rid of the murderous filth that littered our streets and preyed on our kind. They were here because of fools dabbling in dark magic centuries ago. And now their numbers were greater, and pure humans were on the brink of extinction. I believed in what The Order was trying to do. I even believed in their methods, although I would have preferred killing immortals and supernaturals rather than locking them up, but something had shifted within The Order. I left because of it, and now here I was again, supporting a cause that had been distorted, finding myself at their mercy again.

Jack was heading my way as I stomped my way down to the armory. Maybe he would sense my mood and—

"You look like you're in a mood," Jack said as he slowed his jog next to me.

"And you have horrible survival instincts," I grumbled.

"You headed to the armory?"

I ignored him, my patience waning, but he still followed close behind. I scanned my thumbprint at the door of the armory and pushed it open when the lock released. When Jack tried to follow me in, I pushed my hand into his chest. "Where do you think you're going?"

"Aww, come on, Elijah. I've never been in there," he whined like a pathetic teenager.

"Because you don't belong in there. Now, go," I seethed.

He studied me for a moment and backed up a few steps. "You're going on a mission, aren't you?"

"Why else would I be here?" Jack was getting tiresome.

"Take me with you."

I threw my head back, releasing an epic laugh, and then stopped abruptly and responded, "No."

"Why? I've been through all the training, and I was good enough for them to make me a commander."

"You babysit recruits. That hardly qualifies you for battle." I crossed my arms, waiting for a sound rebuttal.

"That stereotype is exactly why I need to go with you.

To prove I'm capable. I'm a Potential for the Elite program, and this would look good."

I had seen Jack fight in his final test against an immortal, but they had been imprisoned and half-starved. Hardly a real challenge. If I brought him with me, he could be killed but, really, what did I care? "Fine, but you have to do everything I say, without question."

Jack's eyes lit up.

"And lose the smile. You won't need that where we're going."

The door slammed shut behind us, the LEDs flickering on ahead as we walked down a long hallway and turning off behind us.

"That's not creepy or anything," Jack said, untrusting.

"If someone were to get past our security, it would ensure we still have the advantage in the dark." I shuddered at the thought. If anything with bad intentions were to find a way in here, we would all be dead. This is where the safe was that housed magical objects collected over the centuries, including Abigail's charm that had brought me back from the dead. Only, the safe contained a fake charm now since I switched it out to return the original to Abigail where it belonged. Magical objects had a way of finding the people they were meant to be with, and that charm didn't end up with Abigail by mistake. I'd be dead if she didn't have it.

The exterior building buzzed with some sort of universal energy. The Order wouldn't admit that it was magic since that went against our code, but they had done a lot of things in recent years that crossed the line. We were barreling down a path that wasn't much better than those we fought against.

However, in case someone was to get past the magic and lead-lined walls, the armory had many fail-safes, so it was doubtful anything would survive this hallway, but nothing was out of the realm of possibility.

I scanned us through two more doors, bypassing the usual weapons of guns, arrows, and knives. I went straight for the Elite weapons assembled by weaponry and engineer specialists. The same ones that the Elites were brandishing the night they had come for Abigail. They were armed and ready to take down anything that got in their way, only the Hunters had managed to escape, something that was damn near impossible against an Elite. Wes had offered to save me that night and I feared he would have. That he would change me into what I hated the most, but Abigail was the one who had saved me. She understood me. She put what I would want before herself. And the thought that Wes had the ability to care enough about her to save his enemy had confused me. It caused me to second-guess my years of blinding hatred and perpetual unhappiness. Now, I had to capture Wes, virtually sentencing him to a life of torture. I wasn't sure how I felt about it.

I snatched up a device that looked similar to a Taser gun, only much more dangerous. Non-humans weren't affected by electrical impulses, so this had been fashioned to inject them with a serum, temporarily shutting down their seemingly human functions, giving us enough time to apprehend them. It had been what Penelope used on Abigail when she kidnapped her. It was thought to kill humans, so the fact that Penelope was brazen enough to use it on her was infuriating, but it also proved she knew all along that Abigail was a Chosen. *The* Chosen. And the only way she could possibly know that was if the council had told her.

"Dude, don't point that thing at me." Jack put his hands up defensively and moved out of range as I checked the Taser.

"Relax. It's not loaded." I opened a box that contained the miniscule needles filled with serum, gathered a handful, and secured them in a little pouch, tossing them into a large army backpack.

"Those are the backpacks the Elites carry. Are you an Elite?" Jack looked stunned.

I scoffed, but didn't answer. I was beyond an Elite. There wasn't a name for what I was. No other human was as strong or as smart as me. The Order tested my abilities in the trials to the point where I was damn near death. James finally stepped in when they wouldn't listen to my father. The pain still pulsed through my veins, a permanent scar on my childhood. I wanted to make them pay for what they had put me through, but in the end, I understood this battle was bigger than me. Bigger than an orphaned boy with no hopes or dreams. They had given me a purpose and, although my faith in it had faded, it made me what I was today. A weapon. And until Abigail, a well-guarded one. No emotions, no pain. But then I had seen those honey-dipped eyes, and my walls crumbled.

Midnight Winters is available now.

Acknowledgments

I have so much to say and yet, not enough. Publishing again terrifies me. Everything that comes with putting myself out there scares me. But then I remember, writing is not about how many read it or what people think of it. It's about doing what I love and having the courage to try. To pick myself up, brush off the fears, and stand tall. Words give me life, stories give me a voice, and publishing tells my children to never give up. To chase the dream. No matter what your heart sings, it only matters if you listen. I'm listening.

I have an amazing team behind me and publishing wouldn't be possible without them. To Paige Maroney Smith, my editor who has been with me since my first book, thank you. My manuscript would be a grammatical nightmare without your expertise. To Catherine Jones, my beta reader whom I stumbled upon a few years ago, thank you for taking a hot mess and making it shine. Your advice, notes, and friendship has given me the confidence to come back to the publishing world. You are nothing short of amazing. New to my team Cassy Roop with Pink Ink Designs, thank you for capturing the true essence of this book and designing the perfect cover.

To anybody out there who chooses to spend their hard earned money on a complete unknown, thank you. Your purchase means the world to me, and believe it or not, strengthens my confidence. The only reason I publish is to bring my stories to life in the eyes of others. Otherwise, I would keep them safely tucked away.

And lastly, I will always be thankful for my husband's support and for the loves of my life, my children. Life is fuller with them.

About the Author

DANI HART graduated from the University of Southern California with a degree in Theatre and a concentration in Screenwriting. To find other books by this author, please visit her website, danihartbooks.com. You can also find her on Facebook and Instagram.

28943713R00262